# CASTLE OF HORROR

## ANTHOLOGY

### VOLUME 5

CASTLE BRIDGE MEDIA
DENVER, COLORADO, USA

CASTLE BRIDGE MEDIA
Denver, Colorado
Edited by Jason Henderson
Edited & Designed by In Churl Yo
Cover Composite by In Churl Yo
Cover Photos by Francisco Andreotti/Unsplash
and Lyudmila2509/Shutterstock


ISBN: 978-1-7364726-4-4



Listen to the Castle of Horror Podcast
www.spreaker.com/show/castle-of-horror-podcast

Or find us online at:
www.facebook.com/castleofhorrorpodcast

# TABLE OF CONTENTS

# INTRODUCTION

WELCOME TO VOLUME 5 OF the *Castle of Horror Anthology!*

I'm not sure there's ever been anything quite like this collection that we're calling *Thinly Veiled.* The assignment I sent it out to the writers was: "We're going to be taking properties that do not belong to us. And we're going to be *suggesting* them, veiling them, camouflaging them just enough that we don't get sued." In other words, we would not be taking the existing properties, we would be building new properties that were on the margins of existing cultural phenomena. You would be able to read the story and squint and see the homage.

All of the stories here are parodies. They chiefly comment on the underlying work, but one thing people miss is that parody doesn't have to be comedic—some of the stories here are very serious, such as Alethea Kontis' odd, sad story of the woman married to a very famous, eccentric candy maker.

We wanted to create *Thinly Veiled* because the pop culture that we obsess about creates the texture of our lives. If you ask people who were alive then what they remember about the 1970s, they will tell you what they were doing and what they were wearing—but in their mind, if we're honest, I think a lot of what they would recall is pop culture, especially in the world of television. I absolutely expected that we would be seeing stories based on properties like *Sanford and Son*, *The Odd Couple* and *M*A*S*H*. You can't think of the 70s and *not* think of these properties.

But: why the 1970s?

The 70s is one of those decades that we don't quite know what to do with. Almost no one remembers it as their *favorite* decade. The early 1960s—the Kennedy era—is marked by an exuberance born of continued economic expansion and a sense that in the United States, anything would be possible. The late 1960s changed all that. The US found itself in a wave of intense emotion amid the civil rights and antiwar movements. Those intense cultural moments, regardless of how alarming and exciting, all wash into nostalgia today, exactly as people have a nostalgia for the grueling years of World War II.

The 1970s are not so fondly remembered. The decade was marked by a pronounced energy crisis, the resignation in disgrace of the President of the United States, and the sad end of the Vietnam War. It is a decade that many people prefer not to remember at all.

Yet our memories of 1970s pop culture are vivid. Sitcoms like *Happy Days* and *M*A*S*H,* both of which took place in earlier eras, became cultural touchstones, possibly because exhausted Americans were enthusiastic about imagining themselves in any other time. *Happy Days* itself became a sort of extended universe, spinning off with *Mork and Mindy, Laverne and Shirley,* and titles that are completely forgotten today, like the fantasy series *Out of the Blue*.

While the realm of television was one of bright and colorful escapism—which makes sense for passing the time with one's family—the world of movies went in an entirely different direction. Movies in the 70s were much more likely to have a downbeat ending than at any other time. The cities presented in the movies of the 1970s were completely different from the gleaming Technicolor visions of the Doris Day and Rock Hudson comedies of the 60s; in the 1970s, cities teemed with pollution and crime.

The pop culture of the 1970s tells us something. And horror gives us the opportunity to look at the fears that lie underneath those statements.

So what do we have on the block for you this time?

In *All My Sins,* Charles R. Rutledge gives us a much more exciting and action-oriented version of [redacted] than that soap opera ever allowed.

Jeremiah Dylan Cook wryly comments on the cultural phenomenon of the Satanic Panic in his story *The Blood-Inked Comic Book.*

Heath Shelby manages to combine the obsession with Bigfoot with certain other adventure stories in his story *Fouke.*

Henry Herz's parody *The Crowe Family* wonders what the would have been like if they had been immortal monsters who played death metal.

Dennis K. Crosby gives us a look at in *The Boneyard*, which is as strangely sweet as it is demonic.

James A. Moore delivers a pitch-perfect parody of in *The Shreveport Slasher.*

Rob Nisbet delivers a mind-boggling commentary on the oddness of , with *Those Meddling Kids*.

John Pritchard brings us a look at the movie phenomena that were and combines them as *Three Days of the Jackal.*

My own story is a look at the bizarre retcon that the sitcom underwent when it switched from a single-camera to a multi-camera setup, in the process erasing both a living room and a major character.

In Churl Yo gives us his take on the enormous cultural phenomenon of with *East, Down and Bound.*

Bryan Young gives us a very well-observed and terrifying view of horror coming to the world of in *A Funny Thing Happened on the Way to the War*.

Tony Jones delivers a very strange fantasy version of in *Fear to Tread.*

Alethea Kontis turns in a character study called *Confessions of the Ex-Future-Mrs. X*, the aforementioned beautiful and sad look at a woman in the orbit of ██████.

And finally, Scott Pearson gives us a knowing and exact parody of the sitcom form (with a level of violence that never would occur in a 1970s multi-camera sitcom) with *The Murder Couple*.

Just for fun, I've redacted all the names of the shows that these stories are based on, but I'm hoping that you'll be able to tell. And in fact, I hope you visit us on Facebook and see if you can name them all. I'm also hoping that this is not the last *Thinly Veiled*. I can't wait to see a *Thinly Veiled 80s* and a *Thinly Veiled 90s*.

So welcome back to the Castle of Horror. I hope you enjoy your stay. ♜

—Jason Henderson, Co-Publisher, Denver, Colorado

# EAST, DOWN AND BOUND

*By In Churl Yo*

RABBIT TOOK HIS FOOT OFF the pedal and jerked the wheel hard, inertia pulling the rear end of his Pontiac Firebird around in a spray of gravel until the car was facing the direction he had come from, then he gunned it out of the pendulum swing back onto the blacktop like a bullet.

If he had really just seen what he thought he'd seen, there wasn't a moment to lose. But since he'd been hauling ass at 90 miles per hour, Rabbit couldn't be sure about anything, only that whatever it was didn't seem quite right.

Still, the absolute last thing he needed to be doing at this moment was to go out of his way looking for trouble, especially when for the past sixteen hours and nine-hundred-fifty miles, trouble had done a pretty good job looking for him. But he was already traveling fast in the wrong direction now, adding miles back onto his journey away from his destination. He was committed.

Was it a bad decision? Hell, probably. Although it couldn't be worse than the horrendously bad decision Rabbit had already made yesterday, but then, a bet was a bet.

A bet was a bet, and you don't get upset.

Not that it was like Rabbit to have regrets about anything anyways. Still, as he rolled up onto two vehicles pulled off on the side of the road, he felt a tinge of it hit the base of his skull just as he turned the engine off and got out of his car. When he had driven past here a few minutes ago all he could make out was what he thought was a group of guys surrounding a lady in a wedding dress.

Or maybe it was a bunch of cows being herded around by a fancy goat?

Either way, it wasn't something you'd expect to see on some backroad in rural Arkansas. But hey, Rabbit wasn't from around here. Who was he to say what was normal? He was really hoping it would be cows though, and not a bunch of fidgety thugs harassing a defenseless woman.

"Yo, fellas! What's going on here? Everything okay?" Rabbit asked with as much authority as he could muster. The odds were against him, five to one, so yeah, not good, but the bride probably had it worse. Way worse.

"Oh, shit. Look at this, boys! We got ourselves a *see*-maritan," the big one said, squaring his shoulders as he approached Rabbit, "and he's a

Chinaman, too. You lost, Chinaman?"

"I'm Korean, but hey, we all look alike, right?"

The big one glanced past Rabbit, smiled, and finished off the beer he was drinking before chucking it into the woods. They'd all been drinking for a while now from the looks of it. "That's a sweet ride you got there, Chinaman. After we take the girl, we're gonna take your Trans Am, too. You understand Eng-rish, right? How's that sound?"

"Terrible. That sounds terrible, man," Rabbit replied, "but that's not how this is going to go down." He could hear the woman struggling to break free from the others, who were restraining her out of sight behind the cars.

"It ain't?"

"Nah, man. Instead, I'm going to take the girl with me in the Trans Am, and you guys are going to go somewhere and sleep it off, maybe to one of your sister-wives' places. Or cousin-wives. I don't really care which."

That set the big one off. "The fuck did you just say to me?!"

"Easy there, Deliverance," warned Rabbit, as he pulled out a snub-nose revolver he had tucked into his jeans at the small of his back. "I don't want to murder anyone today, so just do what I say, okay?"

All the piss left the big one immediately, and Rabbit pushed him back toward his friends. Even with the gun things could still get squirrelly, especially if one of these bozos got to the shotgun that was mounted on the rear window of the pickup they were driving. "Move. Over there, man,"

Rabbit barked, and pointed the pistol back toward the brush away from the road and the cars.

Once they'd been herded back at a safe distance from them, Rabbit glanced at the woman in the wedding gown and asked, "Hey, uh, you okay, lady?" She was red-faced and had been crying but still had her clothes on, which he took as a win. At least there was some good to be had with the bad. That wasn't always the case.

She nodded, then wiped her nose. "Give me the gun."

Rabbit thought about it. Seriously. "Nah, how about we blow this taco stand instead? The last thing either of us needs is the fuzz on our tails for multiple homicide. I've got enough trouble following me as it is. Come on, I'll give you a ride."

"Shoot the tires then, and the radiator, and the fucking windshield," she said while flipping them off with both hands. "Don't worry about my Ford Pinto. That horse is dead." It was hollow consolation, but Rabbit obliged, getting off four shots while she grabbed a duffle bag from her broken-down car. Then they both carefully backed away to his ride and a moment later were on the road again, safe, and making speed headed in the right direction.

With the windows down and that business behind them, the tension slowly began to dissolve away into the warm, Southern wind. He heard her exhaling several times into the breeze and took it as a good sign. He saw her long auburn hair flittering over her dark eyes and resisted the urge to curl it behind her ear. Then a speaker hissed to life and popped static, announcing that someone was about to speak.

"Breaker, breaker, this is Seoul Man. You out there, Rabbit?"

His new passenger looked at him and asked, "Are you the Rabbit?"

Rabbit smiled at her and grabbed the CB mike off its cradle. "10-4, Seoul Man. I hear you. Come back."

"Where the hell are you, Rabbit? We're losing minutes, son!"

"I had to pick something up. Chillax, man."

"You're supposed to be blocking for me," Seoul Man complained. "I'm all exposed and shit up here."

"First, stop cursing. It ain't cool. There could be kids out there listening. Second, take a quick look out of your sideview." Rabbit punched the accelerator and floated over into the left lane, passing Seoul Man's black and gold Kenworth 18-wheel rig without much effort. Seoul Man pulled down on his air horn in three short bursts, signaling back a greeting to his partner. Rabbit nodded and chided, "See, you get all worried over nothing."

"I'll stop worrying when we make it back to Atlanta," Seoul Man replied then looked down at the Pontiac Firebird which, with its T-roof windows off, offered him an unobstructed view into the cabin. "I see what you picked up there. Does she have a name?"

Rabbit looked at his passenger and wondered aloud, "Do you?"

"Terry. My name is Terry," she said. He hadn't noticed her changing clothes beneath the large, frilly wedding gown. “Don’t look at me.”

He tried not to. “Her name is Terry.”

“What’s that she’s wearing?” Seoul Man asked.

“A wedding dress. I don’t know why.”

Now fully clothed in a blue button-down and bell bottoms, Terry stripped off the gown and threw it out of the car, letting the wind carry it into the Arkansas countryside.

“What’s she wearing now?” Seoul Man teased, bowling over in laughter while looking at his dog Red, a 10-year-old Korean Jindo, as if he were in on the joke.

“Your friend is funny,” Terry said.

“He likes to think so,” Rabbit replied. “You know, you’re actually the *second* bride I’ve had to answer to in as many hours. What do you—”

“I got cold feet.”

“Well, okay, you’re—”

“A woman is entitled to change her mind, isn’t she? Regardless of the circumstances. Or timing. It’s 1977, for Pete’s sake,” she exclaimed.

“Sure, but—”

“What are *you* running from, Rabbit?”

He glanced sideways at Terry and contemplated whether he should tell her the truth. Back where he came from the truth could get you killed. Back where he came from, you did your best to keep your head down and not get noticed. Sharing anything real was for suckers.

"Nothing," Rabbit answered. "I'm not running from anything. I'm just running."

# # #

There was no warning. The brown Pontiac LeMans pursuit vehicle sporting twin bubblegum machines on top rolled up against them fast, its front tires crushing Bobby and Seth like they were a couple of Rocky Mountain cow elks crossing the interstate near Little Rock during rush hour.

Except they weren't elks. They were brothers, and Tucker, the biggest one of their gang of five, had grown up just down the road from Bobby and Seth, played hide and seek with them in the woods, shot his first six-point buck with them on his tenth birthday. Now they were both gone, and it was all his fault.

He was the one who had decided to pull over to the side of the road when they came across that crazy ass bride. He was the one who had figured they should take advantage of her being out here in the middle of bum fuck all by her lonesome.

How'd that turn out? Well, the bride was filched by some lunatic Korean with a gun, and when they tried to chop her crappy Ford Pinto into parts and make a little cash for their trouble, Bobby and Seth ended up becoming a couple of gooey skid marks on the side of the road.

Tucker saw it happen. He was changing a tire on his pickup when the LeMans barreled into them without slowing down. They looked like ragdolls—knocked down, rolled over, and done gone in a split second. It had to have been an accident, right? What kind of lawman would intentionally drive his car into a couple of pedestrians like that? What kind of man would murder his friends in cold blood?

It took a second for Tucker to register it. It took another to process it. Then grief and shock took ahold of him, and he stood, dropped the tire iron, and took a step towards them. That's when he saw the driver step out of his vehicle, the sun glinting off his aviator sunglasses and the five-point star pinned to his shirt—the biggest damn sheriff Tucker had ever seen, probably six-foot tall and about half as wide, full of piss, vinegar, and a shit ton of potential energy.

Tucker opened his mouth to scream, but the scream stuck in his throat as the sheriff pulled out his revolver and shot his buddy Waylon square in the face. Waylon didn't even want to be out here. He was supposed to be home today studying for his city college mid-term, but they made him come. When Jeb saw what was happening and tried to bolt, the lawman sniped him in the back. Jeb had always been reckoned as a fool and a cheat, so Tucker wasn't shedding any tears, except now there wasn't anyone else around to get shot except for him.

Betsy. She'd save him. Tucker lunged through the open door of his truck and reached for his Remington 12-guage resting on the gun rack. The shotgun had been a birthday gift from his dad, the first one he'd ever owned. Tucker had named her Betsy, after some girl he had seen on TV. She was just about the prettiest thing he'd ever laid his eyes on. The girl was awful cute, too.

He stretched an arm over his head, pulled the door handle, and rolled out of the opposite side of his truck into a shallow ditch, away from the lawman.

Clutching Betsy, Tucker tried not to lose his shit but was failing. He took thee shallow breaths then stood, leaning against the truck bed, his chin tucked into his shoulder, his good eye focused on the sight at the end of shotgun barrel, and searched for a target.

Except he couldn't find one. The sheriff was gone.

Tucker ducked back down, his head spinning. He was ready to bolt, felt it in his chest, this need to run, but he couldn't make his legs move. He couldn't get his body to do what his mind wanted it to do, even though he knew he was a dead man if he stayed put. Tucker looked across the empty asphalt road that lay perpendicular to him into the dense brush past it, and something inside him clicked.

*Go. Now.*

He ran as fast as he could, the gun clenched tightly in both hands, his head down as if at any moment now he was going to be shot at. It took

Tucker all of ten seconds to cross the road and meet the tree line, then he was into the woods, zigzagging a path through it.

Old Man Baker's spread was less than a mile ahead. There was a phone there. There was an old Chevy pickup in the driveway. He could call for help, or hell, drive into the city for it. All Tucker had to do was make it there, and he was home free. All he had to do—

The forest opened up. Tucker lost his balance from the abrupt change in terrain and fell into a creek. An early spring had caused area waterways and lakes to swell, and the water here was a foot deep, cold, and running. He got up from his hands and knees, shook out Betsy. Then he stopped in his tracks.

Not fifty yards upstream, Tucker saw him. The sheriff.

Standing dead center in the creek, unmoving, and staring straight back at him, the lawman stood under a thicket of trees like a darkened shadow cast back upon itself. Too far away for Tucker to get a good shot off but too close for comfort for damn well sure, he decided instead to jump up the far bank and keep running.

Tucker had lettered in track back in the day. He'd stomped around most of these woods for as far back as he could remember. How the hell did that lawman catch up to him so fast? It wasn't natural. All he could do was keep going.

*Don't look back. Don't look back.*

The perimeter of Old Man Baker's farm was marked by a barbed-wire fence that stood over four-feet tall and ran for miles. Practically all of Arkansas was divided in piecemeal by the same kind of fencing—five strands of high-tensile wire nailed from one un-milled, sun-bleached log to the next.

Tucker stopped short of running right into the sharp, rusty metal barrier, but then immediately set about climbing over it. Tetanus was the least of his worries right now. He slung Betsy over his shoulder by her strap and lifted his foot up onto the first wire to see if it would carry his weight. It held. He shifted his body and raised his other leg to throw it over the top of the fence.

But then something hard slammed into his back. Tucker gasped and lost his breath, but before he could take in another, pain gripped his body as a dozen jagged barbs dug through his clothes and into his skin, grabbing ahold of him. He hung there suspended in the air and screamed just as two powerful hands ripped him from the wire fence and threw him to the ground.

There was blood everywhere. Between that, the sweat and tears, and the bright afternoon sun, Tucker couldn't see who stood over him, just a looming silhouette, but there was no doubt. "Why?" he asked the lawman, barely able to get the word out.

The sheriff kicked him in the solar plexus with his steel-tipped boot, and Tucker curled into a ball, the blow knocking out what little wind he had left in him. He began to hyperventilate and could hardly tell that he'd been sat up and leaned against a fence post. He could hardly feel the ring of barbed wire being curled around his neck. But what happened next, he felt.

The wire constricted against his skin, each barb a tiny saw blade, the pressure cutting off his airway. It was as if he were being choked and decapitated at the same time. Tucker clawed at the wire with his hands, unable to loosen its grip on him. All he managed to do was cut his fingertips and palms to shreds.

Then the pressure relaxed, and Tucker gulped for air.

"The bride," a voice growled.

Tucker fought through the fog of pain. "What?" he replied.

The wire tightened again, and this time, it ran across his neck, the metal digging a trench into his skin as it was pulled along. Tucker screamed until it stopped.

"THE *BRIDE*," the voice bellowed.

"She's… gone," he whispered. "She took off with… that…"

A hard slap brought Tucker back to consciousness.

"THE CAR?"

"What? Oh, yeah, that was… a sweet ride. Trans Am. Black."

"LICENSE PLATE?"

Tucker started to laugh. "Yeah, I remember. That asshole… had a vanity plate. Georgia. R-A-B-B-T-1."

The sheriff dropped the wire and took a few steps back. The sounds of a nearby Carolina Chickadee with its call-and-response chirping accompanied the lower tones of Tucker's labored wheezing. Then the unmistakable clack of a hammer being pulled back produced a sharp crescendo proceeding the final glorious climax—a single gunshot, not an uncommon noise in the Arkansas back country, which echoed briefly across the landscape before dying, disturbing no one.

# # #

"What makes you think I'm running from something anyway?" Rabbit asked.

He couldn't let it go. They hadn't spoken to each other much since she had asked him the question, but the conversation was still stuck in his brain. Rabbit glanced down at the trip meter and watched it tick across the 100-mile mark. They had traveled 100 miles closer toward the finish line in the past hour without incident and were 100 miles away from where he had rescued Terry, which was when he last reset the counter.

She stopped tap dancing with her bare feet on the windshield and looked at him sporting a crooked smile on her face. "You're kidding, right?"

"What? Tell me!"

"Alright, Rabbit, fine. Let's start with the obvious. You're driving like a bat out of hell!"

"So what? I like going fast."

"You've got all sorts of people on the radio warning you about Smokey sightings. I assume that has nothing to do with avoiding forest fires."

Rabbit nodded. "You would be correct."

"Not to mention your pal, Seoul Man. He's driving that 18-wheeler for a reason. My guess is he's hauling something stolen or illegal. Am I getting warm?"

"You're smoking hot," he replied, "and you might also be correct."

Terry smiled at him. "It must be important for you to be risking so much. It's not like you're just going to get a speeding ticket if you get caught, you know."

There was no doubt about that. Rabbit simply sighed and kept his eyes on the road ahead.

"I mean," she continued, "with you being Oriental and all."

He gave her a sideways glance and grinned. "Right."

"Hey, don't get me wrong. I'm a half-Irish Yankee from New York. I love everyone. Live and let live. Except most in the Deep South probably don't feel that way, and I doubt those people on the radio would be helping you if they knew you were Oriental."

"We say Asian-American now."

Terry grimaced. "Oh! Damn it. I knew that. Sorry."

She was right of course, but Rabbit had enough sense not to say no to his Uncle Lee when he asked you to complete a task, even when it involved risking your neck over something that might seem frivolous, because saying no just wasn't an option. Ever. So, he weighed the odds of racing across the countryside on some fool's errand versus disappointing his uncle, which usually didn't end very well for the disappointer. Bet or no bet, the errand still came out on top.

"I expect you know all of this already," Terry continued. "Why else would you wear that ridiculous hat?"

Rabbit feigned offense and ran his finger along the brim of the tan Stetson on his head. "I love this hat. It looks good on me."

"And that turquoise inlaid belt buckle and red shirt?"

"I had no idea you were such a fashionista," he replied. "I dress like this all the time. They call me the Korean Cowboy back in Atlanta."

"Uh-huh," she said unconvinced before turning serious. "You're in camouflage. You're hoping you can sneak across proverbial enemy lines by wearing their uniform and speaking their language. It's a good plan, except why do I get the feeling that you're out here looking for attention?"

"What can I say? Life is complicated."

"That's not a denial, Rabbit."

"Well, I'm pretty complicated, too."

"Birds of a feather," said Terry, who began dancing on the windshield again, this time calling out her moves as she made them. "Paradiddle, *step*. Paradiddle, *stomp*."

Rabbit spied a passing roadside mile marker, then picked up the CB transmitter. "Seoul Man, this is Rabbit. You got your ears on?"

A half-second later, the speaker cackled, "You got the Seoul Man, you lucky devil."

"Hey, man. We should pit stop before we cross The Big Muddy, maybe get a little food and fuel in us while we're still considered respectable."

"Speak for yourself. I was born respectable," Seoul Man replied. "But I could really go for a Diablo sandwich, and Red's looking a little thin in the skin, too. We ran out of *kimbap* and *kkakdugi* an hour ago."

Rabbit nodded. "Why don't you stop at the next Choke and Puke. I'm going to run ahead and drop Terry off at a bus station. We'll meet up again in Mississippi. Oh, and grab me a burger, would you?"

"That's a big 10-4, Rabbit. I'll catch you on the flip side." Seoul Man tossed the CB mike onto his dashboard, then reached out and rubbed Red's belly. The dog leaned into his hand and growled with pleasure while kicking its leg involuntarily.

Seoul Man liked being on the road. He liked the freedom it offered, even if it was only short-lived, even if it was all just a lie. Because eventually the journey ended, and his sorry life working for someone else, answering to his landlord or the Georgia Power Company or his bookie, would tie his hands again and keep him confined to a life of responsibility and restriction. Reality was always going to be the ultimate destination no matter the direction or distance he traveled, and no secret back road shortcut, no gleaming new superhighway or belt loop would ever change that.

But here behind the wheel, up high with the whole world in front of you, rolling 50,000 pounds of steel at 90 miles an hour with no traffic and a tail wind backing you up? There was nothing else like it and nothing else Seoul Man would trade for it.

If he and Rabbit could just do what's never been done before and win that damn bet, maybe he'd never have to. Maybe he could just stay on the road, going nowhere and everywhere forever, and make that his reality instead.

Something in his sideview mirror caught Seoul Man's eye and shook him out of his daydream. "Damn it," he whispered, then downshifted his rig to slow his speed without being too obvious about it.

A patrol car was coming up behind him fast. Really fast.

There wasn't anything he could do about it now, but maybe... "Breaker for the Rabbit," he said, trying to hide the panic in his voice. "You read?"

"Go for Rabbit."

Seoul Man exhaled. "You're not going to believe this. I've got a Smokey on my tail. Came up on me out of nowhere."

"Where are you, man?" asked Rabbit.

"I'm somewhere near mile marker 84."

"That's ten minutes behind me. Five if I boogie."

The truck driver cursed. "You're supposed to be blocking for me!"

"Blockers go in *front* of the runner," Rabbit replied. "I can't block your front and your behind at the same time. Just pull over as slow as you can and stall. I'm already on my way."

Seoul Man sat up straight in his seat and eyed the patrol car as it finally caught up to him. Hanging right off his back bumper, he could see the twin bubblegum machines rolling bright blue lights on the car's rooftop but heard no siren wails. Maybe he was the silent but deadly type?

Just as Seoul Man was about to ease off his accelerator, the brown Pontiac Lemans pursuit vehicle pulled around him and sped up in the passing lane until it was ahead of him, then it continued going on its way. Relieved, the truck driver grabbed his CB transmitter and clicked the channel open. "Rabbit, this is Seoul Man. Come back."

"I'm here. We're only a couple of minutes out."

"You can slow it down. Smokey passed me going about a 120 like I was standing still."

"Aren't you a lucky so-and-so?"

"Something else. The damn sheriff was sporting Texas plates."

"Texas? You sure?"

"Pretty sure," he replied sarcastically.

"What the hell is a Texas County Mountie doing in Arkansas?" Rabbit asked. He looked over at Terry, who shrugged her shoulders in obvious bewilderment, which he shared.

"Like I'm supposed to know," said Seoul Man.

Rabbit tried to logic out the reason but then decided there was no way he'd be able to and shook it from his mind. "Well, we're going to pull over and let him go by, then we'll rendezvous at the Choke and Puke when the coast is clear. Copy that, Seoul Man?"

"Copy, brother."

Rabbit searched for a side road, quickly found a nondescript, paved single-lane peaking between two patches of high brush, and turned onto it. He drove fifty yards and put the Pontiac Firebird in park, then both Terry and he turned around in their seats and looked back toward the main road, waiting for the Smokey to drive by.

Instead, the patrol car executed a power slide onto the end of the side road in a cloud of dust—the suspension still rocking by the time the wind settled down again—and sat there staring back at them, as if daring Rabbit to make the next move.

He looked at Terry. She bit her lip and groaned.

Tires spun on asphalt as Rabbit stomped the accelerator, the smell of burnt rubber filling the air. The Trans Am hit 60 miles per hour in 8.4 seconds and was already a quarter mile down the road in less than four more. A quick glance in the rearview confirmed they were being followed, and a smile grew on Rabbit's face.

"You don't have to do this to impress me, you know," Terry said.

"Actually, I often do things to impress myself," he replied.

They glided around a sharp turn in the road, which was nothing more than a long-neglected stretch of county road filled with cracks, divots, and the occasional roadkill. Rabbit thought they were able to pad the distance between them as the sheriff started lagging a bit behind, which was good, because he had no idea where he was going.

When they reached 90 miles per hour and started to catch air with every roll in the road, Terry turned toward Rabbit and said, "Before we die, I wanted make sure I got a chance to say thank you for saving my life—you know, from that rape gang thing back there."

Rabbit shook his head. "Think nothing of it. Besides, we're not dead yet!"

He pulled onto a dirt road, and the ruts rumbled beneath their wheels causing them to slow down. Rabbit cursed under his breath. This was not what he'd had in mind. An opening came up on his left, and he swerved into the front yard of a cabin, likely someone's summer vacation home. The wide, flat area allowed him to gain some speed again, and he was eventually able to make his way back to an adjacent road that was nicer, straighter, and kinder to their backsides.

The sheriff, somehow, was still behind them.

Better them than Seoul Man. That was the whole point, right?

After a slight curve, they entered a straightaway, and Rabbit really opened the engine up, hitting 80 miles per hour in no time and climbing still, until in the distance, he saw something blocking the road.

A construction sign. Standing squat across the entire lane, it indicated in no uncertain terms that the bridge ahead was out. "That's not good," Rabbit said and slammed on his brakes. He slid the Pontiac Firebird around in a quick 180 and peeled out back the way they came, hoping to find another turn off somewhere.

"It would be better with a *whole* bridge," Terry offered.

Once they were able to gain traction again, Rabbit straightened the car out and sped off, only to see the sheriff closing the distance between them ahead. He had no interest in playing chicken with the lawman. "That's worse," he sighed, then turned the car around again, performing the same maneuver he had before only this time in reverse.

Now they were headed toward the sign again, their speed increasing.

A concerned look came over Terry's face. "Why don't you just drop me off here. I'll catch a cab."

Rabbit shook his head. "Too late now!" The Trans Am crashed through the wooden barrier and then another before hitting the bridge's broken slats at an incline, sending them airborne over the river and high into the air in what felt like slow motion. This allowed plenty of time for doubt and no small amount of fear to wind its way into the hearts of both passengers, each powerless to stop whatever fate had waiting for them on the other side.

# # #

*Nineteen Hours, Forty-Seven Minutes and Twelve Seconds Earlier.*

Rabbit tried hard to stifle a laugh. The groom, dressed in a traditional blue *hanbok*, was having trouble staying upright with the bride (who also wore a customary red *hanbok*) on his back.

She wasn't overweight by any means. In fact, his cousin had lost quite a bit of weight leading up to her wedding, but her fiancée was shorter than she was and a bit thinner to boot. Not exactly the ideal specimen for a man marrying into the kind of family he was about to join, but his ancestral line was good, which counted for a lot, and quite wealthy, which counted even more. Of course, all the important details had been worked out long before the lucky couple had ever met, as was the case with most arranged marriages.

The piggyback ride was part of the *paebaek* ceremony. In Korean tradition, the *paebaek* celebrated the joining of two families and acted as a formal introduction of the bride into the groom's family. Carrying his new wife on his back symbolized the husband's commitment to support her from this day forward 'til death did they part, in this case literally, but the poor guy was having a hard time of it. A couple of groomsmen had to step in and help him out.

Rabbit allowed himself a smile and took a drink of his *soju*. Any bigger show of emotion from him might be interpreted the wrong way, and he knew better than to embarrass his family by creating a scene, especially on a day like today.

Just to be sure, Rabbit scanned the room to make sure no one had seen him laughing at the groom, and that's when he saw his Uncle Lee staring right back at him. He sat up straight in his chair, put his drink down, and watched his uncle get up from his seat and walk to an adjacent room.

Someone tapped him on the shoulder, and Rabbit closed his eyes for a beat before looking up behind him. His other cousin, who was the spitting image of his father, only smaller, stood over him smirking. A quick tilt from his cousin's head told Rabbit to follow him, and the pair exited the reception to where his uncle was waiting for them.

"*Keun-a-beo-ji*," said Rabbit while bowing to his uncle, "thank you for inviting me here on your daughter's special day."

Uncle Lee waved him off, then put his hand on Rabbit's shoulder. "What do you think of him?"

"The groom? He looks… kind."

"Kind, eh? Well, that's better than stupid at least. I love my children and pray for their eternal happiness, and that goes for you too, my young nephew, no matter the circumstances. Now, how have you been, Rabbit?"

"I'm fine, thank you. Is there something I can do for you?"

Uncle Lee looked at his son and said, "You see? Straight to the point.

You could learn a lot from your cousin. Rabbit knows the ropes, and he's the best driver we've got. That warehouse job he pulled was fucking brilliant, not to mention very lucrative for us."

Everyone outside the family called the father and son Big Lee and Little Lee but never to their faces. Rabbit knew better than to call either one of them by name.

"Rabbit's not that good, *a-boe-ji*," said Little Lee. "He's lucky, that's all."

"You think so, eh? What about you, Rabbit?"

"Who am I to argue with my *hyong-nim*?"

Uncle Lee moved to sit down on a nearby chair. "Your humility is unwarranted," he replied, "and it makes you look weak. Nevertheless, I believe I may have a way for you to prove without a doubt that you are the best while also solving a problem for me. How does a bet sound to you?"

"A bet?"

"Our new in-laws are staying with us for a few more days, and I want to celebrate with them in style. For my daughter, your sweet *sachon*, I need you to go to Texarkana, pick up some Coors Banquet beer for us, and be back in 28 hours."

Rabbit considered what Uncle Lee was asking from him. "Getting to Texarkana and back in 28 hours shouldn't be a problem..."

"It ain't never been done before, hot shit," Little Lee interrupted.

"But if you take Coors beer east of Texas, that's bootlegging," Rabbit continued.

"If you make this run for me," said Uncle Lee, "I'll give you $80,000. That's three grand an hour if you make it back in time."

Little Lee turned to face his father and whispered, "*A-boe-ji*, I don't believe that's necessary…"

Uncle Lee offered his son a stern look, which shut him up immediately, and then asked, "Will you do this for me, Rabbit? Will you take this bet?"

"Of course," he replied without hesitation. "It would be my honor."

"We'll need 400 cases," Uncle Lee said while getting up to leave. "My son will help to arrange everything for you and give you what you need. Just remember, our influence ends at the city limits. After that, you're on your own. A stranger in a strange land…"

Rabbit bowed as his uncle walked back toward the reception hall and disappeared into the crowd. The enormity of what he'd agreed to was just beginning to sink in.

"Are you scared?" Little Lee asked, his voice more than a little condescending, but Rabbit remained silent. "You should be. But I don't care if you've got to fight through a whole army of Grand Wizards or the God-damn Texas Rangers… you fail to bring that beer back to Atlanta in 28 hours and embarrass my father, family or no family, I'll hunt your ass down and kill you myself. Is that fucking clear? Now, how much cash do you need to make this happen?"

Little Lee pulled out a fat stack of hundreds and started flipping through them. As Rabbit watched him count off bill after bill, he thought there might not be enough money in the whole world that would get him safely through this.

But a bet was a bet.

# # #

*Twenty Hours, Twenty-Nine Minutes and Eight Seconds Later.*

They were lost, which was better than being dead. Better still, they had eluded the sheriff, who had made the correct decision not to follow them over what was left of Mulberry Bridge. That the Trans Am was able to make the jump at all was no small feat, but to still be running and gunning without breaking down or falling apart after that landing was an absolute, bona fide miracle.

Rabbit wasted no time tearing through the countryside, searching for a way back to the state road and Seoul Man, who had gone on ahead without them.

"I think I've seen that barn before," said Terry. "We're not lost, are we?"

"Of course, you've seen that barn. It's the same as every other barn out here. Big. Wood. Red. Besides, I know exactly where we're going."

"Oh, do you now? Where?"

Rabbit pointed at the road ahead of them. "That way."

"And here I was getting worried…"

He tried not to think of the minutes they were losing. He tried not to think of his Uncle Lee, or his cousins, or Seoul Man out there all by himself. But it was all beginning to weigh on him now, and frustration was setting in. Terry saw the look on his face and placed her hand on his.

"Hey, we'll get there," she said. Rabbit just nodded and kept his eyes on the road.

"Look, whatever's going on, I know you're in deep with a lot at stake," Terry continued, "but I also know what that feels like, Rabbit. Sometimes you've just got to push that noise out of your head, reach down deep inside yourself, and find that part of you that will do whatever it takes, no matter the cost. I've done it before. You can, too."

She made it sound so easy. Maybe it was.

Then as if on cue, they dead ended onto a two-lane road. *Finally.* Rabbit immediately pointed the Pontiac Firebird east and took off with as much speed as the engine could handle. They were coming up on the Choke and Puke, where he and Seoul Man had eaten on the way out to Texarkana, and if they were lucky, his partner might still be there now, assuming he waited for them.

"Breaker, breaker, this is the Rabbit. Is the Seoul Man out there? Am I hitting you, son?"

No response. Rabbit tried a few more times, and his worry grew after each attempt came back with nothing but static in reply. He flashed a look of concern toward Terry, then replaced the CB mike back onto its cradle. If he could drive any faster, he would, but they were already pushing well over 100 miles per hour, the needle tacked past where the numbers ended on the speedometer.

The Choke and Puke was a mom-and-pop diner in the middle of nowhere, little more than a blip on the side of the road near the Mississippi, and the food was fine and precisely what you'd expect to be served there—sandwiches, burgers, the expected assortment of fried foods. As they approached the restaurant, Rabbit sighed when he saw Seoul Man's semi sitting in the parking lot, its cab facing their direction. When they got closer, the truck started flashing its headlights at them.

Rabbit pulled the Trans Am over onto the side of the road.

"What's wrong?" asked Terry. "Isn't that Seoul Man's truck? We were supposed to meet him here, right?"

"Right," he replied, staring at the truck in the distance, and yet, Rabbit couldn't quash the urge to keep his foot pressed firmly on the brake. Something felt off to him.

The 18-wheeler started to shake then, as its engine came to life and its gears were shifted, and the truck began rolling toward them. Rabbit reached again for the CB. "Seoul Man, this is Rabbit. If you read, please respond. You out there?" Nothing.

"Maybe his radio's broken?" Terry suggested, but Rabbit wasn't convinced. That might explain a few things but not everything, and certainly not this.

The truck was gaining speed now on a direct course for them.

Then a thought popped into Rabbit's head: *We're about to get rammed.* But there wasn't enough time for a U-turn, so he slid the Trans Am into reverse and punched the accelerator. The semi was just off their front bumper now, close enough for the smell of spent diesel fuel and heat off the radiator to saturate the air around them.

Rabbit cursed. He had to divide his attention between the truck and the road now, using his mirrors to navigate backwards. As they slowly began to inch away, he glanced up at the 18-wheeler's cabin to confirm what he already knew: Seoul Man wasn't behind the wheel. Instead, he could just make out the profile of a massive figure in a cowboy hat and sunglasses, sporting shiny emblems pinned to his chest and lapels.

"The sheriff!" Rabbit shouted over the rumble of the semi.

"What?!" Terry yelled back.

"The sheriff! From Texas!" He pointed at the truck with his chin, but either she couldn't hear him or didn't believe him, because all Terry did was offer him a confused look back.

The semi rolled over to their left as if to pass them, but Rabbit used the opportunity to spin the Pontiac Firebird around 180 degrees to his right and shift the car into drive. Just as the transmission engaged and they started moving forward, something landed on the back of their car, shattering the rear window with a crash.

Terry screamed. Rabbit spun around to see Seoul Man's dog Red strung along on the broken glass, its body mutilated and bleeding everywhere.

Rabbit closed his eyes, trying to fight away the fear he had for his friend. This wasn't about getting arrested or winning a bet anymore. This was about life and death and Seoul Man being missing, his dog dead, and someone else driving his truck. Rabbit was going to have to change his strategy. He was going to need some help to get out of this alive.

The Trans Am, able to get to its top speed faster, pulled away from the 18-wheeler and turned onto the next exit down the road, a curving onramp that took them toward the one place Rabbit had made a point of avoiding this entire trip: a divided highway.

While a highway might have been easier to travel on, they were patrolled more frequently and offered little to no cover if you needed to shake someone while being pursued. Long stretches often lacked turn offs or exits for miles, a recipe for disaster if you needed to evade someone. But highways were also the one place you were guaranteed to find something else in abundance: other trucks. That's what Rabbit hoped to find, and he wasn't disappointed. They quickly came upon a convoy of 18-wheelers traveling in the righthand lane less than a mile away.

"Breaker 1-9, breaker 1-9. I see a portable gas station ahead of me at highway marker 48. Do you copy?" Rabbit transmitted the message on his CB radio, hoping to hear back from a semi-truck hauling a fuel trailer at the rear of the convoy.

"Hey, is this the Rabbit? This is Mr. D, and I'm gear jamming this rolling refinery. You got another Smokey on your tail?"

"This is the Rabbit. That's a big 10-4, except Smokey's driving a black Kenworth, fully loaded. Can you help us by running a little interference?"

"Come ahead there, Rabbit. We'll slip you into our house and lock the door behind you. The welcome mat is out, and you're coming home!"

The Firebird revved its engine and sped ahead, passing Mr. D into the heart of the convoy. If everything went according to plan, one of the other trucks would move in behind him, blocking both lanes of traffic and slowing everything down, which would let Rabbit escape with the sheriff unable to follow.

He turned to Terry and nodded. "This might actually work," he said and almost allowed himself a beat to relax when the CB cackled back to life.

"Breaker, breaker. This is Smokey Bear. I'm a Texas sheriff in a Kenworth 18-wheeler pursuing a black Trans Am driven by the Rabbit. He's wanted for murder, rape, and kidnapping. Any of you truckers who help him will be charged with aiding and abetting a fugitive."

All the color left Rabbit's face. Terry grabbed the microphone from his hand and pushed the transmit button. "That's a lie," she said. "You're going to believe some crazy guy in truck who says he's a sheriff over the Rabbit? The Rabbit's one of you! He's fighting for you!"

"The Rabbit is an ORIENTAL who's just *pretending* to be one of you," said the sheriff. "There's no way that slanty-eyed foreigner is from the South! He's probably a sumbitch rice farmer from China!"

The bottom fell out of Rabbit's stomach. Whatever advantage he'd had by coming onto the highway was surely gone now. One thing was for sure, he couldn't count on anyone else for help after that little announcement. He was on his own and likely up against more than one opponent.

"We need to go," said Terry. "*Now*."

Rabbit shrugged. "I'll try." He floored the gas pedal, and the Trans Am roared to life, moving forward in the left lane passing the long line of semis to their right, until an orange Allied moving truck pulled out in front of them and hit its brakes.

"Shit!" Rabbit yelled, doing his best to avoid rear-ending the massive trailer. Their speed was rapidly decreasing now, as the moving truck forced them to slow down. There was nothing else to do—a ditch on their left prevented them from going around.

Just as the they reached the back end of the convoy again, another truck rammed them from behind, pinning the Trans Am between two 18-wheelers. Rabbit saw the familiar front end of Seoul Man's rig in his rearview. The sheriff had them trapped right where he wanted.

Even with the accelerator pressed all the way down, nothing Rabbit did would free them. The Pontiac Firebird groaned from the immense pressure being exerted onto its frame, its hood buckling and bending now. They'd be dead in the water soon and just plain dead not long after.

So, this was it. Not only had Rabbit lost the bet, but he'd also lost his friend, his pretty companion, and his life all in one day. For some reason, he took comfort in the fact that he wasn't just unlucky, he was truly, *exceptionally* unlucky. The odds, it seemed, were never in his favor at all, not by a longshot.

Rabbit turned to look at Terry, fully prepared to say something embarrassing to her, when a familiar fuel truck in the righthand lane collided with the Allied semi in front of them, sending it off into a ditch while freeing the Trans Am at the same time.

An opening appeared on the highway to their right, and Rabbit quickly turned toward an exit ramp, the Pontiac Firebird wobbling as it traveled. "Thank you, Mr. D. I don't know how to thank you," he said over the CB, overcome with emotion.

"You can thank me by not getting caught," Mr. D replied. "I don't like liars, and I hate racist assholes even more. You have a good day, Rabbit, and a better one tomorrow."

There was some luck to be had after all, but it was short lived. Every warning light on the Trans Am's dashboard had lit up, and whatever power the engine had left was failing. Rabbit had managed to drive them around a bend onto small two-lane road before the car finally stalled. He looked in his mirror and saw the Kenworth approaching.

"Put your seatbelt on!" Rabbit screamed. Terry scrambled to find the buckle, her hands frantically working to put the loose ends together. "Do it now!"

The piercing wail of the 18-wheeler's horn filled Rabbit's ears followed by the rumble of a diesel engine, then…

# # #

Silence. Darkness. And, slowly, pain.

Light appeared at the edge of Rabbit's vision, a pinhole's worth at first, and then all at once, like a flashing studio camera, it flared while coming sharply into focus. The intensity of it blinded him for a moment, and he thought he might throw up. Instead, the nausea quickly subsided, but the pain intensified—his head, his right arm and lower back all throbbed in agony.

He looked around and saw blood. It was definitely blood. On his boots.

On his jeans.

He wasn't in his car. There were rocks and grass beneath him.

He was being held. Someone's arm was around his chest.

Rabbit tried to lift his head up and immediately regretted it, but despite the pain and dizziness, as he became more aware of his surroundings, he could also feel his mind shrieking at him. Something was wrong. Something besides the accident.

Something *important*.

Then he felt an object digging at his temple. It was hard. Cold. Rabbit didn't like it.

"Get up," a familiar voice said. He knew that voice. A woman. Sexy, too. Her name… was Terry? Yes! That sounded right. Terry, the bride he had rescued.

"YOU," a different voice bellowed, "STOP!" He knew that voice, too, and something about it snapped him back to full consciousness. Rabbit looked up, and in the distance, saw the man whose voice he'd recognized.

The sheriff.

*Shit.*

"I'll kill him. You know I will," Terry said, her voice behind Rabbit and right in his ear. He tried to turn around to look at her, but something pushed his head back. It was the barrel of his snub-nose revolver. She had taken it from the glove compartment and now had it pointed at Rabbit's head.

"What's happening? Terry, what are you doing?!" he asked.

"Whatever it takes," she answered. "No matter the cost."

The sheriff continued to walk toward her, undeterred by her threat to kill Rabbit, his own massive handgun pointed directly at them. "YOU KILLED HIM!" the lawman roared.

"He was an idiot," Terry stated matter-of-factly. "You *knew* he was an idiot."

"MY SON! MY JUNIOR!"

"One less idiot in the world. I couldn't marry him, but I couldn't let him live, either."

"DIE, DIE, DIE!"

She let Rabbit go, and he dropped to the ground just as the sheriff and Terry opened fire at each other. A bullet still managed to strike Rabbit in the shoulder, and yet despite the rolling pain of being shot by a large caliber bullet, he was somehow able to stay out of harm's way. Moments later Terry fell on top of him, and he knew immediately by the heaviness of her body that she was likely dead.

He pushed her over and was confronted by an empty stare that gazed far beyond him into nothingness, confirming her fate. Rabbit sat up and fought the urge to cry because he couldn't decide whether it would've been out of sadness or relief, not that he could feel anything now anyways. He was mostly numb, which is why he had no reaction at all when he saw the sheriff still standing a few yards in front of him, placing fresh bullets into his revolver.

"Hey, man," said Rabbit, "I didn't kill your boy, man. I'm innocent."

The lawman loaded the final round into its chamber, then spun the cylinder with his finger before flicking it back into place with a twist of his hand. Next Rabbit heard the tell-tale clack of a hammer being drawn and knew the sound that would soon follow…

A *thump*.

But he saw the sheriff's body flying before he heard it. Then Rabbit caught the high-pitched squeal of brakes in dire need of pads as a rusted-out tow truck stopped in front of him, its driver jumping out and running toward him now.

"Rabbit, are you okay?"

"Seoul Man?! You're… not dead."

"Hell no, son. I was in the Choke and Puke having a Diablo sandwich and a Dr. Pepper when I heard that damn sheriff stealing my truck outside. I've been a step behind you ever since."

"He… killed Red. I thought he killed you, too," said Rabbit.

The news about his dog hit Seoul Man hard. "Nah, I *avenged* Red. That sheriff is toast," Seoul Man declared, tears welling up in his eyes. "I sent that fucker back to hell, which means we need to get out of here fast. Can you walk?"

Rabbit nodded. His partner helped him back to Seoul Man's 18-wheeler and gave him an assist climbing into the cab. A moment later, the Kenworth started right up again.

"You know, we have about seven hours left to make it to Atlanta before the deadline," Seoul Man said, "and there's still 400 cases of Coors in the trailer. What do you think, man?"

Rabbit took a deep breath and thought about their odds before a wide, toothy grin suddenly appeared on his face. "I think we've got a long way to go and a short time to get there, *chingu*. Let's fucking roll." ♜

# YOU ARE CORDIALLY INVITED TO AN EVENING OF HORROR AT THE SECRET HILLS GOLF AND COUNTRY CLUB

*By Madeline Ashby*

THE SECRET HILLS GOLF AND Country Club appeared at the end of a long and winding drive whose turns occasionally narrowed to chokepoints that squeezed the Continentals and Caprices so close Marcia could smell the cigarettes in their ashtrays. It being private property on unincorporated land, the rules determining the width of the asphalt were more like preferences than anything else. During a daytime luncheon, this wasn't much to worry about. But on a night like tonight, when there was a crowd, it meant a slow red flow of taillights bleeding out of the roughs and fairways.

"You're driving back," she said.

"10-4," Daryl said.

"And if you have to hang back to have one more coffee with Bud or Slim just to sober up, I'm getting a ride with someone else. I'm not staying until three in the morning, like last year."

"That wasn't last year; it was two years ago. And it wasn't Halloween, it was the Christmas party."

Marcia ashed outside the window. "I just want to be home when Clover gets home."

He reached over and squeezed her knee. His hand stayed there. She hadn't realized how cold she was until the warmth of his skin pushed itself against hers. "We will be. Don't worry."

Daryl was going as The King, all in yellow, with a gold lamé cape that matched his huge sunglasses. He caught it in the car door after they sidled into one of the last available parking spaces. They were late. The sun was almost down. But Elvis' hair took Daryl a full hour, and perfecting his impressions in the bedroom mirror took even longer.

Marcia was going as a fortune teller. Technically she should have gone as Priscilla Presley, or Ann-Margaret, or even Nancy Sinatra. The club awarded extra points for couples' costumes. But finding a Priscilla Presley wig was almost impossible on such short notice, and anyway she'd had to take Clover for her B-12 and iron shots that weekend, because Dr. McLaughlin had miraculously found time to squeeze her in ahead of schedule. Clover had fumed the whole way there and back, because driving to the next town over burned up her Saturday, when she and her girlfriends were supposed to be shopping for their own Halloween costumes.

"I'll have to go as a ghost," she complained. "It's corny."

"Go as a black cat," Marcia had advised. "You still have that black leotard from dance class, and those black tights, and those black leg warmers. And those black stage shoes, the ones that don't make any noise."

"I don't even know where my dance clothes are anymore, Mom."

But Marcia knew where they were. Marcia drew them out from an old Sears box under the bed, where she'd wrapped them in tissue with a sachet of dried rosemary, bay leaves, and cloves.

"How come you always do this with my clothes?" Clover had asked, and Marcia had explained that it was always best to pack clothes away with a sachet, when they were being stored for any meaningful length of time.

Clover had held the little bag of cheesecloth tied with black ribbon at arm's length. "It's weird."

"It's something grown-up ladies do," Marcia had said.

The wind kicked up as they made their way to the broad oak doors of the country club. Leaves skittered across the parking lot. The fading sun muted their colours. Soon the trees would be made anonymous by the night, when the velvet lawns turned grey and the water features hosted sleeping swans. At the door, while some new kid from the next town took her coat and gave Daryl a number, Marcia turned to watch the dusk falling. She memorized their car's position in the lot. Maybe it was a mistake to ask Daryl to drive them back. She was faster than he was. She could find the car faster, start it faster, get them on the road faster.

"Mar," he said, with a hand at her elbow. "It's time."

She took one last drag and let her cigarette drop. Then she stubbed it out, the orange spark and black ash mingling briefly under her shoe, and turned to go in.

# # #

If the decorations had changed between this Halloween and the last, Marcia could not tell. As usual, every surface was draped in stretch cotton spiderwebs. As usual, the punch bowl was a livid red, and full of icy "hands" clearly fashioned from water frozen in tied-off dishwashing gloves. There were cheese balls meant to look like brains, made of Philadelphia and cold baby shrimp, bathed in cocktail sauce. There were black candles in every sconce. Organ music played on the speakers. Toccata and Fugue, over and over.

"Manhattan?" Daryl asked.

She shook her head. "Martini."

"That's my girl." He kissed her temple and pushed off, into the crowd of Draculas and Frankensteins and wolf-men. On his way to the bar, a matched set of Frankensteins — Larry and Bitsy Logan, from over on Crane Avenue — stopped him and made him say "Thank you, thank you very much." Her martini, Marcia realized, would be a long time coming.

"What are you supposed to be?"

Marcia turned. Jeannie Crandall and Ginger Hayes stood behind her. Jeannie was Genie, from the show, complete with a huge blonde wig and pink nylon harem pants that looked suspiciously like repurposed pyjamas. Ginger was Ginger, in a tropical two-piece and fake eyelashes, clutching a cigarette holder with nothing in it. They were their own matched set, in a way, which made sense given how much time they spent together on the tennis court. Their husbands, as usual, were somewhere else.

"I'm a fortune teller," Marcia said.

"Oh, that's ballsy," Jeannie said, and Ginger gasped and smacked her across the arm. "What?" Jeannie asked, slurping something orange from a champagne flute. "It is ballsy. I can say that. It's ballsy, going as a fortune teller when our illustrious hostess always goes as Morgan the Fairy or whatever it is."

"It's Morgan Le Fay," Marcia said. "It's from the Arthur legend."

Jeannie made a snoring noise. "It's from Snoozeville," she said. "I don't know why she and he always go as the same thing every year. Merlin and Morgan. They're the same costume, anyway, with the hoods and the, you know, embroidery."

"The runes," Marcia said, just as Ginger said, "The symbols."

The other women drank their orange concoction. A boy in a white jacket passed by, and Jeannie lifted another of the drinks from his tray and handed it to Marcia. "Here. It's rum and orange sherbet and ginger ale. I think."

"Probably Quaaludes," Ginger said, and downed the rest of hers.

"I wish," Jeannie muttered. Her gaze fluttered over Marcia's costume. "So you're like a Gypsy?"

"No," Marcia said. "More like those storefront fortune tellers in the city, with the neon signs."

"Well, those aren't very scary. Those are just little old ladies trying to bulk up their Social Security checks."

"Then I'm the spectre of dying alone in poverty, I guess," Marcia said.

Jeannie and Ginger went silent. They shared a glance out of their corner of their eyes. And as one, they laughed, and Ginger said, "You are just too funny, Marcia," and Jeannie said, "Isn't she funny, Daryl, darling?"

And then Daryl was there, and he took the orange monstrosity out of her hand and replaced it with something clear and strong. His arm slid around her. He smelled like the pomade he'd used to Elvis up his hair, and the shoe polish he'd used to make the sideburns.

"She's the best," he said.

Ginger eyed Marcia's husband up and down, and her arm tightened its link with Jeannie's. "How's Clover?" she asked, brightly. "Still dancing?"

"She runs track, now," Daryl said. "Cross country."

"Oh," said Ginger and Jeannie, at once. Their disappointment was obvious. They were clearly about to say something more when the room hushed and the crowd parted. In strode their hosts, the Llewellyns.

The Llewellyns, Martin and Myra, had opened the Secret Hills Golf and Country Club almost thirty years ago. The couple came over from England after the war and bought the land sight unseen. It started as a target range: skeet shooting, archery, rifles. They even allowed camping. But the permits and the insurance were a legal nightmare, and the acreage was costing them a fortune in taxes, and so they sculpted the land, trimmed the hedges, and manicured the lawns. They planted traps. The course was a success, and the business grew: a tennis court, a pool, a sauna, a Tudor-style clubhouse with vaulted ceilings and dark beams. Since then they had franchised. Now there were Llewellyn-owned country clubs all up and down the Eastern seaboard. Daryl had explained it all, when they first visited together.

"I used to caddy, here, when I was a kid," he had said, "so if we wanted to get married here, we could."

Which of course they did, when they saw the deal Martin was willing to cut them on the venue. Marcia suspected they were like many other couples at the Halloween party, in that way. The club had been part of their lives since they were kids. It was an oasis for them as it once was for their parents: a place where time moved slower, and people were more polite, and the standards of behaviour were high but simple. They received a free month's membership at the club as part of the wedding package, and after that it just seemed like too much trouble to quit — it would be insulting Martin and

Myra, they felt, to leave the community so soon. And the Llewellyns had been so helpful. Myra had introduced them to their real estate agent. Without Doris, they would never have found the house.

Martin Llewellyn's sonorous voice filled the lounge. "Friends, we thank you for joining us once again, on this most special evening."

There was a murmur of assent.

"We have prepared for you all the usual festivities. You will notice the themes of each room: the colours are in the same order as before, with black of course being the last." Martin smiled at his own joke. Everyone else smiled, too.

"In the Black Room, at the stroke of midnight, we shall find the winners of this evening's drawing. As usual, there is one ticket per household. Gentlemen, I suggest you give your ladies your tickets now, before you get too deep in the scotch."

Most of the men laughed. Daryl didn't.

"And now that night has fallen, you will please excuse us if we lock the doors behind us," Martin continued. "You all know the rules. No running out on the grounds. The valets have your keys, and they have been instructed not to give them up until you can demonstrate the proper sobriety." He cleared his throat. "The conservatory transoms have been opened in the Green Room for those of you who wish to smoke. There is plenty of food and drink, and billiards, and darts, and all manner of games of chance."

Silence. Myra Llewellyn gave her husband a tiny frown. "And ladies," she added, in her own silvery voice, "should you require a rest, the Violet Room has been furnished with more than the usual number of settees."

"They bought us fainting couches," Marcia whispered.

"Later," Daryl murmured, without moving his lips very much at all.

"But before the night wears on, might I suggest making use of this evening's photographer?" Myra gestured at a long-haired man carrying a huge Minolta on a black and orange bandolier. He was dressed like a foreign correspondent embedded in Hanoi. Or perhaps that was simply how photographers always dressed. "You'll want evidence," Myra continued, "of having been here tonight."

At the back of the room, a woman made a choking sound. As one, the club turned to her. It was Bitsy Logan, Bride of Frankenstein. "Went down the wrong pipe," she croaked. Her husband rubbed her back. Bitsy wiped her eyes.

"We know you could be elsewhere, this evening," Martin said, now, more quietly. "It means so much that you have chosen to be with us."

In the hall, the huge clock struck eight.

# # #

Marcia was two martinis deep when Fiona Henstridge asked her about the Black Room.

"Is it true what they say? That you can find out about the winners ahead of time?"

"I suppose," Marcia answered, dabbing her nose with the puff from her compact. The women's restroom was a haze of smoke already. "The balls are in there. I don't know when exactly they draw them, but…"

Fiona watched her in the mirror. "Has anyone ever done it? Looked ahead?"

"I don't know. Maybe. But I think we would have heard about it, if they did."

Her eyeliner was already beginning to smear. She'd put too much on, for the sake of her costume. Now she looked like a raccoon. Maybe she would be a raccoon, next year. Maybe Clover could be a raccoon. If Clover still did Halloween. If Clover was still-

"Do you think the kids are still out trick or treating? The little ones, I mean?"

"Probably not." Marcia rifled through her bag for her lipstick. Somehow it was always at the bottom, and never in the slot explicitly intended for that purpose. "It's late. And it's cold."

"Is Clover babysitting?" Fiona asked. "Philip is out with friends," she continued, without waiting for an answer. "By the lake, I think."

Marcia didn't ask which lake. She knew the local lakes. She knew how broad they were, how deep. Sometimes the lakes were dangerous. There were all sorts of dangerous places tucked away in Secret Hills. Lakes and cliffs and condemned homes and sticky railroad tracks and empty fields and sometimes even your own basement. Her fingers locked around her lipstick and she uncapped it with unusual force. She pulled her lips into a tragedy mask and began swiping on colour. In the store, she'd dithered between Maple Red and Appleshine. Clover cheekily suggested that Marcia simply buy both and give her the other one, and that way they could trade whenever they felt like it.

"Clover is babysitting." She blotted. "Lots of the girls are."

"You don't think any of them have done something stupid, do you? Like drinking? Or leaving the doors unlocked?"

Once, Clover had fallen asleep with the doors unlocked while Marcia went out for milk. Marcia grounded her for a week. It never happened again.

"I doubt it," Marcia said. "They're smart kids. They know what can happen if they're not careful."

"Jon says they're lucky," Fiona said. "It's not like they still have the draft."

Marcia thought of the little squirrel cage with the red balls in the Black Room. "I suppose."

Behind them, in the mirror, they watched Doris Hansen run into a bathroom stall, crying. A cluster of her friends followed a half-step behind.

"Clover's an only child, isn't she?"

Marcia raised her eyes to meet Fiona's, in the mirror. "Yes, she is."

"That must be so hard for you. Not having more. Everyone says that four is too many, but honestly I wish we could have five." Fiona smiled. "It's too late to start again, I suppose, isn't it?"

Something inside Marcia twisted. She felt it in her uterus, and her arms, and everywhere that had held Clover's body close to her own. "Sometimes I'm sad that Clover doesn't have a brother or sister." She snapped her bag shut and stood. She watched the other woman in the mirror, surrounded by all the other women of Secret Hills wreathed in blue smoke and White Shoulders. "But her life is good. Our life is good. That's the whole point of living here, isn't it? Isn't that why we all agreed to it? Wasn't that the deal?"

# # #

"Do you think anybody goes inside the Black Room ahead of time?" Marcia asked Daryl, when they reconnected in the Orange Room. He'd taken up residence there, since his costume somewhat matched the decor. The photographer took their picture as they talked. Daryl was rubbing her feet. Marcia had long since kicked off her shoes. They were giving her blisters.

"Probably not," he said. "I mean, it's possible someone's tried. But I don't think Martin would like it."

"But it's not locked."

"Not, it's not locked. Anybody can go in." Daryl looked down the hall, into the other rooms. "I think that's part of the whole thing. Forbidden fruit, and all that. It's a test, kind of."

"Do you think they choose the numbers ahead of time?"

Daryl shrugged. "I don't know. Sometimes I think it's random, and other times I think it's planned."

"Like life," Marcia said.

Daryl frowned at her empty glass. "Jesus, how many of those have you had?" He motioned to a boy in a white jacket. "Hi. Hello. Could you please get my wife some water? Thanks."

"I'm fine," Marcia insisted. "I've been sticking to gin. It's the sugary stuff that gets you wrecked."

In the corner, Ginger Hayes vomited very neatly into a potted plant.

"Do you want to go look?" Daryl asked.

She looked up at him through her lashes. "Seriously?"

"Yeah. Seriously. I'll go with you, if you want to." His gaze fell. "But you'd have to really want to."

Marcia considered. She imagined herself striding through all the rooms, through the haze of smoke and past all the other revellers, and pushing her way into the Black Room room with its single red bulb. The numbers would be there, waiting. She could check them against the ticket. She could know the truth. Get it over with. Right now.

"It's like that experiment with the cat in the box," she murmured. "Until you know whether you've won or lost, either is equally possible."

The boy in the white jacket returned with two glasses of water. Daryl took them from the tray. When they each had a glass, he made sure their eyes met before he clinked them together. "Like life."

The water tasted vaguely chlorinated, as though it had been drawn from some emergency supply and not the tap. Maybe the Llewellyns had learned to keep a stock of things like that during the Blitz. This place would be a good spot to wait out something like a war, or a plague. Marcia drained her entire glass in one go.

"All right," she said. "I want to see."

# # #

The Black Room was larger than she'd expected. Perhaps because she'd always crowded into it with the others, her sense of it had remained hot and small and stuffy, thick with the funeral home smell of unwashed velvet and old lipstick. In reality it was a large room, quite possibly a second ballroom, possibly even the room she'd been married in. Which reminded her all over again of why she'd come.

A single red bulb hung over a small table laden with two red candles, a squirrel cage full of red balls, a book, and a fountain pen. Marcia hastened over. The twin blisters over her Achilles tendons enervated her. They were like two hounds nipping at her heels.

"So this is it." She ran her hands over the book. It felt much older than it looked from a distance. The leather was a curious texture. And the binding was knotted together with something like violin strings.

"Maybe this wasn't such a good idea," Daryl said. "I mean, no one's ever really gone looking. Not even when I was a kid."

The alcohol seemed to evaporate from Marcia's body instantly, leaving behind only the clean, sharp quality of the gin in the centre of her mind. And just like that, the question she'd never asked hung before her like an apple low on the branch. All she had to do was take it.

"How long have you known? About the draw? Did you know about the draw when you were a kid? You grew up here, after all."

Daryl blinked. Under his shoe polish sideburns, he was sweating. The single red bulb made it too dim to see, but she could smell it blooming off him in anxious waves. It was his home late sweat, his gone-too-long Saturday afternoon sweat, his "I don't know what you want me to say," sweat. It was as strong an indictment as a whiff of another woman's White Shoulders.

"I mean, growing up, we knew that people sometimes disappeared," he said. "Bad kids. You know, kids who stayed out late. Girls who parked. You know, greasers and fairies and the like. Kids who couldn't hack it in class and they left once the school year really got going."

Marcia's fingers splayed over the book. She had opened it without meaning to, without even looking at it, so fixed was her gaze on her husband. Under her fingers, the letters felt embossed somehow. As though with a little training she could know the names and numbers without looking. Like typing. Or feeding a punch card computer.

"Bad kids," she said.

"Girls, mostly, and sometimes their boyfriends." He grinned. "See? We've got nothing to worry about! Clover doesn't date!"

Marcia's palms pressed flat to the pages of the book. The leather creaked under her hands as she leaned forward. "So you knew. Before we came here. Before we were married. Before Clover. You knew."

"I wouldn't say that. We suspected. Me and my friends. Not even that. It was a campfire story! Something we'd scare girls with on the way home!"

"Girls who parked, presumably."

Daryl gave her a look that implied her listening to him so carefully and remembering what he'd just said was somehow a low and petty betrayal. Just as he attempted to protest, the Llewellyns swept into the room.

"Ah, Marcia," they said, as though they'd expected her. "Fiona thought we might find you here."

"No one likes a tattle-tale," Marcia said.

Both Llewellyns gave the same brittle, pitying smile that they frequently afforded to American jokes.

"Reading ahead, are you?" Mr. Llwellyn arched one magnificent eyebrow. "Young Daryl over here has always told us that you were quite the reader."

"What else has he told you?"

The three of them shared a look. "Only how much he loves you, my dear girl," Mrs. Llewellyn said. "He was so excited to marry you. I remember it like it was yesterday. Why, we'd known him since he was a tiny thing, and saw him grow up all elbows and knees and spots here where he caddied, and we were so pleased for him-

"That's right," Marcia said. "You caddied, here. You knew about the Halloween party."

"It wasn't always Halloween," Mr. Llewellyn said.

"Yes, sometimes it was the first of May," said his wife.

"But that has different connotations on these shores," Mr. Llewellyn finished. "And it's best done at harvest time, I should think."

"And once we realized it could be a fancy dress party…" Mrs. Llewellyn gestured at her own robes, covered in runes, and the crescent moon that hung just above her navel. All these years, Marcia had thought it was just a big silver hippie pendant. But no, it was a knife. Like the kind used to cut linoleum. "Well, it just seemed meant to be, after that."

Marcia's fingers drifted over the fountain pen to the left of the book.

"You knew," she said to Daryl, "and you bought us here anyway."

"Of course he did!" said Mr. Llewellyn. "What young man in his position wouldn't? We have a stable, safe, clean, prosperous community here, full of like-minded people who share the same traditional values that have stood the test of time. Of course he wanted to bring you here, and raise your child here. The cities are in decay. The back-to-the-landers are poor farmers and worse lovers. The children grow up without fathers, without any discipline. They grow up soft. But here, here we know when to use the carrot, and when to use the stick."

Marcia was aware of the Llewellyn's coming gradually closer. Their robes were so long she couldn't see their feet. They appeared to float across the blackened floor.

"It's good for them, you see, in the end," Mrs. Llewellyn agreed. "It gives them a greater appreciation for life."

She said "appreciation" with an S where the C should be. Marcia wondered if she would be able to make the same sound if she were missing all her teeth.

"And it ensures the continuation of our community," her husband added.

Marcia picked up the book and held it close. She watched their eyes widen in the dark. "So how does it work?" she asked. "Your hand goes in the cage, you pick a number from the cage, and it corresponds to a raffle ticket. It's random. Right?"

"More or less," Mr. Llwellyn said.

“Well, which is it? More, or less?” Marcia flipped the book open to the last page and then turned it around. Under her fingers, she could feel the numbers, spiky and crawling, alive somehow in the dull red light. “Because it doesn’t look random, to me. It looks like you’ve chosen ahead of time. It looks like you’ve rigged the game. All the way into the next century.”

Daryl stepped back. “That’s impossible.”

“Shut the fuck up, Daryl.”

“Hey! Don’t take that tone of voice with me, or I’ll-”

“You’ll what?” Marcia snapped the book shut. She held it high, but close to the candle flame. A little too close, for the Llewellyn’s comfort. “What’ll you do, Daryl? Divorce me? If it takes Clover out of the game, then please, go right ahead. Divorce me.”

Daryl paled. “I don’t want that! I don’t want to divorce you. I want to stay married to you until the day I die. I want us to grow old together. I want us to eat dinner at four o’clock and slow everyone down on the interchange and get one of those tiny dogs no one likes.” He swallowed. “I want you to forgive me. Can you do that? I promise you that all I wanted was what I thought was best for us. If I had thought the city was best, we would have gone there. And we’d run have risks there, too. You know what it’s like. This is the safest place, and I brought you here because I love you. Do you think you can forgive that?”

Marcia wondered if she could. She wondered what would happen if and when Clover's number came up. It might not. In some years, the number corresponded to a raffle ticket that didn't show up in their country club. But she suspected that it corresponded to another ticket, in another club, in another town. There were more, up and down the seaboard. There were other Clovers, everywhere. Could she forgive that? Really? And if the worst were to happen, and Clover was gone, what would be left? Only the knowledge of what her husband had always known. It would stretch between them forever, like the vast expanse of their manicured lawn slowly going yellow in summer heat.

Somehow, Daryl was still talking.

"Honey, you're drunk. And tired. And nervous. We all are. Just put the book down, okay?"

"Please, Marcia." Mrs. Llewellyn had drawn into herself like a mantis about to strike. "Let's discuss this like adults."

"Our whole community is in that book," Mr. Llewellyn said, in his gentlest voice. "You don't want to wipe all that away, do you? You don't want to destroy all this."

Finally, Marcia looked down at the book's pages. And there were the numbers, alive and writhing, crawling all over her fingers like fire ants, leaving little pricks of blood and smears of carbon black in their wake as they scurried inside the binding and between the pages. They crawled up inside her sleeves and under her collar and into her mouth and over her eyes. When she spoke her voice was full of them: humming, resonant, certain.

"Oh," she said. "But I do."

When she held the book over the candle, three things happened. First, the others shouted at her to stop. Second, the numbers went up like sparks, burning before the pages or the binding or the covers. And third, as the leather began to burn, fire licked up the black velvet curtains all around them. In the distance, she heard screams. And she remembered all the locked doors, and all the rules, and thought of Clover safe at home, her black cat face rising from her book as she smelled fire just over the hills. ♜

# THE BLOOD-INKED COMIC BOOK

*By Jeremiah Dylan Cook*

I STARED DOWN AT THE ASHTRAY on the tiny table. The noxious stink of cigarettes reminded me of how Johnny's body smelled during his metamorphosis. Detective Ketch sat opposite me in the claustrophobic interrogation room. The cop's black mustache stood in stark contrast to his white hair. His aviator glasses seemed to take up most of his face.

Ketch tapped his cigarette on the ashtray. "Alright, Mr. Roy, what's your story?"

My stomach growled. I'd never replaced the contents of my gut after puking yesterday. I itched at where my torn shirt was irritating my skin. No one had offered me new clothes, so I'd remained in my blood-stained denim shirt and corduroy pants. I pushed my shaggy hair back and felt a day's worth of grease that needed to be shampooed away.

Ketch knocked on the table. “I don’t have all day, Mr. Roy.”

“It’s going to sound crazy.”

“That’s fine. I’ve heard crazy before. Hell, I run into crazy every time I pass through the Bowery.”

“You’ve never heard this kind of crazy.”

“Kid, last year, during the bicentennial, there were 1,622 homicides in this city. I was the first one at the scene for a lot of those. Nothing you say will shock me.” Ketch took a drag on his cigarette.

“Have you heard of the band Smooch?”

“Sure. Those four guys who dress up in black leather and paint their faces with flames. I hear they put on great live shows.”

“It all started when their lead singer came into the Astonishing Comics office.”

# # #

Mr. Lieber drove a toy car around his desk while I sat next to him, ready to jot down notes. His aged frame and snowy beard made him look a bit like Santa Clause. While Mr. Lieber’s name was on most of Astonishing Comic’s work as the writer, I was the guy who truly wrote the dialogue, the descriptions, and everything beyond the vague outline Mr. Lieber gave me. Still, everyone, including me, loved Mr. Lieber for creating iconic characters such as The Fabulous Five, Moth-Man, the Z-People, and Doctor Destruction. He'd been serving as both a writer and the editor-in-chief for over a decade now.

The office walls were plastered in art from the various comics currently being published. There was also a calendar covered in upcoming deadlines. The rest of the room was relatively spartan, with an empty trashcan being the only other piece of furniture besides the three chairs and desk. Outside of Mr. Lieber's glass door, the day-to-day operations hummed along. Artists sketched on tall standing easels, while writers clacked the keys of their typewriters in cubicles stretching to the windows, where you got a small glimpse of the midtown skyline. A vast mural of Astonishing Comics' characters hung over the room with the slogan "Enter the Astonishing Universe" underneath.

"Where is this guy? He was supposed to be here an hour ago. I want my lunch." Mr. Lieber drove the toy car off his desk and into the trash.

"Speak of the devil, and he will appear." A tall man wearing black boots, black jeans, and a long black coat stood just across the desk.

I hadn't heard the door into the office open, nor had I seen him walk in. Sweat beaded on my brow as the cool air became stifling. The man's face was painted with red and yellow flames framed by his long brown hair. From my research on Smooch, I knew this guy was Damien Hellbound, the lead singer.

Mr. Lieber sat forward. "Don't you ever take that stuff off your face?"

"No." Damien reached into his jacket and produced a manilla envelope. "This contains documents showing how many sales we've had in the last three years. My bandmates and I believe a partnership with Astonishing Comics could be beneficial for both of us."

"You don't need to convince us. Your tunes are all over the radio. We'd be happy to work with Smooch." Mr. Lieber stroked his beard. "Heck, this meeting is really just so Roy here can hear what you want and go write it up."

Damien's gaze fell on me for the first time, and when I tried to return eye contact, it felt like I was staring at the sun. I looked away and saw spots popping up in my vision. After several blinks, my eyesight returned to normal.

Damien put the envelope back in his jacket. "You can write whatever you want. My band has only one request."

Mr. Lieber snapped his fingers at me. "Name it."

My pen hovered over my notepad as I waited to write down whatever our guest said.

"We want to mix our blood with the comic's ink."

"What?" Mr. Lieber let out a nervous laugh.

"It will drive publicity for the comic, increase sales, and allow us to reach a greater audience of children." Damien reached back into his jacket and pulled out a rolled-up sheet of paper. "If we have a deal, I just need to get the writer's signature on this contract. Management will be in touch to finalize the rest of the details."

I looked at Mr. Lieber and shook my head. Nothing about this felt right. Hellbound clearly had issues we didn't need to be associated with.

"Lighten up, Roy." Mr. Lieber gestured for the contract. "Kids love this kind of kooky stuff. It will be great. Sign the document and get started on the comic. We'll have Smooch face off against Doctor Destruction in a big double-sized issue spectacular. It'll be great."

Damien unrolled the document on the desk. I leaned over and scanned it, but I couldn't make out the writing. It was in another language. The paper didn't look like paper either. It looked closer to a thin sliver of skin. I reached forward with my pen, but Damien held out a hand for me to stop.

"Use this." He removed a quill that looked like it'd been carved from someone's fingerbone.

I took the writing instrument and signed my name where Damien pointed. The ink was scarlet, and I had to press down hard to scratch my full name, Thomas Roy, into the material. As I managed to complete the final letter in my last name, I felt sick, like I'd swallowed a rock that was passing through my intestines.

"What language is this?" I asked.

"Ancient Babylonian." Damien rolled up the contract and returned it to his jacket. "We'll meet you at the ink plant in thirteen weeks. The comic must be ready to be printed by then."

"We'll make it our number one priority." Mr. Lieber stood up and offered his hand.

Damien turned away and left the office, disappearing around a corner outside.

"Christ, and I thought the hippies were weird. This new wave of pseudo-satanism is something else." Mr. Lieber sat back in his chair.

"I don't know if I'd call it pseudo. Are we really going to print a comic for this guy and let the band toss their blood into it?" I asked.

"Of course. That guy may be crazy, but he's right. It'll be great publicity, and printing anything with Smooch is guaranteed to make a mint."

# # #

Ketch lit up a second cigarette. "And did you make a mint?"

"Yes. Lieber was entirely correct. Smooch: An Astonishing Comics Special was released three months ago, and it sold out within a week of release."

"Why don't you tell me about Johnny now?"

"I'm not ready to talk about him yet."

"You're trying my patience, kid." Ketch let out a puff of smoke. "This better be going somewhere."

"We started getting calls from parents pretty soon after the Smooch comic came out. They were all saying their kids had started to act up after they'd read the issue. I thought it was the usual moral panic over whatever kids liked. But I couldn't deny that Mr. Lieber had come back shaken from his trip to the ink plant. He retired abruptly and wouldn't talk about what he'd seen, except to say the bandmembers had indeed dropped their blood into the ink. Lieber's smiling in all the publicity stills we put in the comic, so I really can't say what he could've seen."

"He's an old man. Maybe his egg just cracked?"

"I don't think that's the case at all, but he was lucky he left when he did. I was promoted to his position, and I had to meet with the owner's son, Dan, to hear about how much he liked the Smooch comic a week after I started."

# # #

Mr. Lieber's seat still didn't fit me right, and I jotted down a note to pull in my old chair from the bullpen. Stacks of paper covered my desk, and I was totally overwhelmed by the sudden jump in responsibilities. I'd need to create a system to manage everything soon or risk getting so far behind on deadlines that I'd start missing shipping dates.

Outside the office, the artists and writers had gone home for the night. Only a few hallway lights remained on for the cleaning staff. I returned my attention to a page I was editing. I made several notes for the writer to shorten his dialogue and provided some directions for the inker before moving onto a new page.

The office door opened with a squeak, and a gust of warm air came in. I looked up to see Mel Moore, the President of Astonishing Comics, standing there with a grin. He wore shorts that didn't reach the middle of his thighs and a polo, which exposed his sprawling chest hair. A tennis racket hung in his right arm. Our parent company subjected us to Moore because he'd once interned for the Times, and his family made up most of the company's board. His pre-teen son stood behind him in a plaid suit.

Mel walked in and tapped my desk with his racket. "Sorry to barge in on you, but I've got a tennis match with some friends at the gym downstairs. I was hoping you could watch my son Dan until I got back. He's been dying to discuss the Smooch comic with you."

I struggled to keep my facial expression neutral as I seethed with frustration. "Sure. I'd be happy to."

"Great. I'll be back soon." Moore left.

Despite my annoyance, I reminded myself not to take anything out on Moore's son, who wasn't responsible for his father. "Come on in, Dan. Grab a seat. I'll be with you in a second."

Dan walked across the office and sat down as I finished marking up another page.

"So, what's on your mind?"

While the kid was tall for his age, baby fat still clung to his face giving him a bloated visage.

Tears started to fall from Dan's eyes. "Why did you let them do it?"

"Do what? What's wrong?"

"Haven't you read the comic? Didn't you write it?" Dan cried as snot joined the tears.

I looked around for tissues. "The Smooch one? Yeah, I wrote the whole thing. They go to Doctor Destruction's castle and stop him from invading the United States. Pretty standard stuff. I'm sorry it upset you so much."

"That's not what happens at all. That's just what they want you to think. There's more in the pages, in the ink." Dan pulled out a heavily crumpled and rolled-up copy of the comic and laid it on my desk. "I've been changing ever since I read it, and I'm hearing voices. They're telling me to do horrible things."

My mouth hung open as I struggled to compose a response. "Have you told your dad about any of this?"

"They won't let me. They hold my tongue down when I try. I can only talk to you because you signed the pact." Blood started to mix with the snot streaming out of Dan's nose. "They're inside of me."

I stood up and walked over to the door, which I opened. "Let's get you back to your dad. I'll bring you to the gym."

# # #

"Sounds like a crazy kid." Ketch paced back and forth.

I slumped down in my chair. “He wasn’t. My work had changed him. It let something enter his body.”

“Ever considered you’re crazy too? It’s hard for crazy to recognize crazy. Artist types like you are always going off their rockers, aren’t they?” Ketch sat back down. “Why don’t you tell me about Johnny now?”

“My encounter with Dan made me start taking the calls we’d been getting from parents more seriously, and I remembered that I’d given the comic to Johnny in a comp box.”

“Comp box?” Ketch asked.

“They’re boxes filled with all the comics we produce for a month. A lot of our employees and some special friends and family get them. Johnny got one because he liked Astonishing Comics, and he was cheap market research for me.”

“Alright, so what did he think of the Smooch comic?”

# # #

My sister, Tabitha, unlocked two deadbolts and removed three chains from her front door. I rushed in to escape the sour milk stench of the hallway. She had several scented candles burning around the kitchen to keep the outside odors at bay. I picked up hints of vanilla and cinnamon.

“Sorry about the smell. Old Mrs. Magdalena was jumped for her groceries yesterday, and the robbers spilled her milk all over. What is this city coming to?" Tabitha shoved a can of mace into her purse.

I realized my sister was dressed for work at the diner. She wore her hair in a bun that vaguely reminded me of Princess Lara from the movie Space Battles, and her faded red blouse bore the food stains of past shifts. After my experience with Dan, I was uncomfortable at the thought of being left alone with another kid, even one I knew as well as my nephew.

"I didn't realize you were heading out."

"You don't mind, do you? You said you wanted to talk to Johnny, and I figured you two could catch up and play a game or something while I worked. It'll only be a short shift." Tabitha stood in the doorway, ready to leave.

"Sure."

"Thanks. I'll bring you back the last slice of pie from the diner." Tabitha pulled the door shut and left.

My sister's apartment was always a mess. The sink was filled with dirty dishes that had been left to suffer the ravages of time, her fold up kitchen table was covered in magazine clippings, and greasy pans littered the stove. I thought that even without the spilled milk outside, she would've needed the candles to hide the stink within. Still, I couldn't judge her housekeeping too harshly, considering Johnny's dad had split five years ago, and she was on her own to work and raise him. I re-locked the door and deposited an envelope filled with money on the table. I helped her out as often as I could.

Johnny sat on the couch in the living room facing the lone, dirty window. A brick wall was the only view out there, but some sunlight still managed to creep through. My pulse quickened when I realized he was reading the Smooch comic.

He turned to me and smiled. “Hi, Uncle Tom. You look like you’ve seen a ghost.”

I sat down in a small chair next to the couch, opposite the rabbit-eared television. “Sorry, Johnny. I just came to ask you about how you were enjoying that exact comic, and I was surprised to see it in your hands.”

“Is it true the band put their blood in the ink?” Johnny asked.

My nephew had just hit double digits, and his current obsession was the syndicated show Galaxy Hop. Figures, most of which I’d bought him, littered the floor, and he wore a yellow t-shirt with a small bottle cap I’d fashioned into a star-shaped Galaxyfleet communicator. He’d even taken to gelling his hair like his favorite character, Captain Cork. I’d been meaning to take him to see Space Battles, which I knew would blow his mind, for several months.

“Yeah. They had the blood drawn and mixed with the ink up at our plant near Buffalo. What did you think of the story?”

Johnny couldn’t keep a sour expression off his face. “I don’t really like how the band gets their powers from demons because demons are supposed to be bad. I rooted for Doctor Destruction to beat them, and I was disappointed when he didn't."

"Fair point." Relief flooded into me over the normal response. "I did write that issue, though. You could at least pretend to have liked it."

"Well, even though I didn't like it. I've read it thirteen times. I don't know why, but I keep wanting to re-read it." Johnny turned a page in the comic.

Over his shoulder, I could see the art of the four band members battling Doctor Destruction on a bridge above a lake of lava. Each member of Smooch was adorned in black armor, and their faces were all painted with flames. Doctor Destruction wore a mustard-yellow tunic and a flowing crimson cape with a hood, which hid his scarred face. As I stared at the art, the lava seemed to boil and steam for real. I smelled the rotten egg scent of brimstone.

I got out of the chair and snatched the comic from his hand. "Well, thirteen times is probably good enough. Let me get rid of this for you."

Johnny smiled up at me. "Why so scared Uncle Tom? Is it because you know Johnny's about to burn?"

"What?"

"You signed the contract. You let them put their blood in the ink. You gave us permission to do this." My nephew's face had twisted into an expression of cynical contempt far beyond his years.

"You're scaring me, Johnny. Why don't you stop the possessed act? Did your mom let you watch The Expulsionist recently? Did that horror flick warp your brain?"

Smoke curled out from Johnny's ears, nose, and mouth. "Help me, Uncle Tom. I don't know what's happening."

My nephew's forehead started to blacken and char as his cheeks bubbled with heat that I could feel warming my skin. Adrenaline flooded through my body, and I raced into the kitchen to look for a fire extinguisher. I tossed everything out of the cabinets as I searched them. There was nothing to put out a fire. I opened the fridge and was relieved to discover a full pitcher of water, which I grabbed. When I returned to the living room, Johnny's face was engulfed in a blaze of flames.

The white of his skull was visible in several spots, and his melted eyes ran down his face like eggy tears.

I poured the water over his head, and steam issued forth to fill the room. The smell reminded me of melted plastic. I started coughing. Johnny swung his arms wildly in a blind panic and tore my denim shirt while smearing me with his blood. Once I'd gotten out of his reach, I went back to the kitchen for more water. I couldn't take what I'd seen and puked all over the dirty dishes in the sink.

"Don't worry, Mr. Roy, I'll take good care of Johnny's body."

I turned around to see my nephew standing in the doorway to the kitchen. His head was devoid of skin, and flames erupted from the base of his neck. His arms had turned black and scaly. Long talons had sprouted from the end of his fingers. Bat-like wings tore through the back of his shirt as I looked on in horror. A pair of protrusions grew from his crown, and I realized he now had horns.

# # #

"Stop right there." Ketch pounded on the door. "I'm done with this ridiculousness. You're going back into a cell until you're ready to tell me what really happened to your nephew."

I wiped away tears. "I knew you wouldn't believe me. How do you explain what your officers found at my sister's place?"

"We found a door that had been smashed open without being unlocked, and we found signs of intense heat. That's it. You want my theory? I think you accidentally burned your nephew's face off while trying to cook him dinner and came up with this story to cope with your guilt. Everything we found there was staged by you. My only question is, where did you hide his body?"

"After I woke up from passing out, I came right here. I didn't have time to change anything in the apartment."

A uniformed cop opened the door to the interrogation room.

Ketch stepped into the hallway. "Take this guy back to the holding cells for now. And call up a shrink. This guy needs an evaluation."

"If I was really so damaged that I concocted this story to hide from my feelings, why would I have come to the police and not made up a story that kept me out of jail?"

The uniformed cop came in and slapped cuffs back on me.

Ketch smiled. "You're a comics guy. You live in a world of good and evil, and you knew you needed to be punished.

I was led into the hallway. "Look into the other kids who read the comic."

"How many kids would that be?" Ketch laughed.

"Millions," I whispered.

# # #

I lay on a bench, turned away from the other inhabitants of general population, and stared at a concrete wall. The dim lighting flickered on and off as the single bulb above buzzed loudly. The entire room smelled of urine. I couldn't wait for the psychiatrist to arrive so I could be pronounced insane and get transferred to a private, padded room. Behind me, I heard cops unlock the cell door every few minutes and take or add someone new to the cage.

The bulb above shattered, startling me into sitting up and turning around. I found myself alone. The six benches between me and the other wall were empty. Moonlight from the tiny, unreachable window illuminated the toilet in the corner. A little light still found its way in from deeper in the police station and cast inky tendrils of shadow through the steel bars keeping me imprisoned.

Out of the darkness in the middle of the room stepped Damien Hellbound. "I have an offer for you." The painted fire on his face seemed to writhe like real flames.

I reached down and pinched my thigh to ensure I was awake. "What's that?"

"We'll give you your nephew back. But in exchange, you must produce more blood comics for us."

I laughed. "Are you going to put the skin back on his face first?"

"Don't underestimate the power of the pit. He'll be returned as he was before Zarthusala took control of his flesh." Hellbound's eyes glowed like burning coals.

I looked away and stared at my feet. "You want me to let the forces of hell enslave the souls of millions of children in exchange for my nephew? I love the kid, and I'm tempted, but I can't say that deal seems like a fair exchange."

"We have no power over souls, only flesh. We can provide messages and guidance, but humans must freely choose to do evil to condemn their souls to our clutches. And the vast majority of the children who read our work will not become like Johnny. Your nephew was a special case because he shared a blood bond with you, the signer of the contract. That gave us extra liberties with his form."

"So, what happens to the vast majority?"

"They're encouraged to do small evils. They'll lie more, disrespect authority, have pre-marital sex, commit minor theft. In other words, they'll do normal kid stuff. We don't even need to have the whelps in this city read our comics. They're rotten enough on their own. We're using your comics to pierce the heartland. A select number of children will become special sleeper agents, but we may never even need to activate them. Who can say when the almighty will finally kick off Armageddon?"

"I see."

"So, do we have a deal?"

I pictured my nephew playing with his toys and reading comics. "Yes."

Hellbound walked forward, stepping on the shattered lightbulb's glass. He presented another contract and bone quill. I took the skin-like paper, laid it on the bench, and scratched out my name, just like I'd done before.

"What happens if someone stops me from fulfilling my end of this bargain?"

"Johnny will be set ablaze again. This time Zarthusala will keep his flesh." Hellbound collected the contract. "We'll be in touch with further instructions on which comics we'd like our ink run in and when."

A clamor of voices filled the room as the other jailed individuals reappeared in the cage with me. They were complaining about the broken light. The cell door opened, and several cops came in to clean up the area and handle the commotion. One of the officers was my former interrogator.

Ketch made a beeline to me. “You’re free to go. Your nephew returned to your sister’s place without a scratch. Thanks for wasting our time. I still think you should wait around to see the shrink.”

Despite the detective’s ire, the news relieved me. My nephew was safe, and my sister wasn’t childless. Hellbound had made good on his promise quicker than I’d imagined possible. Once I checked in with Johnny to confirm he was truly back to normal, it would be time to start preparing to hold up my end of the bargain. While my body was uninjured, I knew my soul would soon be damned. ♜

# THE CROWE FAMILY: A PARODY

*By Henry Herz*

I BLASTED OUT THE FINAL minor key on my heavily distorted bass guitar as we finished a second encore with our smash hit, "Come On Get Morbid." Our new style of rock, death metal, was wildly popular. During the standing room-only concert, we had to turn up the volume of our music to drown out the crowd's roars.

Once the enthusiastic cheering subsided, Chris threw his drumsticks into the crowd. Tracy set down her tambourine and waded with Chris into the audience. The rest of our family band wove backstage through a crowd of black T-shirted groupies to a green room featuring a fully stocked bar and trays of sandwiches and snacks.

No stranger to monstrous appetites, I long ago learned to control mine. Sadly, I couldn't say that for my bandmates. I knew from experience that "eight-year-old" Chris and "seven-year-old" Tracy would be getting into mischief of one kind or another – tying shoelaces together, picking pockets, and pinching rear ends. Hefting his Ovation Breadwinner electric guitar, "eighteen-year-old" Keith stood like a smiling Greek god rising from a tempest-tossed sea of eager girls.

"Nice bass playing tonight, Danny," said our "thirty-something" hazel-eyed blonde lead singer, Shirley – or "Mom" as we called her.

"Thanks," I replied in my squeaky ten-year-old's voice.

Tall, thin piano player Laurie stood in front of a mirror. Her long brown hair framed green eyes in a pretty sixteen-year-old face. Personally, I have no use for mirrors, but even so, who stares at themselves like that?

When she didn't think I'd notice, Mom guided a fit, smiling fan out of the green room, her intentions very different than those of the poor unsuspecting man.

*Helvete!* I cursed in Norwegian, pushing my way through the groupies in pursuit. Bursting into the hallway, I checked both directions. *Where are they?* I sniffed for human blood. *Ah, the janitor's closet.* I rushed over and yanked open the door – luckily before Mom had sprouted the fangs and long, snake-like tail of a lamia and devoured the poor bastard. "Take a hike!" I ordered.

The human frowned at the interruption, having no way to know I'd just saved him from becoming Mom's late-night supper. And adults don't typically take orders from a red-headed, freckle-faced boy. But since I was an eight-hundred-year-old Nordic vampire, my gaze held menace and power atypical of a child. He removed his arms from around Mom's waist and departed in a hurry.

*You're welcome.* Reaching up, I grasped Shirley's shoulders. "What are you doing? We agreed not to hunt at concert venues. It'll be too easy for the police to track the murders to us. You need to be more discreet." Having more self-discipline than the others when it came to preying on humans, I'd become the de facto leader of our shape-shifting pack.

She flashed a seductive smile – purely reflexively. She knows it doesn't work on me. "Oh, Danny." My original name was Halfdan, but we adopted modern American ones. "Why do you still struggle against your nature? Stop pretending to be something you're not. We're monsters. Humans are food, not friends."

I shook my head from side to side. I'd grown accustomed to the luxurious lifestyle our music income afforded us. I wouldn't let my unruly "family" threaten that. "Come on, let's go home." I undertook the Sisyphean task of herding my bandmates to our repurposed school bus parked in the lot.

# # #

Mom drove us home, scowling all the way. Mature pines surrounded our opulent 4,000 square foot house on a five-acre lot in Woodland, California.

The arboreal aroma reminded me of childhood. More and more, I found myself pining for the fjords. Woodland's greatest claim to fame was being forty miles from Napa Valley. That may not seem impressive, but seclusion is especially prized when you have secret identities to preserve. And it tickled me that we monsters resided in Yolo County. It may be true "you only live once," but we live for a very long time.

Even though it was late, I asked the others to join me in the living room. An enormous grey Italian distressed leather sectional sofa dominated the ash hardwood-floored room. I considered my "family" members individually as they took their places. The two youngest, Tracy and Chris, were natural born havoc makers. That was no surprise since Tracy was a brownie and Chris an imp – literally as well as figuratively. But since they weren't killers, they didn't threaten our livelihood as pop stars. As an incubus, Keith possessed an insatiable appetite for bedding women. But he only broke their hearts; he didn't eat them.

That left Mom and Laurie. Both required unfailing vigilance on my part to keep our concerts homicide-free. Being a wendigo, Laurie harbored cannibalistic instincts similar to Mom's. As my gaze lingered on her, I belatedly noticed her distended stomach. I sniffed and caught the faint scent of human blood. "Dammit, Laurie! I may be guilty of conspicuous consumption." I patted the absurdly expensive sofa before pointing at her belly. "But that's the wrong kind of conspicuous consumption. You ate someone at a public concert."

Laurie smiled sheepishly and shrugged. "Sorry." Her expression showed no remorse. "I was in the mood for Asian food. And now I'm hungry again."

My face flushed with cold undead blood. I stood and swept my arm at the floor-to-ceiling travertine fireplace surround and the wide windows offering unobstructed forest views. "Listen. We cannot enjoy these luxuries without money. If people end up dead at every Woodland concert, the money that funds our fancy cars, jewelry, and designer clothes will dry up."

Mom made a sour face while Chris and Tracy played patty-cake. Keith walked to the kitchen for his own snack, past Laurie who curled up to sleep off hers.

I stormed out of the room. If I can't get them to rein in their instincts, we'll have to break up the band. But then how would I afford dining at the finest restaurants or maintaining a respectable wine cellar? Do I want to revert to the monster I truly am? To live in a rough, dark cave with bat guano on the floor, emerging only to drain the blood of the occasional hiker? No thanks.

I stomped into my bedroom. I love the finer things. I deserve them. But how can I keep them? A blur of motion outside my window caught my eye. An owl swept past. Inspiration struck. What if we went on tour? Any murders committed by Mom and Laurie would be spread out geographically. We'd play for larger audiences, where some amount of mayhem would be normal. And we'd earn more money. Yes. Expanding our hunting grounds would make it much less likely that any dining faux pas could be traced to us.

The following morning, I dialed the executive director of our recording studio. Being one of their bigger-name bands gave us access and influence. "Bob. Hey, this is Danny Crowe."

"Danny! Great to hear from you, little guy. How's my favorite bass player?"

His patronizing and insincerity nauseated me. "I'm good. Listen, Mom asked me to call you. We'd like to start touring at larger venues across northern California. Can you assign someone to schedule gigs, arrange hotels rooms, and act as an in-person concierge?" In the two seconds before he responded, I could almost hear the cash register sounds ringing in his money-hungry mind.

"Absolutely, Danny. I know the perfect guy. Reuben's our best tour manager. I'll have him in Woodland in two days." He gave me Reuben's phone number.

"Fantastic. I'll tell Mom. Thanks, Bob." I hung up and let the others know. They seemed indifferent, except for Chris and Tracy, who giggled with excitement at the prospect of new crowds in which to run amok.

# # #

Mid-afternoon two days later, our tour manager Reuben drove up in a beat-up BMW M535i. His eyes bulged at the sight of our massive home's stone exterior and man-made waterfall. Mom invited him to meet with all of us. His gaze swept the interior of our house and I sensed his pulse race as he took in the original Mondrian self-portrait hanging in our entryway, our five-figure home stereo system, and the stunning kitchen counters in darkly veined Calacatta marble. *Ah, he appreciates the finer things – a man after my own heart.*

By the way, the claim that vampires can't withstand daylight is dead wrong. Let's put a stake through that falsehood right now. Shapeshifters lose their powers between sunrise and sunset. That's why we hunted at night.

"I'm Shirley. Please, have a seat, Reuben," said Mom, ever the gracious host. "Would you like a glass of red wine?" He nodded enthusiastically and she opened a bottle of 1976 Châteauneuf-du-Pape. As a "ten-year-old," I couldn't drink wine in front of Reuben, but I vowed to enjoy some later with a roast saddle of lamb and greens.

"Have you scheduled any gigs yet?" I asked after Mom introduced everyone. *Laurie's eyeing him like she's a hungry kid at a fair and he's a corndog.*

"Ha. I like a young man who gets right to business. As a matter of fact, I did." He beamed as if he'd accomplished something Herculean, like swimming across the North Sea, which, I can say from personal experience, isn't easy. "I booked you Thursday two weeks from now at UC Berkeley and in San Jose the week after that. If that goes well, we can book Reno, Nevada, if you're game."

I smiled. *As far as Mom and Laurie are concerned, you're game.*

Having been properly coached in advance by me, my family nodded and made the appropriate "ooh" and "ah" sounds.

Encouraged, Reuben waxed poetic about the "lavish" hotel accommodations. I could tell that he'd never been in a true luxury hotel in his polyester-suited life. Tacky wall art, shag carpet, and meals barely one step up from fast food were practically guaranteed. But that was the price I had to pay for keeping the band together and the money flowing. Sigh.

Reuben looked at his watch.

*As if you have more important matters to attend to than us.*

"Thank you for the wine. It was a pleasure to meet all of you. I'll be back at noon the Thursday of the show. I'll drive my car and lead you to the hotel."

# # #

With two weeks to kill, so to speak, I decided that the preservation of our luxury lifestyle deserved some form of commemoration. I had our bus exterior painted in red, blue, and yellow rectilinear shapes with thick black borders strongly reminiscent of the neoplasticism painting, Composizione 1921. Back in the 1880's, I'd lived in Winterswijk, The Netherlands, where I befriended young Piet Mondrian. He grew up to become one of my favorite artists, and the paint scheme was also in fond memory of him. What can I say? Even vampires can be sentimental.

Our music featured deep growling vocals, aggressive drumming, and abrupt tempo and key changes. It was we who created the death metal sub-genre of rock. I'd considered other band names like Venom, Celtic Frost, and Slayer. But in the end, I'm always a sucker for word play. We were A Murder of Crowes.

Excited at the prospect of keeping my bandmates' predations under control, I penned a new song – "Doesn't Somebody Want to be Hunted." Keith quickly composed a melody, and the others dived in with gusto to flesh out the song. It may seem odd, but I relished situations where we acted like a real family.

At dinner the night before our concert, I laid down some rules. "In order for this tour to work..." I made eye contact with Mom and Laurie. "... you two have to alternate. That means only one of you gets to kill after our next concert. Since Laurie ate last, it's Mom's turn tomorrow."

A scowl marred Laurie's face, while Shirley offered me a warm maternal smile. "Thank you, dear."

"What about me?" cried Chris, followed immediately by Tracy's, "and me?"

I sighed. "As long as no one dies, you're still free to be hooligans."

"YAY!" they cheered. They were both over a century old. But their small size and near-constant mischief-making aligned nicely with their disguises as young children.

# # #

The next day, Reuben arrived at our home promptly at noon. He parked next to our bus as we finished loading our instruments. "Hey, nice Picasso paint scheme, guys."

The smell of his cheap cologne wafted on the brisk morning breeze. I tried not to let that, or his lack of art knowledge, spoil my mood. This was a big day for The Crowe Family, after all.

Reuben seemed giddy, probably at the prospect of the financial windfall our tour represented to him personally. He mused aloud about buying the latest model BMW.

I turned my head away, so he wouldn't see my sneer. *Maybe first buy yourself a decent suit, drittsekk.*

# # #

We drove westward. Mom followed Reuben, maneuvering our bus into the parking lot at our Berkeley hotel.

Our tour manager popped out of his car. "Here we are," he announced unnecessarily. He led us into the lobby and checked us in, making a point to let all the staff know that we were VIPs.

We followed him into the elevator, six shapeshifters and an ambulatory snack. He unlocked the first room with a dramatic sweep of an arm. "You guys can relax now. Let's plan to drive to the venue at 3 PM. That will leave us time for a sound check and dinner in the green room."

At the word "dinner," Mom smiled at Reuben a bit too intently for my comfort. I rested a hand on her arm.

But, Reuben wasn't quite through. He made a point of dramatically confirming that the mini bar was fully stocked. When he swooned over liquor brands suitable only for well drinks, I rolled my eyes.

*Ugh. I'll need to eat somewhere else beforehand – I can't abide green room food.* I blinked. It struck me that Reuben's superficiality was a shallow human reflection of my own. *Reflection? Really, Halfdan? A vampire joke?* Humor aside, the insight bothered me more than I expected. I shoved away the unpleasant thought to focus on tonight's song order. *We could start with "I'll Eat You Halfway" and close with "Am I Bruising You?"*

# # #

The warm-up band left the stage and the audience gave us a raucous welcome. They did indeed have an appetite for "I'll Eat You Halfway," shaking their fists to the beat. Keith's smile told me he anticipated casting his net in a sea of frenzied college girls tonight. He was on fire. His palm muting and tremolo picking combined with Chris's double kick and blast beat drumming got the humans in a frenzy of death metal adoration.

*Their blood is up and so is ours.*

This was the largest venue we'd ever played. Despite some minor hiccups setting up the sound system, the concert went well. We'd packed the house and rocked them on their asses. I even spotted tears in the eyes of a front row fan when we played "I Really Want to Gnaw You."

We finished two encores to standing ovations. We bowed a final time and left the stage. As usual, Chris and Tracy turned invisible and melted into the crowd to play their pranks. Mom hurried toward the green room, an anticipatory grin on her face. After hydrating with a gin and tonic, she excused herself. Keith chose not one, but two eager fangirls and wandered off to find a private space to indulge himself.

I'd asked everyone to meet us back at the bus by 1 AM. And by prior arrangement, Reuben took a taxi back to the hotel. Mom would drive us there after the evening's... goings-on. I stayed in the green room, mostly to keep an eye on Laurie, who was no doubt jealous of Mom's hunting license tonight.

# # #

Eventually, Mom, Keith, Chris, and Tracy met Laurie and I at the bus, all four sporting blissful expressions on their faces. That only made Laurie's scowl deepen as Mom drove us back to our hotel.

I extended my hand toward Mom, palm upward. I liked to keep track of things, so Mom and Laurie always brought me the wallet of their victims. "How was dinner?"

Mom sighed with content. "Delicious. I was going to eat organic – we're in Berkeley, after all. But then I decided I was in the mood for Italian." She passed me the wallet.

Pulling out the driver's license, I read it aloud. "Marco Vargassi." *Vargassi*. Bells went off in my head. I sat up. "Was he alone when you chose him?"

"No. There were two big men with him." She shrugged. "But we left them to get a motel room. I only needed it for a half hour, though I did leave a rather big mess for the maids to clean up tomorrow morning."

"A motel? You know our rule is to allow no witnesses!" I yelled, anger getting the better of me. "The motel lobby undoubtedly had a security camera. I checked the driver's license for Marco's age. *Helvete*!" I slammed my hand on the bus seat. "This wasn't just any human. Marco is... I mean was, the son of crime lord Big Tony Vargassi. It's only a matter of time before his bodyguards go looking for him. Even if they can't find him tonight, his murder will be discovered tomorrow morning by the motel. Then, it won't take long for Vargassi's men to get their hands on the security video."

We parked at our hotel and I assembled everyone in my room.

"Why don't we drive back to Woodland tonight?" suggested Chris.

I shook my head. "If we check out of the hotel tonight, it'll look suspicious. We can't assume Big Tony won't involve the police. Some of them may be on his payroll. No, we need to stay until the morning."

Laurie lifted a slender wrist to check her watch. "It's two AM. We have about four hours until sunrise."

I turned to Chris. "Please turn invisible and keep watch in the hotel lobby. If anyone asks at the front desk for us, call me on a hotel phone and then try to delay them."

"How, Danny?"

"You're an imp," I replied, raising my arms. "You're the mischief expert. Use your imagination." *Calm yourself.* "Trip them. Push all the elevator buttons. Untie their shoelaces. That kind of thing. If no one comes for us, we'll meet you in the lobby at 6 AM."

Chris nodded and left, while Mom drew the curtains.

Before I called the front desk to let them know of our early check out, I told the others, "We should all stay in my room tonight. They'll almost certainly attack Mom's room first."

# # #

Imps, vampires, and incubi don't need to sleep, so I sat near the phone. Keith gathered up everyone's suitcases while Mom and Laurie laid on the king-size bed to rest. Tracy arranged seat cushions on the floor, forming a makeshift mattress for herself.

Our room phone rang around 5:30 AM. I snatched up the receiver before the first ring finished.

Chris whispered over the phone. "A woman and a big man – both wearing grey suits with bulges under the left armpit."

"Got it. Try to slow them down." I hung up.

Keith had already woken Mom, Laurie, and Tracy.

I ran my hand through my hair. "It's a man and woman in grey suits. Their bullets can't hurt us before sunrise, but I'd rather do this without them firing at all. It'd be even better if we didn't have to kill them."

Laurie stomped her foot as I shared the plan. *You were hoping for a morning snack.*

"You three, stay here." I took Mom's key and rushed into her room with Keith.

Two minutes later, someone knocked on the door.

Act natural. "Who is it?"

"Hotel security. Is Shirley Crowe in there? We'd like to speak with her."

"She's in the bathroom, but come on in." I opened the door.

The assassins shared a quick glance.

I suspected their exchange was less about finding a ten- and eighteen-year-old fully dressed so early in the morning, and more about realizing they now have to kill two more people, including a kid. But they didn't hesitate to enter.

*This is not going to end the way you expect. You're messing with the wrong band.* I gestured to the chairs. "Have a seat." As the man turned to sit, I lunged with the full speed and strength of a vampire. I threw a punch to his jaw that laid him out face down on the ugly carpet.

Before his partner could draw her weapon, Keith stepped in front of her. I swear I saw his smile sparkle.

The woman gazed into his warm light brown eyes and forgot why she was here.

I tore up a bedsheet, using strips to gag and tie up the unconscious man, while Keith disabled the women using his preferred method.

The door opened and Chris popped into view. "I delayed them as long as I could."

"You did great," I replied, patting his back. "Go let the others know it's time to check out and head home." With a final tug of a torn sheet, I finished restraining the man and turned to Keith. "You about done?"

He sat up on the bed, the woman now naked and asleep beside him. "Yeah. Not my best work, but I perform better when I'm not rushed and don't have an audience."

I wrinkled my face. "Don't flatter yourself. I wasn't watching. How much time do we have?"

Keith shrugged. "It's not an exact science, but she should be dreaming blissfully about me for at least half an hour."

I rolled my eyes with 800 years of experience as a ten-year old. "Okay, let's get out of here." I hung a "Do not disturb" sign on the handle and locked the door behind us.

We grabbed our suitcases, checked out, and hustled into our bus. And none too soon because the sun had risen. We were mortal again until sunset.

Mom stopped our bus at the parking lot exit, waiting for a gap in traffic to merge onto the street. Five gunshots cracked out in rapid succession, punching through the roof of our bus. I glanced back at the hotel. A fourth-floor window has been shot out. *That was our floor. The female assassin must have woken up sooner than Keith expected. I should've tied her up.*

Tracy screamed.

Chris gasped and fell to the floor of the bus. He'd taken hits in his upper left thigh and the right side of his chest.

"Go! Go! Go!" I yelled at Mom as I rushed to Chris's side.

Mom slammed on the gas. Our bus shot out into traffic. Car brakes squealed and the crunch of fender benders followed. She floored our bus to its maximum speed.

Tracy knelt at Chris's head. "Hold on, Chris."

I assessed his wounds. A tourniquet would keep him from bleeding out from his leg wound. But Chris's shortness of breath, jugular vein distension, and expanded right chest told me he had a tension pneumothorax. *Your right lung's collapsed.*

Chris looked me in the eyes. His wound was mortal without immediate medical treatment – treatment none of us were equipped to give. He knew it too. *Helvete!*

I took his hand in mine and held it until the imp's eyes closed for the final time.

"I guess we need a new drummer," said Laurie, the heartless bitch.

Tracy burst into tears and I burst into a stream of profanity, half directed at the assassin and half at Laurie.

# # #

Mom drove us home without further incident. "I'll deal with the damage to the bus," Keith volunteered. He retrieved a hammer from the garage and went to work tapping flat the torn metal edges of the bullet holes.

At least that'll make the damage less noticeable to casual inspection, I thought. I'll need to contact a discreet auto body repair shop.

Mom and I gently removed Chris's small body from the bus. I told Laurie to clean up the blood out of the bus. My stomach twisted at her smile.

*She's not finicky about whose blood she consumes.* "For Loki's sake, use a sponge with soap and water."

Mom helped me bury Chris in the yard within earshot of a tinkling fountain.

What have I done? My love of luxury has indirectly cost Chris his life. I've become a shadow of the fierce predator I once was. That must change.

I gathered everyone in the study, running my hand along the wall. The luxurious walnut paneling had lost its luster for me. "Listen up. Our home address isn't published, but it's only a matter of time before Big Tony's armed thugs show up. So, do we stay or do we run away?"

"We are monsters!" Mom cried. "We do not flee from humans. We prey upon them."

Laurie nodded her agreement. "We are why they fear the dark."

Battle lust even took over little Tracy. "It's been a while since we had humans to our house for dinner."

I pointed out the window at the sun, high in the sky. "Well, if they arrive before sunset, we can't access our powers. Bullets can kill you in your human form just like they did Chris."

A practical point, yet I felt ashamed that modernity had so tamed my natural ferocity. "I checked and today's sunset'll be at 6:15. We need to prepare in case we have visitors before that."

# # #

We barricaded the front and back doors. At the sound of car tires on the dirt road leading to our house, I checked my watch. *It's still 20 minutes before sundown.*

Tracy, Keith, and I peered through a slit in the blinds of a second story window as a BMW pulled into our driveway. I sighed. "It's just Reuben," I called to the others. "Don't show yourselves and don't answer the door. He'll go away, eventually."

My plan lasted all of three minutes. Two late-model Mercedes sedans pulled up, each with a driver and three passengers. I caught myself admiring the cars. *Focus*! I recognized the male and female assassins from the hotel. "Eight thugs," I called out. *They must've followed Reuben.*

Having nearly reached our front door, Reuben turned to face the newcomers. "Whoa. Hey there, guys. I'm the Crowe Family's tour manager."

I shook my head. You have no idea who you're dealing with, Reuben. Still, maybe you can help delay them.

Reuben gave them his trademark big, fake smile. "Listen fellas... ma'am. The Crowe Family really appreciates your support. But this is their home. It's not right for you to show up here unannounced. If you want to see them in person, their next concert is in San Jo–"

The assassin from the hotel drew her silenced Beretta 92 pistol from a left-side shoulder holster. It had an equally silencing effect on Reuben. "Are they home?"

*Ah, you're the leader. I'm gonna call you Snow White and the others the seven dwarfs.*

Reuben put his hands in the air. "I... I think so. But I'm not sure. What's going on here? Are you the police?"

The dwarfs snickered as Snow White gestured with her chin. "Check the bus."

Reuben tried to regain a bit of authority. "C'mon, now. That's private property. Do you have a warrant?"

In lieu of the proper paperwork, Snow White put a nine-millimeter round through poor Reuben's forehead. He toppled backward.

Tracy grumbled in Gaelic. I don't speak the language, but it sounded like a curse. Brownies are slow to anger, but never forget a grudge. Or forgive.

"Nothing but music equipment in the bus, boss."

Snow White nodded acknowledgement. "Hide the body."

Two dwarfs unceremoniously dragged Reuben behind some bushes so that he wouldn't be visible from the road. We get little traffic, but professionals avoid taking unnecessary risks.

Tracy put her hand on my forearm. Anger blazed on her freckled face. "I'll climb out a side window and try to slow them. They won't shoot a 'little girl.' I hope."

I didn't like her chances, but if the thugs broke in before sunset, we were all dead anyway. "Go."

A moment later, our doorbell rang.

*Smart.* You never knew if someone would open the door and save you the trouble of forcing it.

It rang again. "Kick it open," Snow White ordered.

"What's going on?" asked Tracy, stepping into view from around the right front corner of the house. She raised her hands when the dwarfs pointed their guns at her.

Don't shoot her.

Snow White holstered her gun. "Come here, sweetie. What's your name?"

Tracy offered a well-practiced timid smile and stepped forward. "Tracy."

"Tracy, is your mommy home?"

Tracy burst into mock tears, playing the part of a distraught human child.

Snow White rolled her eyes and grabbed Tracy's wrist. "Shirley Crowe! We've got your daughter. Come on out and nothing bad will happen to her."

At 'bad will happen,' Tracy squirmed and bawled even louder.

Snow White scowled at the tantrum. "I'm gonna sit in the car with the kid. Kick in the door and take care of business."

Keith whispered to me. "I'm not gay, but I'd be willing to take one for the team. Unfortunately, my power only works against women."

"Right. Go tell Mom and Laurie to hide. You too."

A dwarf started kicking the front door as Snow White sat with Tracy in the front seat of a Benz.

I looked at my watch. *6:05*.

We had a beautiful thick oaken front door. It stood up well to the dwarfs' determined kicks, but not to repeated pistol shots. Two dwarfs shoved with their shoulders to dislodge our barricade of piled furniture.

*I hope the others have hidden well.* I sprinted to the kitchen, snatched a chef's knife, and hid in a lower kitchen cabinet – one of the few benefits conferred by being trapped inside a weak ten-year-old human's body. My hands trembled and sweat pooled under my arms. *This must be what human prey feel when they're hunted by us. I'm barely able to keep from soiling myself. What an ignoble end to a long life.* I couldn't swallow.

We didn't have guns, but our assailants couldn't assume that was the case. The sounds of measured footsteps followed calls of "clear" confirmed they were well-trained and not taking any chances. *They're clearing the ground floor first, room-by-room. I should've hidden in the attic.*

The tone of a dwarf's footsteps changed when he trod on travertine tile. *He's in the kitchen!* Faint hinge squeaking told me he was checking the kitchen cabinets, one by one.

The sounds of the dwarf's search echoed loudly in my panicked ears. My heart pounded like I'd run a sprint and my palms felt as clammy as a corpse's. *Oh, how the mighty have fallen. So, this is what it feels like to cower in pathetic terror at the prospect of my demise.* In the depths of despair, I briefly contemplated pleading for mercy or trying to flee. I took a quivering breath. *No.* If I were to die, I'd do so with dignity. I gritted my teeth and tightened my grip on the knife handle. *It won't matter. This guy's a pro. He's not gonna lower his face to within slashing distance. This is it.*

As I checked my watch, the dwarf opened my cabinet door. *6:16.* I smiled.

# # #

It didn't take long for Mom, Laurie, and I to finish off the seven dwarfs. Their bullets had no effect on us and the damage they caused to the house interior didn't even bother me. I glanced out a window in time to see Keith saunter out the front door. *He must've found a good hiding place.*

Snow White still held Tracy in the car's front seat. But the screams of her men had drained the blood from her face. She drew her gun and aimed it at Keith. But at the incubus's supernaturally seductive smile, she put away her weapon, entranced.

Before Keith reached the car, Tracy slid a stiletto from a wrist sheath hidden under her long-sleeved shirt and plunged it repeatedly through Snow White's neck.

*Never piss off a brownie,* I noted. The example of a normally carefree brownie tapping into her inner monster to avenge the death of her friend shamed me. *It's time for me to revert to my true vampiric nature.*

After Mom and Laurie ate their fill, we loaded the thug's remains—and I mean both definitions of the term—into the trunks of their cars. With satiated grins, Mom and Laurie drove off to dump the cars far from here.

That'll only delay the inevitable. This beautiful home and lifestyle are forfeit. Big Tony's men will keep coming for us. He won't forget that Mom murdered his son. It was time to break up the band.

# # #

I swore off frivolous luxury and travelled to the east coast, taking up abode in a hilly maple and oak forest. To paraphrase my former acquaintance, Thoreau: "I went to the woods because I wished to live deliberately, to front only the essential facts of life, and see if I could not learn what it had to teach. I wanted to live deep and suck out all the marrow of humans, to live so sturdily and Spartan-like as to put to rout all that was alive, to cut a broad swath and shave close, to hunt humans into a corner."

But living without toilet paper got old real fast. Six months later, I rejoined society, earning a living by competing in celebrity boxing and wrestling matches.

*Author's Note*

This story is an homage to and parody of The Partridge Family. Below is a list of story references to that legendary musical group.

- The Crowe surname is, of course, an avian wink at the Partridge surname. The Crowe family's death metal sound is about as far as one can get from the Partridge Family's wholesome pop rock.
- For reasons unknown, the Partridge Family's school bus was painted in the style of Piet Mondrian's Composizione 1921.
- The Partridge Family recorded a number of songs, including: "Come On Get Happy (not Morbid)", "Doesn't Somebody Want to Be Wanted (not Hunted)", "I'll Meet (not Eat) You Halfway", "Am I Losing (not Bruising) You?", and "I Really Want to Know (not Gnaw) You". Performance videos are available online for your nostalgic viewing.
- The character names reflect the corresponding TV character's name: Shirley Jones portrayed mother Shirley Partridge, David Cassidy portrayed Keith Partridge, Susan Dey portrayed Laurie Partridge, Danny Bonaduce portrayed Danny Partridge, Brian Forster portrayed Chris Partridge (seasons 2-4), Suzanne Crough portrayed Tracy Partridge, and Dave Madden

portrayed band manager Reuben Kincaid.

• The Crowe Family needed a new drummer, just like The Partridge Family after season one.

• The Partridge Family TV show was set in a fictional San Pueblo, CA, "forty miles from Napa Valley." Woodland, CA in Yolo County meets that specification.

• After The Partridge Family broke up, Danny Bonaduce earned a living primarily as an on-air radio personality and by participating in celebrity boxing and wrestling matches.

The story also contains winks at Maurice Sendak's *Where the Wild Things Are*, Finding Nemo, Monty Python, and Jim Butcher's The Dresden Files.

*Helvete* is Norwegian for hell. *Drittsekk* is Norwegian for shit sack.

Venom, Celtic Frost, and Slayer are the names of actual death metal bands. ♜

# THE BONEYARD

*By Dennis K. Crosby*

IT WASN'T THE SOUND OF a ravenous animal that awoke Lawrence Sanders. The guttural growl reminiscent of rolling thunder was like a lullaby. The feel of warm saliva dripping on his face though, that was an entirely different sensation. He bypassed the initial disorientation people generally feel when they first wake up and escalated to full panic at the sight of a snarling two-headed dog proudly displaying its razor-sharp fangs and blood-stained muzzles. He wanted it to be a dream. Like those dreams he had as a kid. He wanted to believe that this was just like those apparitions he spied from the holes in the blankets he covered his head with on the nights of rare Los Angeles thunderstorms. The ghosts his father swore were fanciful, frightful tricks of light to a kid with a vivid imagination. Most of all, he wanted his death to come quickly. The thought of being torn apart by this creature caused tears to well in the corner of his eyes. He wanted it all to go away. So, he whispered it.

What did he have to lose?

"Go. Away."

It was soft. It was more of a hope, than a command. And yet it had the desired effect. The animal, the creature, the dog, stopped snarling. Both heads licked their muzzles and bent down to sniff Lawrence. It let out a low growl, then licked his face—both heads, on either side. Without warning, it leapt from Lawrence's bed and trotted off through the open bedroom door and down the hall.

Lawrence was frozen in place. The only sound, his heartbeat. He wanted to move. He *needed* to move. He had to make sure the thing didn't get his father, asleep down the hall. Forcing some movement, Lawrence left his bed, grabbed the baseball bat leaning against his closet door, then bounded down the hall.

Making his way to his father's room, he was relieved to see that the door was closed. He opened it to check, just in case. Peering inside, he was shocked to find that his father was not in bed. It was still made from the morning. Had he fallen asleep downstairs again? Closing the door, Lawrence moved toward the stairs, the sound of wind catching his attention. From the top of the staircase, he could see that the front door was open.

CRACK!

BOOM!

The sound outside startled Lawrence. Something was happening. That thing, that dog, was rummaging through the junkyard. Had to be what that noise was. Was his father out there with it? Had it found him?

Lawrence descended the stairs and walked out the door, bat at the ready for defense. He thought back to the first time he'd ventured out into the Boneyard late at night. He was seven, and he'd heard yelling and the clang of metal. After leaving his bed, he ventured out toward the source and found his father, Frederick, swinging a blue hued sword through the neck of a man… with horns and reddish black skin. It was the last thing he saw before a blinding light seemingly knocked him out. When he awoke, it was morning, he was in his bed, and his father was sitting on the edge.

"Good morning," Frederick said.

"Hey, Pop."

"Feeling okay?"

"Um, I think so. But…Pop, there was this noise last night and I went out to see…"

"Hold on, son. We should talk."

"About the devil thing?" Lawrence asked with anticipation.

"Devil? What? No, son…about your sleep walking. We need to make a doctor's appointment. Now, I know you hate doctors and needles and stuff, but we need to look out for your well-being."

"Sleepwalking?"

"Yeah, son. Sleepwalking."

As the memory invaded his mind, Lawrence felt pangs of anger and frustration. That hadn't been the first time Lawrence had witnessed something strange in the Boneyard, and it wasn't the last time his father had dismissed it as the fanciful thoughts of a precocious child. Was tonight going to be more of the same? Lawrence wasn't a boy anymore. He stayed with his father all these years because the man was old. It didn't seem he had many years left in him. He didn't want to think in such terms, but his father's death would mean his freedom. Lawrence would sell the Boneyard, despite his father's protestations that it was his legacy. No…he'd sell it, and he'd move on.

Finally.

Lawrence heard the sound again beyond the mound of junk that had been accumulated over the last few days. There was a clank, and a glow of white light. Moving closer, he saw the dog again, both heads staring and growling at a strobing white light beneath a vintage porcelain tub. A tub he was desperate to sell because of its rarity. A tub that sat in that same space, year after year after year. Lawrence edged closer, careful not to startle the beast. Inadvertently, he stepped on a thin piece of plywood. The crack caught the attention of the dog, who turned to Lawrence, staring…at first.

"Go. Away."

It worked the first time, so why not try it again.

But the dog didn't back away. If anything, he doubled down on his growling and added some barking for measure.

Finding some courage, or falling off the cliff of stupidity, it was a fine line for Lawrence, he charged at the beast with his bat raised. Somehow, it was enough. The dog backed up, turned, and scurried away a short distance.

"Stay back," demanded Lawrence, pointing at the dog with his bat.

Turning his attention to the glow, now just steps away, Lawrence inched closer. The glow seemed to be coming from the ground, but…that didn't make sense. The Boneyard was nothing but a large lot of dirt and salvaged junk. There was nothing beneath it. Especially nothing that should be glowing.

And now humming?

"What the hell is this?" he whispered to himself.

Kneeling, Lawrence stretched out his hand and touched the glowing dirt. As he did, the two-headed dog growled and began to stalk toward him. Lawrence shifted at the sound of the animal coming closer and scraped his hand against the jagged porcelain edge beneath the tub, tearing his skin, as he lost his balance. Awareness of the animal was dulled by the realization of the burn of a cut and warm liquid in his hand. A hand now planted on the ground as he caught himself.

A bloodied hand on the ground.

A bloodied hand on the source of the pulsating light emanating from the ground.

Without warning, the dog stopped. Lawrence was curious about this abrupt change, but pleased, nevertheless. The pleasure washed away quickly though as the animal lowered its haunches as if primed for attack. Yet, it didn't move. It wasn't in attack mode; it was preparing for defense. In fact, as Lawrence looked closer, the animal wasn't focused on him anymore, but the spot where his hand was. Daring to glance away, Lawrence looked down to find that the pulsating white glow, was now red. The humming that began minutes earlier, was now a wail. A primal, evil, ear piercing wail.

Lawrence scrambled away, no longer concerned about the dog. He covered his ears as the sound got louder. The red light pulsated faster, smoke billowed from the ground, barking was drowned by the sound of a malevolent scream and the vibration of metal, wood, and porcelain. Then, seemingly in slow motion, the ground exploded. Shards of debris flew into the air. Light and wind were expelled from the earth and Lawrence covered his head in protection. When he dared to look up, he found that the two-headed beast had moved closer, standing now between him and the indescribable scene in front of him. It barked, desperately, furiously, as a dark, translucent figure arose from the depths beneath.

The figure was cloaked, large, menacing, with two bright green orbs for eyes. Lawrence could not make out its features, but he could feel its evil. He could feel the cold, emotionless threat of death. The thing hung in the air, smelling of rotten flesh and mildew, despite its transparent appearance.

The smell was so overpowering Lawrence could taste it. It seemed to phase between solid and intangible, flickering like a television searching for a signal. The dog barked, trying to scare it off, trying to guard Lawrence, but with the wave of a skeletal hand, the animal was flung to the side.

"Ahhhhhhhhhh!"

The scream was not from Lawrence, but his father, who ran forward with a blue hued sword toward the dark figure.

"Get away from him, damn you!" Frederick screamed.

"You!" said the entity with a slow drawl.

Lawrence couldn't see it, but he knew the entity was grinning. That was confirmed when he heard the sinister laugh fill his ears.

"I'll kill you last," promised the entity right before it shot into the air.

There was immediate silence as it left. Silence that was soon filled by the sound of Frederick's voice.

"Son. Son. Are you okay?"

Frederick moved in, staring at Lawrence. In his father's eyes, he saw fear, he saw concern, and he saw…disappointment?

"Pop…I…"

"Oh son. Dammit. What have you done?"

"Pop…"

Lawrence was at a loss for words. He wanted to speak, to ask questions, to do…something. Anything. Anything other than what he felt was about to happen as tears once again welled in his eyes. The image of his father was blurred, but he could make out the movement. Then he felt the tight embrace of his father, his Pop, and he softly wept.

"You big dummy," said Frederick.

"Pop…"

"It's all right, son," Frederick said softly. "It's about time we had a talk about a few things."

# # #

Lawrence walked back into the house, behind his father, dazed and confused. He'd seen enough weirdness around the Boneyard to last three lifetimes. But this? This was on an entirely different level of weird.

Lawrence looked over to find his father walking to the card table with a giant leatherbound book and an armful of eyeglasses. That reality, that normalcy, brought him back to the present.

"Sit down, son."

Lawrence walked to the small table and sat in the old metal folding chair. His lingering gaze at Frederick was a combination of curiosity and contempt. It was met with frankness, a touch of pity, and a lot of, "oh, that mess out there was nothing". Lawrence then lowered his eyes to look at the book his father was nervously tapping his fingers on. Up close, the cover looked less like leather and more like…

"What is that?" Lawrence asked.

The cover was odd, bumpy, and coarse. It was dark, reddish black, with a strange, yet familiar texture. Some parts of it were porous. It seemed to have tiny follicles of…hair?

"Nope!" Lawrence exclaimed, backing up out of his chair almost tripping over it.

"Son, please, calm down."

"Calm down? Calm down? Tell me that book isn't covered in human skin and I'll calm down."

"It's not covered in human skin, son. Don't be ridiculous."

Lawrence gave a skeptical look then slowly moved forward, picking up his chair from the ground to resume his seat at the table.

"As you can see," Frederick began, "it's a lot like your Aunt Edna. So clearly, it's demon skin."

"Pop, please. I've asked you a hundred time to leave Aunt Edna alone."

"Son, I'm not…you know what, never mind. It'll become clear soon," Frederick said.

Lawrence watched impatiently as Frederick sorted through dozens of eyeglasses. It was hard to fathom that at one point, he found this amusing. His father's eyesight seemed to deteriorate more and more each year, yet he'd never throw out his old glasses. Some were simple reading glasses, some were prescription, but in a house that was a constant mess, in the middle of a salvage yard, it was all junk to Lawrence. Beyond that, every deficiency in his father was yet another attempt by the universe to keep him from leaving.

“Ah, here we go,” Frederick said, finding a pair of glasses that suited him.

“Can we get on with it?” Lawrence asked hurriedly.

Frederick opened the old book and when Lawrence looked at it, he saw nothing. The pages were empty. He grabbed it from his father and began rifling through it to find every page, blank. His frustration grew.

“C’mon, Pop,” Lawrence began, “we got real problems. A two headed dog, a ghost or spirit or something flying out of the ground, and don’t get me started on you with that sword. I knew I wasn’t imagining things when I was a kid. And now you’re wasting time on a blank book? Either tell me what’s going on, or—”

Lawrence stopped as Frederick grabbed the hand he’d scraped on the porcelain tub. Frederick forced it open and slammed it down onto the blank pages. Within seconds, words and images appeared. Lawrence, mouth agape, said nothing as he turned more pages to find more words and images becoming visible.

“Now you see what I see,” said Frederick.

“I don’t…I don’t understand. What is all this?”

"This book contains a lot of history, your history, and a lot of secrets, too."

"And my blood—"

"Activates it," said Frederick. "Or you can wear the right glasses. All these glasses are for different books, or different hidden messages."

"Why my blood?" Lawrence asked.

"I wasn't kidding about your Aunt Edna. This book is made of skin like hers. Demon skin. Her great-great grandfather's to be exact. The ink is the blood of demons and can only be activated by blood of its kind."

Once again, Lawrence was silent, as he tried to process his father's words. They didn't make sense. None of it made sense. Yet, somehow, in the back of his mind, he knew the words true.

"I'm a…demon," Lawrence said.

"Yes, son. Well…in part."

"Just like my mother."

Lawrence, distracted from the realization of his heritage, was unprepared for the crash behind him as the front door blew open to allow entry to an invisible force hidden within a heavy wind. The howling and screeching disoriented him as he tried to stand his ground. His father, completely caught off guard, was blown back from his chair and pinned against the wall. Lawrence shielded his eyes from the rush of air and began walking toward his father, only to be stopped by the invisible force he'd sensed seconds ago.

"Oh no!" Frederick screamed to Lawrence. "This is the big one! Lizbetta, it's my time! I'm coming to join ya honey!"

Lawrence heard that same phrase from his father almost weekly for most of his life, but this was the first time he felt it was real. Whatever was stopping him from reaching his father, whatever was keeping his father pinned against the wall, four feet off the ground, whatever was causing the small tornado in his home, was trying to communicate.

*You, Prince of the Damned, you have unleashed the Primeval, your blood has doomed us all!*

"Who…who are you?" Lawrence asked.

*Kill him!*

*Yes, kill him!*

*Must appeal to the Primeval with his blood!*

Lawrence heard multiple voices, whispers, shouts, screams, pleas, all demanding his blood, his sacrifice…his life. He could not fathom why they referred to him as the Prince of the Damned, but he was determined to get to his father, to free him, and escape this madness. As he struggled to break invisible chains, he saw movement from the corner of his eye.

A dark brown, worm-like creature, slick with mucus, skittered across the floor on a thousand tiny legs. Unaffected by the rushing winds swirling in the house, it moved with purpose. It moved with hunger.

It moved toward his father.

Across the floor, past Lawrence, and to the wall, it hurried along, only to stop abruptly. The small creature, perhaps the size of a loaf of bread, undulated, then looked up, as if sizing up its prey. Lawrence could see Frederick's eyes go wide with recognition. It was easy to see that his father knew what was about to happen. Lawrence, maybe instinctively, knew as well. The thought made him shudder.

The tiny creature moved to the wall, and began to scale it, reaching Frederick's foot. It crawled on his shoe, then scurried up his leg, his thigh, his torso, to his chest, where it rested a moment.

A barb extended from the creature's tail, razor sharp, dripping with the same clear slime that coated its body. Lawrence watched the tail raise, and then strike his father. As Frederick screamed, the creature scurried upwards and entered his mouth. Lawrence, still frozen, could only watch in horror as the thing fought to enter Frederick. His father's throat enlarged as the creature forced its way in.

"Pop!"

As the last of the creature entered, Frederick's eyes, wide from shock, turned completely black. His body pulled itself from the wall and he slowly floated down to the ground. He stretched out his arm, opened his hand, nodded, and the winds stop. Immediately, Lawrence felt the invisible force release its hold upon him. He wanted to run to his father, but he wasn't even sure it was him anymore.

“Pop?” he asked, cautiously. “Pop…you in there?”

“I am here son.”

The tone and cadence were all wrong. It was mechanical, inhuman, otherworldly. Whatever stood before him was not Frederick Sanders.

“Who are you? You’re not my father, now tell me, who are you?”

In an instant, Frederick was in front of Lawrence, a hand around his son’s throat, lifting him off the ground. Lawrence gripped his father’s arm, holding on, silently pleading with the black eyed being, to no avail.

“You will listen, you will take heed, and you will act,” said whatever was inhabiting Frederick.

Lawrence was lowered to the floor, littered with glass, papers, and anything else not bolted down in the living room. His legs were wobbly, mostly from fear and anxiety. Catching his breath, bent over, with hands on his knees, he once again wished silently for all of this to be a terrible dream. He wished his father would burst into his room and awaken him from his nightmare. He wanted to see his friends, Raul and Jose, his Aunt Edna, if for nothing else than to prove that she was no demon and simply the continued victim of his father’s insults. He wished hard for all those things. But he knew they were simply wishes on the winds.

“I’m…I’m listening,” said Lawrence.

“I am your father, and I am something else, something more.”

Lawrence stood at attention. Not wanting to miss a word. He looked deep in the blackened eyes of his father, searching for some recognition, some proof that his words rang true. That the man, the being before him, was truly Frederick. He could find nothing, yet strangely, the fear and concern he'd felt still seemed to subside. Innately, he knew he was in no danger.

A satisfying change of pace from what he'd been feeling the rest of the night.

"Who…I'm sorry, what…are you?" asked Lawrence.

"I am Frederick, but more than that, I am a Sentinel, guardian of the Gates of the Damned."

"The Gates of the Damned?"

"Yes, son. This place, this salvage yard, sits atop those gates. And we are charged with protecting it."

"We?"

"Think back to all those times you saw something strange, heard weird noises, or felt that something wasn't quite right. Those apparitions you saw as a boy—"

"The ones you told me were my imagination?"

"Yes," said Frederick. "Those were revenants. Souls trapped between this world and the next, seeking some sort of absolution so they could move on. In their quest, they served as…guards, of a sort. I can't be everywhere and awake at all times, after all."

Lawrence let the words sink in. As fantastic as it sounded, something in the story rang true. Reminiscing, he recalled that the apparitions he saw, never tried to harm him. In fact, they never came near him. They floated about, gave an occasional glance, but never acted in a malicious manner.

"So they work for you?" asked Lawrence.

"In a manner of speaking."

"Where were they tonight?"

"Scattered, likely fearful of the growing presence in the Vacant Space."

"The Vacant Space?"

"It's a place, a…space, a netherworld, where the most dangerous of entities was kept."

"The Primeval?"

"Yes."

He connected the dots, somewhat shocked at his growing acceptance of current events. He sought further connection with his father. The voice had softened, sounding less robotic, settling back into the cadence he'd always known. His eyes too began to soften. The onyx orbs changed slowly into something…else.

Purple.

Violet.

Blue.

Silver.

They seemed to stay there. Steady, shiny, almost metallic. Lawrence noticed the slack in Frederick's shoulders, as if he were settling into himself. As if he were becoming whole again…just as he said a few minutes ago.

"Pop?"

"I told you, it's me, son. It just takes a minute to adjust when I'm first integrated."

"Integrated? Like, there's two parts of you?"

"In a sense, yes. To do what needs to be done, I must serve as a host body, for something to possess. I need the help in augmenting power I already have."

"Like a…demon?"

"Yes, but I'm a little different. We don't have a lot of time to dig into that right now. We have to get to work on stopping the Primeval."

"From doing what?"

"Finding the path to a permanent corporeal foothold on this world."

"This is all just too—"

Lawrence's words were cut off by two growls from behind. He froze in place because of all the sounds he'd heard that night, this one cut to his very soul.

If he had one.

"Pop…"

"It's okay, son. No need to worry about her?"

"Her?"

"Yeah…her. Come here, Bella."

At Frederick's urging, the dog trotted over, and Lawrence could do nothing but look on in stunned silence.

"She was your first pet. Obviously, we couldn't keep her around and take her for walks. Watts is a tough neighborhood, but it ain't ready for nothing like this," said Frederick, stroking the heads of the animal at his feet.

"She tried to attack me," said Lawrence.

"No, you big dummy," Frederick began, "she was trying to protect you because she sensed the danger. She's been trained to come around if the Revenants vanish, 'cause if they're gone, something wicked is on the way. She was trying to keep you safe, and trying to keep you from the Vacant Space, because she knows son…she knows."

"Knows what?"

"That you are the key to opening it. Or rather, your blood is."

"Why my blood?"

"The Primeval is so powerful that it can only be contained by itself. The seal keeping it within the Vacant Space was consecrated with its own blood. In this instance, the blood of its progeny. By extension, it can only be opened by its own blood, or the blood of its decedent."

Lawrence felt his own blood retreat from his extremities. He went numb, legs slack, and it took sheer will to keep himself upright. Thoughts swirled about in his mind, each fighting for prime position, but he was in no position to give them an audience.

Bella's barking fit came out of nowhere, but it was a welcomed distraction for Lawrence. He turned to the source of her angst and found a creature most foul standing in the doorway. Its feminine features were hidden from the leathery brown skin, fangs, and horns on either side of its forehead. Its eyes were red, malevolent, its snarl menacing, and the two silver daggers it held, in a tight grip, spoke volumes of its intentions.

"Dammit!" Frederick exclaimed.

There was nothing nearby except an old, rusted letter opener, but Lawrence didn't care. He'd been through enough this evening and was determined to find some way, any way, to take control of his fears. He couldn't let his father down again. The stakes were high tonight. There was much to learn, but he wouldn't let ignorance give rice to cowardice. With the letter opener in hand, he rushed the demon at the door.

It roared at him.

Smoke escaped its nostrils.

As Lawrence approached, prepared to stab the thing, it dropped one of its daggers, grabbed his arm, and lifted him in the air. Feet dangling, Lawrence tried to kick, tried anything that would get him free. The demon looked at him, set him down, and said, "Enough!"

"That voice," Lawrence thought to himself.

"You old fish-eyed, ignorant fool," said the demon, turning its attention to Frederick, "what the hell did you do now?"

"Aunt…Edna?"

# # #

"Edna, I told you, don't come in my house looking like that," said Frederick.

"I'll come in here looking any way I please," said Edna.

"Well, your human face is the lesser of two evils. Two very ugly evils. Give me that, at least."

Lawrence, once again in awe of everything happening, stood, mouth agape, watching this demon morph into an image he'd known his entire life. His Aunt Edna was a rough and tumble kind of lady. She appeared sweet and pious, but she suffered no fools. Lawrence was quickly learning that the piety he'd once admired was nothing more than a cover. Demons, after all, didn't worship the Lord, did they?

"Lawrence, honey, are you okay?"

He was speechless.

"Lawrence?" she asked again.

Still nothing.

"Well now you done gone and done it, Frederick. I told you that you should have told him long ago. Now look at him. In shock."

"Probably just in shock because he didn't realize you could get uglier."

"Watch it sucker! Just 'cause you got that sword, don't mean I won't get a couple licks in right across your lip!"

As his father and aunt began to square off, Lawrence, exhausted in every way, turned to them, and screamed, "STOP IT!"

His words froze the two. They stopped and turned to face him. In their faces he saw concern, and maybe, just maybe, a little guilt.

"Now I've had about enough of you two. Especially tonight of all nights. You should have told me," said Lawrence, pointing to his father. "You should have told me as soon as you knew I was aware that things were strange around here."

"Mm-hmm," said Edna, eyeing Frederick.

"And you," began Lawrence, looking at Edna, "if you knew something was up, especially about my mother, and if you knew he wouldn't tell me, then you should have. How could you? She was your sister. I'm her only son. I deserved to know."

"I wanted to—" started Edna.

"Look son, this is my fault," said Frederick. "You're probably right. I should have told you."

"Then why didn't you?"

"In my mind, I think I thought I was protecting you."

"Nice job," said Lawrence and Edna in unison.

Lawrence walked over to the book, Frederick opened earlier. He picked it up and began turning pages.

"You said this book has secrets and history in it?"

"That's right, son."

"Does it tell us how to stop the Primeval?"

"It does. But we don't need that. I already know."

"How?" asked Lawrence. "How do we kill it?"

"It can't be killed," said Edna.

"No, it can't be. She's right," agreed Frederick.

"Then what do can do?" asked Lawrence.

"We have to lock it back up," said Frederick.

"We don't know where it's gone though. How do we find it and get it back here?"

Lawrence watched as his aunt and his father regarded one another, sharing a glance that betrayed a common knowledge. Once again, they were holding something back. Once again, Lawrence was getting angry. He felt himself begin to tremble. Before long, he wasn't the only thing shaking. Glass rattled, some cracked, pictures fell from the walls. He heard a pipe burst in the kitchen followed by the spray of water.

"Earthquake!" screamed Edna.

"No," said Frederick. "That's no earthquake. It's Lawrence."

Lawrence heard the words and quickly realized that he was indeed the cause. He could feel some sense of control, but little ability. It made him wonder if he'd been the cause of other quakes when he was mad. Lawrence closed his eyes, took deep breaths, and calmed himself. As he did, the shaking and rattling slowed. The only sound, the hissing from the burst pipe in the kitchen.

"Tell me what you're holding back from me," he said calmy.

"The Primeval is still non corporeal. Powerful, but non corporeal. Once he's solid, he'll be almost unbeatable. He's probably on his way to do just that," said Frederick.

"On his way where?" asked Lawrence.

"To your mother's resting place," said Frederick.

"The only way he can stay, is through his own blood," began Edna, "so he'll go for the one thing that can make him whole…her heart."

"Her…heart? Then we need to go. We need to stop him. We need to get to the cemetery."

"Hold on, son. Just hold on. Your mother isn't at the cemetery. That's just where we had the service. There's a marker, but that was just for appearances."

"Then where is she?"

"In the catacombs beneath St. Augustine's," said Frederick.

Ignoring the urge to lash out, Lawrence put the book down and walked to his father. He looked at the old man. His wrinkles, his salt and pepper hair, contrasted by the metallic silver eyes staring back. There was much to talk about. But now was not the time.

"We need to get there, and fast. He's probably already found her."

"It's doubtful, but you're right, we do need to get there. We can trap him, bring him back, and throw him back into the Vacant Space."

"Well let's go. I'll drive. C'mon Pop!"

"There's a faster way, son."

Lawrence watched his father walk over the small wooden desk where the phone and liquor sat. The decrepit old thing was good for little else. His father faced the edge, near the drawer that was always stuck. Frederick lifted a bottle of whiskey, slammed it down, then reached up to tilt a book, tapped his fingers against two other books, before finally slapping the desk and kicking his leg underneath. When he finished the bizarre ritual, the drawer automatically opened.

"What the…," said Lawrence, his words trailing off.

Frederick retrieved three things from the drawer. Two black spheres, slightly smaller than billiard balls, and a gold box.

"These will transport us to the catacombs, and we can use this box to trap him," said Frederick.

"Fine," began Lawrence, "let's go."

Standing next to Lawrence, with Edna looking on, Frederick slammed one of the orbs to the ground. A brilliant light filled the room, and once gone, so too were Sanders and son.

# # #

Lawrence materialized in the catacombs beneath St. Augustine's with his father. It was dark, the only illumination coming from the blue hued sword Frederick brought. The ominous tunnel smelled of rat feces, mold, and decay. The gray concrete blocks were covered with damp algae. In some areas, the walls seemed to move. Upon closer inspection though, they were simply covered with all manner of insects.

Some feasting on others.

The two men moved forward across a ground slick with mud, animal carcasses, and fragments of human skulls. The scene was a strange juxtaposition against any reality. Lawrence, dressed in bell bottomed blue jeans and a turtleneck, next to his father, the gray-haired Frederick, dressed in tan pants, with a brown tattered cardigan sweater over a plain white shirt, in a seemingly endless tunnel on their way to possible death.

A gust of wind rushed through the tunnel, carrying the moans and screams of the damned. The hair on the back of Lawrence's neck was at attention. Among the whispers, he heard his name.

*Lawrence, Prince of the Damned.*

*It's him!*

*He's here!*

*Kill him!*

*He must be killed!*

"Pop?"

"What?"

"You hear that?"

"Hear what, son?"

"Those voices. Calling my name."

Lawrence stopped as Frederick did. The sword, now between them, cast a blue glow across his father's face.

"They're calling for you, son," whispered Frederick.

"Why me?!"

"Would you hush," Frederick demanded in a loud whisper. "You need to keep your voice down."

"Pop, there's things here that want to kill me. How do you expect me to remain calm?"

"I expect you to do what's needed, Lawrence. That's all. No more, no less."

"What the hell does that mean?"

"We'll find out soon enough. Now come on, before the hellhounds come."

"The what?"

"Boy, hush and come on."

As they trudged forward, the whispers continued. More voices joined the cacophony of chants calling for Lawrence's death. Had his offense, his mistake, been that dire? He couldn't say. He didn't need to. The damned were doing it for him.

"Just up ahead, son," whispered Frederick.

In the distance, Lawrence saw flickering light. There was a sound carried on the wind. Grunting. The sound of someone…straining. Edging closer, Lawrence and his father saw the source of the sound. It wasn't just one person, but three. All three were working to open a granite sarcophagus.

The Primeval floated above them, his green eyes shining bright, his boney hand directing the trio of men like a band leader.

"Pop? Mom is in there?" asked Lawrence, keeping his voice low.

"Yes."

"He's, controlling them? He can do that? Those poor people. We have to help them."

"Look closer, son."

Lawrence followed his father's direction and studied the men. In awe of the spectacle before him, he'd completely overlooked the fact that all the men…wore suits. Their skin seemed odd, too. They were black men, but their skin was ashen, grayed…decayed. As they continued to push the heavy stone lid, Lawrence saw blood dripping from the mouth of one, yet the man continued as if he hadn't noticed. No, not a man. These were not men at all. At least, not anymore.

"Pop, are they…dead?"

Frederick nodded.

"He can do that? He can control the dead?"

Frederick nodded again.

Lawrence lamented, backed against the wall, and began rethinking the decision to go after the Primeval. As thoughts ran through his mind, he felt a strange sensation on his head.

Then in his hair.

Then his face.

Then his arms.

Lawrence found himself covered in insects and bugs. Spiders crawled near is ear, and a millipede skittered across his cheek. His hair felt alive as something burrowed through his afro and made its way to his scalp. Just as the zombies made a final push to get the lid off, Lawrence screamed. His arms flailed about as he tried to clear his body of the tiny creatures crawling all over him. The sound of the lid was not enough to mask his cry or his antics. The zombies and the Primeval took notice.

"Get them," said the ghostly apparition floating overhead.

The three undead creatures bounded toward Lawrence and his father. Their eyes were vacant, soulless. All three seemed to have dried blood dripping from open mouths. Bloodied gums highlighted black and yellow teeth. Their motives were innate, autonomic, and primal.

They wanted to feed.

“Hang back, son,” said Frederick, handing over the gold box.

Lawrence watched in awe as his father, looking no more imposing than a resident of a retirement home, moved with agility, speed, and grace toward the three mindless drones of the Primeval. With his sword he took the leg of the lead zombie, who shook it off with indifference and began to crawl along the ground toward Frederick. As his father contended with the other two, Lawrence searched for something to use as a weapon. Palming a large rock, he moved with purpose toward the undead creature and hit it in the head, then backed away.

It turned awkwardly then began scurrying toward him, seemingly picking up speed.

He hit it again.

It kept coming.

Another hit.

Now it was on him.

Lawrence toppled back as the thing grabbed his leg. Smashing at its hands had no effect. Before long, its bloodied mouth clamped down on Lawrence’s leg. He let out a scream as teeth tore into skin. The zombie gnawed, its head thrashing back and forth. It ripped a chunk of flesh from Lawrence just as his father pulled it away by its remaining leg. Frederick brought his tip of his blade down into the zombie’s skull, killing him…again.

The Primeval's laughter filled the cavern. Lawrence's leg gushed blood, soaking his pants and ground beneath him. He looked back at his father, then at the Primeval. His father had a knowing look, but it was filled with dread.

"Prince of the Damned, indeed," taunted the Primeval.

"Pop?"

"We have to get out of here, son."

"No! Pop! Wait! We can stop him."

Lawrence knew there was no stopping his father though, who moved with singular purpose. Frederick had the second orb in hand when he reached Lawrence. The two shared a glance, then looked back at the Primeval who was hovering directly over the body of Lizbetta Sanders.

"Mom," whispered Lawrence.

"Come on, son."

"We have to stay, Pop."

"This isn't where we make our stand son. He won't find what he's looking for here."

With that, Frederick slammed the final orb to the ground. Light filled the cavern, and once gone, so too, were Sanders and son.

In the corner, covered with insects, was the gold box that was to be the Primeval's transportation to the Vacant Space.

# # #

Back at the Boneyard, Lawrence and Frederick materialized near the site of the Primeval's escape. Frederick knelt to check the wound on Lawrence's leg. He said nothing, making Lawrence even more uneasy.

"Am I gonna turn into one of them? Am I gonna die, Pop?"

"Nope," said Frederick quickly. "You'll die, but not from this."

Lawrence stared at his father who made no eye contact. He then watched as his Frederick shifted from him and began moving shards of porcelain to clear the entrance to the Primeval's former cell. Seeing the strain on the old man's body, Lawrence moved to offer assistance.

"I got it," bit Frederick.

"Pop, come on."

"Come on, what?" Frederick asked rhetorically.

Lawrence said nothing. What could he say? His inept actions cost them everything that night. He'd unleashed the ultimate evil on the world and was bitten by a zombie. His night was only getting better and better with each passing second.

"Look…man, what was I supposed to do? Just let you die?"

"Yes!" Frederick exclaimed before slamming a large piece of porcelain to the ground.

Lawrence jumped in his own skin as his father screamed. He'd never seen him that angry. There'd been years of disappointment, years of love, compassion, even empathy when comforting the boy he once was. His father had been many things over the years. But never angry. Not like this. Frederick's reaction only further drove home how serious the night's events were.

"My job, my only job in life, is to keep you and this world safe. If that means I give up my life, then fine. I'm gonna be all right because you're safe, and then I can get back to your mother."

He'd always assumed that his father's devotion to his mother was just the overly hopeful rhetoric of a Christian who believed in being reunited with a loved one in the afterlife. Realization grew tonight though. There was the very real possibility that he would, in fact, see her again. If there is a world beyond this one, with strange creatures and magical beings…why couldn't they be reunited?

"Pop, I get it. But come on man, I only learned about all this stuff tonight. Now how can you expect me to be okay with this and just know what to do. You've known about this for sixty years. I've known about it for sixty minutes. Give me a break."

Silence held the microphone on the night's stage. A light breeze scattered loose dirt on the ground. Both men, father, and son, stared at each other. In unison, their shoulders lowered, they took deep breaths, and each seemed to take stock of the moment, of the night, of their lives.

"Five hundred," said Frederick.

"Say what?"

"Five hundred," repeated Frederick. "I've known about this for five hundred years, not sixty."

"I thought you said you weren't a—"

"The thing inside me, is from down there," said Frederick, pointing down. "We work in tandem when things get serious. But me, I'm from upstairs, the Golden City. I was cast out and sentenced to be a Sentinel. I age, because technically I'm not immortal, but I still have some skill. Especially when I'm integrated."

"Cast out? Because…of mom?"

Frederick's slow nod almost crushed Lawrence. If not for the knowing and loving smile that went with it, Lawrence would have caved under the weight of guilt, the oppression of a burden that wasn't his to bear. In that smile and slow nod, a love like no other was expressed.

"What do we need to do?" he asked.

"He'll be back here. He'll want to destroy this thing to make sure he can't be locked in again."

"We don't have the box. So, we lure him in and close it?"

"And seal it with your blood," said Frederick.

"But, what about the heart? He's too powerful now."

"You can beat him, son. You have the power."

"I couldn't even fight a zombie, Pop. You said yourself, this bite isn't going to kill me, but he will."

"No, son. I said, you'll die, but not from that bite. You see, to beat him, you do have to die. Just…in a different way."

"Pop, I don't have—"

Lawrence's words stopped at the first pinprick he felt. The breaking of skin in his chest, followed by a rush of heat, a heat so intense that the cool night air brought no comfort. His breath caught in his throat as he felt the invasion in his body. In a split second, shock and awareness smacked him across the face, as he realized the blue hued sword of his father pierced his heart.

"Pop?" he whispered.

The last sound he heard was the crack of lightening from above.

The last thing he saw was his father struck in the chest and hurled back against a large mound of junk as the Primeval landed with authority and purpose.

The last thing he felt was his head hit the ground.

And then the darkness came.

# # #

For the second time in as many hours, Lawrence felt wet, warm, canine drool hit his face. That was followed by the feel of a rough, wet, warm tongue on his cheek. He moved slowly, feeling aches, mostly in his chest, right in the spot his father impaled him with a sword. He sat up, gaining his bearings, Bella still licking him—both heads alternating.

"Ok, ok…enough. I'm up," said Lawrence.

He pushed her away and got to his feet. Instinctively, he moved his hand to his chest, feeling for a wound. All he felt, was the scar. He felt something else, too. A buzz, or tingle—something he couldn't quite put his finger on. His body simply felt…alive. Electric, almost. As if it surged with power waiting to be unleashed.

Boom!

The sound shook Lawrence from his daze. Following it, he found his father engaged with The Primeval. For an old man, his father was surprisingly quick and agile. He ducked punches, countered with his own, blocked kicks, and dove away from what could have been fatal blows. The Primeval seemed frustrated. He was still flickering like an old television. Strange. They'd left him alone with his mother's body. He should have found what he needed. What had happened to keep him in this state? In the distance, Lawrence saw his father's sword, the agent of his own death.

Why? Why'd you do it, Pop?

You must have known I'd come back, right?

What am I supposed to do now?

Bella's barking brought him back to the present, alerting the combatants to his position. The distraction was enough to give The Primeval time to quickly retrieve the blue hued sword and drive it into Frederick's abdomen, sending him to his knees.

"POPPPPPP!" screamed Lawrence.

Rushing to him Lawrence absently waved his hand, tossing the Primeval aside like a rag doll. Reaching his father, Lawrence knelt. His breathing was heavy. His thoughts scattered as he searched for a way to help his father.

"Pop? Pop? What can I do? How do I fix this?"

"Son," began Frederick, "there's no fix. This is the end. This is your time."

The strain of Frederick pulling the blade from his body broke Lawrence's heart. Watching his father slump down to the ground almost broke him.

"Blood of my blood," said a sinister voice from behind.

Lawrence's body strummed again. That feeling of power surging through him, now a pleasant shock to his system.

"This…is your…time," said Frederick.

"Blood. Of. My. Blood."

Lawrence rose to his feet at that. The creature had the audacity to sound impatient and condescending after what he'd done. Turning to face the Primeval, Lawrence's face flushed with heat. Anger filled him and he needed an outlet.

"You killed my father," said Lawrence with disturbing calm.

"You can't kill me, boy," said the entity.

"I know. But I can put you back in your box."

The Primeval laughed mockingly.

"Boy, please. Your father is dead. You can't even fathom the enormity of this. And. You. Are. Alone."

The Primeval pulled his hood back to reveal a dark, emaciated face with sunken eyes that continued to glow green…only brighter. He continued to laugh, revealing a mouth with jagged teeth atop gums that seemed to ooze black liquid. The entity raised its arms and in an instant, Lawrence was surrounded by walking, mindless, and hungry zombies. One of them, slightly more aware than the others, carried the gold box he'd dropped in the catacombs. His mind seemed to dissolve with each step and before long, he dropped the box, kicking it toward other piles of debris and junk in the Boneyard.

Lawrence didn't know what to do. There were so many of them. He was healed and he felt strong and powerful, but he was unsure about how to direct it. Taking a moment to consider his father, he reached for the sword, which surprisingly flew to his hand, and he prepared to attack.

"Hold on, nephew."

Lawrence turned to find his Aunt Edna standing there. She gave a quick glance at Frederick's body, then turned toward Lawrence again. She put two fingers in her mouth and whistled. From other sections of the Boneyard people appeared.

Not just any people.

His family.

His Aunt Rosa, Uncle Ed, and Aunt Hazy. His cousins were among them, too. They'd never been particularly close, but he was happy to see them now.

"You take care of him," said Edna, pointing to the Primeval. "We'll take care of the others."

As she said that, she transformed again into the demon form he'd seen earlier. Looking around, the rest of the family followed suit. All demons. At once, they attacked the mindless undead creatures filling the Boneyard.

Lawrence moved forward to engage the Primeval.

He took one punch from the boney yet powerful hand and simply turned his head, going with the momentum, but he didn't fall. He took a second punch and did the same. When the next punch came, Lawrence caught it, squeezed, then countered with his own sending the Primeval back several feet.

Lawrence now heard the internal hum in his body. He was filled with power. Power that he finally felt able to command. The Primeval was still flickering, struggling to stay solid. It would make it difficult to subdue him. He needed a way to get him into the Vacant Space. What happened in the catacombs that kept him from her heart?

Her…heart.

Her heart?

Of course!

He hadn't seen it until now. It was the reason his father told him the Primeval wouldn't find what he was looking for. It wasn't in the sarcophagus.

*He* was his mother's heart. In that moment, he knew what he needed to do. But first, a distraction.

Letting his instincts take over, he held his arms out and closed his eyes. Winds picked up within the Boneyard. Once again, debris flew, crashing into fixed structures. When Lawrence opened his eyes, they glowed, casting a shade of blue, not unlike his fathers' sword. A low murmur echoed throughout the Boneyard.

*Kill him!*

*Yes, kill him!*

*Must appeal to the Primeval with his blood!*

The voices were back. All this time, they hadn't been calling for his head. They been urging Lawrence to fulfil his duty as Prince of the Damned.

And then it happened.

Bones sprang from the ground. Dozens, hundreds rose from the dirt as far as the eye could see…and they came together. The reformed skeletons lurched forward, each step seemingly the last. Despite their fragile appearance, they held strong. Their skulls were sinister. Cracked, slack-jawed, mindless, yet full of purpose, determined to bend to the will of their master—the Prince of the Damned.

"You think this brittle army of bones can defeat me, boy?"

"What you want, is right here," said Lawrence. "I am my mother's heart. Her blood. *Your* blood. You can live again…through me. So come and get me."

The Primeval sprang forward, squared off against a skeleton and struck. The skull landed on the ground. With only his will and desire for vengeance, Lawrence urged the skeleton to continue. From all sides, skeletons converged on the Primeval like locusts, hungry for their next meal. They tore at him, scratched and bit, mindlessly, primal obedience their only guide. He continued to flicker, but there were so many of them he had no time to remain intangible enough to flee. As he watched, Lawrence felt a nudge against his leg. Bella had arrived, in one of her mouths, the gold box.

Each time the Primeval broke free, he became solid enough to be dragged back down. Lawrence stepped forward, taunting him. The Primeval stretched out enough to grab Lawrence's arm. The contact enough to keep him tangible. The skeleton's clung to him, pulling him back, and pulling Lawrence in as well. As they did, Lawrence opened the box.

The Primeval struggled, but the sheer numbers made it impossible to break free. The magic of the box sought out its prey, sought the blood it was to hold. Both Lawrence and the Primeval succumbed to its power. The Primeval tightened hid grip onto Lawrence and the box fell to the ground. Both were drawn in.

"You'll go with me, so-called Prince of the Damned," said the evil entity.

Lawrence responded only with a smile.

His eyes became a shiny blue and in seconds, the skeletons released their grip on the Primeval, shifting their efforts to Lawrence. From nowhere,

Bella arrived, and with an insatiable bloodlust, she gnawed at the forearms of the Primeval, severing them, allowing the box to take him completely as the skeleton army pulled Lawrence back.

Lawrence closed quickly closed the lid, grabbed his father's sword by the blade and pulled it with the other, cutting his palm, allowing blood to flow freely. He let it drip over the gold box. Once covered, the crimson liquid automatically hardened, sealing the evil inside. He then walked to the entrance to the Vacant Space, dropped the box inside, covered it, and sealed the lid with his blood as well.

His family surrounded him, their battles completed. There was no talk, no congratulations, just looks of understanding and reverence. Lawrence then looked to his father's body.

It stirred.

# # #

"Is this the big one, Pop?" asked Lawrence.

"Yeah, son. It is," Frederick managed to say. "You…you…you hear that Lizbetta? I'm coming to join…you…honey."

Lawrence held his father, feeling the stabs of a thousand memories. The memories were bittersweet. Some good, most filled with stupid arguments, threats of leaving, blame for feeling held back from having a much different life. But the events of this night, answered the question of why. In this moment, Lawrence understood why his father manipulated him into staying.

"Hey, hey son, you remember…when you were a little boy…just… learning how to talk, and you couldn't…you…you couldn't say daddy? You remember that son?"

"Yeah, Pop. I remember."

"You remember…what you said…in…instead?"

"I called you," Lawrence started, pausing as a lump formed in his throat, "I said dummy."

The sound of Frederick trying to laugh was the final stab. Lawrence let the first tear fall. Then the second. Each holding an "I'm sorry, Pop" or an "I forgive you, Pop".

"Yeah…yeah…you said…you said dummy. Then I called you a dummy, and we laughed and laughed," Frederick said, before letting out a series of coughs.

"Yeah, we did, Pop."

"Hey…hey son? You know when I call you that, you know I don't mean that…right?"

"Yeah, Pop. I know."

And he did know. Somewhere, deep down he'd always known. It was their thing, their secret handshake, their special code. The unspoken *I love you* between two stubborn men forever devoted to each other. Lawrence knew that this man was his anchor, but not in the way he'd openly complained. Frederick wasn't an anchor holding him back. Frederick was the anchor to his humanity.

"I…I…I gotta go now, son. You're gonna stay, right? You're gonna stay and manage the Boneyard?"

"I will, Pop. I'll make you proud."

"I'll see you…on the other…side. Big dummy," Frederick said, with a final grin, before drifting off into the dark abyss of death.

"I love you, too, Pop." ♜

# THOSE MEDDLING KIDS

*By Rob Nisbet*

IT WAS DARK; OF COURSE it was. It was always dark, and often foggy with occasional lightning, when The Mystery Gang turned up for the latest of their weekly adventures.

The big key grated in the lock, the imposing double glass doors swung inward, creaking ominously on protesting hinges, and from outside four faces peered around the door frame into the gloom; five if you included Patchy, the talking dog, who appeared at ground level.

"Creep-y!" growled Patchy, his little black eyes wide amongst his white fur.

"You're not wrong there, Patch," agreed Norman. He craned his long neck into the darkness as if unwilling to allow the rest of his gangly body over the threshold. He ran his fingers nervously through his shaggy mop of orange hair. "Why can't ghosts haunt nice well-lit places where there are no shadows or black-as-night corners?"

"Come on, Norman." Gordon pushed himself bravely forward, pocketing the heavy key as he did so. "There must be a light switch here somewhere." He patted the wall by the doors. "Found it," he said.

A moment later, they were all blinking in the glare as neon tubes flickered into life. "Reception area," Gordon announced, looking around the functional open space and the vacant semi-circular desk facing them.

"Nobody at home," Norman sounded relieved. "We might as well come back in the daytime. You know – when there are people about, and daylight."

"Daylight," agreed Patchy, trotting cautiously by Norman's ankles.

"Oh, you two are incorrigible!" Vera bustled forward, peering around over the top of her just-for-show glasses.

"Hear that, Patch?" said Norman. "We're in-corrig… Whatever *she* said."

Patchy gave a furry snigger.

Undaunted, Vera strode up to the curved reception desk. On the wall behind it, a large sign spelled out BLAKE in bold yellow letters. "The Blake cartoon studio," she informed them wisely. "That means we're in the right place."

Daisy, the remaining member of The Mystery Gang, allowed her eyelashes to shiver in Gordon's direction. She shrugged her skimpy leather jacket over her shoulders. "I hope I'll be warm enough. I never know what to wear for ghost hunting in a cartoon studio." She pulled ineffectually at the short skirt that perfectly matched the pink of her chiffon scarf.

It hadn't slipped Gordon's notice that the skirt did little to cover Daisy's perfect legs. The curve of his lustful heart could be seen throbbing against his tight white shirt. "Let's split up," he said, "and look for clues."

This generally involved Norman and Patchy going one way; Gordon and Daisy, accompanied by her perfect legs, going another; with the diminutive Vera joining whichever team would require the most plot exposition.

"Hey," said Vera before they could split up, "I think I've found something." She lifted a newspaper from the reception desk; a narrow column on the first page had been circled with a bold red marker. Vera squinted, then pushed her glasses out of the way, into her hairline. "Listen to this…

> *Police are investigating reported sightings of a ghost in the studio belonging to murdered cartoon pioneer, Gerald Blake. Mr Blake was found last month, brutally stabbed in his office on the third floor. The investigations into the murder have been hampered recently by apparent sightings of Mr Blake's ghost which, reports state, has been haunting the building where he was killed. A close associate: Mr Richard*

> *Sanderfield, of the Sanderfield animation company said: "The animation world has lost one of its pioneers. Blake's is one of the oldest companies, producing fondly remembered traditional cartoons."*
>
> *Readers may find it interesting to know that Sanderfield had offered to buy the whole Blake operation just weeks before the murder took place. It is rumored that he planned to revive the old studio, modernizing Blake's dated processes using Sanderfield's cutting edge Animation Dome technology.*
>
> *Traditionalists however have pointed out the popularity of Blake's cartoons, the best known of which is The Mystery Gang. They point out that these traditional cartoons are more popular than the technically advanced realistic images produced by Sanderfield's Dome."*

Gordon rubbed at his manly jaw. "That's the ghost we've been asked to investigate," he said, patting the pocket that contained the note that had accompanied the bulky key. He narrowed his eyes thoughtfully. "And there's some useful background information there too. Is there a helpful picture of Blake in that article?"

"There is." Vera held up the page showing the others the grim heavily bearded face.

Norman shuddered. "I don't fancy, you know, meeting *his* ghost on a dark night. What about you, Patch?"

"No way!" said Patchy peering up through his white fluff at the picture.

"There's the elevator," said Gordon. "The article said the crime took place on the third floor. Daisy, Vera and I should take a look, while Norman and Patchy scout around down here."

"Suits me." Norman leant on the desk, talking to an imaginary receptionist. "Tell me, my good woman; is the ghost receiving visitors tonight?"

With a juddering moan that echoed throughout the entrance hall, a transparent specter rose as if through the floor behind the desk. It was a bearded man, the image of the murdered cartoonist, Gerald Blake. His eyes glowed a fiery red and his mouth twisted into a growl.

"Zoinks!" Norman leapt back.

The specter passed through the desk, reaching out his hands like claws towards the astounded Mystery Gang.

"Run!" advised Norman, demonstrating the maneuver towards the glass entrance doors.

Patchy's little legs pinwheeled in the air, then, suddenly finding purchase on the floor, he sped after his master.

The ghost blurred across the room, past Norman and Patchy, appearing at the doors with another growling moan. Patchy practically turned himself inside out to retreat towards the desk.

"It's Blake's ghost!" informed the normally rational Vera, helpfully.

Forgetting that they were going to split into two groups, everyone scattered in panic.

The ghost seemed satisfied with this reaction and floated threateningly just above the tiled floor to the center of the room.

Patchy passed the reception desk at speed, then, with a sound suspiciously like the twang of a coiled spring, he bounced off some invisible barrier, rubbing at his flattened nose with a surprised paw.

"What's up, Patch?" asked Norman, just as he too ran headfirst into another invisible wall. A throbbing bump grew out of his skull, surrounded by a halo of tweeting blue birds.

Around the reception area, each of the Mystery Gang had hit a wall they couldn't see. The ghost's beard split with a roar of mocking laughter. It glared at them with its eerie red eyes, swept across the floor, and passed straight through the door of what might have been a broom cupboard.

"If anyone asks me to fetch a broom, I'm outta here," informed Norman.

"Hang on a moment…" Vera peered around the room over the top of her glasses. "Look at us! All five of us have reached some kind of invisible barrier, and we've formed a perfect circle." A lightbulb pinged into existence above her head. "Zinkies! I have a horrible suspicion about this."

Vera became motionless as the scene froze then faded to be replaced by a bag of dogfood.

Jolly music appeared, together with a cartoon west-highland terrier complete with dotted bib and brandishing a knife and fork.

The dog burst into song.

Patchy Snacks, Patchy Snacks, they're so *crunchy*.

Patchy Snacks, Patchy Snacks, they're so *munchy*.

When you have a *mystery* to solve, that's proving hard to crack,

Remember you can do it when you have a *Patchy Snack!*

"Hang on a moment…" Vera peered around the room over the top of her glasses. "Look at us! All five of us have reached some kind of invisible barrier, and we've formed a perfect circle." A lightbulb pinged into existence above her head. "Zinkies! I have a horrible suspicion about this."

"Hey, Vera," said Gordon. "Was that some kind of echo? Didn't you just say all that?"

"Yes." Vera pinched at her chin thoughtfully. "I couldn't help it; it was like a reprise. Hey, did anyone else have the impression that we were interrupted just now by a commercial break?"

"Patchy snacks," said Patchy with a slobbery slurp of his little pink tongue.

"Yeah, Patchy snacks," agreed Norman. He delved into a pocket with an appreciative slurp of his own and produced a handful of kibble that he shared with Patchy.

Vera was looking worried. “Like I said, I have a horrible suspicion about this. And that commercial appearing at a vital plot point could be a clue.”

“A clue!” Daisy placed a delicate hand on her slim hips and fluttered her eyelashes towards Gordon in excitement. “Now we’re getting somewhere.”

“*Somewhere*, yes,” Vera frowned through the ideas flitting through her head. “But not, perhaps where we think we are.”

“Concentrate, everyone,” said Gordon manfully as if in a significant close-up. “This could be important.”

“I don’t think we are in the Blake studio at all,” explained Vera. “We have reached some kind of invisible boundary - and formed a perfect circle. I think we are actually inside the Sanderfield Animation Dome!”

“Wow!” said Norman, not sure that he had understood what Vera had said. “That’s just, wow!”

“Yeah,” Patchy agreed with a cautious wag of his little white tail, “wow!”

“So, what about the ghost?” fluttered Daisy, with a graceful gesture to the broom cupboard.

Gordon gritted his perfect teeth which pinged with a reflected sparkle. “The ghost seemed genuine,” he said. “That was no man in a mask; he was transparent, and he can pass through solid objects.”

“Oh, I don’t think he was real,” said Vera. “I think he was a very clever animation, like a realistic cartoon. I think this whole scene has been generated by Sanderfield within his Dome, and we're trapped within it."

"So, we're inside an animated scenario…" Gordon reiterated, to make sure everyone understood.

Vera nodded. "I read an article recently about Sanderfield's animation process. He can generate an astonishingly realistic setting within his Dome, which can then be filmed. The process has been used in several big movies, but it's expensive tech. Rumors are the Sanderfield studios are not doing well."

"This is realistic, all right," agreed Gordon, looking around. "It had *us* fooled. So, how do we get out of here?"

"There must be a control panel around here somewhere," said Vera. "Feel around the walls."

They ran their hands over the invisible circular wall of the Dome. The walls were smooth except for the broom cupboard.

"Makes sense," said Norman tapping at the door with a visible shudder. "Nobody's gonna look for controls in a haunted broom cupboard."

"Except we now know that this is an animation," said Gordon. "For once we know the ghost *isn't* real – we're perfectly safe. Open the door, Norman."

"Why me?" Norman turned around to find all his friends had taken a step back, even Patchy. He had the impression of canned laughter taunting him. "Ok," he said resigned. "Here goes…" He tugged at the door, and the bearded, red-eyed ghost of Gerald Blake lunged out at him. "Zoinks!"

Norman's shaggy hair stood up in orange spikes, he fled across the tiled floor diving behind the reception desk. After a few seconds, his head reappeared, eyes mega-wide with caution.

The ghost had stopped its pursuit and stood motionless and transparent in the center of the room. At the cupboard, Vera had found the control panel and twisted at a complicated dial. The ghost began to revolve. She prodded a few buttons and the ghost responded with growls and grasping sweeps of its claw-like hands.

"I think this is an animated rehearsal," said Vera. "But I think it proves that Sanderfield has been faking the haunting of Blake's studio." Vera sounded very pleased with herself. "No doubt, with his own animation company in financial difficulties, he wanted to take over Blake's popular and successful cartoon industry."

Daisy fluttered her eyelashes in confusion. "But why does Sanderfield have this elaborate recreation of Blake's reception area in his Dome?" she asked.

"That's the most horrible part," said Vera. She paused, blinking through her glasses, as if expecting another commercial break to burst over this significant plot development. "I believe it was Sanderfield who murdered Blake, and all this was set up as a rehearsal for the actual crime. When Blake refused to sell Sanderfield his cartoon company, Sanderfield killed him. And since then, he has been haunting the Blake studios to bring down the price."

"That's despicable," said Gordon, like a true hero.

"Despicable!" agreed Patchy, furrily.

"And," added Vera, "I might be able to prove it." She twisted various dials on the control panel, lights flashed, and she flicked some complicated switches. "There is a useful purple button to reactivate a previous scenario," she explained. "Here goes…"

The motionless ghostly figure in the center of the room faded away. Then the whole room disappeared too. For a moment, the panels of Sanderfield's vast Animation Dome could be seen arching above them. It resembled a cathedral of interlocking hexagons, like a giant beehive. Then, one by one, the hexagons became projections of a new scene. The Mystery Gang found themselves in a cramped elevator – with a furtive-looking stranger.

"That's Sanderfield," said Vera in an unnecessary whisper. The man was cloaked in a non-descript coat. He had a pointed nose, swept back greying hair and eyes that glinted like struck flint. "Don't worry; we're not part of this scenario, so he can't see or hear us. I think this is Sanderfield's animated rehearsal for when he broke into the Blake studios."

The elevator pinged at the third floor and the door slid open. The Mystery Gang followed Sanderfield out and along a corridor. Offices lined the passage on both sides, and between the doors stood man-sized publicity cut outs of Blake's famous cartoon characters.

"Hey, it's the Boneflints," said Norman as they passed a cluster of caveman characters. "I used to love that show."

"Me too," said Patchy, and began to hum the theme tune.

Gordon beckoned at them. "Keep up you two."

The stealthy image of Sanderfield paused outside a more imposing doorway – Blake's office. The cut outs by this door were of his most famous cartoon show, The Mystery Gang. Gordon, Daisy, Vera, Norman and Patchy frowned at these flat characters. Perhaps it was their faces, or their clothes, but there was something uncomfortably familiar about them. But there was no time to think about this. Sanderfield pushed open Blake's office door and strode inside.

"Blake!" roared Sanderfield, unaware of his audience which had shuffled in behind him, "I'm gonna give you one last chance. Will you sell me your studio or not?"

Blake had risen from behind a wooden desk, his eyes were wide with realistically animated surprise. He shook his bearded face from side to side. "My cartoons are the pinnacle of my life's work," he said. "They are not some special effect for your struggling film company – my answer, for the final time, is still no. I shall never sell to you, Sanderfield."

"Then you leave me just one option." Sanderfield pulled a long thin blade from within his coat, swept up to Blake, and thrust the knife into him three times.

Daisy screeched. "Oh, it's horrible, I can't look!"

Gordon was quick to offer her a comforting arm around her narrow waist. "Don't worry," he said manfully as Blake collapsed to the floor in a pool of animated blood. "This isn't real, is it Vera?"

"This is a practice-run for Sanderfield's attack," Vera confirmed. "I think it proves though that Sanderfield was the killer. We need to show this evidence to the police."

"No chance." The voice was unmistakably Sanderfield's, but it didn't come from the image of the man who stood with the dripping knife. There were now two Sanderfields: the animation they had been watching, and the *real* man who now stood in the office doorway. He narrowed his flinty eyes. "How clever of Blake to enlist the help of *you*, his solvers of mysteries, he obviously realized that only cartoon characters could investigate in a realm of animation."

"What do you mean, *cartoon characters?*" Peering over her glasses, Vera too narrowed her eyes, but not so flintily.

Sanderfield produced a hand-held control device. "You are about to find out." He pressed a sequence of buttons. The animated Sanderfield with his knife, and the slumped Blake, vanished, even the pool of blood disappeared. "I'm going to enjoy this," said Sanderfield; his voice sounded like a threat. He stepped back into the corridor and slammed the door behind him.

"I don't like the sound of that," said Vera.

"Nor me," said Daisy.

"Nor me," said Norman.

"Nor me too," said Patchy.

"Let's split up and get out of here," said Gordon, tightening his grip on Daisy's narrow waist.

Vera blinked thoughtfully behind her glasses. "We are inside Sanderfield's Animation Dome. Somehow, we got in here when we entered the reception area. I'd suggest we all go down in the elevator and try the main double doors. Then we can contact the police."

"Sounds like a plan," said Norman. "Hey, you don't suppose there's anything, you know, *creepy* behind that closed door, do you?"

Gordon stepped bravely forward. "Haven't you learned anything, Norman?" He pulled open the door. "This place is just an animation; we're real; nothing here can harm us."

They filed out into the corridor, to be faced with the cardboard cut-outs of The Mystery Gang.

"I've got a nasty feeling about this," said Vera. She turned to Gordon. "What exactly did that note say, the one with the key?"

Gordon fished about in his rugged pocket for the key that had opened the door to the reception area. Then, delving deeper, he produced a note. He cleared his throat. "My dear Mystery Gang," he read, "I am depending on you to solve the haunting of my cartoon studio, and I enclose a key to the main door. Regards and best wishes, Gerald Blake (deceased)."

"A letter from Blake's ghost!" Norman's teeth began to rattle like castanets.

"Yeah, Blake's ghost!" echoed Patchy, his teeth joining in with a salsa rhythm.

"It's more serious than that." Vera gestured at the cut-out display figures. "They are *The Mystery Gang*. They are characters from a cartoon. Look familiar?"

"Hey Patch," said Norman. "This guy looks kinda funky – shaggy hair and he has a cute little westie too."

"It's you!" barked Patchy. "And me!"

Vera pulled off her glasses to be certain. "Zinkies! It's all of us!"

Gordon stared at the square jaw of his double and at the arms folded across the heroic white shirt he wore. Then he looked down at himself and his friends around him with a dawning understanding. He held out a hand, examining it closely. "Vera's right. I never realized it before, but we do seem a little two-dimensional."

"And our clothes," said Daisy, pulling at her matching pink skirt and scarf. "There is no shade or texture to them, just a uniform color."

Vera nodded. "That's the difference between Blake's traditional cartoons and Sanderfield's realistic animation process. That proves it; we're cartoon investigators!"

"And, Blake," reasoned Daisy with a rare burst of intellect, "wants us to look into the fake haunting of his studio."

"And therefore solve his murder," finished Gordon. "We need to get to the police as soon as possible."

They all agreed and were secretly relieved to leave their eerie cardboard doppelgangers and head to the elevator. Only Patchy seemed troubled by the recent revelation. "But," he whimpered, "we're a cartoon!"

"Says the talking dog." Norman reached down to scratch behind Patchy's little pointed ears. "I guess, deep down, we've always suspected we were different. Hey, we're unique!"

They descended to the reception area and crossed the tiled floor. Gordon noticed Vera's worried frown. "We're not as safe as we thought we were," she confided. "The only *real* person here is Sanderfield, controlling his Dome. We are cartoon characters in an animated environment – anything could happen."

"Then the sooner we get outta here, the better." Gordon reached for the double doors. There was the shadow of a figure beyond the glass.

A voice called from the darkness outside. "Parcel for Mr Gordon Smith."

Gordon opened the door and was handed an Acme cardboard box. The delivery man turned and was gone before any of The Mystery Gang noticed his swept-back grey hair or the flinty glint of his eyes.

Intrigued, Gordon flipped open the lid and pulled out a bowling-ball sized black sphere. It was heavy, had a burning fuse on the top and the word

BOMB stenciled in helpful white letters on one side.

"Acme Products," said a cheerful voiceover, as stacks of cardboard boxes replaced the reception area scene. "Need a can of polka-dot paint? No problem! Or how about a can of empty blackness for painting holes and useful tunnels?"

An assortment of anvils appeared.

"Our ever-popular anvils are available for immediate delivery, and, for a limited time only, why not upgrade to a heavy safe, or, for that touch of sophistication, a grand piano?"

The anvil selection faded.

"Acme Products," reiterated the voiceover, "for your every need."

Intrigued, Gordon flipped open the lid and pulled out a bowling-ball sized black sphere. It was heavy, had a burning fuse on the top and the word BOMB stenciled in helpful white letters on one side.

"Run!" yelled Vera.

Everyone ran for cover leaping behind the reception desk. Left holding the fizzing bomb, Gordon heroically drew back his arm, aiming to fling it through the doors. But the fuse had burnt down. The word KA-BLAM! exploded through the reception hall in a jagged starburst that blasted the desk back against the wall. A few seconds later, four horrified faces appeared over the top.

Daisy screamed.

Gordon gore was spattered everywhere. A section of square jaw was embedded in the wall where a perfect tooth glinted amongst the dripping redness.

"He's gone to pieces!" Norman exclaimed. He meant it seriously, but the laugh track sounded amused.

Vera glanced distastefully across the Gordon-spattered tiles to the relatively unmarked doors. "We've got to get out of here!" she yelled.

She, Daisy, Norman and Patchy began to squelch their way through the slimy pieces. Then Sanderfield appeared in the doorway, blocking their escape. "Not so fast," he said in a voice that made their black outlines quaver. "You know *too* much. Do you think I'm going to let you testify against me?" He produced his hand-held control device again and spun an intricately calibrated dial. The interior of the Animation Dome spun in sympathy. The reception area swirled and darkened to an absolute blackness. The bewildered eyes of The Mystery Gang blinked white in the darkness, Daisy's eyelashes fluttered, and the Dome suddenly brightened around them.

They were outside. A harsh white sun burnt down on a breath-taking scene of rugged canyons and boulders, throwing the barren landscape into stark brown light and shade. Deserted gullies and mountain ridges zig-zagged high above and far below them. The bleached skull of a horned ox emphasized the desolation.

Patchy's little furry chin thudded to the ground in surprise. "Where are we?" he asked, easing his jaw back into place with a trembling paw.

"We're still in Sanderfield's Dome," said Vera, peering warily over her glasses. The perspective of the scene was perfect, appearing to stretch for miles. "This is a new animated scenario."

Daisy was spraying the dry dusty ground with the force of her tears. "W-what happened to Gordon?" she sobbed, dabbing her eyes with her pink scarf.

"That poses an interesting metaphysical conjecture," Vera mused. "Can a cartoon character, who's not technically alive, be blown apart like that?"

This was too profound a question for afternoon viewing. Daisy gave an elegant sniff as a perfectly rendered vulture wheeled on spread wings through the pale blue sky high above them. "If I'd known we'd end up hiking," she said, "I'd have worn more sensible shoes."

"Like these?" Asked Norman. He gestured to an elegant pair of ladies hiking boots that rested by a convenient low flat rock, not far from the edge of a dizzying precipice.

"They're my size," said Daisy in delight. She fluttered her eyes around the scene as if the appearance of these perfect boots might somehow be suspicious. There was no sign of life in any direction, except up, where a second vulture had joined the first in a sweeping dance.

Daisy used her scarf to flick the dust from the convenient rock, then sat to try on the boots.

"Those boots are an anachronism," said Vera. "An odd thing to find in the middle of a deserted mountain range." She looked around. "I wonder…" She held out her arms in front of her, resembling the fake zombie The Mystery Gang had encountered exactly two weeks ago. She continued to walk until her hands found the invisible curved wall of the Animation Dome. "Somewhere around here…" she muttered, feeling around the wall. She stopped at a smooth rock face, felt it carefully with her fingers, then pulled open the Dome's control panel.

"Wow!" barked Patchy, suitably impressed by the patch of technology that looked so out of place in the otherwise desolate landscape.

"Yeah, wow," agreed Norman.

"I don't know enough about photo-realistic animation to cancel this scenario," said Vera. "But if I recalibrate this morphic imageizer…" She recalibrated the morphic imageizer, and a rock near her feet transformed into a telephone.

"Hey, double-wow!" praised Norman.

Vera squatted down, picked up the receiver and dialed 911. "Police? Yes, I'm calling from the Sanderfield Animation Studio. I have important information about a murder."

From behind another rock, Sanderfield appeared, the blazing sun catching his swept-back hair, turning it to silver. He glared at Vera and twisted a few dials on his hand-held control device. The receiver in her hand glowed red with heat. She dropped it quickly as it and the telephone melted into the parched ground. "Clever," he sneered. "But not clever enough." At the push of a few more buttons, an Acme parcel appeared on the ground at the edge of the dizzying precipice and close to where Daisy had just finished lacing up her new boots. "I see my parcel has arrived," he said.

Daisy stood, fluttering her eyelashes in suspicion as Sanderfield approached. He whisked away the cardboard packaging, like a magician, revealing a heavy iron anvil. This too, glinted in the sunlight. A long coil of rope had been tied around the anvil in a decorative bow.

"Amazing what you can get by mail-order these days," said Sanderfield with a flinty sweep of his eyes around what remained of The Mystery Gang. He kicked at the anvil, sending it, and a cascade of gravel, plummeting over the edge of the precipice. It fell with a fading whistle of air, unravelling the long coil of rope at the cliff edge. "You may be wondering what is tied to the other end of that rope," he said as it uncoiled swiftly. "At the other end are two thin wires," he turned villainously to Daisy, "which are attached to the heels of the boots you are wearing."

Daisy screeched.

Norman and Patchy's eyes popped out on horrified stalks as they realized how little rope was left at the cliff edge. Vera started to run towards the disappearing coils. But too late.

Still screeching, Daisy had her perfect legs yanked from beneath her. She fell upon her face, eyes wide with terror, fingernails scoring the dusty rock as she was pulled over the edge.

Vera squinted down the vast drop as Daisy quickly became too small to see (even without her glasses). Eventually a puff of Daisy dust at the bottom of the ravine revealed the impact of the anvil and their friend.

"Two down," gloated Sanderfield; "three to go…" He twisted at his control device and the mountainous landscape swirled into blackness.

"Where are we now?" asked Patchy.

Norman looked around at the tall trees and shrubs; the blackness had been replaced by a tangle of greenery. "I don't know, Patch. And where's Vera?"

Patchy sniffed at the air with his little black nose. His white fur stiffened into a pointed arrow-shape. "This way," he said.

Keeping his nose to the undergrowth, Patchy pushed through the bushes sniffing out the trail at ground level as Norman was snagged by twigs and thorns.

"Is this Sanderfield's next diabolical plan?" Norman wondered, with a shiver that visibly trickled down his spine. "Death by, you know, a thousand scratches."

"Help!"

"Hey, that's Vera's voice." Norman redoubled his efforts. "Well done, Patch, you've found her." He reached into a pocket and they shared a handful of Patchy Snacks in celebration.

"Help!" cried Vera again, closer this time.

Pushing through a final hedgerow, Norman and Patchy found themselves at a clear stripe of land which cut through the trees and shrubs. It was a railway line. It stretched away for as far as they could see in both directions. And just ahead of them, cocooned in rope, Vera lay across the tracks.

"Norman! Patchy! Over here, I can't move!"

Her diminutive size meant that Vera fitted snuggly across the wooden sleepers, her feet resting on one rail, and her head on the other.

Norman tried to find an end to the rope so that he could untie it. But it was cartoon rope and there wasn't one. Furthermore, the rope bound Vera to the tracks and a sleeper set into the ground; there was no way to remove her.

"Find the Dome control panel," Vera said. "I think I can talk you through a way to delete this rope."

Norman and Patchy left the railway line on opposite sides, feeling through the tangle of undergrowth for the invisible wall. Then Patchy glanced back. "Train!" he yelped.

The inevitable train had appeared in the distance, chugging with clouds of steam, the coupling bar pounding at the wheels. Patchy's eyes popped again, somehow allowing him a close-up vision of Sanderfield on the footplate. The villain's eyes looked flintier than ever, and his silver hair swept back as he pressed home a lever for maximum speed.

Vera had felt the tremble of the tracks. "Hurry!" she screeched.

"Hey, I've found it!" Norman flicked open the control panel which seemed to hang impossibly in the middle of a thorned hedge. He balked, with a gulp that set his Adam's-apple bouncing in his throat, at the complex mechanisms inside. "What do I do?!" he yelled through the bushes to where he could just see Vera and the railway.

"No time for lessons," Vera yelled. "The main dial in the middle controls most of the image detail. Give it a twist – now!"

Norman gave it a twist. The train raced even faster.

Vera, even with her glasses, had no trouble spotting the fast-approaching train. She screwed up her eyes. "Twist it the other way!"

Too late. As Norman twisted the dial in reverse, there was a sickening thud and a spray of unpleasantness as the train zoomed past. The whistle sounded in triumph and Norman was sure he could hear Sanderfield cackling with laughter.

Norman thought he might throw up, but that seemed inappropriate for a kids' cartoon show.

Shaking bits of Vera and her smashed glasses from his shaggy orange hair, Norman called to Patchy. "Patchy, here boy!" Patchy pushed through the bushes and looked up at his master who was staring intently at the Dome control mechanisms. "We should be able to use the Animation Dome to our advantage," he said with admirable approaching-a-commercial determination. "This dial controls the image detail – apparently." His eyes grew heavy with confusion and his shoulders sank. He sighed. "It's no good, Patchy," he said. "I'll never work this out."

"Perhaps I could help with that."

Norman and Patchy whirled round. Behind them, transparent and red-eyed, floated Gerald Blake's ghost.

"The Gerald Blake Studios proudly present - *The Mystery Gang*," announced the voiceover.

Norman and Patchy threw Patchy Snacks into the air and caught them in their mouths.

Gordon folded his arms in a heroic pose.

Daisy looked glamourous, hands on hips.

And Vera blinked knowledgeably over her glasses.

"Of all his cartoons, The Mystery Gang was Gerald Blake's personal favorite," enthused the voiceover. "He thought of Gordon, Daisy, Vera, Norman and Patchy as if they were personal friends. All episodes are now available to buy on Betamax in stunning color."

The BLAKE logo appeared in bold yellow.

"Why not enjoy The Mystery Gang whenever you wish?" the voiceover queried. "Available now at a store near you!"

"Perhaps I could help with that."

Norman and Patchy whirled round. Behind them, transparent and red-eyed, floated Gerald Blake's ghost.

Patchy was about to leap into Norman's arms for protection. But he found Norman had already leapt into his own little paws. They faced each other. "Zoinks!" they said.

Norman tried to be brave. "You're, you know, just an animation, right?" he asked, hopefully.

The ghost looked apologetic. "I sent you the note and the key that got you into this adventure," he said, trying not to look too terrifyingly transparent, red-eyed, or floaty. "I'm on your side. I wanted you and the gang to investigate the false haunting of my studio, but your friend Gordon was right, I wanted you to investigate my murder too."

Norman gave a massive nervous gulp. "Yeah, well we're not doing too well there."

Patchy shook himself, spraying Vera viscera over the undergrowth and the incongruous Dome control panel.

"We all know Sanderfield is guilty," said Norman. "We just need to catch him."

Wavy undulations appeared in the forest scene around them. "That," said the ghost, as squiggle-vision indicated a jump forward in time, "is where I may be able to help."

"There," said Norman some hours later. "We're all set."

"All set," echoed Patchy, from ground level.

"We can't fail," said Norman.

"Can't fail," agreed Patchy.

The ghost of Gerald Blake wasn't so certain. His glowing red eyes surveyed the elaborate trap that his two cartoon characters had created. With his guidance, they had manipulated the Animation Dome controls. They now stood in an abandoned amusement park. The rusting rides rose around them and had been augmented with cables, seesaws, and other objects for their scheme to work.

"Exactly a week ago," Norman explained, "we were in an abandoned amusement park, just like this one. The local real estate salesman was keeping the public away by making it seem haunted by a creepy clown. Only *he* knew that the park was built on a valuable zinc mine." He waved proudly at the contraption around them. "We trapped the ghostly clown, who turned out to be the realtor in a glowing mask."

Blake's ghost hovered next to a towering sandwich where practically every filling Norman and Patchy could think of was slotted between two slices of bread. "So, you plan to trap Sanderfield in the same way, and turn him over to the police." He floated up among the fairground rides, his obvious misgivings as transparent as his body. "Talk me through it," he asked. "Why, for example, is there a suit of armor?"

"Hey, there's *always* a suit of armor," Norman explained reasonably. He was holding the pole of a large fishing net, and waved it at the teetering sandwich garnished with sliced tomato, Patchy Snacks, and an olive. "The trap starts here. Nobody, not even a villain like Sanderfield, could resist one of Patchy's mega-wiches."

The ghost's eyes glowed doubtfully.

"When he eats the sandwich, he unbalances the seesaw, which presses the start button of the rusty and disused Ferris wheel…"

Patchy sniffed the air and gave a warning yelp. With a tinkling shimmer, Blake's ghost vanished immediately.

Sanderfield appeared from behind the entrance to the log flume. "Well," he said, casting his flinty gaze around the altered scene in his Animation Dome. "You *have* been busy."

"Hungry?" asked Norman, a look of friendly innocence on his face.

Sanderfield took a couple of slow steps towards them. His flinty gaze assessed the enormous sandwich and the contraption that appeared to be linked to it. He reached up to the decorative garnish and, with exaggerated care, removed the olive. The sandwich swayed precariously and rose minutely on one end of the seesaw; the other end dropped minutely towards the Ferris wheel control. "Quite tasty for an animated olive," said Sanderfield with flinty appreciation. "But then you must admit that my Dome technology is far more realistic than anything Blake and his flat cartoons could achieve."

The two-dimensional Patchy was not going to be side-tracked. "Still hungry?" He trotted over to the seesaw, a cloth draped over a front paw in his best impression of a waiter, and subtly gestured up at the mega-wich.

Sanderfield seemed drawn in, then, with one hand, he grabbed the squirming Patchy by the collar, and shoving with the other hand, he demolished the sandwich tower. The far end of the seesaw dropped, switching on the Ferris wheel. Jolly fairground music and lights heralded the sweep of the nearest swinging pod from which dangled a large hook. Sanderfield ducked out of the way as the hook caught Patchy's collar.

"Patchy!" The trap had been set in motion. There was nothing Norman could do except bite at his fingernails in nervous agitation. Nail parings had piled up to his knees by the time Patchy had travelled to the top of the Ferris wheel. Norman strained his gangly neck as, high above him, the arm of a strategically placed suit of armor knocked Patchy from the hook. Patchy yelped and clung for a dizzying moment to the armored arm, which became detached from the armored shoulder. He hung there for a bewildering moment, until he realized there was nothing supporting him - then he fell. "N-o-r-m-a-n! Help!" he yelled, flapping his little legs as he plummeted down to the next stage of the trap. He landed with a stretchy rubber 'spoing' onto the rusty and disused trampoline pit below. The first trampoline had been angled to bounce him onto a series of further trampolines that threw him in balletic arcs into a waiting car poised at the top of a rusty and disused roller coaster. Patchy managed to catch a little of his furry breath, then he felt the car waver and trundle slowly forward - easing over the dip of a chasmic plunge. He clung to a bar in front of his seat, his little pointed ears were swept back, so far back that they followed him downhill and only caught up with him as he began to climb the next slope. Somewhere far below, Norman was shouting something about a banana.

"What did you say?" yelled Patchy as he swooped through another dip in the track.

Blake's bearded ghost shimmered into existence on the seat next to him. "He said something about a banana."

They reached the next peak, then whizzed down towards a loop-the-loop. Patchy screwed his little black eyes shut as they met the loop with a sickening *whoooosh*. They whirled around, then upward again to where the track ended in a rusted gap. The car, with Patchy and Blake's ghost, tumbled towards the animated sky, slowed, then thudded, as planned, into the helter-skelter. Gripping a sacking mat, they spiraled together down to the base, then slid along the ground, screeching to a stop, as expected, inches before the lake-like tank that contained the track of the log flume.

"Phew," said Patchy, relieved that he'd finally stopped moving.

“Phew,” said Blake’s ghost for similar reasons. Then he tapped Patchy on a furry shoulder, pointing out the two policemen that had appeared from behind the log flume’s cabin. “The cavalry,” he added, then faded away with a ghostly shimmer.

Sanderfield hadn’t noticed the police; he was too busy with a flinty sneer of derision. “Call that contraption a trap?”

Patchy knew that there was a further stage to their elaborate snare: the banana skin which now lay by the side of the helter-skelter mat. The intention had been for Sanderfield to slip on it, ending up in the log-flume tank, from which he would have been scooped by Norman and his enormous fishing net. Speaking of which…

Brandishing his net, Norman approached. “No tricks, Sanderfield,” he warned.

“Yeah, no tricks,” echoed Patchy. He trotted off the mat, glaring at Sanderfield with one eye. The other eye he kept trained hopefully on the two policemen: they must have received Vera’s phone call and come to investigate. Having thus run out of eyes, Patchy was unable to avoid the strategic banana peel. His little legs whirled and slipped in surprise beneath him, and he toppled ears-first into the tank.

“Hang in there, Patchy!” Norman swung his net out over the water. “Doggy paddle.”

Sanderfield chortled. “Oh, this is too easy.” He prodded his hand-held control device, and the point of a deep grey dorsal fin broke the surface of the water.

"Shark!" yelled Norman, feeling that Patchy ought to know.

"Sharks, *plural*," corrected Sanderfield, then thought he should clarify further. "*Hungry* sharks."

Three more fins appeared, circling Patchy, who doggy paddled with such force that he rose from the water with a spluttering yelp. The hungriest shark grinned hugely beneath him with a great many sharp teeth. Patchy tumbled teethwards and managed to keep the shark's jaws apart with his hind legs.

Norman shot a glare at Sanderfield. "I won't let you add Patchy to your crimes!"

This seemed to awaken some interest in the two policemen. As serious officers of law enforcement, they hadn't much enthusiasm for the juvenile animation playing out in the Dome around them. From their point of view, their suspect, Sanderfield, was watching some slapstick fairground scene with obviously cartoon characters: a two-dimensional man with a fishing net and a talking dog. But now the man had mentioned crimes, so they thought they'd better pay attention.

Norman seemed to realize this but couldn't allow himself to be distracted. He beat at the toothy shark with his net. Patchy leaped free and began a frantic circling of the tank, swiftly followed by four fishy fins.

"Wasn't killing Blake enough?" Norman demanded in a loud clear voice aimed somewhere between Sanderfield and the police officers. "Now you're killing off his characters too!"

Sanderfield twiddled with his control device, and four more fins appeared. "Blake was a fool," he declared. "He should have sold his company to me, then I wouldn't have needed to kill him."

"You still intend to buy it," provoked Norman, swinging his net out into the water. "That's why you've been faking the hauntings to bring down the price!"

Sanderfield gave a flinty chuckle, adding a few poisonous jellyfish to the tank. "And then…" his voice became wistful in its imaginings, "I'll re-create all his out-of-date traditional cartoons using my superior Dome technology. I can't help but succeed. I'll be the new king of the animated world!"

The police had heard enough. Sanderfield had been their obvious suspect all along and now they had heard his confession. Perhaps he had been motivated by some egotistical madness. Certainly, it was now obvious to them that killing Blake had driven him insane. Why else would he be animating this attack on The Mystery Gang? It was almost a sacrilege: both policemen had loved that show.

All four legs flailing, Patchy swam into Norman's net, and was lifted free as the sharks snapped and snarled in the frothing water. A triumphant *Ta-Dah!* fanfared over the scene as the police stepped forward either side of the astonished Sanderfield.

"All the evidence you need is here," called Norman, waving his net and the soggy Patchy towards the Dome's control panel. "There's a handy purple-button gismo to re-play previous scenarios, including his rehearsal of Blake's murder."

Sanderfield gnashed his teeth. If he'd been a cartoon, his ears would have been steaming with fury. Then he seemed to deflate, and his eyes lost some of their flintiness. The police pulled his arms behind his back and cuffed him.

Patchy jumped from the dripping net and shook himself dry.

Blake's ghost shimmered back into existence to shake Patchy's paw and Norman's hand. "Thank you," he said. "I knew you would solve this mystery."

Norman and Patchy grinned, sharing a handful of Patchy Snacks in celebration. And, through the magic of animation, where anything can happen, Gordon appeared, arms folded; Daisy appeared, hands on hips; and Vera appeared, peering over her glasses.

Gerald Blake (deceased), surrounded by his Mystery Gang, watched his killer being led away.

Sanderfield glared back at them. "I'd have got away with it too," he snapped, "if it weren't for those…" his intended words trailed away, totally unsuitable for daytime schedules.

Patchy gave a close-up snigger - then faded into the end credits. ♜

# THREE DAYS OF THE JACKAL

*By John Pritchard*

IF I HADN'T TAKEN PITY on that beggar, I'd be living a dull and normal life right now, not sleeping with a gun under my pillow – on those nights when I can get to sleep at all.

I saw him as I came up from the subway. He was sitting with his back against the wall, a blanket wrapped around him. Not a rarity, of course, and normally I would have walked right past. But this time I paused. Maybe it was a hangover from Christmas – the guy could have been a shepherd from two thousand years ago, too cold to move, although his flock had scattered.

He sensed me wavering and raised his eyes.

*He's not from here*, my first impression told me – though how the hell can you tell that in New York? I thought that he was maybe Middle Eastern. His cheeks were grizzled, and his hair cropped short. He stared at me, expressionless, not speaking. There was something almost knowing in his gaze.

Maybe – being a Catholic girl – I thought about St Martin, who gave a beggar half his cloak, one snowy winter's day. Well, I wasn't going to give this guy the fur coat I got for Christmas (A fake fur coat, but even so). Then again, in Martin's day, you couldn't buy a coffee from a vendor on the sidewalk.

'Pardon me, sir – can I get you a hot drink?'

A flicker of something crossed his face. No doubt I had surprised him, but after a moment he inclined his head. I went to the hot drink stand and bought two coffees. I was a tad surprised myself, to tell the truth. A grimy chunk of frozen snow still lingered in the gutter. I went back to the guy and passed his coffee down to him.

'Thank you, Miss.' He took a sip and savored it like whisky, then settled back. 'Are you on your way to work?' I wasn't really sure about his accent – American underpinned by something else.

'Yeah,' I said. 'Nine to five stuck in an office. Guess I'm lucky.' I smiled wryly and was going to turn away, but something about his somber features stopped me.

'Do you live in this city, Miss?' he asked.

I was on my guard at once, of course, but a polite reply cost nothing. I was one in about eight million, after all. 'All my life,' I said, like I was ancient, instead of very nearly twenty-two.

He nodded, then glanced off across the street – and maybe further. His eyes seemed to lose focus on the things in front of us. When he spoke, like a man pronouncing judgment, it was as if he had the whole damn city in his view.

'The jackals will be there, and her great ones will be gone. They will say, there is no longer a kingdom there, and all her chiefs will have come to an end.'

I scrunched up my face in puzzlement. His gaze returned to me and he reached up and pushed something into my hand. My fingers closed reflexively around it. Through my glove I could feel a small, hard object, bundled in a cloth. I opened my hand and stared at it, then looked at him again.

'You gave me your gift,' he said. 'I give you mine.'

I nodded, still nonplussed, not even sure if I should thank him. He raised his cup to me, then drank again. I turned and walked away, joining the flow along the sidewalk. After a minute I glanced back, just to check he wasn't coming after me.

As soon as I had gone around the corner, I stopped to examine the thing he'd given me. It was wrapped in a threadbare piece of rag. I undid it cautiously and found there was a piece of bone inside.

I couldn't tell if it was animal or human, but it certainly looked old and fragile, not just yellowish but turning brown. It might have been a finger bone or something. I hadn't a clue what I should make of it. A part of me was ready to put it in the nearest trashcan. But a bone isn't just a piece of trash. And the guy had offered it respectfully. Perhaps it was a good-luck charm of some sort. I hesitated briefly and then dropped it in my bag to join all the other clutter that I carried. With a last glance back, I carried on toward the poky office where I worked.

# # #

By lunchtime I had more or less forgotten the encounter – or pushed it to the back of my mind, at least. Life's too short to get hung up on stuff like that.

Steve and I had stepped outside onto the fire escape to smoke and have a private talk. Things were starting to look like they might get serious, and I wanted to be clear about where we stood. It wasn't the sort of talk you wanted Carol overhearing, or Brad watching with his crooked little smile.

Apart from that, I always liked the view from the fourth floor. It was cold – I drew my fur coat tight – but that emphasized the freshness of the air. The traffic fumes below us lay like mist over a swamp, in contrast to the pale blue of the sky. The blocks and towers still hemmed us in, but I felt less claustrophobic. In the distance, the new World Trade Center was growing a little taller every day.

*They will say there is no longer a kingdom there...*

So yeah, at the back of my mind, that nameless beggar was still squatting. I drew on my cigarette and breathed a plume of smoke into the chilly air. Those words he'd quoted sounded like the Bible – one of the prophets maybe, though I don't know a whole lot about those guys.

'Hey, Sue,' said Steve. 'Did you just remember that you left the gas on?'

I let my frowning face go smooth again.

'My place is always shipshape when I shut the door behind me.' In fact it was a total mess, most days. He grinned at my mock-straitlaced tone, then glanced towards the street. 'So you don't need anyone to double-check…?'

He said it idly enough, but I felt a little kick inside my chest. Not just at the thought of spending the night together. It's the little domestic details afterwards that make it real. I knew damn well what the others thought about me – that I was just the pouting office blonde, always looking for a guy who she could twist around her finger. Even Beth on the reception desk looked snootily at me. But Steve was a smart guy. We shared some interests and we liked spending time in each other's company.

We'd left the fire door ajar behind us, but as I leaned back, trying to act as casual as him, I accidentally pushed it closed. There was no outside handle. 'Oh shit,' I said and straightened up again.

'Well,' said Steve, 'there are worse people I could be stuck outside with.'

'Sure,' I said. 'It's freezing, though.'

Still grinning, he went over to the door and thumped on it. I stepped aside. My cigarette was finished, and I flicked it away and bent over the rail to watch it drop like a single glowing snowflake to the alley. The cars kept up their clamor on the street. I'd thought I didn't care about the gossip in the office, but the thought of their faces when we came back in brought a tinge of warmth to my cold cheeks. I turned to pick my bag up as Steve banged at the door again.

There was a sudden crunching noise and he flinched back.

His heel struck my bag and knocked it off the platform before I could even lunge for it. For a moment I just stared in disbelief as it dropped away. It felt like I was watching in slow-motion. I rounded on Steve as he lurched and caught himself. *For God's sake*, I was going to say, but the words stuck in my throat. His face had gone as pale as flour and I noticed a raw cut across his cheek that began to fill with bright red as I watched it. My gaze went to the door. There was a small but jagged hole punched through the wood.

A larger shard had come away and a piece of it must have hit him in the face. I stared at it – we both did – without knowing what had made it, not thinking of a bullet till another one came out through the same hole.

I heard no shot, just the dull thud of the impact, which sounded like a hammer striking meat. Steve's body was thrown back against the guardrail and tipped over it. I glimpsed his shocked white face, and he was gone.

I looked away instinctively. For a moment I stood frozen. The city's noise receded till it felt as if the world had dropped away. Then I heard the door lock start to rattle. It broke the spell. I turned and took off down the iron steps.

As I reached the next platform, I heard the door shoved open. I swung onto the next flight down and something caught my eye. Steve hadn't plummeted into the alley. His legs had tangled in the guardrail and his body was still dangling there, upside down and dripping like a carcass on a meat hook. I stopped and stared in horror. Then I glimpsed a dark shape moving into view at the top of the steps. A man in a fedora, the wide brim shadowing his face. He pointed a metallic tube at me. *Gun*, I thought and went down the flight so quickly that I thought I'd trip and do a nose-dive. I could hear him coming after me, the clank of his footfalls steady and relentless. As I turned to go down the next flight, I'm pretty sure he took a shot at me through the fire escape's skeletal frame. Again, I didn't hear it, but something struck the railing a few inches from my hand and deflected with a high-pitched whine. I gasped and kept on going. A part of me found time to wonder what I'd do if the drop-ladder was stuck. The steps seemed almost vertical, but I somehow kept my balance till I reached the platform on the second floor. I realized I was whimpering as I fumbled with the ladder. It extended with a clatter and I clambered awkwardly down to the ground.

My bag lay crumpled nearby. I lunged to scoop it up, and not because a girl needs makeup even when a killer's chasing her. I didn't just trust in my good looks to get me out of trouble.

At the bottom of the bag I had a pistol of my own.

But I knew I had no time to try and grab it. The guy was thundering down toward me, only yards away from a clear shot. Sobbing for breath, I fled along the alley and round the corner, hitting someone, reeling clear of him and running on. My knee-boots weren't exactly meant for running but I didn't pause or look behind me, weaving my way through curious passers-by till I reached the haven of the subway station. I rushed down to the platforms, saw a waiting train, and ran to get on board. Throwing myself onto a seat I filled my lungs at last and felt the strength drain out of me.

The car just sat there, whirring to itself.

After a moment I sat up and craned forward, looking back along the platform, searching for a shape pursuing me. I was wheezing like a little girl on sports day and felt the wetness on my cheeks. *Oh God*, I thought, *come on, come on, come on…*

The doors rattled shut. I slumped back, hardly daring to believe it as the train moved off and began to pick up speed. And just before the gaping tunnel took us, I thought I caught a fleeting glimpse of a figure on the platform, giving chase.

# # #

There were four other people in the office, and he took them all. Our neighbors never heard a thing. I heard later about the gun he used. Turns out it was a Welrod silent pistol, a gun the British made in World War Two. They used to issue it to secret agents. It makes less noise than a guy does when he coughs into his hand.

He'd have met Beth first, at her desk in the front office. I imagine she gave him her usual sweet smile. In response he brought his pistol up and shot her in the forehead. The Welrod fires a bullet on the small side – .32 – but to compensate for that, this joker used exploding ammo. So the shot that tore into Beth's brain blew half her head away.

I don't want to think about what splattered on the wall behind her. But that was poor Beth out of it. Maybe Carol, just beyond the inner door, heard a noise like a rotten apple getting stamped on. I wonder what thought filled her mind as a man stepped through the doorway unannounced.

You know, there's a curious thing about the Welrod. It's not an automatic and you have to operate a kind of bolt to eject the empty shell and put a fresh round in the chamber. So what kind of killer chooses that for a job where several victims are involved?

An ice-cold killer, you might say – machinelike and efficient. But something else occurs to me. Each time a cobra bites, it needs to take time to recharge its poison. But its gaze keeps its next victim mesmerized.

Carol would have blinked through her big glasses. She might have had the time to ask him "Can I help you, sir?" before he shot her through the heart, which the bullet then burst open. She was wearing a white blouse, as well. Just imagine how much Tide that stain would need.

Across the room, I reckon Brad sat dumbstruck for a moment, but then he rose to the occasion. It seems he pitched a ledger at the man, who swatted it aside, then calmly worked the pistol's action and shot our office hero in the chest, dead center so the bullet blew his breastbone into fragments which pierced his heart and lungs like shrapnel. The blow sat Brad back down, already dead.

Howard, being the boss, retreated smartly to his office and tried to wedge a chair against the door. Maybe he thought he could buy time to dial 911, or perhaps it was just instinct taking hold. Either way, the killer made short work of getting in and dispatched him with another head shot. Coming out, he'd have seen our empty desks, just as Steve banged for attention on the fire door.

Even before I heard all that, I knew how narrowly I had escaped.

I had ridden the train to the end of the line and still sat trembling when the last of the passengers had got off. My bag was in my lap and my right hand was inside, touching the pistol. It kept me anchored to my sanity.

The gun was illegal, I didn't have a permit. But my dad insisted that I carry it. He knew I liked the James Bond books so he got me a Beretta, the snub-nosed pocket model that was 007's first gun. A ladies' gun, according to its critics. Well, right now it suited *this* lady just fine.

We'd come from beneath the city like a slow train out of Hell, but at last I saw the wintry sun again. The light was already waning though, the short day almost over. The thought of encroaching darkness scared me stiff.

Manhattan's towers were still looming on the skyline. I had to get home, and that meant riding this train back again, against the rush-hour tide, into the city. A man was waiting for me there. He'd shot my boyfriend dead in front of me. And something told me that he wasn't finished. I fingered the Beretta's frame and waited for the first lurch of the car.

# # #

I thought I'd made it. I got to my street corner and was pretty sure no-one had followed me. The subway journey had turned into a nightmare. I had to change trains at West Fourth Street and almost panicked as the crowd closed in. Each jostle felt like someone trying to grab me. Each man in a hat seemed to catch my eye and stare. The tide of commuters flowed like sinners marching to their judgment. Finally I got my train, and from there it was only a couple of uptown stops.

My mind was fixed on the refuge of my second-floor apartment. I guess I was still in shock and all that mattered was to get through my front door and then lock it on the garish, swarming city. I wasn't in any hurry to call the cops. I've had bad experiences with New York's finest and wasn't sure I could trust them even now. I glanced back one more time and picked my pace up. I was almost home when something caught my eye and stopped me short.

On the opposite sidewalk a man was standing underneath the streetlight, but its glow showed me no details; he was just a shadow in a coat and a hat. From the lift of his head I could tell that he was staring at my building, and maybe my apartment window. There was an ageless patience in his stance.

I watched him, motionless, my heartbeat racing as the terror I had battened down came bubbling up again. His head didn't turn. Perhaps he hadn't seen me. I slowly began to back away, and still he didn't stir. I turned round and retraced my steps, looking back over my shoulder. The man maintained his vigil, a dark shape under the light. He was still there as I hurried round the corner. I felt my tight chest loosen with relief.

I kept on walking with no thought of where I might be headed, only conscious I was putting distance between me and him. I came to Broadway, stopped at last and watched the traffic passing. There were sirens wailing somewhere like lost souls. The evening air was cold and getting colder. I hadn't the first idea where I should go.

Familiar though the city is, I'm off the streets by nightfall unless I've got a gang of friends with me. It sometimes feels like there's a junkie under every stone, ready to crawl out like a vampire once the sun's gone down. I love the place and hate it too. It's full of predators and a girl has got to watch her step – every minute, every day.

But the peril I sensed now was something different. I thought of Steve's limp body hanging from the fire escape. I didn't know then what had happened to the others, but my instinct told me it was something bad. So who was this man and why had he attacked us? Was he alone or working with a team? I wondered if Howard had pissed off the mob somehow. Perhaps we were even book-keeping for them...

I went to a movie theater and watched a double bill that I hadn't the slightest interest in. I felt no safer, sitting in the dark, but it got me through the next few hours. I kept my bag hugged to me and took comfort from the closeness of my gun.

After that I walked some more but felt very exposed, so I headed for a late-night bar. I knew the bartender and trusted him to step in if somebody pestered me. The place was almost empty. I chatted briefly with the guy, then took my drink to the farthest booth and nursed it.

Like the poem says, the hours crawled by like years.

At the lowest point, in the small hours of the morning, a paranoid thought wormed its way into my brain. Because it wasn't just me who'd escaped the faceless killer. Lisa, our filing clerk, had called in sick with a bad cold. At the time I'd rolled my eyes at Steve. Sure, I got on well with her, but she was a precious little miss who wouldn't step outside if she didn't look her best. But now I began to wonder if it was just coincidence, or had she somehow known what was going to happen?

If the mob had hit us, maybe she'd tipped them off.

With the thought still wriggling in my mind, I nodded off at last and slept with my head laid on the table, dreaming of a city in ruins where jackals flitted through the empty streets.

# # #

The bartender let me sleep, then brought me coffee. I sat back feeling stiff and clammy in my slept-in clothes. He asked if I wanted to talk about it and I said I didn't. I paid the tab and gave him a good tip.

Back on the street in the early morning daylight, I found I had an appetite again. I had breakfast in a diner and felt better, till I saw the front page of the Daily News. FIVE SLAIN IN OFFICE MASSACRE it shouted. Maybe a part of me had thought that yesterday had just been a bad dream.

I was numb for a while, but then I had the urge to confront Lisa. The nagging suspicion of last night had grown into a sick conviction now. I remembered her furtive phone calls and her new, expensive coat – the signs of a new relationship, or so I had assumed.

I knew she lived in Brooklyn, I had visited one time, so that was where I took the train to now. I felt my fear return as I went down the subway steps, but at least there would be witnesses if anybody made a grab for me. The train crossed the bridge and I basked in the sunlight through the dirty windows. My right hand rested on my bag as my restless gaze moved up and down the car.

Her street felt like a refuge from the city. It was quiet and lined with leafless trees, with a view of the looming towers at one end. Her apartment was in the basement of a brownstone. I went down the stoop and rang the bell. I had to ring again before she opened up.

My first thought was, she wasn't lying when she said she had a cold. She was wearing a bathrobe and looked washed out. But she'd obviously been crying a lot as well. Her puffy eyes opened wide with shock when she found me on the doorstep. 'Susan!' she blurted. 'Where have you *been*? The cops are looking for you everywhere.'

'I guess you heard about the others,' I said flatly. 'I got away, but the guy's still out there. Nowhere feels safe.' I heard a sudden tremor in my voice. She drew me in and put her arms around me. I realized I was going to cry and bit my lip to keep the sobs in check.

'Come on,' she said. I wiped my eyes and closed the door behind me, then followed her down the narrow hallway to the living room. 'A detective came here yesterday,' she told me fretfully. 'Said that everybody else was dead but you had disappeared. They didn't even know if you escaped or got abducted! He called again this morning asking if I'd heard from you.'

'There was this guy…' I said, but couldn't put it into words: that sense of having glimpsed the Devil and survived. 'You look like you could use a drink,' she said and went to get one. I felt too restless to sit down and stood looking round at her tasteful furnishings. The windows were covered with iron grilles. It felt odd, being below the sidewalk. As if the house had begun to sink into the earth.

Lisa came back with a glass of whisky. 'Medicinal,' she said. 'You're lucky that I've got some left!' I resisted the urge to knock it back and took a cautious sip. She pushed back her disheveled hair. 'We have to call the cops. The detective left his number.' She went through into the passage and I listened to her dialing as I drank a little more.

'Detective, hi. It's Lisa Weintraub, you spoke with me a little while ago?' She told him that I'd showed up on her doorstep and was ready to be interviewed.

The worm of paranoia twitched again.

Was it really a detective she was talking to, I wondered? Or was she telling a hit man that his target had just walked into a trap? I went to the open door and watched her talking. She flashed me a reassuring smile and I turned away again. The window grilles made the front room feel oppressive, like a prison. I swallowed the rest of the whisky, felt it sear down through my chest.

When she hung up and came back in, I drew the Beretta and pointed it at her.

She stopped and stared at it. Her mouth fell open. Then she looked into my face and my expression seemed to scare her even more.

'Who was that you were talking to?' I asked through gritted teeth.

'I told you, that detective. Jesus, Susan!' She took a slow step backward and I flexed my fingers round the trembling gun. 'Why weren't you in the office?' I demanded.

'I was sick,' she bleated, 'I really was.' Her face, already pasty, had gone white.

I gestured with the gun for her to move clear of the doorway. She edged around me, one hand raised as if she hoped to fend the bullets off. A detached part of me was actually appalled to see her cringing and know I was the cause of it. But my survival instinct would not be denied.

My mouth was dry. I licked my lips. 'I'm leaving now,' I told her. 'And if I find you sold us out…'

A shadow fell across the windowpane.

I couldn't believe the person she had called had come this quickly. Perhaps it was the mailman. Lisa tore her frightened gaze away from me and turned appealingly towards the window.

There was no shot, just the crack of breaking glass. It blended with a crunch-splat sound as the silent pistol's bullet penetrated Lisa's brow and then exploded in her brain. Her head flipped back and she went down on the spot, as if she'd fainted. The walls were abruptly flecked with red, and something hot and sticky splashed my cheek.

I stumbled back and turned toward the window. An indistinct figure was peering through the grille. For a moment I stood paralyzed but then I swung the gun up and pulled the trigger, but it wouldn't move. The pistol had a grip-safety on the back edge of the butt, but I couldn't have held it tighter if I tried. I took it in both hands and squeezed, but the damn thing had jammed solid. And the man was moving to the door. I guessed it wouldn't slow him down too much.

With a whimper of dismay I turned and fled through the apartment, past bookshelves and an open door that gave a glimpse of Lisa's unmade bed. There was no way through the kitchen. I ducked back into the passage and heard a splintering noise behind me as I made for the door at the far end. It was locked and for a moment I was overwhelmed by panic, then I noticed a key hanging on a nearby hook. With a frantic backward glance, I fumbled it into the keyhole. It turned in the lock, a heavenly sound, and I opened the door and ran into the backyard.

I unbolted the high back gate and kept on going. The gun was in my pocket now and my bag swung from my shoulder by its strap. As I followed the lane, I realized what had locked the pistol's trigger. Beside myself with fear and rage, I'd forgotten to flick the safety switch to 'fire'. There was no time now to stop and try and draw it. I didn't risk another look, but the guy was surely breathing down my neck.

I came to the next street and turned right, towards the intersection. Just short of it, a police cruiser was sitting at the curb. The cop inside it almost spilled his coffee when I banged on his window. His eyes got wide when he saw my blood-smeared face. Stepping back to let him out, I glanced towards the lane but there was no sign of my pursuer. I fumbled in my coat and pulled out my concealed pistol right in front of him. I remembered to flick the safety this time. Then he slapped the gun out of my hand.

It clattered on the pavement and I lunged to scoop it up, but the cop grabbed me and dragged me back. 'There's a killer coming after me!' I wailed, twisting my head to look, convinced I'd see the guy emerging. But still he didn't show himself. The cop was unimpressed. He shoved me up against the car and pulled my hands behind me. Terror surged into my throat as I felt the handcuffs close around my wrists. I screamed at him to let me go, that a murderer was coming – and then I just screamed for the sake of it.

# # #

He drove me to the station house and by the time we got there I'd already begun to think this was the safest place to be. Lisa's neighbor had reported someone breaking in and they found her body soon enough.

I told the grim detectives everything.

But they seemed no more impressed than the patrolman. *So you fled two crime scenes in twenty-four hours, and your whole office has been wiped out – apart from you. The second time, you had the victim's blood splashed on your face. And you were carrying a gun without a permit. You ever hear of the Sullivan Act? You could get twenty years just for that…*

They kept on at me for hours and then they left me there to stew. The interview room had no windows and I'd lost all track of time. My watch said two-fifteen, but was that afternoon or morning? I huddled in my coat on the hard chair.

I didn't want to call my dad. Of course he'd come straight here, with a lawyer who might get me out – but that could put him in the line of fire. Better to sit tight and wait. The cops had nothing on me. They'd have to let me go eventually.

At last fatigue caught up with me and I slumped over the table. When I woke with a start I was no longer on my own. A man in scruffy clothes and an old trench coat sat facing me, his face expressionless.

I didn't know the guy, yet he was curiously familiar. I sat back and blinked muzzily at him. Then it struck me, and I thought I must be dreaming. It was the beggar I'd bought coffee for.

'Good to see you again, Miss,' he said.

I frowned at him in bleary bafflement.

'Detective Mattara,' he went on, by way of introduction. 'I need to ask you some questions, but you could probably do with a smoke before we start.'

He offered a pack of Marlboros. I lit one from his lighter, drew the stimulating smoke into my lungs. Sitting back again, I eyed his clothes. 'Are you working undercover?'

'Deep cover,' he said drily. 'Very deep.' He rummaged in his coat and laid my Beretta on the table. 'My colleagues are a mite disturbed by this.'

'Wait till forensics check it out,' I countered. 'It hasn't been fired; it's still got all eight rounds. I only just remembered to take the goddamn safety off!'

He inclined his head to show he took my point, 'It wasn't used in any of the murders. The caliber's too small and it's not nearly quiet enough.' He studied me, his dark brown eyes unblinking. 'Something else you had in your possession was more significant.'

He dug in his pocket again and put something else beside the pistol. I knew what it was but could only stare as he unwrapped the cloth to reveal that piece of bone.

I looked at him accusingly. 'You gave me that yourself!'

He nodded, maddeningly calm. 'Can you tell what it is?'

'I don't know. A finger bone or something?'

'A finger bone.' He eased back in his chair. The street-smell he gave off was pretty rancid, but I knew that I could use a bath myself.

'How old is it?' I asked after a moment. I'd carried it for a day, forgotten, but now something about it was making my skin crawl.

'Older than this city. Older than America. Maybe older than the first city on earth.' He reached out with own finger to touch it, very gently. 'Do you know much about ancient Egypt, Miss?'

I drew on my cigarette and shrugged. 'Just pyramids and pharaohs, stuff like that.'

‘There’s a group of people out there,’ he said slowly. ‘I suppose you could describe them as a cult. They believe this piece of bone is from the finger of Anubis – the jackal-headed god of the Egyptian underworld.’

‘Yeah?’ I peered doubtfully at the discoloured fragment.

‘Many years ago,’ Mattara said, ‘a skeleton was found, or rather the remains of one, deep in the Sinai desert. A beast-and-human hybrid of some kind. The bones had been scattered. These people believe that if they’re brought together – every knuckle, every vertebra – Anubis will rise to walk the earth again.’

‘And is that bad?’ I asked.

He smiled thinly. ‘It’s a matter of conjecture, naturally. Some people think that if something that old was returned to life, decompressing ages of deep time, it could bring decay to anything it touched. And that decay would spread like a contagion, till the cities of the world were laid to waste.’

I let out a stream of smoke. ‘And you believe that?’

Mattara shrugged. ‘It doesn’t matter what outsiders think. These people want to bring the bones together. There are others who have tried to thwart them. Some bones were hidden, some taken overseas. A while ago, this one came to my attention. Now the cult has sent someone to get it back.’

I thought of the dark shape at Lisa’s window, the figure clanking down the fire escape. ‘So this is the guy with the silenced gun? Who is he?’

‘We don’t know much about him. He has a reputation in the underworld.

They call him the Gray Reaper. The Stone Killer.'

I felt the coldness creep under my coat.

I was staring at the bone but then I looked up at Mattara. 'And you gave me that, knowing he'd come after me?'

'A calculated risk,' he said. 'I was hoping he'd break cover.'

'Screw you,' I snapped. 'He killed my friends! He almost killed me too.'

'It's a good thing you're a fortunate young woman.'

I was trembling with anger now. I wanted to rake my nails across his face.

'Did you let him know where Lisa lived, you bastard?'

Mattara shook his head. 'He tracked you there. He would have come for you in that bar last night if he hadn't sensed that I was keeping watch.'

I looked at the bone again, like I thought it might be radioactive. 'Just take the damn thing back again and settle this between the two of you.'

He shook his head. 'It was a gift and you accepted it. You own it now. You can try to lose it, but it will find its way back to your hands.'

That was ridiculous, of course. It was just a piece of bone that some fruitcakes thought belonged to their false god. I pushed it towards him, glowering a challenge. He pushed it back, his gaze intensely calm.

I couldn't believe the cops would do this, even in New York. No way would the Police Chief have approved. I wondered then if Mattara had gone so deep undercover that he'd lost touch with reality. Was that scarier than the story he had told?

'You think I'll just go out and act as bait again?' I asked him.

'Don't worry, I'll be close behind,' he said. 'And maybe this will help to reassure you.' He slid the Beretta over to me too.

I stared at it, then back at him. He nodded. 'You can carry that right out of here, and we'll turn a blind eye.'

I chewed at my lip, then took the gun and turned it in my fingers. It seemed as puny as a toy, but I felt a little better holding it. I met Mattara's gaze again, then put it in my pocket. After a moment's hesitation, I picked up the finger bone as well.

'When the bastard makes his move,' I said, 'make sure you blow his head off.'

My heart was thumping heavily, but I knew that I was trapped and had no choice.

# # #

He left me in the room. His odor lingered. I waited, nodded off again and woke to the sound of voices and slammed doors. A little while later, one of the cops who'd interviewed me first came in and told me I could go but there would be a lot more questions later on.

I didn't argue, just signed the forms he put in front of me. We went upstairs. The desk sergeant returned my bag. The lightweight Beretta seemed to weigh like lead in my coat pocket. I wasn't sure who Mattara had cleared that with, and I wasn't going to ask.

'Is Detective Mattara around?' I asked. The sergeant eyed me dourly. 'That guy from the Thirteenth, you mean? He left a while ago.'

'Oh. Right.' I glanced towards the doors and the cold sunlight beyond them. My faltering courage failed completely then. I leaned appealingly towards the sergeant. 'Please, I need police protection. I can't walk out of here.'

He gave me that dead-eyed look again. 'Lady, it seems to me that you only need protecting from yourself.'

'There's a murderer after me. He's killed six people!'

'Well, I don't think you need to worry about him no more. There was a guy hanging round outside last night who fitted your description. When a couple of officers checked him out, he ran. They chased him as far as the bridge and he jumped off into the river. That's over a hundred feet straight down. The guy went under like a stone, of course.'

*Like a stone,* I thought, and nodded dumbly. The sergeant returned to his ledger. There was nothing more to say. I turned away and went outside. The winter sun seemed dazzling after hours of flat, fluorescent light. My head felt thick and heavy with fatigue. But adrenalin was buzzing in my bloodstream. I looked around me. Traffic passed; pedestrians bustled by. I had no sense of anybody watching. If what the sergeant said was right, then perhaps Mattara had no more use for me.

I decided to return to my apartment. A fatalistic part of me accepted I had nowhere else to go. But I didn't want to travel there directly. Better to wander for a while and see if anyone was following.

Another thing: I balked at going down into the subway. After everything I'd been through, going down the steps into that stifling space would be like descending into Hell. But if I carried on through Brooklyn, I could take the elevated train – climb up from the street, not burrow under it.

I walked for a long time, changing direction randomly, and turning to check behind myself. I couldn't see anybody trailing me. But the fine hairs at the back of my neck kept prickling, and a knot of fear sat in my belly. My hand stayed in the pocket of my coat.

I thought about dropping the piece of bone through a grating in the gutter. Could Mattara keep track of it somehow? I told myself I was being paranoid. Yet I imagined it glowing in my inside pocket, like a cigarette butt I thought I had crushed out but which could set my coat on fire before I knew it. Despite the cold, I felt sweat run down my ribs.

I could see the elevated tracks crossing the street ahead, with a station beyond the intersection. Sixty-Second Street. As I made toward the steps up to the platform, the sense of someone behind me grew so strong that I swung around to look, my nerve-ends tingling. But once again there was nobody there.

Wiping my hand across my lips, I turned toward the stairs and saw a figure stepping out from under them. A tall man in a dark coat that looked slimy in the shadow of the looming iron bridge. He didn't have a hat; his hair was plastered to his skull. His face had the livid color of the sky before a storm. But it was the eyes that held me and transfixed me. They shone like freshly coughed-up phlegm. Their cold gaze almost made me wet myself.

He looked like a man fished out of the East River, but one who's been down there much longer than a day. I knew it was him: the Gray Reaper. The Stone Killer. It was as if he'd always known where I would finish up.

He brought up a long pistol that looked like a piece of plumbing and pointed it deliberately at me.

I braced myself for the blow I knew was coming, the gun forgotten in my pocket even though my hand was touching it. But then his gaze flicked away from me, as if he'd been distracted. His face remained expressionless, and yet his body seemed to stiffen up. His lips moved silently – I sensed a word of recognition. Then he swung the pistol to my left and fired.

The clicking of the mechanism was louder than the discharge. He turned away and lunged towards the stairs. My legs gave way and I slumped down to the sidewalk, but a surge of desperate fury flooded me. I pulled out my Beretta, flicked the safety and began to shoot as he bounded up the steps. He seemed to move as quickly as a spider, but I kept firing as I rolled onto my side. Some of the bullets missed but others hit him in the back, and he stumbled jerkily and spread his hands. The gun locked open. I realized it was empty. Gasping I watched as the man fell backward, tumbling toward me down the steps.

I tried to squirm away as his body fetched up next to me. He wasn't dead. He began to raise himself. I sensed somebody striding up and turned. It was Mattara. He leveled a big revolver and fired it into the man's head.

The skull exploded like a rotten pumpkin, the contents black and stinking of decay. I cried out as I got some of it on me. The Stone Killer flopped onto his belly like a broken doll.

Mattara turned to me. I held my hands up, the gun still clutched in one of them, convinced that he was going to shoot me next. But he just gave a grim smile. 'You did well, Susan. Now you must bear the bone, and keep it safe.'

He turned and walked away, even as a crowd began to gather. I watched him cross the street and vanish. Mostly I felt stunned. But my nerves were crackling with exhilaration, as if I'd passed some kind of test and life would never be the same again.

A woman gave a stifled cry. The corpse oozed its foul contents. I lay where I was and waited for the cops.

# # #

In the end they had to let me go. It was way too complicated. I'd shot a wanted murderer, but someone else gave him the coup de grace. And the autopsy suggested that the body was of someone who'd been dead for a long time. Plus, I was unsurprised to learn, there was no Detective Mattara. Not in the Thirteenth Precinct nor the whole NYPD.

They took away my gun, of course. But I got myself another. Someone guarding a sacred relic needs the means to defend it, and herself. Maybe one day that cult will send another killer for it. I'll wait for him in this concrete jungle, knowing that all these lives depend on me.

Like I said, I hate this city, and I love it. Its streets are full of predators. But sometimes there are guardian angels too. ♜

# FOUKE

*By Heath Shelby*

*9:35am*

*April 25, 1974*

BOBBY WAYNE HATED CHANGE, ALMOST as much as he hated the uncertainty that change brought. And here he was, caught up in a storm of both change and uncertainty.

Bobby, his wife Leigh Ann and their three children had packed their meager belongings into their station wagon and left their home in West Monroe, Louisiana early that morning and drove to Fouke, Arkansas for a new start.

Bobby's younger brother Charlie and his wife Carol loaded up their beat-up Chevy pickup and joined the caravan. It was Charlie who had approached Bobby with the idea of starting over in Fouke. The Waynes' cousin, Cody Harmon, had recently been hired at the Double S Ranch south of Fouke. While on a fishing trip last weekend, Cody mentioned to Charlie that he needed a few good workers, and the pay was almost twice what he and Bobby were making at the factory in West Monroe. After a couple of days of arm-twisting and convincing from Charlie and Leigh Ann, Bobby threw caution to the wind and decided that Fouke was his family's future.

"You okay?"

Bobby had felt Leigh Ann's eyes on him for the past 30 miles. He was surprised she waited this long to say something.

"Yeah. Just thinking."

Out of the corner of his eye, Bobby could see Leigh Ann chewing on her bottom lip. This was Leigh Ann's telltale sign of wanting to say something.

"What is it?"

"Nothing."

It had been a long, quiet drive from West Monroe. Too quiet. Bobby had decided to leave out early enough to stop at a truck stop for a big family breakfast. With their bellies full, the kids fell asleep about 10 minutes into the drive. Leigh Ann had fretted, squirmed in her seat, and chewed on her bottom lip since then. But she never spoke a word until now.

"Honey, I know something has been on your mind since we pulled out of the truck stop. Just spit it out."

Leigh Ann looked warily at Bobby and gently nodded her head.

"I'm just worried."

Bobby waited for Leigh Ann to reveal the source of her concern. When it didn't come, Bobby sighed and tried to prod his wife along, "About?"

"Do you think everything is gonna be okay?"

"Honey, I'm the one who doesn't like change. Where's this coming from?"

"Do you know how to do ranch work?"

"Well, it's not the Old West. Me and Charlie will just be working around the farm. Feeding the cows, fixing fences, taking the cows to auction. I think we'll be fine. And the pay is more than what we were making at the factory. Wouldn't you like to have some extra money? Maybe get you a color TV?"

Leigh Ann smiled.

"I'm not much for TV, but I guess it would be nice to be able to get the kids some new clothes…maybe get me a new dress…"

"Heck, yeah! We'll get you a new red dress and we'll go out at paint the town!"

Leigh Ann laughed and slapped Bobby playfully on the arm.

"Can you paint the town in Fouke?"

"Well, we may be the first!"

Leigh Ann's smile was quickly replaced by a concerned frown.

"Where are we gonna live?"

"That's taken care of. Charlie said we are supposed to meet a Mr. Smith at the Fouke Filling Station. He is supposed to have a place big enough for all of us just outside of town."

"How are we supposed to pay for it? We have enough for groceries and gas, but that's all until your first paycheck."

"That's the best part. Apparently, Mr. Smith is friends with our new boss and he's good with waiting until we get paid before he charges us any rent."

Leigh Ann mumbled, "Sounds almost too good to be true…"

"What was that?"

Leigh Ann smiled, leaned over, and gave her husband a quick peck on the cheek.

"Nothing."

The Fouke Filling Station was a run-down garage on the side of the road just inside the city limits of Fouke. Bobby pulled the family station wagon beside the station's single gas pump and a spry older gentleman wearing a greasy set of blue coveralls approached the driver's side window.

"You folks need a fill-up?"

Before Bobby could answer, the man grabbed a squeegee and began washing the bugs and road grime off the station wagon's windshield.

"Yeah, fill her up… could you direct us to a Mr. Smith?"

The old man stopped washing the windshield, leaned in close to the glass and squinted at the driver.

"Who's askin'?"

"Bobby and Charlie Wayne. We're supposed to begin work at the Double S Ranch on Monday morning."

The old man leaned closer to the windshield and tapped the oval badge sown to the right breast pocket of his coveralls.

"Says right here that you've found John Smith. I've been expectin' you boys!"

John Smith walked around the station wagon, looking in each window, before turning around to wave at Charlie and Carol Wayne, as they pulled in behind the station wagon.

"Got yerself a crew, dontcha?"

"Daddy, he talks funny!"

Startled, Bobby turned and looked in the backseat to see his six-year-old daughter Katey wide awake, while her two brothers yawned and stretched themselves awake.

"Kateybug, that's not polite."

The old man laughed out loud and said, "No, that's alright. I do talk a little funny. I'm from Slidell, Louisiana. Where are you from?"

Katey looked at her mom and dad to see if it was safe to talk to this stranger. Leigh Ann nodded slightly.

"I'm Katey. Everyone calls me Kateybug. I'm six and I'm from

West Monroe!"

"Well, Kateybug, it's nice to meet you! I'm Mr. Smith. Everyone calls me Mr. Smith!"

"Mr. Smith, this is my wife Leigh Ann. And next to Kateybug, that's Jesse. He's 10. And next to him is our oldest boy, Bobby, Jr. Junior is 12."

Mr. Smith leaned down and offered a friendly smile. "Nice to meet, y'all!"

Leigh Ann leaned toward the driver's window and asked, "Did you say you were from Slidell?"

"Yes, ma'am! I moved from Slidell to Fouke back in '65."

"The only folks I know who lived in Slidell worked at the NASA thing…the Mississippi Test Operations…did you work there, too?"

The old man laughed and went back to finish the windshield.

"Yea…you found me out…I'm a rocket scientist workin' as a gas jockey!"

Everyone in the station wagon broke out in laughter, except for Leigh Ann, who blushed and quietly said, "I'm sorry."

Mr. Smith dropped his squeegee back into a bucket of dirty water and shook his head.

"Ma'am, I am just messin' with ya."

As Mr. Smith grabbed the nozzle to begin filling up the Waynes' car, a heavyset man wearing a black ballcap that looked to be two sizes too small for his head, stepped out of the filling station toting a bottle of Dr. Pepper.

"Howdy, folks," said Black Ballcap, as he saluted the Waynes with a tip of his Dr. Pepper bottle.

From the back of the car, Mr. Smith hollered, “Don’t mind that ole fool! That’s Elmer. He drinks all my sodee pops.”

Elmer offered the Waynes another tip-of-the-bottle salute before taking a big swig of his Dr. Pepper.

Bobby got out of the car, stretched, and waved at his brother. Charlie climbed out of his pickup truck and walked over to his brother.

“Mr. Smith, me and Charlie sure do appreciate you helping us out with a place to stay. We’re supposed to get paid next Friday, and we will bring you some money for the rent then.”

Mr. Smith replaced the nozzle on the gas pump and waved his hands in the air.

“You boys don’t worry ‘bout it. I know ole man Simpson out there at the ranch. I know yer good fer it. Hang on and I’ll git the keys to yer place.”

As Mr. Smith walked into the filling station, Elmer walked over to the brothers.

“You boys gonna start working at the ranch?”

“Yep. Our cousin Cody is the foreman out there.”

Elmer’s face lit up.

“I know Cody. He’s a good ole boy. We go fishin’ a lot.”

Charlie placed his hand on his brother’s shoulder and said, “Speaking of which, since we ain't gotta work till Monday, what's someone do for fun around here besides hunting and fishing?"

Elmer quickly replied, "Go to Texarkana."

Mr. Smith came out of the filling station just in time to hear Elmer's reply.

"Like I said, don't listen to that ole fool. All's he's good fer is drinkin' all my sodee pops."

Mr. Smith handed Bobby a set of keys and looked back at Elmer.

"Hey, you ole fool. Why dontcha make yerself useful and drive these folks out to the Ford place, so's they don't get lost."

Elmer nodded at Mr. Smith and replied, "Sure, but it's gonna cost ya!"

"Let me guess…you want another sodee pop?"

Elmer tipped his now empty Dr. Pepper bottle toward Mr. Smith as he reached into the cooler for another one.

"Come on, folks! Follow me!"

A short drive through town and a bumpy ride down a dirt road later, Elmer led the Waynes to their new home. The Ford house was a single story, three-bedroom wood structure that Mr. Smith had kept up for potential renters. There just wasn't a big demand for rent houses in Fouke.

The Ford house sat at the end of a dirt road, surrounded by thick woods and a soybean field. A big front yard complete with a large oak tree with a tire swing would give the kids hours and hours of enjoyment. A big front porch that stretched across the front of the house would give the adults plenty of space to relax and watch the kids have their fun.

While his family began to unpack and inspect their surroundings, Bobby walked up to Elmer's pickup truck.

"Thank you, Elmer. We really appreciate it."

"You're welcome. I would help you folks get settled in, but I have a Dr. Pepper calling my name back at John's place!"

Charlie and Carol pulled up next to Elmer, parked their pickup and opened their doors. Two big hunting dogs jumped out of the pickup and took off barking across the yard.

"Nice looking hounds you got there!"

Charlie beamed, "That's our pride and joy, Roscoe and Buford. Best huntin' dogs in three states."

Elmer watched the dogs circle the yard before looking back at Charlie. "You might wanna keep them hounds inside at night. There's all kinds of critters that roam around these parts when the sun goes down."

"Critters?"

"Yeah…you know…critters like bears, panthers and such."

Charlie looked at his dogs and then looked back at Elmer to see if he was serious.

He was.

In fact, in the short time they had known Elmer, this was the first time they noticed that he wasn't smiling from ear to ear.

"Yeah…I'll bring 'em in at night."

"Good deal. Oh, and if y'all need anything, there ain't no phone in that house. You got electricity, gas for the stove and water, but you ain't got a phone. You'll have to drive a mile back up the road to Ole Man Prince's house for the nearest phone."

Bobby spoke up, more than a little concerned, "Why would we need a phone bad enough that we'd have to drive a mile away to use it?"

"You boys can never tell…someone might have an accident or something…or you may wanna call ole Elmer and invite him out for a cold Dr. Pepper!"

The brothers laughed nervously as Elmer climbed in and started up his pickup truck, tipped an empty Dr. Pepper bottle at them and drove away.

The Waynes spent most of the day unpacking and settling into their new home. Between the two families, there wasn't a lot to unpack. The kids had their bedroom set up in no time and spent most of the rest of the day playing in the yard with Roscoe and Buford. Meanwhile, Leigh Ann and Carol had set up the adults' bedrooms and unpacked the few groceries they had brought with them. Bobby and Charlie had spent all day unloading and moving furniture and worked up an appetite for the beans and cornbread that the wives prepared for supper.

As the sun started going down, the family was already dozing off in the living room. Remembering what Elmer had told them, Bobby walked over and nudged his sleeping brother as he snored on the couch.

"Hey! Wake up! You need to go get the dogs. It's almost dark."

Charlie sat up, yawned, and said, "Yeah, yeah…I'm on my way."

Charlie walked out to the front porch and called for his dogs, "ROSCOE!! BUFORD!! Here, boys!"

From behind the house somewhere in the woods, Charlie could hear his dogs barking. The sun had already gone down, and it was hard to see anything but trees and lightning bugs, but Charlie could hear his dogs barking. Charlie noticed the dogs' barking wasn't their typical playful barking. They weren't even barking like they had treed something. This barking was more menacing. As if the dogs were trying to ward off imminent danger.

Worried, Charlie began walking towards the woods. The Waynes never thought to bring a flashlight, so Charlie had to rely on what little light remained in the Fouke dusk.

The dogs suddenly stopped barking.

Charlie stopped at the edge of the woods and listened.

Charlie heard nothing. Everything had gone quiet. The birds had stopped chirping. The frogs had stopped croaking. It even seemed as if the insects had stopped buzzing about.

Charlie softly spoke, the sound of his own voice chilling the blood in his veins, "Roscoe? Buford?"

Charlie was answered by a bloodcurdling, "YELP!"

Charlie was knocked off his feet when Roscoe and Buford bolted from the woods, making a beeline for the house. Charlie picked himself up off the ground and called to his dogs, "Hey! Where are y'all going?!"

Behind Charlie in the woods, the silence was replaced by the sound of breaking limbs and crunching leaves, as if something big was running through the woods. Slowly, Charlie began walking backward to the house when the silence returned. Suddenly, a strong, musty odor filled the air. The smell was so strong, it caught Charlie off guard, causing him to cough. Charlie's cough was almost instantly answered by a sound that reminded him of a buck's snort.

HUFF!

Charlie coughed again. This time, Charlie was answered by a low, guttural growl, that proceeded to get louder and louder.

grrrrAWWRRRRLLLL!

Charlie ran back to the house where Bobby was waiting on the porch for him.

"Hey, little brother! What's wrong? You look like you've seen a ghost."

Charlie looked at his brother and glanced back to the woods. "Did the dogs get in?"

"Yeah. They're acting like they saw a ghost, too. They've been crouched in the corner, shaking all over like they're freezin' their butts off."

Charlie took one last look at the woods before grabbing his brother by the arm. "Let's get inside."

*7:15am April 26, 1974*

The aroma of frying eggs and fresh coffee greeted Bobby as he walked into the kitchen. Charlie was already at the table, but instead of eating, he was staring out the window, intently watching the woods behind the house. Charlie jumped as his brother clapped him on the back.

"How'd you sleep, little brother?"

"I didn't. It was a long night…"

Carol placed a plate of eggs and toast on the table for Bobby and interjected, "He didn't even come to bed last night. I think he sat right there all night."

Bobby glanced out the window to see if he could see what was of such interest to Charlie.

"What's up?"

"Nothin'…"

Bobby looked at Carol and shrugged his shoulders.

Leigh Ann handed her husband a steaming cup of coffee.

"Here. Drink this and tell me what we are gonna do today."

Bobby took a sip of his coffee and pointed toward the open, bare cupboards.

"How 'bout we go into town and get some groceries. Maybe me and Charlie will go get some haircuts so we will look presentable for our new jobs."

"Before we do all of that, how 'bout we stop at the house down the road so you can call your cousin and let him know you're in town."

"Sounds like a plan!"

Junior carried his now-clean plate to the sink and turned to ask his dad, "Pa, can me and Jesse stay home and take y'all's guns and go squirrel hunting?"

Before Bobby could answer, Charlie quickly snapped, "No sir! You boys stay outta them woods!"

Junior looked at his dad, who could only shrug his shoulders once again.

Charlie carried his untouched breakfast to the counter and poured his cold coffee down the sink. Without saying a word, Charlie opened the backdoor and followed Roscoe and Buford outside.

Trying to alleviate to tension in the kitchen, Leigh Ann hugged Junior and said, "Alright! Everyone get ready! We're leaving for town in five minutes. Jesse, help your sister clean up her breakfast. Junior, get some food and water for the dogs. We'll leave them here in the kitchen while we are gone."

Bobby pulled the packed station wagon off on the side of the road next to an old shack at the end of the gravel road that led to their house.

"This must be Ole Man Prince's place that Elmer told us about."

Leigh Ann playfully slapped her husband's arm. "Don't let him hear you call him that. Be a gentleman. How about 'Mr. Prince?'"

"Yes, ma'am…Come on, Charlie. Let's go 'be gentlemen' and introduce ourselves to 'Mr. Prince.'"

The brothers got out of the car and walked across a yard that hadn't been mowed for a couple of weeks. The knee-high grass nearly obscured a push mower and a couple of cinder blocks. Bobby walked up onto the porch and knocked on the screen door.

"Yeah! Hold yer horses! I'm comin'!"

Bobby stepped back as the screen door flew upon to reveal an old man wearing overalls and a frown that held up a hand-rolled cigarette.

"Mr. Prince?"

"Yep. Jack Prince at yer service."

"Sir, my name is Bobby Wayne. This is my brother Charlie. We're staying in the Ford house down the road there. Elmer down at the filling station told us if we ever needed to use the phone, to come see you."

"Yeah. I got a phone. But if'n you wanna use it, you boys are gonna have to do me a favor."

"Sure…you need help mowing your yard?"

Jack Prince looked out at his yard and then looked back at the brothers with a dumbfounded look on his face.

"My yard? What's wrong with my yard?"

Bobby looked at Charlie, realizing he had put his foot in his mouth.

The old man answered his own question. "There's nothin' wrong with my yard. If'n you boys want to use the phone, I'm gonna need you to run an errand for me. Go to the store and get me some Prince Albert and some rollin' papers. I got the money in here. Come on!"

Without waiting for the brothers, Jack Prince disappeared back into his house.

Bobby looked back at Charlie, unsure of what to do next.

"You boys! I said, 'come on!'"

Bobby and Charlie jogged across Ole Man Prince's yard and hopped into the waiting station wagon.

"Well, that didn't take long."

"Nope. I got ahold of Cody and he told us to be at the ranch Monday morning at six. Oh…here."

Bobby handed Leigh Ann a crumpled ten-dollar bill.

"What's this for?"

"The cost of doing business with Mr. Prince. Add a can of Prince Albert and some rollin' papers to the shopping list."

"We don't have a big list. What are we supposed to do while y'all are getting haircuts?"

Bobby thought for a minute and replied, "How 'bout y'all drop me and Charlie off at the barbershop, then y'all go to the store. Y'all can bring the groceries – and the Prince Albert – back home and then come back to town and pick us up."

"You're just trying to get out of unloading the car and putting up the groceries."

After a short drive into town, Bobby turned the station wagon over to Leigh Ann as he and his brother walked up to Butch's Barbershop, a small building on Main Street. Upon opening the door, the brothers were greeted by the smell of aftershave and the sound of Jack Greene's "There Goes My Everything" coming from a small radio on the backbar.

"Man, I love that song."

The barber immediately smiled at Bobby and said, "Me, too! They play the good stuff on KTFS. My son works there."

"We're new in town and we haven't even had time to listen to the radio yet."

"Where are you boys from?"

"We just got in from West Monroe, Louisiana. I'm Bobby and that's my brother Charlie."

The barber walked out from behind the barber chair and offered his hand for a greeting.

“I’m Butch Henry. If y’all need a haircut, have a seat.”

Bobby sat down in the barber chair, while Charlie took a seat against the wall and waited his turn.

Butch draped a hair cloth around Bobby and asked, “What will it be? A little off the ears?”

“How ‘bout a flattop? We’re starting a new job Monday and we’re gonna need to stay cool.”

“Where are y’all working at?”

“Down at the Double S.”

“Where are you boys staying?”

“We’re renting the old Ford house just outside of town.”

An awkward silence immediately filled the barbershop…a silence that was suddenly broken by the sound of Charlie snoring.

Bobby and Butch shared a laugh before the barber asked, “Did he have a long night?”

“I guess…CHARLIE! Wake up!”

Charlie quickly sat up and apologized, “Oh…I’m sorry.”

“Son, did you have a long night last night?”

Charlie looked hesitantly at Butch and muttered, “Yeah…I guess you could say that…”

Butch stopped cutting Bobby’s hair, stepped from behind the barber chair and squinted at Charlie.

"You saw it, didn't you?"

Charlie turned pale. His lips moved, but no words came out.

"You know who I'm talking about…Mr. Hairy and Scary."

Bobby looked from Butch to Charlie and asked his brother, "What's he talking about?"

Butch walked back behind the barber chair and resumed cutting Bobby's hair.

"Your brother has seen Fouke's most famous celebrity: the Fouke Monster."

"The what?"

"The Fouke Monster. It's some kind of big creature that roams around in our woods and down around Boggy Creek. I've been here in the shop since '68, and in that time, I have heard several stories. Folks have been seeing the monster crossing the road, walking in the woods, and sneaking through their yards."

Charlie was wide awake now.

"What is it?"

"No one knows for sure. But it's harmless. It just shows up and scares the stew outta you every now and then, but it's never hurt anyone."

Quietly, Charlie said, "Yet…"

After dropping off Ole Man Prince's Prince Albert and rolling papers, Leigh Ann parked the station wagon in front of their rental house. As soon as she put the car in park, Leigh Ann could tell something was wrong. When the family had left earlier, they had left the dogs in the kitchen. However, Roscoe was now sitting on the front porch.

"Leigh Ann, didn't we leave the dogs in the house?"

"Yes, we did…how did Roscoe get out?"

The family climbed out of the car, but Roscoe didn't run to greet anyone. Roscoe refused to leave the porch. The dog shivered, whined, and laid down by the front door.

"Aunt Carol, what's wrong with Roscoe?"

"Kateybug, I don't know."

As the family walked toward the porch, they could hear Buford barking in the woods behind the house.

Jesse took off running toward the woods as fast as his little legs would carry him.

"JESSE! Get back here!"

Junior took off after his little brother and hollered back to his mother, "Don't worry, Mom! I'll get him and we'll get Buford."

"Honey, be careful! And get your butt back here so we can go get your dad and your uncle!"

While Leigh Ann watched her sons run into the woods, Carol grabbed the bags of groceries out of the back of the station wagon and led her niece to the porch.

"Kateybug, open the door and let Roscoe in."

As soon as Katey opened the front door, Roscoe bolted inside and laid down besides the couch in the living room.

Carol carried the grocery bags into the kitchen, placed them on the table and took in a scene of absolute chaos. Chairs were turned over; the garbage can was overturned, and shards of glass covered the floor.

"Leigh Ann…you better get in here!"

Leigh Ann walked into the kitchen and was taken aback by the mess.

"What happened in here?"

"It looks like the dogs went nuts…and then jumped out the window."

Leigh Ann bent down to examine the glass covering the kitchen floor.

"If they jumped out of the window…then why is the glass in here?"

"Leigh Ann, I think someone tried to break in here!"

"I'm gonna get the boys out of the woods. Carol, I need you to run back up the road to Mr. Prince and call the sheriff."

Junior caught up with his brother just as Jesse reached the woods.

"Jesse! Uncle Charlie told us to stay out of the woods! We've gotta get home!"

"I'm not going anywhere until I find Buford!"

Junior could hear Buford barking somewhere in the distance.

"Junior, he's just over that ridge right there. Can't you hear him?"

Junior looked back at the house and then back to the ridge, as Buford barked again.

"Junior…please!"

"Okay. Let's hurry up before Mom comes lookin' for us!"

Junior and Jesse made their way up the ridge. At the bottom of the ridge, they could see Buford at the edge of a small pond. Buford was barking at something out in the middle of the pond. Junior couldn't make out what Buford was so upset at, so he grabbed Jesse's hand and walked down the ridge toward the pond.

Buford paced the water's edge, oblivious to the brothers' approach. Buford continued barking at something in the pond. Junior and Jesse could now see the source of Buford's frustration, but they weren't sure what it was. In the middle of the pond was some type of large animal, covered with dark, brown hair.

"Buford! What are you barking at?!"

Buford stopped barking and turned to look at the brothers.

So did the creature in the water.

Junior could see the creature more clearly now, but he wished he couldn't. The creature appeared to be standing waist deep in the pond. The creature was standing upright on two legs, but Junior couldn't be sure. He was too distracted by the creature's man-like face staring at them. Even from a distance, Junior could see what appeared to be anger in its – red? – eyes.

The creature looked back at Buford and utter a grunt. The creature then turned its head toward the brothers, opened its mouth – which Junior could see was filled with lots of large, sharp teeth – and unleashed a bloodcurdling scream.

SCRREEEEE!!!

"Junior…what is –"

"Buford! Come on, boy!"

Buford took off running toward the brothers.

The creature eased its way across the pond. Then with a burst of unnatural speed, it exploded from the pond and ran right toward the brothers on top of the ridge. Sheer terror had paralyzed both brothers as they couldn't believe what they were seeing.

A chilling howl echoed through the woods as the enraged creature closed the distance between them.

ARRROOOOOOOO!!!

Junior couldn't help but notice that the creature had abnormally long arms that extended below its knees. As the creature ran, its arms didn't move at all, hanging almost motionless at its sides as its long legs and long strides carried the creature quickly up the ridge.

"Jesse! RUN!!"

Junior grabbed his brother's left hand and together they ran faster than they had ever run before, trying to ignore the howls and the sounds of something big and fast crashing through the woods after them.

The brothers burst out of the woods just as Buford blew past them. Seeing the house and their perceived safety so close, the brothers both screamed at the top of their lungs, "MOM!!! MOM!!!"

Leigh Ann ran around the corner of the house and was almost knocked over by Buford, as the dog ran around the house and headed right for the front door. Leigh Ann dropped to her knees and wrapped her crying sons in a frantic embrace.

"What's wrong, boys?!"

"Mom! There's something chasing us!"

Leigh Ann looked and saw nothing but the dark, thick woods behind the house…and what appeared to be two red eyes peering out of the darkness back at her.

As Leigh Ann was hugging her sons and trying to calm them down, a Miller County Sheriff's Department car pulled into the yard. Two officers jumped out of the car and ran over to Leigh Ann and her crying sons.

"Ma'am, are you okay?"

A tall, lanky officer with genuine concern in his eyes knelt next to Leigh Ann and her sons.

"Yessir…it's been a crazy day…"

"Yes, ma'am. That's what I hear. I'm Sheriff Alan Vines and that ole boy over there is Deputy William McCartney. We had a call to come out here because of a break in?"

Carol walked out onto the porch. "Yes, sir. That was me. Someone tried to break into the kitchen while we were in town."

Deputy McCartney removed his mirrored sunglasses and said, "We don't have a lot of break ins out here. Most folks around these parts don't even lock their doors at night."

Sheriff Vines turned his attention to the two upset boys. "Hey, guys. There's nothing to worry about. Whoever tried to break in is long gone. We'll find them and lock them up for you."

Leigh Ann stood up and pulled her sons close to her. "I'm afraid that's not what has the boys so upset. They said there was something chasing them in the woods."

Sheriff Vines and Deputy McCartney exchanged a look that said they knew more about the situation than Leigh Ann did.

"Something was chasing you in the woods?"

Junior looked at Sheriff Vines through his tear-filled eyes. "Yessir…"

Deputy McCartney interjected, "It was probably a panther. Game and

Fish claims that we don't have any panthers in Arkansas, but we are ate up with 'em down here."

Sheriff Vines patted Junior on the back. "Yep. I bet it was a panther. We'll check it out in a bit, but first let's see about this break in."

The officers followed Carol into the kitchen to observe the mess. Deputy McCartney walked around the kitchen and stopped at the broken window.

"Ma'am, was anything taken? Anything missing?"

Leigh Ann walked into the kitchen with her children peeking out from behind her. "Nothing is missing that we can tell. We don't have that much. We just moved here for our husbands' new jobs. I can't imagine why anyone would try to break in."

"Where are your husbands at now, if you don't mind me asking?"

"We dropped them off in town to get haircuts while we brought some groceries home."

Sheriff Vines nodded. "I tell you what. Why don't y'all go pick up your husbands while me and Will stick around and check out this break in. We'll even go out and investigate the woods and see if we can find out what was chasing the boys. We'll wait here until y'all get back."

"Okay…kids, go get in the car so we can go get your dad and Uncle Charlie."

" – and he said it was probably just a panther. He said he and the deputy would hang out and investigate the break in and look for some tracks while we picked y'all up."

For most of the ride back to the house, Leigh Ann had filled her husband and brother-in-law in on the chaotic chain of events that had occurred during their absence. Now that Leigh Ann had concluded her unbelievable tale, Bobby sat slack jawed in the backseat next to Charlie, who closed his eyes and shook his head.

"Pa…"

Junior tapped his dad on the shoulder, as he had been taking in the story from the back of the station wagon along with his younger siblings.

"Yeah, son?"

"It wasn't a panther."

Charlie muttered, "No…it's not a panther."

Leigh Ann parked the station wagon in front of the house and was immediately greeted by Sheriff Vines as she and her family climbed out of the vehicle.

"Sheriff, this is my husband Bobby and his brother Charlie."

Sheriff Vines walked over and shook hands with the brothers. "Sorry we're meeting under these circumstances."

"Yes, sir. Did you guys find anything that will help you find out who broke into the place?"

"No, sir –"

"Sheriff, I couldn't find any tracks out there in the woods."

Deputy McCartney walked around the corner of the house, wiping the sweat from his forehead with a handkerchief. "I checked all the way to the pond and back. Nothing."

Junior tugged on his dad's shirttail, "Pa…"

Bobby gently waved his hand, which was Junior's sign to wait until the grown folks were finished talking.

Sheriff Vines looked down and slowly shook his head. Bobby knew what was coming next.

"I'm sorry, folks. We couldn't find anything. If y'all have any more trouble – be it a would-be burglar or a panther – just give us a call and we'll come back out here. Deputy, let's roll."

Both officers waved goodbye to the bewildered Wayne family, got in their cruiser, and drove away.

Leigh Ann looked at her frightened children and then looked to her husband for an answer.

"What do we do know?"

Bobby wrapped an arm around his wife and squeezed her tight. "We go clean up the mess…and try not to make any more messes for the rest of the day."

Once the kitchen was cleaned up and the broken window boarded up, Leigh Ann and Carol cooked a big lunch for the family. After the events of the morning and the filling meal, most of the family took a well-deserved nap. However, Bobby was too troubled to sleep.

"Charlie, let's go for a walk."

Charlie left the room and returned with his single shot breakover .410 shotgun in one hand and Bobby's bolt-action .30-06 rifle in the other.

"Are we going huntin'?"

"Bobby, after what happened last night and this morning, we aren't going outside without a little backup."

Bobby thought about it for a moment. "The sun's still up and we're just walking around the yard. I doubt we're gonna see anything."

Undeterred, Charlie opened the front door and hollered, "Roscoe! Buford! C'mon boys!"

Charlie's dogs walked up to the door but refused to follow their master outside.

Charlie knelt and patted his dogs on their heads. "Boys, it's okay. C'mon. Let's go outside." Hesitantly, the dogs followed Charlie and Bobby outside.

"What's wrong with the hounds?"

"I don't know, but I can tell you it's not a panther."

"So, little brother…you gonna tell me what happened last night?"

Charlie stopped walking and looked at his brother. "Bobby, there's something out there in the woods. Something big. Something that's got the dogs…and me…and now your boys all scared."

"What do you think it is?"

Charlie shook his head. "I don't know. I not sure I really want to know."

"Maybe it's a bear."

"Bobby, I've never heard a bear sound like that."

Bobby walked on beside his brother, not really knowing what to say. As the brothers walked around the corner of the house, they noticed the dogs standing at the edge of the yard, facing the woods, not moving, and not barking. The dogs had their hackles up and were both growling lowly at the woods.

Charlie approached his dogs and whispered, "What is it, boys?"

Bobby looked towards the woods and could just barely make out a dark object at the edge of the thick foliage. "Charlie…is that…a panther?"

At the edge of the woods, the brothers could see an animal covered with brown hair apparently grazing or eating something on the ground. The creature was on four legs and was about three feet off the ground, just visible through the high weeds leading into the woods.

"Bobby, I don't think that's a panther…I don't see a tail. Maybe a bear?"

"I don't know what it is, but I bet that's the thing that scared the boys." Bobby pulled his rifle up to his shoulder and sighted in the mysterious creature. Bobby took a deep breath, held it, and pulled the trigger.

BLAM!!

The creature quickly stood up two legs and turned toward the source of the shot. That's when the brothers could see it wasn't a four-legged animal. Maybe four or five feet tall, the enraged animal raised two abnormally long arms above its head before leveling one arm and a single finger in the direction of the brothers. The creature then opened its mouth unnaturally wide and unleashed a high-pitched scream that sent the dogs running back to the house.

SCREEEEEEE!!!

Bobby pulled his rifle back up to his shoulder and aimed for a second shot. The creature stopped screaming but left its fang-filled mouth wide open and its accusing finger pointed at the brothers. Then the creature slowly backed into the woods until it blended in with the darkness and was simply gone.

Bobby lowered his rifle and looked at his brother in disbelief.

"So…still think we have a panther problem?"

Suppertime was a somber time. The kids picked at their food, while the adults sat in silence contemplating the events of the day. Even the dogs weren't begging for table scraps.

Leigh Ann sighed loudly, jolting the entire family from their collective malaise. "Oh, well…kids, if you aren't going to eat anymore, let's get ready for bed." Carol helped the kids gather up their dirty dishes and carry everything to the kitchen sink, while Bobby and Charlie continued to pick at the food on their plates.

Leigh Ann pulled her sons close to her and ruffled their hair. "You boys go brush your teeth and hurry up so your sister can get in there and get ready for bed."

In unison, Junior and Jesse replied, "Yes, ma'am."

"Kateybug, while you're waiting on your brothers, would you help Aunt Carol dry the dishes?"

"Aw, mom! Do I have to?"

"Five minutes tops. It won't kill you. I promise."

Katey lowered her head, accepting defeat and muttered, "Yes, ma'am."

Carol handed her niece a dish towel and together they tackled the nightly task that never took the five minutes Leigh Ann suggested.

From the back of the house, Junior yelled, "Mom! We're done in here!"

Leigh Ann turned to her daughter. "Kateybug, you can go –"

Katey dropped her damp dish towel on the kitchen counter and ran toward the bathroom before her mom could finish what she was saying.

Katey's nighttime routine took a little longer than everyone else's. For Katey, "getting ready for bed" wasn't just about putting on a nightgown and brushing her teeth. It was about "showtime" – time spent in front of the mirror with Katey singing her favorite song, which this week just happened to one of her dad's favorite songs, Johnny Horton's "Ole Slew Foot."

However, before she could begin tonight's performance, Katey had to do something about the smell. Her mom had always told Katey that the only thing worse than boys was boys and beans. It was nights like this one that helped Katey understand exactly what her mom was talking about.

Katey was about to climb up onto the commode to open the small window above, but she could see through the reflection in the mirror that the curtains were moving as a gentle breeze blew through. But the breeze was not blowing the smell anywhere. If anything, the smell seemed to be getting worse.

Katey decided that tonight's show must go on, although it would be an abbreviated set due to the smell. Katey grabbed her toothbrush, flipped her hair, looked in the mirror and began singing, "*High on the mountain, tell me what you see...*"

Ooooooooo...

Katey stopped singing and listened intently. It sounded like something was cooing along with her, but now she couldn't hear anything.

"Bear tracks bear tracks lookin' back at me. Better get your rifle boy before it's too late 'cause the bear's got a little pig and headed through the gate. He's big around the middle and he's broad across the rump..."

That word "rump" always made Katey giggle. However, Katey's laughter came to a stop when she saw the bathroom window curtains moving, but not because of the wind. Katey could see in the mirror a big hairy hand with long black claws reach through the window.

"MOM!!!!"

Katey dropped her toothbrush and ran out of the bathroom straight into her mom and dad.

Leigh Ann dropped to her knees and grabbed her daughter by the shoulders. "Kateybug! What's wrong with you?!"

Tears streamed down Katey's cheeks as she tried to tell her parents what happened. "There was…a monster…"

Bobby joined his wife on the floor beside their daughter. "A monster?"

Katey nodded her head and swiped at the tears covering her cheeks. "Uh, huh…a monster…it was trying to get in the bathroom!"

Bobby got to his feet and went into the bathroom. Nothing looked out of place, but there was an awful stench that filled the room. A musty stench that smelled like rotting flesh.

Bobby returned to the hall to find the entire family gathered in frightened anticipation. "There's nothing in there. It stinks to high heaven, but there's no monster in there."

Katy buried her head against her mom's chest and unleashed a new wave of tears. Leigh Ann picked her daughter up and hugged her tight. "It's okay. Let's get you kids to bed. Everything will be better in the morning."

Katy lifted her head off her mother's shoulder. "Mom? Can I sleep with you and Daddy?"

Leigh Ann looked to her husband for an answer. Bobby nodded his head. “Yeah, she can sleep in our bed. Y’all go on to bed. I’m gonna stay up for a while.”

Leigh Ann and Carol corralled the kids and headed down the hallway toward the bedrooms. “Don’t stay up too late.”

“I won’t.”

Charlie walked over to his brother and whispered, “You don’t think Kateybug saw that thing we saw today, do you?”

Bobby never took his eyes off the bathroom window and replied, “I hope not…I really hope not.”

It didn’t take long for the family to fall asleep. Not long after that, despite his best attempts to stay awake and keep watch, Bobby fell into a fitful sleep on the couch in the living room. Vivid images of what he and his brother had seen in the afternoon kept him tossing and turning.

CREAK! CREAK! CREAK!

Bobby jolted awake at the sound of someone – or something – walking across the wooden front porch just on the other side of the big picture window behind the couch. In the corner of the living room, Roscoe and Buford growled, but didn’t move closer to the door.

CREAK! CREAK!

The footsteps stopped and the noise was replaced by the sound of the front door's doorknob turning. Bobby quickly crawled across the couch and turned the lock on the deadbolt. As soon as the deadbolt clicked, the doorknob stopped turning. The dogs stopped growling, laid down in the corner of the room and began whining.

CREAK!CREAK!CREAK!CREAK!CREAK!

Whatever was on the front porch ran away quickly. Bobby followed suit and ran down the hall to get his rifle. As Bobby ran back down the hall with his rifle in hand, Charlie came out of his bedroom with his shotgun in his hands.

"What's wrong?!"

"Someone – or something – was trying to get in the front door!"

"What are we doing?"

"Get your boots on. We're gonna go out there and put a stop to this."

Bobby and Charlie opened the front door and eased out into the still darkness. The wind had stopped blowing. The crickets weren't chirping. A thick musty odor settled around the house.

The brothers stepped into the yard with their guards and their guns up. The moon was shining bright enough for the brothers to see clearly across the backyard all the way to the woods. As the brothers began to investigate behind the house, they were stopped in their tracks by the sound of a snapping twig behind them.

The brothers turned with their guns aimed high, but they didn't see anything except their vehicles parked by the big oak tree with the tire swing, which was swaying back and forth.

Charlie lowered his shotgun. "Hmmm…that's odd…"

"What?"

Charlie pointed toward the tire swing. "Why is that swing moving?"

"The wind, maybe?"

"But the wind's not blowing."

Bobby looked at the tree closer and noticed there was something standing behind it. A tall silhouette was partially visible leaning out from behind the tree.

Bobby pointed at the tree. "Do you see that?"

The silhouette eased behind the tree.

"I saw…something…but there's nothing there now…"

HUFF! HUFF! HUFF!

The sound of heavy breathing caused the brothers to turn around and look at the backyard in time to see a tall, wide shadow with strangely long, dangling arms and red eyes rushing right at them!

RAWRRRRR!!!

The shadowy figure unleashed a rage-filled howl as it plowed into the brothers. The impact sent the brothers sprawling and scrambling for their guns.

Charlie was the first to find his gun and get back to his feet. Instead of aiming for their assailant, Charlie bolted for the porch. “Bobby! Over here! Back to the house!”

The impact with the mysterious creature had nearly knocked Bobby unconscious. He could hear his brother, but Bobby was so rattled, he couldn’t see Charlie and he couldn’t find his rifle.

“Bobby! Come on!”

Bobby decided to leave his missing rifle behind and make a run for the porch. Charlie threw the front door open. “Get in here!”

Just as Bobby reached the porch, a large hairy creature stepped between him and the front door. The creature was a good two feet taller than Bobby, covered in hair and producing the foul odor that had filled the air the moment the brothers stepped outside. Bobby looked up into the creature’s face, which was humanlike, but only if a human was covered in hair, in a rage and had a mouth full of big sharp teeth.

Bobby tried to run around the creature, but a huge hand with large claws snatched Bobby off the ground by his neck. The creature lifted Bobby up and looked at his would-be victim eye to eye. Bobby struggled to breathe, while the creature blew fetid breath into Bobby’s face and tightened his grip.

Just as he was about to pass out, the creature released Bobby’s throat, tossing him into the house and into Charlie. The commotion had awakened the rest of the family, who stood in the hallway watching in awestruck horror.

Leigh Ann had the wherewithal to rush past the pile of brothers on the floor, slam the front door and lock the deadbolt.

"What was that?!"

Bobby couldn't answer his wife. He could barely catch his breath. It felt like his throat had been crushed. Bobby tried to massage his neck, only to draw his hand back when it became wet. Bobby looked at his hand and saw that it was soaked in blood.

"Honey! You're bleeding!" Leigh Ann rushed to her husband and was shocked to see four large gashes across the back of his neck.

"Carol! Get me a towel or something! That thing almost cut Bobby's head off!"

The kids were huddled together in the hall crying hysterically.

"Kids, take the dogs, go back to your bedroom and lock the door. It will be okay." Leigh Ann tried to sound as calm as possible, even though she was soaked in her husband's blood.

The kids looked questionably back at their mom.

"Go on. I promise…it will be okay." If she hadn't been covered in blood, Leigh Ann might have believed it herself.

As Carol returned with a towel, the kids ran to their bedroom with the dogs in tow and followed Leigh Ann's instruction. While Leigh Ann tried to clean up her husband and stop his bleeding, Carol went to check on Charlie.

"What was that?"

"I don't know…but there's more than one out there. There was one out in the –"

WHAM!!

Charlie's answer was cut off by a large object bouncing off the front door.

WHAM! WHAM! WHAM!

Several large objects were bouncing off the door, the walls, and the roof. The creatures were throwing things at the house.

Charlie picked himself up off the floor and walked to the door with his shotgun raised.

CRASH!!

The picture window above the couch imploded as a huge tree limb was thrown into the house, sending shattered glass all over the living room.

Carol and Leigh Ann screamed, as Charlie aimed his shotgun at the broken window and fired.

BLAMMM!

The bombardment stopped and everything again went quiet.

ROWWRRRRR!!

The silence was broken by a mournful howl that sounded like it was coming from all sides of the house.

RAWWRRRRR! RUWWRRRRR!

The howl was almost immediately answered by two more distinctly different howls.

"How many of those things are out there?!"

The howls stopped. Charlie looked at Carol, unsure of what to do next and completely unnerved by the sudden growing silence.

CREAK. CREAK. CREAK. CREAK.

Something was walking slowly on the porch.

Charlie's eyes went to the door as something tried to turn the doorknob to gain entry. Charlie quickly reloaded his shotgun, raised the gun, and aimed it at the door.

The doorknob stopped turning.

Charlie lowered his shotgun.

KER-RASSSHHH!

The front door exploded into a shower of broken wood and splinters as one of the creatures hammered its way through the obstacle!

RAWWRRRRR!

The tall hairy creature leaned into the doorway and unleashed a howl that would haunt the Wayne family for the rest of their lives. Charlie stepped between the creature and his family, aimed his shotgun at the creature's head and pulled the trigger.

BLAMMM!

The blast hit the creature square in the face, but as the gun smoke cleared, it became clear that the shot didn't do any damage at all to the creature. As Charlie reloaded his shotgun, the creature stepped back out of the doorway and disappeared into the darkness.

Carol ran to her husband and hugged him. As her tears soaked Charlie's t-shirt, Carol pressed her face against her husband's chest and asked, "Is… it…gone?"

"I don't know, but we are! Get the kids and the dogs. I'll help Leigh Ann with Bobby. Grab whatever you can because we ain't coming back!"

In less than 10 minutes, the Wayne family had grabbed a handful of belongings, piled into their vehicles, and sped away from the Ford house.

*6:35am April 27, 1974*

Jack Prince looked forward to Saturday morning because that was the one day of the week when he didn't have to watch his diet. That meant that each Saturday morning began with a plateful of biscuits and gravy. However, this Saturday morning, Jack had to set his breakfast beside the stove to allow it to cool while he made an important phone call.

Jack's call was answered on the second ring. *"Yes."*

"Thought you'd like to know they didn't even last through the weekend."

"Is that so?"

"Yep. They flew out of here a little after midnight."

"Good to know. Thanks for the call."

"Glad to help. I've got a plate of biscuits and gravy callin' my name. You oughtta come by and I'll fix you a plate."

CLICK!

Jack's invitation went unanswered as the other party on the line abruptly ended the call.

John Smith hung up the phone in the Fouke Filling Station, went to the front door of the garage and locked the door. Smith flipped the "OPEN" sign over to "SORRY, WE ARE CLOSED" and went to the back room in the garage.

Smith approached a large metal cabinet at the back of the room and turned a handle on one of the cabinet's doors to the right. However, the cabinet's door didn't open. Instead, the metal cabinet slowly slid away from the wall, revealing a set of shiny metal doors. Smith typed in a series of numbers on the keypad to the right of the doors and stood back as the doors to a large elevator opened for him.

Smith inserted a key on the panel inside the elevator and the doors closed. In a matter of seconds, the doors reopened, as Smith had been transported to a large facility beneath his garage. Smith stepped out of the elevator and was immediately greeted by two armed guards in military garb saluting him.

"As you were."

Smith walked past the guards and entered a huge laboratory, where he was immediately greeted by a tall man with a shaved head and a white beard wearing a white lab coat.

"Commander! We weren't expecting you this early." Dr. Stephen Hammonds was caught off guard by Smith's appearance.

"At ease, Dr. Hammonds. Our test subjects have left the testing grounds. I just want a status report."

"Yes, sir. If you will step over here. Dr. Henderson and I were just finishing the latest diagnostics."

Dr. Grant Henderson joined the two men as they circled a table in an examining room. On the table was a stocky, hairy creature with abnormally long arms.

"Grant, if you would…"

"Yes, Dr. Hammonds. Commander, as you can see, this unit – the AR2 – is the powerhouse of our collection. However, we discovered that the unit was not waterproof. It ended up in a pond and the water apparently short circuited the servos that operate its arms. But even without the use of its arms, we have discovered that the unit is still a force to be –"

"Why was the AR2 in the pond?"

Dr. Henderson looked to Dr. Hammonds for help. Hammonds stepped forward. "Commander, we are still having an issue with the larger units.

Their inner mechanisms produce a higher pitch sound that apparently only canines can hear."

"You're telling me dogs chased our million-dollar project into a pond?"

"I'm afraid so, sir…but we only had that issue with the AR2. As you are aware, the AR1 was built for stealth –"

"I'm also aware that because of its size, that unit is of no use to the program other than to make the locals think that they have a panther problem."

Smith walked past an exam table containing the smaller creature known as AR1. "I'm interested on where we stand with the AR3."

Dr. Hammonds rushed across the room in order to intercept Smith as he entered the exam room containing a creature standing erect inside a big stasis tube. The creature was muscular, covered in dark brown hair and nearly eight feet tall.

"What is that smell?!"

"Commander, that's the only problem we are reporting with this unit. We used a different type of synthetic skin on this unit. The good news is two-fold: the skin is waterproof and, as we learned overnight, it's also impervious to gunshots. The problem is that the mechanisms that power this unit are running hot. When the mechanisms get too hot, they begin to 'cook' the synthetic skin, which is where that rotten smell is coming from."

Smith walked around the stasis tube, inspecting the AR3. "So, you're telling me that the AR3 is ready to go as soon as you can install a better cooling unit, so it doesn't cook from the inside out?"

Dr. Henderson quickly interjected, "Yes, sir! We even corrected the issue with the red ocular devices. On the AR1 and AR2, every time we would activate the view ports to see what was happening, their eyes would shine red. Not so with the AR3."

"Excuse me, Commander…"

Smith turned around and saw Major JoAnn Tapp standing at the edge of the exam room. Tapp was Smith's right-hand person in the operation and she often knew more about what was going on than anyone else did.

"Yes, Major?"

"Mr. Jones is on the phone and wants to speak with you immediately."

Without saying another word, Smith walked past the doctors and followed Major Tapp to an office down the hall. Smith nodded at Major Tapp, entered the office, and closed the door behind him. Once settled behind the desk at the back of the room, Smith took a deep breath and picked up the phone.

"Mr. Jones?"

"Smith, I received a report that a test subject has been admitted to a Texarkana hospital. Can we control the situation?"

"Yes, sir. As long as our checks clear, Deputy McCartney will keep things covered up."

"So, where do we stand?"

"Sir, we are almost there."

"What's the hold up?"

"A simple cooling unit. A week. Two weeks tops."

"Excellent. This is why we recruited you from the Mississippi Test Operations. Your operation has far exceeded our projects in California and in the Pacific Northwest. We need a unit from your operation to be up and running to perfection as soon as possible so we can put a stop to Goldman's six-million-dollar pet project once and for all."

"Trust me, sir. Colonel Austin won't know what hit him." ♜

# ALL MY SINS

*By Charles R. Rutledge*

*"In thy orisons, be all my sins remembered." Hamlet. Act III. Scene I*

*Caulkin Harbor, Massachusetts. 1971*

BARABBAS CAULKIN SAT IN THE drawing room of the mansion known as Caulkin House, listening to his family talk. To many people, the chatter about day-to-day things might have seemed boring or tiresome, but it was something Barabbas enjoyed. He had spent so many years alone, he was happy to be part of a true family, even if the other people in the room were only cousins, and distant cousins at that.

"So has Carrie Nevins decided to accept our offer?" Elspeth Bradford said.

The former Elspeth Caulkin was a widow, and she and her daughter,

Marilyn, had returned to Elspeth's family home after the death of Elspeth's husband.

Robert Caulkin, who stood by the fire with a snifter of brandy, said, "Yes, she said she could start in two weeks, Beth. Until then we'll just have to try and keep Derek focused on his studies."

"Derek's been so quiet since Livie left," Marilyn said. "I think Carrie will make a wonderful governess."

"I quite agree," interjected Barabbas. Derek Caulkin was Robert's son. His governess, a young woman named Olivia Danvers, had recently married, and given up her position. There had been a time when Barabbas had harbored tender feelings for 'Livie' as she was called, but as often happened with him, his rather unusual life had gotten in the way.

Barabbas was startled from his reverie by three knocks on the front door. He Heard Mrs. Pearson, the housekeeper, cross the marble floor of the foyer. A few moments later, she appeared in the doorway to the drawing room.

"Someone is asking for you, Mr. Barabbas," Mrs. Pearson said. "She wouldn't give her name."

"Rather late for anyone to be calling," Robert said, arching an eyebrow. No one could arch an eyebrow like Robert.

"Indeed, Robert," Barabbas said, getting to his feet. "I'll go and see who it is."

As Barabbas left the drawing room, he was surprised to see that the woman, whoever she was, had apparently declined to come inside as well as refusing to give a name. The front doors were partially open, and he could see someone standing outside in the shadows. He felt a flicker of apprehension.

He stepped to the doorway and said, “I’m Barabbas Caulkin.”

“Oh, I know who you are, Barabbas,” the woman said.

She came out of the shadows into the scant light filtering through the doors. She was a slender woman with auburn hair and dark eyes.

Barabbas said, “I’m afraid you have me at a disadvantage.”

“You don’t remember me. I’m not surprised. There were many like me.”

Barabbas said, “Would you like to come inside where we can talk?”

“I think it’s better if we talk out here. In fact, you might want to join me outside. You wouldn’t want your family to hear what I have to say.”

“I don’t understand.”

The woman smiled, showing long, sharp, teeth that gleamed white in the dim light. “Do you understand now?”

Unease spiked into panic. Barabbas said, “You’re…”

“Yes. I’m one of yours. Though you’re no longer one of us, are you?”

Barabbas stepped outside and closed the door behind him. The night was cold, but not cold enough to explain the trembling in his hands. “What do you want?”

“We’ll get to that. Look at you. You’re afraid of me. You know how easily I could kill you. But don’t worry. We’re not going to start with you.”

“We?” Barabbas said.

“Yes, I’m not alone. Some other old friends have come to pay their respects. And some new ones.”

“Listen to me…” Barabbas began.

“You’re not the master here. Not anymore. You’re weak and fragile now, like your friends and family. We’ve come to show you just how fragile.”

“If it’s revenge you want, then kill me. I deserve it. Just leave my family out of it.”

He didn’t see her move, but the woman’s face was suddenly only inches from his. “That would be too easy. Too merciful. You know what our kind is like, Barabbas. There’s no mercy here.”

Barabbas wanted to look away from the cold, undead eyes. He knew now what every victim of his must have felt. He was helpless. As helpless as if a tiger crouched before him. He was prey.

“What are you going to do?” he managed to stammer.

The woman smiled again and took a step back. “You’ll find out very soon. One word of advice. Don’t go wandering outside. Some of us aren’t as patient as I am.”

With that, the woman began to fade from view. She became mist and drifted away into the darkness. Barabbas could feel his heart hammering. He had to calm himself before he went back inside. What was he going to say to the others? They were all in mortal danger, but how could he warn them?

They didn't know what he had been.

That decision was taken from him. The doors opened and Marilyn looked out at him. Tears ran from her eyes. "Barabbas, you need to come inside. Something terrible has happened."

"What? What is it?"

Marilyn just shook her head and turned in the doorway so Barabbas could enter. He stepped past her with one final look at her face, then hurried into the drawing room. Elspeth sat on the couch with her face in her hands. Robert, who was normally the model of supercilious calm, looked visibly shaken.

"Barabbas," Robert said in a strained voice. "Carrie Nevins is dead. The sheriff just called from her place."

Barabbas said, "Carrie? She can't…"

"I'm afraid it's true. The sheriff said he got an anonymous call and went to check on her. He found her dead in her apartment."

"Did he…did he say how she died?"

Robert nodded. "That's the worst part. He said he normally wouldn't discuss details with civilians, but he felt we needed to know. It appears to be the work of the madman who killed several people in town a few years ago. Carrie's body was completely drained of blood."

Marilyn, who had followed Barabbas inside, said, "And since some of those people died in the woods around Caulkin House, he wanted to warn us, I guess."

Robert nodded. "Yes."

And there it was. No longer a threat. Now a reality. One of the vampires had killed someone Barabbas cared about. They had probably chosen Carrie because she lived alone. But they had wanted to be sure he knew, so they had called the sheriff.

"Are you all right, Barabbas?" Marilyn said. "Do you need to sit down?"

Barabbas realized how stricken he must look. They couldn't know why, of course. Not just because Carrie was dead, but because in some way it was his fault. The question was, who would they attack next? If they were going after the people who were alone first, they might try for Dr. Lydia Kaufmann, the woman who had 'cured' Barabbas of his vampirism. Or they might go after…

Barabbas said, "No, I'm not all right. I need time to think. I'm going home."

Elspeth looked up. Her face was streaked with tears and her mascara was smeared. "Barabbas no! You shouldn't be alone. I know you and Carrie were friends."

"I won't be alone. Eddie is at the cottage. I'm sorry. I must go. I'll call you tomorrow."

Barabbas turned and hurried out of the drawing room before anyone else could offer an objection. He had a sudden suspicion, almost a premonition, that the next target would be Eddie Lucas, his handyman, and really his only servant. Eddie was alone. Even though the woman had told him not to go outside, he had to get to Eddie to warn him.

The 'cottage' was the family name for the original Caulkin residence that had been built in the early 1800s to house the family during the construction of the manor house. It was a good deal larger than the nickname would suggest. Barabbas had lived there in his youth before he had been unfortunate enough to run across a vampire's grave.

The cottage wasn't far from the main house, but the path through the woods was winding and easy to lose if one didn't know their way. Once upon a time, Barabbas could see in the dark, but now he had to move carefully.

"You were warned to stay inside," a voice said from his left.

Barabbas stopped walking. He turned and saw a pale face just visible among the leaves. Then a figure stepped out of the trees and stretched out long fingers tipped with ragged nails.

"Please," Barabbas began.

"Please?" The man said. He was tall and gaunt, with a mane of white hair. Just what you'd think a vampire would look like. "Please don't kill you? I begged that of you once, a long time ago."

Barabbas said, "I couldn't control myself then. You know what it's like."

"Yes. I know what it's like. I can't control myself either, and I don't want to. Celia said any of us could kill you if we caught you outside. Just your luck to run into three of us."

Barabbas became aware of the other two even as the man spoke. He turned and saw two women, one black and one white, coming toward him on the path. They smiled at him with sharp teeth. Neither of them looked familiar. Had he killed these two people as well? Or were they the victims of his victims?

It didn't matter. They were about to kill him. And then they'd kill everyone he cared about. The three vampires began to close in. Barabbas thought of trying to dodge past, but he knew how fast the creatures were. He saw their mouths open wide, and their hands stretch out like talons.

Then he saw something else. A shadow loomed up behind the vampire with the white hair. Something glittered, and Barabbas heard a whistling hiss, and then the vampire's head came off. The other two vampires turned toward their fallen comrade as he crumpled to the ground.

A giant figure stood just behind the headless vampire. It was the largest man Barabbas had ever seen. He couldn't see him well in the darkness, but the man had to be at least seven feet tall.

One of the two women launched herself at the big man, screeching like a cat in rage. The man moved far more quickly than anyone would expect from someone so large, and Barabbas again saw the glint of metal. Now he could see the man wielded a large ax with two blades.

The ax swung up, then back down toward the vampire's head. The woman twisted to the side so that the blade missed her skull, but it struck her in the shoulder, severing her arm. She fell to the ground screaming. How had the weapon harmed her? That should have been impossible.

The giant was merciless. He stepped forward and struck the vampire again, this time splitting her head down the middle. Barabbas looked back, expecting to see the last of the trio rushing to attack, but she was gone. Apparently, she wanted nothing to do with the big man.

"Thank you," Barabbas said. "I'd be dead now if you hadn't come along."

"You should get indoors," the man said. "There are more of these things."

Barabbas said, "I know. I'm the reason they're here. And getting inside won't help. These aren't the kind of vampires that need an invitation to enter a house."

The man turned cold blue eyes on Barabbas. "What do you mean you're the reason they're here?"

"I can't stop to explain now. I think a friend is in danger from the vampires. Come with me, and I'll tell you everything."

"Lead on. I'll follow."

"Thank you. I'm Barabbas Caulkin. Do you mind telling me who you are?"

"I'm Kharrn," the man said, as if that explained everything.

Barabbas hurried along the path. He could see the lights of the cottage now. The front door looked normal. Maybe his premonition was groundless, and Eddie was all right.

He reached the door and went through, with Kharrn close behind. The cottage's foyer wasn't as grand as that of Caulkin house. Barabbas turned to his left and entered a small parlor.

Eddie Lucas lay face-up on the floor. His skin was white the way milk was white, and there was a wound in his throat near his jugular.

Barabbas groaned and knelt beside Eddie. He knew there was no point in checking his pulse, but he did it anyway. Eddie was dead.

"Your friend?" Kharrn said.

"Yes. I'm too late."

"Move away from him. I need to cut off his head, so he doesn't turn."

"I know," Barabbas said. "God help me, I know."

"I'll drag him outside if you want."

Barabbas shook his head. "Just do it."

He turned as Kharrn raised the ax. He knew there was no choice, but he didn't have to watch. He heard the ax blade strike into the floor.

"I'll get something to cover him," Barabbas said. "I'll have to figure out what to do with the body if I survive this."

Kharrn said, "Hurry. I need you to tell me what's going on here and what you have to do with it."

Barabbas went to the Eddie's bedroom and brought back a sheet, which he used to cover the body. Eddie had been the one who had unknowingly released him back into the world. Eddie had begun as a servant and thrall but had somehow become a friend.

Once he had completed his grim task, Barabbas turned back to Kharrn. "I've no idea who you are, or what you're doing here."

"For now, all you need to know is I came here to stop the vampires."

Barabbas gave a short nod. "Here's what I can tell you then. Up until three years ago, I was a vampire myself."

Kharrn raised an eyebrow. "You were cured?"

"Mostly. It turned out the thing that had made me a vampire had a scientific explanation, even if it manifested in what seemed to be a supernatural way. There was an enzyme in my blood, something I received from the vampire that turned me, and a doctor named Lydia Kaufmann developed a sort of anti-venom serum that neutralized the enzyme."

"Then you could cure the others."

"Perhaps. Lydia said I might be an isolated case. And the process took many months, and I must take the serum daily or I'll revert. But here's what matters now. I was turned in 1856 and went on something of a rampage. But unlike some other vampires, I retained enough of my personality to regret what I had done. I managed to kill all the others I had turned, and then had my brother seal me up in the family crypt. I was there for over a century."

Kharrn said, "Were you aware all of that time?"

"No. Thankfully, for most of it, I was in a sort of dormant state. Then in 1968, Eddie Lucas was doing some work on the Caulkin family crypt. He realized one of the walls was hollow and released me by accident.

"I went on a killing spree, famished from my long years of hunger. I killed many men and women before Lydia managed to help me."

"And this time you didn't keep them all from turning."

Barabbas shook his head. "Once my mind was clear, I hunted down as many as I could, but some escaped. And now they've come back, and they plan to kill all my friends and family in revenge. I can't really blame them. I deserve it."

"You do, but your family doesn't. You suspected they would come after your friend, Eddie. Do you have any idea who they might seek out next?"

"Possibly Lydia Kaufmann. She lives alone too. But she lives in town, so they might wait to go after her."

Kharrn said, "You should go back to the main house. Any members of your family are in danger."

"Will you come with me?"

"I will."

They left the cottage, and Eddie's body, and Barabbas was seized by the feeling that he wouldn't be coming back here, one way or another. He noted, as they followed the path, that Kharrn was alert for any other attackers. He seemed very comfortable in the role of warrior and held his ax loosely in his hands.

"Kharrn", Barabbas said. "Your ax cut those vampires down as if they were human beings. Can you tell me how that's possible? Vampires are almost invincible at night."

Kharrn said, "The ax has special properties. It can kill most supernatural beings."

"Where did it come from?"

"It was created by a goddess named Samra thousands of years ago in a time lost age."

"And how did you acquire it, then?"

"You ask a lot of questions. The goddess made the ax for me. It was part of a bargain I made with her."

Barabbas didn't know if the man were mad or just delusional. Still, he had seen so many strange things, perhaps Kharrn was telling the truth. "But that would mean you're as old as the ax."

Kharrn grinned. "Yes, you've lived barely a century. I've lived for twelve thousand years. In that time, I've killed many vampires. And worse things."

Barabbas didn't want to imagine worse things. When they reached the top of the path and came out of the woods, Barabbas saw the doors to Caukin House hung open. He said, "Oh God," and hurried toward the house.

Kharrn caught him by the shoulder. "Careful. They may be waiting inside."

Kharrn took the lead and went into the foyer, scanning his surroundings. Nothing moved. Barabbas followed the big man in, and they went into the drawing room. Two chairs and a coffee table were overturned. Broken bits of one of Elspeth's favorite vases were scattered across the carpet. There were no people in sight.

"It looks as if the vampires have abducted your family," Kharrn said.

Barabbas said, 'But why? Why didn't they just kill them and leave them like they did with Eddie?"

The quiet of the room was broken by the jangling of the telephone on a cabinet near one wall. Barabbas and Kharrn both turned and looked at the ringing instrument.

"Better answer it," said Kharrn.

Barabbas crossed the to the phone and picked up the receiver. A voice said, "You know who this is?"

"Yes," said Barabbas. It was the woman the white-haired vampire had called Celia.

"Come to the Caulkin chapel. Alone. Tell the big man if we see him, we'll kill your family."

"You'll kill them anyway," Barabbas said.

"You'll have to do as I say to find out."

Barabbas hung up the phone and told Kharrn what Celia had said. "There's an old chapel on the estate, about half a mile from here. That's where they're holding Elspeth and the others. I have to go."

Kharrn nodded. "You're right. They'll kill them anyway."

"Why do you think they took them, rather than killing them outright?"

"They're running out of time. It will be morning in a few hours. They wanted to make sure they got another chance at you without me being in the way. Once the sun's up, you could leave town or try and hunt them down. They all came here for you, but they have to sleep somewhere in the daytime."

"There's a crypt under the chapel," Barabbas said. "They could all be resting there. I must go now, Kharrn. Promise me you won't come after me."

"I'll do as they said," Kharrn said. "Though it rankles me."

"Thank you for all you've done. I doubt we'll meet again."

Kharrn nodded, and Barabbas turned and went out into the waning night. The Caulkin estate has several other buildings and houses. The chapel was actually a small church, but it had been deconsecrated years ago, which made it a perfect place for vampires.

As Barabbas approached the chapel, he could see flickering lights through the stained-glass windows. The light would be for his benefit. The vampires didn't need it, but he was sure they wanted him to see whatever they had planned.

Barabbas went through the front doors without hesitating. There was no point in delaying his fate. Once inside, he could see the light came from two small bonfires set on the old cracked, stone floor. The chapel was mostly empty of furniture, with only a few broken pews still in place.

At least a dozen figures were gathered just beyond the fire. Behind them, Robert, Marilyn, and Elspeth were huddled on the floor near what was left of a pulpit.

Celia smiled when she saw Barabbas. “You did as you were told, I see. I have two scouts outside and the big man didn’t follow you. Who is he, by the way?”

“I don’t know. He just showed up. I’ve never seen him before.”

Celia shrugged. “It doesn’t matter. You’re here now and we can end this.”

Barabbas said, “Please let them go. They’ve done nothing to you.”

“You’re right. They’re completely innocent. And so was I when you killed me. Do you know why I chose this spot to bring your family, Barabbas?”

“I’ve no way of knowing that.”

Celia said, “I’ll be glad to tell you. The night you came out of the dark and killed me, I was a week away from taking my final vows to become a nun. Do you know what you did to me? You destroyed my life. You made me abhorrent in the eyes of my god.”

“Believe me, I am so sorry for what I did. Kill me if you will. I don’t argue that I deserve it.”

“You deserve that and far more. Before I take your life, you’re going to see your family die first. And don’t think I’ve forgotten Derek Caulkin. He wasn’t home when we took the others, but we’ll find him and put an end to the Caulkin line.”

Barabbas felt the first twinge of what he had waited for. But he needed more time. He had to stall a little longer. "There's no need for this. You can just kill me and go. Please…"

"Enough of your pleading." Celia swept her arm toward the three people on the floor. "Kill them now. And make sure they suffer."

The other vampires began to move forward, closing a circle of death and terror around the Caulkin family. They were halted when something smashed through one of the stained-glass windows. A round object bounced across the floor and landed almost at Celia's feet. Barabbas could see now that it was a human head. No, not quite human, because the open mouth showed long, sharp, canines.

A moment later, the chapel doors banged open, and a giant figure loomed in the doorway. Kharrn stepped into the sanctuary, firelight reflecting from his cold blue eyes and from the blades of the great ax he held in one hand. In his other hand he carried the head of the second vampire scout. He swung the head by its hair and tossed it so that it rolled along the floor like some obscene bowling ball.

Celia pointed toward Kharrn. "Kill him! All of you. The others can wait."

The vampires started toward Kharrn, but Barabbas noted they didn't move with the certainty one might have expected. The giant man had already destroyed four of their number. Still, they outnumbered Kharrn ten to one.

In contrast, Kharrn didn't hesitate. He rushed into the midst of the vampires, swinging the great ax. The vampires were fast, but bunched together, they initially offered easy targets. Kharrn split one of the creatures from shoulder to waist, and his backswing took another's head.

A tall vampire with lank dark hair managed to get his arms around the big man in an attempt to restrain him. Kharrn rotated the ax in his hand as a smaller man might wield a hatchet and crushed the tall vampire's skull. But the attack had slowed Kharrn's forward momentum, and now the other vampires were grasping at his clothes and limbs.

The big man was incredibly savage, but the vampires, though not as powerful as the legends said, were still much stronger than normal humans. They pressed in around him, hampering his movements. Kharrn decapitated one more of the group before the others pulled him down.

But the change had come. Barabbas felt a sharp pain in his abdomen, and then a feeling of heat spread through his body. He had forgotten what it felt like not to be human. His senses became sharper and power flowed through him.

With a snarl, he rushed forward into the throng of vampires and began grabbing them and pulling them away from Kharrn. His hands became claws, and he tore out one the vampire's throats.

The vampires began stumbling away, confused and dismayed by Barabbas' sudden attack. Kharrn rolled to his feet and caught up his ax. He cut through two more of the vampires before they could get clear. The remaining half dozen grouped together and stood facing Barabbas and Kharrn.

Celia came running toward the group and stopped in front of Barabbas. "You've reverted."

Barabbas bared his sharp teeth. "Yes. I am no longer helpless."

He could see the fear in the woman's eyes. "Your power over me hasn't returned. You're not my master."

"No, I lost that power when I became human. I can't control any of you. But I can destroy you."

"Do you think you can? You're still outnumbered."

Barabbas gave a harsh laugh. He gestured toward Kharrn. "You've seen what this man can do. And I am far older than any of you. I can do things you can't imagine."

The vampire called Celia howled in rage as she lunged for Barabbas. She seemed to move in slow motion to him now. He caught her by the throat and held her at arm's length. She clawed at his arm and he hurled her away. She slammed into one of the walls but scrambled quickly to her feet.

"You were going to kill my family," Barabbas said. He stalked across the room toward Celia. Two of the other vampires tried to get in his way but he swatted them aside. Before they could recover, Kharrn was upon them and the ax did its deadly work.

Barabbas reached Celia. She glared at him. "Do it. You killed me once. Kill me for a final time. Even if I didn't manage to kill your family, somehow

I made you one of us again."

Barabbas bared his fangs and reached out with both hands. His claws tore into Celia's throat and he ripped her head from her body. He had done it without thinking. After almost four years of trying to live a normal life he had reverted to an animal in a matter of minutes.

He whirled around to see that Kharrn had finished the other vampires. The floor of the chapel was strewn with the crumbling bodies of the undead. The big man was making sure none of them would come back by cutting off every head.

Barabbas looked toward the back of the chapel where Elspeth, Robert, and Marilyn still cowered against one wall. They were looking at him now, the way they had looked at Celia and the other vampires. Barabbas wanted to speak to them. To explain.

But he didn't. Instead, he turned and went out the doors into what was left of the night. His family was safe. And they were lost to him.

"Barabbas!" Kharrn called.

Barabbas looked back and saw the big man was following him. "Are you going to kill me now, too, Kharrn?"

Kharrn said, "Do you want me to?"

It wasn't the answer Barabbas had expected. "I don't know. I truly don't."

Kharrn said, "Can you be cured again?"

Barabbas said. "Perhaps. Perhaps not. Lydia warned me not to miss even one night of taking the serum. She said if I reverted, it might not work again."

"You didn't take it tonight on purpose," said Kharrn.

"No, I knew my one hope of escaping what Celia and her follower planned for me was to become what I was. But now I've seen the damage I've caused in so many lives, I don't know what to do."

Kharrn lifted the ax. "If you want, I can end it quickly for you. But that's up to you."

"You'd let me go? Didn't your goddess send you here to destroy the vampires."

Kharrn said, "If you're willing to try and be cured again, I'm willing to let you."

Barabbas felt a familiar sensation on his skin. It would be dawn soon. He needed to find somewhere to sleep. He still had a coffin in the basement of the cottage.

"I don't know what to do, Kharrn, but I don't want you to kill me. Perhaps I'll just walk down to the beach and watch the sun rise. That would end things."

Kharrn nodded. "If that's what you want, I'll stay with you until the end. You repaid any dept you owed me for your life when you pulled those vampires off me. They might have killed me."

Barabbas wasn't sure about that. Kharrn's shirt had been shredded in the fight. He noticed that all the bites, cuts, and gouges on Kharrn's torso were gone. Somehow the big man healed at an amazing rate. Maybe his wild stories were true.

Barabbas said, "Let's walk back toward the cottage. The beach lies in the same direction. I can choose to be or not to be before the sun comes up."

Kharrn said nothing. He slung his ax over one shoulder and fell into step beside Barabbas as he walked toward whatever fate awaited. ♜

# A FUNNY THING HAPPENED ON THE WAY TO THE WAR

*By Bryan Young*

"NURSE," CRIED HAVOC, "IRRIGATE THIS. And hand me that clamp."

"Yes, Captain," she said, doing exactly as she was asked.

"Oh, would you look at that? We found it." With the clamps, Havoc pulled out the piece of shrapnel and it offered a satisfying ding when it hit the metal collection bowl and rolled to a stop. "I think that's the last one."

Havoc was about to ask the nurse to close up, but he was already halfway done with it before he thought about it. The curse of gifted hands. Often, they worked on autopilot. And this kid was going to live, and that's what mattered.

"Ok, bring in the next patient," he said.

But as the nurses worked to move his patient to post-op, the company clerk came in. From behind his big round glasses, he announced, "That's the last one. No more choppers for now."

Relief hit Havoc and he wiped the sweat from his brow with his forearm and went to the locker room where he could take off his smock and mask, wash his face and breathe easy for a minute. The colonel joined Havoc to do the same, as did Chap, Havoc's friend and the second-best surgeon in the camp. He was British and loud, and everyone liked him. He was everybody's chap.

"That was a helluva run, eh, fellas?" Chap said.

"Same as always," the Colonel said. "I think they're even finding new ways to send them in hurt."

Havoc shook his head. "The only thing they're getting better at is helping them lie on their intake forms. Kid I saved today, I swear to God he wasn't more than sixteen."

Chap let out a disgusted sigh. "Well, if there's anything in the world that stays the same throughout history, it's sending babies to war."

"Police action," Havoc said, correcting him.

"Ah, yes. Police action. Can't forget that."

"Will you two knock it off," the colonel spat. "I've been in every war since the great one and there have always been kids that shouldn't have been there. It's as American as apple pie and the amber waves of grain. You catch 'em, you send 'em home. It's the best we can do from here. I promise, the Army won't miss the meat in the grinder. There's plenty where that came from."

"Ah, America," Havoc said. "Home of the free, land of the forgotten veterans."

"You two are the absolute worst, and I swear you'll both rot in hell," came a voice through the curtain. Francis Smithers.

A passable surgeon, but an insufferable buffoon.

"Better to reign in hell than serve in heaven," Havoc said. "Besides, Francis, at least we know how to have fun."

"Fun is all I'm plannin' on 'avin'," Chap said, smiling wide until he broke into a laugh at the expense of Francis.

Havoc joined in and they laughed until Francis turned red.

"You'll see. It'll catch up with you. Both of you. You'll see."

"When it does, I'll offer it a cigar and my hearty congratulations. But in the meantime, I really need to get some strong drink and shuteye." And without another word, Havoc fled to his bunk at the Fox Den. Stripping to his skivvies in the Korean heat and unwinding with a nip of homemade hooch was the right prescription for any ailment. Chap followed like a lost puppy looking for a water bowl.

"You want a martini?" Havoc asked him.

"Boy, do I," Chap said, crowding the still and collecting an empty glass.

They weren't really martinis, but because they were served in martini glasses, they were called martinis. There was something of a placebo effect in place. Moonshine, if presented in a martini glass and with an olive, could almost taste like a martini.

Like everything in the mobile surgical hospital, it was an acquired taste.

Havoc poured Chap's martini, handed him the glass, and drank down his own. Both of them collapsed on their bunks, keeping their drinks upright like the professionals they were. Their hands had to be steady for surgery, sure, but they had to be even steadier for handling beverages.

"Let's have a toast," Chap said, raising his glass from the comfort of their cot.

Havoc raised his glass to join. "Let's have it then."

"Here's to getting out of here, one way or the other."

"Hear, hear!"

And they both drank to that until they passed out.

# # #

Morning came and the only thing it left Havoc with was a hangover and the sweat from the night's heat. The sleep was neither restful nor deep. It just was, which was about as much as he could expect in the middle of a war zone.

He didn't open his eyes at first, but the red tint through his eyelids told him that the sun had risen, gray as though the day might be. The last thing he wanted was to rush getting up. Getting up meant standing up. It meant getting dressed and putting on boots. Sure, he'd walk around in a bathrobe for a while, but being awake also meant more casualties and the last thing Havoc wanted to see were more of those.

Didn't the brass in charge of the war understand that the last thing he wanted to do was deal with dead kids?

Why did anyone want to deal with dead kids?

A bugle went off somewhere, and Havoc had to admit that as bad as the bugle was, that sound was more welcome than the sound of choppers. Choppers meant blood and the only blood he wanted to see was the figurative kind in a Bloody Mary.

"That sounds divine, don't you think, Chap? Why don't we find some tomato juice and make some Bloody Marys?"

But Chap didn't respond.

The louse was probably still asleep.

How he could sleep in the bugling was anyone's guess. Chap was a notoriously heavy sleeper, and it would take a bugle literally aimed three inches from his face to get him to respond to it. How he made it in this man's army with the ability to sleep through Reveille was a shock.

But he was a doctor, not a soldier. Who could blame him?

"Hey, Chap. I said what about some Bloody Marys?"

Chap still made no response.

Havoc rolled over and tried opening his eyes. His vision blurred, but slowly got into focus. The red all over Chap seemed wrong. "Why do you have my bath robe?"

But as the image got more and more clear, Havoc realized that it wasn't his bathrobe on Chap or his cot.

It was blood.

Adrenaline jolted Havoc awake. He sat upright in a flash and did his best to get a better look at the situation. "Chap?"

But Chap wouldn't respond. Couldn't respond.

From the looks of it, his throat had been cut. Sliced from ear to ear.

Instinct kicked in and Havoc's innate sense of invincibility, his utter desire to save anyone and everyone, no matter how dire the wound kicked in. He covered the distance across the Fox Den and his hands immediately went to work, doing what they could do in order to save Chap's life.

But the blood was cold.

And there was a quiet serenity on Chap's face. Almost like a smile, but sadder. More somber. He'd escaped.

He had a ticket home.

Just not to the right one.

Havoc's hands went to work, doing what they could to cover the wound, hold it down, put pressure on it. "You can't do this, Chap."

But Chap didn't know any better.

Havoc looked around for any sign of the knife that was used and wondered if this was something Chap had done himself. Things were rough in Korea, there was no denying that.

And there was no way Chap did this to himself.

Havoc looked around for any tools in arm's length that would help him fix his friend and patch him up and breathe life back into him, but the only thing close by was the still.

"Help! Somebody help me!" he screamed.

There was nothing he could do on his own and he knew it.

Chap's blood covered his hands, and his vision grew blurry again, not from exhaustion this time, but from tears.

"Somebody help me!"

# # #

They had a small memorial for Chap. The Colonel organized it and said a few stirring words that broke everyone's heart. The only person not there was the clerk, assigned to figure out who the hell was responsible for Chap's death. It seemed like a job for someone of more import, but they were in a war. They had to make do.

Predictably, the memorial was interrupted by the whirring blades of a chopper.

All assembled scrambled.

But before Havoc could, the Colonel stopped him. "You okay, son?"

"Do I have a choice?"

"No, but I'll tell you this now, there's no shame in grief. I understand Chap was your best friend. And I understand his loss is great. And it's made worse not knowing what happened to him for sure. But if you need to take the time to get yourself right, Emerson and I can handle the OR for a while. I'll have the clerk call in a sub until we can get Chap's replacement. You just need to say the word."

"No, I'll be fine, Colonel. I think I just need to get my hands dirty in there and save someone for a change."

"I understand. If you change your mind, I'll understand that, too."

"Thanks, Colonel."

"Don't mention it. Let's just get in there and do some good. In Chap's memory."

"Yes, sir," Havoc said quietly.

Havoc spent the next nine hours in the OR, keeping his mouth uncharacteristically shut. He didn't have anything witty to say. All he could do was focus on the work, pulling out shards of metal from the intestines of kids. One had a bullet that needed removing and his intestines resected in four places. Another kid came in with a head wound and a mostly torn-off arm. Another needed a foot amputated. It was a meat grinder, but none of it got to him more than the haunted images of Chap's throat being slit.

This sort of thing shouldn't have happened to anyone, but that it happened to Chap was the travesty.

"You did good in there, given the circumstances, Havoc."

That was the Colonel's voice behind Havoc.

He had barely realized that he'd already taken off his scrubs and his mask. He wore the olive undershirt and green pants that felt like his usual lackadaisical uniform. He just needed his bathrobe and maybe he'd feel comfortable again, even if it were a little warm for the bathrobe. Something about it made him feel like he was home. Which was absurd, he was in the middle of a war, but the fuzzy terry robe helped.

"Thanks, Colonel."

"I want you to get some shuteye. You've had a long day. And we'll work on figuring out what happened to Chap. I don't want you to worry about it at all. And that's an order."

The thought of going back to their shared space and sleeping right next to where Chap had his throat slit didn't sit right with Havoc. Sure, there were guards around and he presumed someone was on the lookout for the murderer, but he wouldn't be able to close his eyes without seeing the ribbons of red, falling into a pool on the ground. The Colonel had made sure that everything was cleaned up while they were working in the OR, but those images were like light tracers behind his eyes, burned there indelibly.

He'd never forget what he'd seen.

Which he found absurd. He couldn't remember half of the gore he'd seen in the OR.

"Is there somewhere else I could sleep, Colonel?"

The Colonel thought for a moment while he did the math and when he came up with the answer, he understood completely. "Oh, yes, of course. Why don't you take the VIP tent for now? And we'll give it a couple of days for the shock to wear off and for us to figure out what exactly happened and who's responsible."

"I appreciate that, sir."

"Now skee-daddle. Get your shut-eye while I get some work done."

"Yes, sir."

# # #

The VIP tent was quiet and haunting in a completely different way than his shared space with Chap would have been. It was designed for one person rather than three or four, so there was much more space. The noises of the place weren't the same either. The still didn't bubble in the corner. The inane chattering of the more pompous of the roommates was absent. The din of the mess tent came from a completely different direction. It was peculiar in every way imaginable.

Aside from the noise, the biggest difference was the dark privacy. The shared tent he and Chap had called home was more mosquito netting for walls that looked out onto the camp than anything. There was next to no privacy in the hot summer. Here, it was just thick canvas, a cloth oven that kept the sun at least out of sight during the day and the moonlight and the bustle of the camp hidden in the night.

Havoc nuzzled into the cot and tested the waters by closing his eyes. But that's when he saw Chap, throat slit and bleeding out, eyes dead.

He opened his eyes and shot upright, gasping for breath.

"Chap..." was all he said.

Eventually, he was able to get to sleep. Of course he couldn't help it. After so much trauma and such a long shift in the OR, sleep would take him by force if it had to. His body was exhausted and no matter how hot and traumatized and uncomfortable as he was, Havoc would have his rest.

But dreams were the problem.

He found himself there at the camp on his first day, lost and confused, without a friend in the world. And then he didn't have his clothes on either. Buck naked. He felt distinctly like he had no interest in being there and just wanted to make it home as fast as he could. But then the dream transitioned from mild discomfort to something far worse and more sinister. Suddenly, Havoc was on the run from something. Or someone. Pursuing him.

It was someone.

Definitely.

And there was something that told him, a flash of dream logic and intuition that told him it was Chap's killer hunting him. Knife drawn, the silent, secret killer followed Havoc across the camp. Past the showers and the latrine, through the OR, where Havoc sought refuge, and then, finally, into the mess tent.

In his dream, Havoc assumed the mess tent would be the best place to thwart the killer. No one in their right mind would go in there, and since you had to be sane to appear insane in the middle of a war, the killer wouldn't enter.

It didn't make a whole lot of sense, but Havoc had to admit it was a dream and the logic was as sound as anything else he came up with.

The sound of fabric tearing startled him. Like a strong pair of hands tearing an old shirt in half. But there was something else to the sound, too. Something menacing. A sharp edge. And it forced Havoc to turn in circles, wondering where it came from. But the mess tent stood empty. Not another soul could be seen. The stomach-turning scent of the food was the only thing to keep him company as he sought the source of the discomfort.

He turned in circles, but he could never quite find the thing that made him feel as though there were something–or someone–lurking just over his shoulder.

Then his chest tightened.

It got harder to breathe.

And Havoc found himself falling into the floor, descending into it like it were made of thick and viscous quicksand.

"No!" he screamed. Or tried to. Like a bad stereotype of a dream. Nothing came out.

The louder he tried to scream, the more his lungs burned.

But still no sound came.

Until he jolted.

Awake, things started to make more sense and less sense all at the same time. Rough hands were smothering him. Whose hands, he didn't know. The darkness was all-consuming except for a strip of light off to the side, a long tear rent in the tent admitted the light. Havoc spent what he assumed would be his last moments wondering if the sound he heard in his dreams had intruded from reality.

"You dirty son of a bitch!" a voice said, somewhere above Havoc. "You'll pay..."

Havoc brought his hands up trying to free his mouth and nose, hoping to free his breath, but it was so difficult. The hands were firm and strong and seemed intent to end him. Desperate, and with burning lungs, Havoc tried bringing a knee up into the groin of his attacker but found that he was trapped tight beneath the blanket. He tried punching around the arms suffocating him, but his own arms were as useless as bullets against a tank.

With time running out, Havoc knew he had to do something drastic.

He bit down on the hand covering his mouth. Hard.

There was a moment where Havoc didn't know if he'd been effective in his attack. Then the copper taste of blood filled his mouth, then a scream filled the air.

Maybe he'd been too disoriented to identify the voice, or maybe he'd gotten some more air, but the scream was unmistakable.

Francis.

The camp's right wing religious nut.

Francis pulled his hands from Havoc's face, which posed a problem. He had to take a deep breath, but that meant swallowing some of the blood inadvertently. As soon as he had enough breath, he spat the chunk of finger up at his attacker.

"What the hell are you doing, Francis?"

Francis contained his screaming and clutched his wounded hand, but that gave Havoc enough time to buck him from his perch, sending him tumbling to the floor. Havoc bolted upright and kicked the blanket from his legs, not wanting to be trapped again. Not with a lunatic on the loose trying to kill him.

When Havoc saw the still-bloody knife on the floor and the slashed tent canvas together, he realized that Francis was the source of his problems. "You killed Chap, didn't you? It wasn't enough to just be a feckless coward of a person, but you had to go and try to kill one of the best guys either of us will ever know? And Chap, too?"

Whether Francis was getting his pain under control or his adrenaline kicked in, Havoc couldn't tell, but he got up to his knees, grabbed his knife with his good hand, and stood.

"What are you going to do?" Havoc stood and raised his fists. "I'm not sleeping like Chap was. I'm not going to just let you do this without a fight."

Francis raised the knife and backed up a step. His left hand bled and bled, dripping crimson stains down the legs of his neatly pressed uniform and pooling on the ground besides. "You, both of you, you and your precious Chap, are exactly what's wrong."

"What's wrong? You don't see either of us sneaking around slitting people's throats. I mean, unless we're doing a cricothyrotomy, but then we're expected to be doing that."

"You're not just what's wrong with this man's Army, you're what's wrong with America and its very soul."

"What in the hell are you talking about?"

Francis stepped closer, pointing the blade right at Havoc's heart. His thin lips, suspicious like a ferret's, curled into a dark snarl. "You. The both of you. Always joking. Never taking anything seriously. The two of you talk like this war –like any war –is a bad thing. And that these brave soldiers are giving up their lives for nothing."

"Francis, what are you talking about? Of course they're giving up their lives for nothing. What does it matter to our way of life, or their way of life, if we control this bit of latitude or that bit of longitude? None of it makes any sense. Next thing you know, we won't just be fighting wars for alleged democracy, we'll be fighting it over resources. For oil, for land, for whatever space-age mineral we decide everything is worth next. None of it matters to how these boys live their lives. And now you want to kill me for seeing things the way they are? Are you insane?"

"No. I'm a patriot. And you're talking like a coward. If it's in the best interests of America, it's in the best interest of the world. And it's worth all the soldier's blood in the Army."

"So what, Francis? Even if that's true, what does it matter? You think you're going to kill people who don't agree with you one at a time?"

"Yes." Francis lunged with the knife.

Havoc jumped back but found himself tumbling over the cot and tearing right through the rip in the back of the canvas VIP tent. He rolled out, finding himself blinded by the harsh Korean sunlight. "Francis, you've gotta knock this off," Havoc yelled, hoping it was loud enough for someone to hear him and offer assistance.

Then he realized he should just yell for help. "Help!"

Turning over in the dirt and scrambling to his feet, Havoc leapt back away from the tent just fast enough to miss Francis stumbling out, knife first. "You all thought I was a joke. But I was the only real American in the bunch."

"Francis, you're insane, which I guess proves your point."

The deranged man lunged toward Havoc and Havoc dodged again. He remembered once being told that if you fight someone with a weapon, you need to understand that worst case scenario, you would be wounded by that weapon in some way during the fight. And Havoc had no interest in being cut open by anyone, least of all Francis Smithers.

"You're still making fun of me to the last, but I'll be the one who laughs last..."

Francis charged Havoc, knife pointed right for his heart.

With nowhere else to go, Havoc closed his eyes and braced for impact.

The knife pierced his stomach with a pain so sharp, Havoc couldn't feel it at first. He knew it was there, though, because he felt the wetness on his shirt. Hotter than sweat. He felt the blood run from his face. This was it.

When he opened his eyes, he saw Francis huddled around his middle, mid-tackle. His hands were obscured and so was the knife, and Havoc was grateful for that small favor. The last thing he wanted to see was a knife sticking out of him.

"Et tu, Brute," Havoc struggled to say. "I thought it would come in the back."

With what strength he had left, he punched down at Francis's exposed back and then shoved him backward. It was as though Francis didn't expect any retaliation, because he fell back like he'd fainted.

Havoc collapsed to the ground, clutching the open wound in his middle.

He blinked, wondering if this was it.

If this were the last thing he'd see and do.

If it was, he hoped they strung Francis up for it.

The guy was a fruit cake wrapped in an American flag.

A shadow appeared over Havoc. "Come to finish the job?"

But the voice that answered wasn't Francis. "You okay, son?"

"Colonel?" Havoc said weakly.

"I brought the MPs. We're going to take care of Smithers. You rest up. We're going to do what we can to that gut shot there."

Havoc lolled his head to the side and saw the MPs struggling with Francis, trying to get him to his feet with a minimum of blood on him.

And then, maybe it was the shock and loss of blood, but Havoc's world went black.

# # #

Havoc's eyes cracked open, and he wished he were having a nightmare.

His vision was blurry, and he could barely make out anything but the bright light.

"Don't worry, we'll get you together," came a voice.

"Get him down, we'll start the surgery," came another voice.

His head was a balloon, filling lightly with more and more air.

"Am I gonna be okay?" he muttered, though he wondered if anyone could hear him.

Someone placed a mask over his face, pumping in the sweet, pungent smell of anesthetic.

He felt severe pain in his middle and tried looking down to see it, but he couldn't quite focus.

"He's still awake," a voice said from somewhere above him.

There was panic in the words, but Havoc couldn't focus enough on why. He knew, though, that something was wrong.

Something wasn't right.

He was in the wrong place.

There must have been a mistake. He should have been the one doing the surgery. He didn't get wounded; he fixed the wounded.

But then the operating surgeon turned to regard him. That little white knit cap and mask obscured their identity and Havoc grew worried about their identity. "Don't worry, Havoc, we're going to fix you up real good," the doctor said.

"Who...?" Havoc muttered. "Who are you?"

The doctor pulled the mask from their face, which should have raised alarms in Havoc, but Havoc just shrugged. Or would have if he could feel his shoulders.

"We're going to make sure you're never a problem again." The doctor turned to the anesthetist. "Go ahead and crank it."

The doctor smiled.

And, as blackness took him for the last time, Havoc realized why he should be alarmed.

The doctor smiled the wide, petty smile of Francis Smithers.

And hummed the national anthem like a lullaby in a nightmare. ♜

# FEAR TO TREAD

*By Tony Jones*

*Fortune's Warehouse, Irvine, CA*

WHUMP. WHUMP.

Sacha felt the latest blows to her face more than she heard them. She'd moved beyond pain into a dull anguish. She'd stopped pulling on the ropes tying her to the chair after the first few punches, the only sounds the fists of Butler's goon striking her face. The goon paused.

Sacha lifted her head and tried to force her eyes open. Her left had clogged shut with blood. Her blood. Her right eye managed a squint through the aching, swollen flesh she used to call her eyelid. She spat blood in no particular direction, catching the goon's shirt. He punched her again.

This is playing hell with my makeup, she thought as she tried to glare at the blonde woman, Tammy, tied to the chair beside her.

'You're supposed to ask questions,' Tammy said to a well-dressed man in his late forties sat behind a desk across the room. Apart from the two women, the well-dressed man and the goon, another half-a-dozen pale men and women looked on bored, as the goon tore a strip from Sacha's bright yellow blouse and wiped the blood from his shirt.

'Maybe I like to see women getting hurt,' the well-dressed man said, rubbing a platinum signet-ring. 'Besides. Harvey here likes his meat tenderised.'

Tammy looked directly at him, as though willing him to say more. The man laughed.

'Don't worry, it'll be your turn soon. Then you'll both talk. Don't worry, I'll make sure I get my diamonds before I let my associates enjoy themselves with what's left of you. Besides… I had to cancel golf, so I need a little… entertainment.'

A door opened. Those stood nearest turned sharply, then relaxed as two men came in, pale as the others, dragging a third man between them. They stopped a few feet in front of the desk and let their burden drop to the floor.

'We found this in the plant room, Mr Butler,' one of them said.

'What was he doing?' the man behind the desk, Butler, asked.

'No idea, we hardly touched him before he was out cold.'

'No matter,' Butler said. He turned to face one of his women. 'Cindy. A little snack for you. Something to show our guests what's in store for them. Something to show how serious the situation is.'

The woman, Cindy, stood tall as Butler talked. She knelt beside the now semi-conscious man on the floor. She smiled.

'No, please no, what's happening?' the man screamed as Cindy smiled wider, revealing a pair of glistening fangs. Taking her time, she reached down to loosen the man's collar and reveal his neck…

# # #

*36 hours earlier, Chandler S Weston Investigators, Wilshire Boulevard, CA*

Tammy sat alone in the office. Glancing at the clock for the dozenth time in as many minutes, she saw it was almost 11 o'clock. Time for coffee. Sure enough, as soon as the smell of fresh coffee wafted across the room, the office door opened. In came Sacha.

Sacha shuffled rather than walked and slumped onto the nearest sofa. She took off her sunglasses to reveal bloodshot eyes, squinting against the light. She hugged herself as she called across to Tammy.

'Is that fresh coffee?'

Tammy poured a cup for herself.

'What happened to you? You look like Hell!' she asked.

'Ha, ha. Not funny. Be an angel, pour me a cup. And have you any Advil?'

Tammy took another cup, filled it, and took it across.

'Thanks.' Sacha took a sip. 'Heaven. What about the Advil?'

'We're out.'

'Any chance you can get some? My head is screaming. I'd go, but I gave the cabbie the last of my money.'

Tammy glared. 'I'm not your servant! Get your own medicine,' she said with a snap.

Sacha pouted. 'I'd do it for you if you were at death's door.'

'More like the door to the nearest bar. What was it last night? Scotch? Rum?'

Sacha winced. 'I think it was a little of both. Together. On ice. Well, until I ran out. Have you any idea how long it takes to make ice?'

Tammy turned her back and sat back down on her own sofa, making a performance out of not looking at her colleague.

Sacha hurled her cup across the room, a trail of dark stain spattering leather furniture and a fine Persian rug before the delicate china shattered on the wall behind the other woman.

Tammy carried on drinking and flicking through a newspaper.

'You could have caught that.'

'You shouldn't have thrown it!'

'You should have gone to the pharmacist!'

'You shouldn't get drunk for no reason every single night of the week!'

'I had a reason!'

As the two women argued, their voices grew louder and louder. They both stood and closed the gap between them, shouting into each other's faces from inches.

'I miss her too!'

'She was my friend as well.'

'If you had any emotions, you'd be upset!'

'I am upset!'

They were shouting over one another. It was all but impossible to tell who was speaking at any one time.

'LADIES!'

A stern voice rang out from one side of the room. It boomed. It rattled pictures, shook ornaments, and set the remaining coffee vibrating in the jug. A smell of sulphur filled the air, and a wave of unnatural heat ruffled the women's hair and clothes. As one, they turned.

There stood a portly figure, with horns, forked tail, blood red leathery skin, glowing red eyes and pointed ears. He was eight inches tall.

The two women bowed their heads.

'Sorry, Malthus,' they said together.

'I should think so,' the demon said. 'We all miss Nana, but she's in a better place now. Or so they say. I think it's overrated.'

'Malthus,' Tammy interrupted.

The demon glared.

'I was talking.' This he said in a slow, measured tone in some ways more disturbing than his previous gargantuan bellows.

Tammy pointed at herself and pulled her tight-fitting blouse forward for a moment. 'You're not dressed,' she said in a loud whisper.

Sacha giggled, then winced again before rubbing her temples.

Malthus clicked his fingers. His diminutive demon form was replaced with the figure of a man in his early forties, thinning dark hair cut smartly over his normal human ears, blue-grey eyes. around five and a half feet tall, and a good fifteen or twenty pounds too heavy. He wore a well-tailored dark-grey suit, crisp white shirt, and country club tie.

He glanced around. The coffee stains had vanished, the broken cup stood back on the side by the now re-filled jug.

'I think coffees all round,' he said. 'How's your head, Sacha?'

'Does it matter?' she answered with a question. 'I'm done here. The team's gone. We were three. Three angels. Now Nana's gone, we might as well give up.'

'Did Nana give up?' Malthus asked. 'She earned her penance, you can too. Or would you rather come back with me and help out? Hell's overflowing with sinners, and if you can't pull yourself together to stop the flow from here, come where you can be more use.'

Sacha went and slumped in her chair, but not so as to spill any coffee.

A chime rang out. Sacha and Tammy bowed their heads, while Malthus scowled.

'We have a case,' an unearthly voice said from all around. 'And before either of you says anything, I know you are only two and the *Covenant* calls for three to fight the good fight.'

There was a pause.

'Have faith.'

Malthus drummed his fingers.

'Malthus,' the voice said. 'I need you to find out everything you can about Don Butler, business owner of this district.'

The demon nodded.

'You ladies need to look into something more immediately pressing. I'll give you the address…'

# # #

*Two hours later, Happy Lion Chinese Restaurant, Downtown LA*

Sacha and Tammy were used to blending in and getting into where they wanted, but the *Happy Lion* was proving an unusually difficult proposition. Police had the front of the building cordoned off, and uniformed officers were taking care to check everyone coming and going. From outside they could tell something had happened on the upper floor, not visible from street level.

'We should fly up and look,' Sacha said.

Tammy turned to her partner and scowled.

'Broad daylight. Wings. How's that going to go down? Shall I call the press first? Give me ten minutes, I'll arrange for a TV crew.'

'What's your idea?'

'We could be insurance investigators, maybe medics?'

'I left my ambulance at home,' Sacha said without looking at Tammy. For a moment Tammy thought she was being serious.'

'Maybe we'll have more luck from the back of the restaurant?' Sacha suggested. Without waiting for an answer, she headed for the 24-hour store next door. Tammy followed. The storekeeper tried to stop them from going through his shop, until Tammy touched his temple for a moment, leaving him in a daze.

'You must teach me that sometime,' Sacha said.

They let themselves out into a deserted alley and listened. There was some activity from the restaurant, but no sign of police.

'Looks like we're clear,' Tammy said.

'Hold on,' Sacha answered, placing a hand on Tammy's shoulder.

A man had entered the alley from the far end. He was too smartly dressed to be a down and out, with dark trousers and a matching dark coat. His face was hard to make out under a dark hat, possibly a fedora, and he moved with purpose in their direction. He paused as he saw them, then carried on.

Tammy and Sacha started a conversation about work and their boss, all the while not looking at the approaching man.

Moments later he'd let himself into the backdoor of the restaurant. Tammy pointed at her wristwatch, raising two fingers. Sacha nodded. Two minutes later they followed the man inside.

They were in a corridor leading to the kitchen. To the side a door led to a storeroom, and through the open door they could see several bodies lying on the ground. Even from ten feet away, both women felt something *wrong* about the dead. They'd seen more corpses than they could count, but these were not normal.

Moving up to the room door, they saw the man leaning over one of the bodies. He was muttering something and holding an object over the corpse.

Tammy rushed in.

'What do you think you're doing?' she shouted at him.

The man carried on muttering and finally waved his hand over the body before standing. Tammy recognised the object the man was holding. A cross. He was in his late twenties, with dark eyes, fair hair, and a dog-collar.

By this time Sacha had entered.

'What's a priest doing at a crime scene blessing the dead?' she asked. 'Don't you have to wait until the funeral or something? I guess times are hard.'

'Don't move!' a woman said from behind. 'Hands where I can see them and turn around slowly.'

Tammy and Sacha turned to see a young woman, early twenties, with red hair, wearing a police uniform.

'I could ask you two the same question,' the woman said.

'I'm Tammy, this is Sacha.'

'Officer Eva Lynch.' Eva waved at the man. 'Carry on Peter.'

The priest nodded and carried on blessing the dead. Sacha looked at Eva, the priest, and the bodies. She knew what was wrong now. The question was, how did this officer Lynch and the priest know to be involved? She reached with her mind and felt the connection between the two humans.

'So,' Sacha said, lowering her hands. 'How come your brother is blessing bodies at a crime scene?'

Tasha raised an eyebrow as Lynch's gun wavered. Tasha lowered her arms at the same time as Lynch lowered her weapon.

'How did you know?' asked Lynch.

'Easy enough,' Sacha answered. 'We're private investigators. We're working a case and suddenly there's a restaurant full of bodies and priest blessing them. You called him Peter, not Father something. You must know him and you've the same eyes, even if the hair's different.'

As Sacha spoke, Lynch nodded.

'I'm guessing you called your brother to bless the bodies told him to sneak in the back of the restaurant while you offered to keep watch. Good planning.'

The young police officer looked at Sacha and Tammy.

'I don't suppose you'd like to tell me what you're working on?' she asked. 'Or why you aren't surprised I'd ask a priest to bless the newly murdered?'

Tammy stepped forward. 'Live in LA long enough, you see plenty of crazy things. If they had killed me, I'd like someone to say a few words for me.'

'I may have only been on the force a couple of years,' Lynch said. 'But I've seen things. This city's going crazy, and not the usual stuff. I've seen cults, magic ceremonies, people claiming to have seen the dead walk. This felt wrong.'

Now it was Tammy's turn to nod. 'Why don't you forget you've seen us,' she said, 'and we won't mention your brother to anybody.'

The red-headed woman took a few seconds to consider her brother, the bodies, Tammy, and Sacha. 'OK,' she said.

Tammy and Sacha took one last look round the storeroom and left. Lynch watched them as they did, making sure they didn't wander off.

# # #

*Three hours later, Ocean Vista Spa, Santa Monica, CA*

Tammy and Sacha lay on massage tables, dressed only in white towels. Classical music was playing softly from speakers near the ceiling, and the white marble floored room was lit by a vast array of scented candles scattered in alcoves around the walls.

'Why are we here, exactly?' Sacha asked.

Tammy answered without opening her eyes or moving her body.

'I thought you could use a massage and a detox. Besides, the person we need to meet isn't due for a while. I checked with reception.'

Sacha raised herself on her elbows, careful to make sure the towel stayed where intended. On a side table sat a jug of fruit juice and ice. She poured a glassful and drank.

'This could really do with some vodka,' she said.

'You saw those bodies,' Tammy said, a statement rather than a question.

'Yes,' Sacha answered, finishing her drink than lying back down. 'All Chinese, likely all from the restaurant, so where were the other side? No signs of bullet wounds, just those expressions and the discolouration round the eyes.'

'You can say it.'

'Looks like vampires to me, or at least a vampire. Even that cop knew something was wrong, without the movie style neck bites. Shame crosses and garlic don't help, never mind sunlight.'

'Agreed. They can even hurt us, particular in this form. That's why we're here. This is where Sophia Caroni comes for her regular spa session.'

'And she is?' asked Sacha.

'A witch.'

'Whose side?'

'Whoever pays the most.' Tammy answered.

'One of Malthus's.'

Tammy sighed. 'Does it matter? She's the nearest thing to an expert in the field. If there's a vampire in LA, she'll know about it.' She sat up. 'Come on, we're due.'

The only other person in the sauna was an overweight, middle-aged woman, wrapped in one of the spa's towels. She was ladling water onto hot coals and ignored them when they entered and sat on the wooden slatted bench.

'Just like home, I imagine,' Tammy said.

The woman paused for a second, then poured another generous load of water, generating a cloud of steam half-filling the room.

Tammy stood, moved to the coals, and extended her left arm. She drew her right hand slowly across, and it seemed the nail on her index finger was unusually long. She used it to trace a thin line along her forearm, from which dripped three vivid scarlet drops.

'I invoke the boon of Hecate,' she intoned. As her blood hit the coals, a sweet aroma filled the sauna. 'I require three questions be answered.'

Sophia Caroni spoke in a broad New Jersey drawl.

'You're the ones work for Malthus,' she said. 'I thought you'd be long gone by now, or did you want to know where would be safe?'

'What do you mean?' Tammy asked.

Sophia laughed, her bloated stomach threatening to dislodge her towel.

'I hear there's only two of you now. That means the *Covenant* is broken. Come the full moon…'

'Come the full moon what?' Tammy asked.

Sophia laughed again. Sacha moved closer. Her brow furrowed.

'Hell is overflowing. There's some don't like the idea of the *Covenant*; some think things should be done differently. Some think it's time for expansion, and they want to strike out.'

'You mean…' Tammy said.

'Wait,' Sacha shouted, grabbing Tammy's already healed arm. 'You've used two questions already!'

Tammy looked first at Sacha, then back to Sophia.

'No, that was conversation. I've not started yet.'

Sophia laughed. 'Your friend can count. Who'd have thought?! You've one question left. And the boon can only be granted once per day, so don't go cutting up any more of that oh-so-pure flesh of yours!'

Tammy thought hard. What question could she ask? She needed to know about the vampire and how Butler fitted into the picture. She had an idea…

# # #

*That evening, the Pacific Yacht Club, Newport Beach, CA*

Thirty or forty people in expensive suits, or even more expensive dresses, thronged the principal reception room and the balconies of the *Pacific Yacht Club*. Most of the men had found an excuse to be on or near the balcony ahead of the swimsuit event. To one side, Don Butler and a few others sat at a table with the best view as one by one, or in pairs, some dozen young women paraded on a small stage, each dressed (if that were the word) in a small bikini or other, barely concealing, item of swimwear.

'Do we really have to do this?' Sacha asked. 'These outfits don't exactly leave much to the imagination, and I've had four propositions already. I wouldn't mind, but they all looked older than Malthus.'

'You heard the witch. Besides, Malthus is sure there's a connection between Butler and the restaurant, so that means it involves the vampire. It may even be here.'

'I still don't know what she meant. All she really said was we should *follow suit*. What does that mean?'

Tammy shrugged, attracting the attention of one of the younger men in the audience as her bikini top threatened to snap open.

'It's the best I could do. The more convoluted the question, the vaguer the answer. There's lots of men in suits here, so — let's mingle.'

Sacha smiled a fake smile as the music changed, and it was her turn to take the stage. She focused on the music, dismal disco covers played by the house band and in the wrong time. As soon as it was over, she made a point of grabbing a drink from one of the equally barely dressed women carrying trays of drinks. She was about to drink when she saw who was carrying them.

'You!'

It was the police officer from earlier. She couldn't remember her name, only the red hair. Whoever had made her wear a polka dot sunshine yellow on a sky-blue swimsuit clearly had no taste.

Sacha concentrated and placed a palm on the woman's forehead for a moment. She'd known Tammy's trick would come in useful, just not how soon she'd get to try it.

'Meet me in five minutes in the ballroom.'

She didn't wait for an answer. Five minutes later, Tammy and she were waiting by the ballroom entrance, talking to a man in his twenties in a blazer wearing a crested tie. As they noticed the police officer (whose name Tammy had remembered, Lynch) arrive, they made their excuses.

'Maybe later,' Sacha said to the young man, then blew him a kiss as the three women went to a corner of the room, Lynch following the other two with a frown, looking round the room, then at the other two.

'How did I… weren't we just talking next door?' Lynch asked.

'We were, now we're here,' Sacha answered. 'More important, why are *you* here?'

'I could ask you the same.' Lynch paused. 'The Department are investigating the guy hosting this event.'

'Donald Butler?' Tammy asked.

'Yes. Though he likes to be called Don. We think he feels it makes him more *mafia*.'

'I didn't realise you were a detective,' Sacha said.

Lynch flushed. 'I'm not. And no sign I ever will be. Have you any idea what it's like being a woman in the police? Endless requests for coffee, suggestions I take traffic control as a career choice. Then there's the *other* requests. And most of those are from married guys as well.'

Sacha and Tammy glanced at each other, each giving a wry smile.

'We can believe it,' Sacha said. 'It's the same all over this world; and the next.'

Lynch frowned. 'What about you?' she asked.

'As we said, we're investigators, looking into the restaurant, and some connected crimes. One of our informers pointed us toward this party.'

Lynch looked round, lowered her voice before moving closer in.

'Butler's been investigated for years. He's half of City Hall in his pocket. He runs clubs, strip joints, handles narcotics, and now he's branching out into diamonds. I heard Butler does after-parties — invites a few friends to his villa next to the yacht club for poker and brings girls back to keep them company. I thought I'd blend in, look around his villa and see what I can find.'

Tammy nodded. 'Good thinking. Similar to our plan. Why don't we divide and conquer?'

# # #

Two hours later the party had moved to the Butler villa. As officer Lynch had said, getting there was easy enough, as long as being leered at by Butler and his cronies counted as easy….

For the first hour, they relegated all the women to fetching drinks or standing meekly behind various poker players. Conversation among the men was limited to money, golf, or cars; they expected the women to keep quiet and smile. Tammy was sure Hell itself couldn't be much worse than this. As for the men, it was all about power. People who lost to Butler he invited to play golf; those foolish enough to win a hand got side-lined in conversation and given the cold shoulder. Tammy wondered what other fate was in store for them.

Neither Sacha nor Tammy was impressed with the quality of play, but then they had certain advantages. Stakes were fairly high, and as the drinks went down, it was easy enough to slip away. Lynch was impatient to get on and made straight for the main staircase, while the other two followed on more casually so as not to draw attention.

'It's OK for you,' Sacha said. 'You didn't have Butler making sure you knew where his bedroom was *for later.*'

'I blame the bikini. Yours doesn't leave a lot to the imagination,' Tammy replied. 'Lynch is taking the top floor. You take the first and I'll see if I can find a study. Stay in touch.'

As she explored, Tammy found kitchens, a landscaped garden, a gym, pool house and more. There was no sign of an office, or anywhere else Butler might conduct business from. Her thoughts kept returning to the poker table. There was something she was missing.

Tammy felt a tingle at the corner of her mind. She lifted her head to stare in the general direction of her companion and thought of Sacha. *What is it?*

*I heard shouts from the top floor. I think Lynch is in trouble.*

Tammy walked briskly towards the staircase, until she was sure nobody could see, then she sprinted to the top floor. She rendezvoused with Sacha outside a closed door. From inside she heard muffled shouts and heard things being thrown. This was accompanied by a man's laughter.

Tammy nodded. Sacha kicked open the door and Tammy rushed in.

In the far corner, Lynch stood, one hand holding a rip in her polka dot swimsuit, the other a desk lamp. She had a nosebleed and a bruise appearing on her face. The room was a bedroom and at the end of the bed nearest the door stood Joey Butler, Don's son. He'd declined the poker tables and taken one of the other women to the swimming pool. Whatever had happened to her wasn't clear. For now, his desires were transparent.

Joey turned at their entry and snarled.

'What do you want? Who do you think you are? Do you know who I am?'

Sacha brushed past Tammy, smiling and running a finger along the top of her outfit. 'We thought we'd joining the party. A man like you has appetites.'

Joey smiled as Sacha stood barely inches from him, stared into his eyes, and raised her hands to his temples. Lynch looked on in surprise, which increased as Joey collapsed in Sacha's arms and she draped him on the bed.

'What did you do?' she asked.

Instead of answering, Tammy walked over to her and helped her arrange her outfit. 'We should get you out of here. You're in no state to carry on for now. Let's get you home.'

As Tammy walked the other woman to the doorway, she grabbed a towel from a side table. 'Put this over you,' she said. She grabbed a face cloth. 'Give me a second.' She wiped the woman's face and as she did, the bruising faded and the nosebleed stopped. Tammy turned back to Sacha.

'I'll take Lynch in our car. Why don't you find out about diamonds?'

Sacha raised an eyebrow, then turned her attention to the man on the bed…

# # #

*8:15 am the following day, S Hill Street, Downtown LA*

Tammy and Sacha watched from a nearby café as a pair of plain cars parked across the street, and a group of what looked to be all men in dark suits donned balaclavas and stormed into van Henke's Jewellers and Diamond Merchants (est. 1909). They continued drinking as though nothing had happened.

'So,' Sacha said between sips. 'I get the poker made you think of card suits, and Lynch had mentioned clubs and diamonds, and Joey had plenty to say about this robbery, but why this time in the morning? Not that I object to a little sleep.'

'Simple really,' Tammy answered. 'To be honest, though, it was Malthus who told me. Diamond merchants keep their stock in time-locked safes, and they are not easy to open overnight. The timer mechanism can't be overridden once set, and so the raid happens first thing once the manager arrives. And it had to be today as they're handling a shipment of black diamonds from South America. It's almost certainly connected to the appearance of the vampire.'

'Or vampires,' Sacha said, finishing her drink. 'Should we go?'

'Two more minutes I think.'

'And what if the vampire is there?' Sacha asked.

'We defeat it, or it defeats us. If we're killed in this form, we return home and can't come back for a century. It won't matter. With the *Covenant* broken, it's over for us anyhow. We simply do what we can.'

'I thought I was the gloomy one,' Sacha said.

'You must have rubbed off on me,' Tammy said. 'Come on, let's look at the action.'

Ten minutes later, they stood in the back room of van Henke's. A man they took for the manager was unconscious in a corner; the raiders had suffered more. Tammy and Sacha had been none too gentle as they fought the men, and Tammy took special pleasure in rendering Joey Butler unconscious, having broken his arm first while interrogating him. Like all pampered bullies, he was a coward with no tolerance for pain and told them everything he knew about his father's plans for the diamonds. No direct mention of a vampire, but confirmation someone *special* was helping the family business.

'Next step the warehouse?' Sacha asked.

'Later on. Butler will be playing golf this afternoon, so we've a chance to search this warehouse Joey told us about when we know he's now there. For now, let's call Eva and get the police to sort this out.'

Sacha frowned before realisation dawned. 'You mean officer Lynch? So she's Eva now?'

'She's been helpful, she can't help trying to be an independent woman in a male dominated organisation trying to get noticed. Would she have taken so many risks if we'd not encouraged her?'

'Maybe not. Anyway, if we've a few hours, I've a hair appointment later this morning. Meet you in the office?'

Tammy sighed. 'Why not? I'll take these diamonds to Malthus; he can stash them somewhere Butler and his like will never see them. Not in this life, anyhow.'

She was already talking to Sacha's back; her partner was on the way out. With only a few days left on Earth before the *Covenant* expired, Tammy was tempted to take some time out as well. After they'd solved the case; vampire permitting.

# # #

*Mid-afternoon, Fortune's Warehouse, Irvine, CA*

The warehouse seemed deserted. It was locked-up, no cars or vans outside and no sign anyone was at home, not even on watch. It didn't fit the profile they'd built of the ruthless villain Butler was.

They gained access through a side door and made their way round to a set of rooms on one side of the building. It took them the best part of an hour to decide the first office was for legitimate business: the books all made sense, filing cabinets seemed full of legitimate transactions, and they paid all the bills., Butler was trading antiques he shipped from around the continent, storing them and reselling. They must be missing something.

They'd started looking round a small storeroom full of old files when Sacha tensed. She held up a hand.

The two of them listened and reached out with other senses. Someone had arrived.

'It might be quicker if we got caught,' Sacha said. 'This is boring.'

Tammy nodded. They carried on opening boxes and feigned surprise when a man in a tight-fitting lime-green patterned shirt opened the door, pointing a gun in their direction.

'What have we here?' he said. 'Guys. I found us some entertainment.' This to some unseen others outside.

Lime-green man gestured with his gun and they followed him back to the main office.

'So, what do you two want? Gerry, search them.'

A heavy-set man with short blond hair smiled as he moved forward and checked Tammy and Sacha very thoroughly. He made sure he checked every part he could, and the two women stared coolly, ignoring the affront.

'Nothing,' Gerry said. 'I could strip them off to make sure.'

'Maybe later.' He turned to face Tammy and Sacha. 'Now, tell me what you're doing, who you work for, and why I shouldn't just let the boys have some fun with you?' he asked with a leer.

'Because if you do, we won't be able to tell Mr Butler where we hid his diamonds,' Tammy said, smiling back.

Lime-green flinched as though struck.

'Tie them to the chairs,' he told Gerry and the others, who used some heavy-grade crate packaging to tie them down. While this was happening, lime-green made a call. It was all apologies and stammers. After, he came back over.

'The boss is on the way. His bringing some people with him. We're to go apart from a couple of us to watch them until he gets here.'

There was some disgruntled muttering from several of the men who'd been looking forward to entertaining themselves at the expense of the women, but it was clear they were far more in fear of Butler than driven by lust. Soon only three remained: lime-green, Gerry and one whose name was never mentioned.

Twenty minutes later, Butler arrived.

'You can go now.'

The three who'd kept watch left meekly by a second door and were replaced by half-a-dozen men and women. Or so they appeared. They were unusually pale. Tammy and Sacha shared a glance as they entered. It was a typical warm day in LA, but the room temperature had dropped several degrees, or so it seemed.

Butler sat behind his desk and indicated to one of his men. He pointed to the two women and held up a finger. The man walked across and struck each of them hard across the face. Once. He stood back, waiting for further instruction.

'That's for what you did to Joey this morning,' Butler said. 'Give me my diamonds and we can make this easy. If not, there's plenty more where that came from. Harvey can do this all day. He's not bothered about hurting women, even ones as attractive as you.'

Tammy stared at Butler. 'And why do you want the diamonds?'

Butler lifted a finger and Harvey struck Tammy across the face once more.

The others seemed content to watch. Not with any emotion, just watching. In some ways, they were more disturbing than the beating.

'Perhaps your friend is more talkative?' Butler said, pointing at Sacha. Harvey hit her a few times, damaging her eyes. She spat blood, catching Harvey on the shirt.

The door opened, and an emotionless voice called from behind. 'We've visitors.'

Butler pointed, and Sacha heard several sets of footsteps move away.

Another gesture and the beating continued…

# # #

…Harvey tore a strip from Sacha's bright yellow blouse and wiped the blood from his shirt.

'Maybe I like to see women getting hurt,' Butler said, rubbing a platinum signet-ring. 'Besides. Harvey here likes his meat tenderised.'

Tammy looked directly at him, as though willing him to say more. The man laughed.

'Don't worry, it'll be your turn soon. Then you'll both talk. Don't worry, I'll make sure I get my diamonds before I let my associates enjoy themselves with what's left of you. Besides… I had to cancel golf, so I need a little… entertainment.'

A door opened. Those stood nearest turned sharply, then relaxed as two men came in, pale as the others, dragging a third man between them. They stopped a few feet in front of the desk and let their burden drop to the floor.

'We found this in the plant room, Mr Butler,' one of them said.

'What was he doing?' Butler, asked.

'No idea, we hardly touched him before he was out cold.'

'No matter,' Butler said. He turned to face one of his women. 'Cindy. A little snack for you. Something to show our guests just what's in store for them. Something to show how serious the situation is.'

The woman, Cindy, stood tall as Butler talked. She knelt beside the now semi-conscious man on the floor. She smiled.

'No, please no, what's happening!' the man screamed as Cindy smiled wider, revealing a pair of glistening fangs. Taking her time, she reached down to loosen the man's collar and reveal his neck.

Sacha tensed. Were all Butler's people vampires? They were

badly outnumbered.

A gun shot rang out from the direction of the room's second door.

'Freeze!'

It was officer Lynch.

The vampire Cindy lowered her mouth. Lynch shot, the bullet hitting Cindy in the arm. Cindy looked up, and smirked.

'I'm afraid bullets won't help you,' Butler said.

Tammy and Sacha were about to act, unable to leave the man to be killed in such a manner.

'Maybe this will help,' Lynch said, smashing her weapon against a fire alarm point. A bell sounded and seconds later water sprayed from the ceiling.

Butler looked puzzled. 'And what use is that?'

The screaming started.

Every single one of Butler's people was screaming. Every part of their exposed flesh was smoking, blistering, boiling away. Butler, Tammy, Sacha, Lynch, and the unconscious man on the ground were all unaffected.

'What have you done?' Butler asked, pointing his gun at Lynch.

Tammy and Sacha knew. Already the wounds on their faces were healing as the spray of water from above soaked their hair, faces and clothes. They felt good. Better than the health spa. Better than they'd felt for a long time.

'I did nothing,' Lynch said. 'It was my brother there. He's a priest. He blessed the water. It's holy water coming down.'

She looked pleased with herself and hadn't spotted the water's effect on the other two.

Butler fired. Twice. Stunned, Lynch collapsed, blood oozing from a pair of bullet-holes in her left side. He turned the gun to point at Sacha and Tammy. By this time, the vampires had ceased their screams, their flesh had vaporised, and they were no more.

'I'll keep this simple,' he said. 'One of you lives, one dies. Whoever tells me where the diamonds are, I won't shoot. I will set the building on fire, but you'll have a chance. Not much chance, but more than none. You choose.'

He pointed the gun first at one, then the other. They both smiled. The water had stopped, but it had been more than enough to repair most of the damage inflicted by Harvey.

'Why?' asked Tammy. 'So you can use it summon more vampires? Why trust you? You're a crook, a killer, a thief, a drug smuggler, a whoremonger and probably a tax evader. Your time is up.'

'You think!' he said, laughing. 'You're the ones whose time is up. The diamonds I can replace. You two, say your prayers. Yes, I'm all the things you said, and more, but I'm also a winner, a survivor, a force of nature.'

'Thank you,' Tammy said. 'That confession was all we needed to hear.'

The two women stood, their bonds snapping. Butler fired, but the bullets made no impact. As he watched in fear, they seemed to grow taller, brighter, more powerful. The last image he had was of wings and a blazing golden light before his eyes saw no more and the radiance cauterised his soul from his wretched corpse and he fell dead to the floor.

# # #

*Two days later, Chandler S Weston Investigators, Wilshire Boulevard, CA*

Tammy and Sacha took one last look around the office. Malthus had asked to meet them at noon. While they waited, they saw a bottle of champagne chilling on the side.

'Nice of Malthus to mark the occasion,' Sacha said, examining the label.

Tammy said nothing.

'We did our best,' Sacha said. 'Today's the full moon. I can't sense anyone else coming down to help us, so it's over. No more *Covenant*, no more weeding out the worst before they get to Hell, and one day they'll start spilling out onto the streets and we watch from up there.' She glanced upwards as she spoke.

Malthus came in, looking fully human and as elegantly attired as ever.

'So, it's farewell?' Tammy asked him.

'Are you going somewhere?' he retorted.

Both women looked at him closely. What game was he playing?

'The *Covenant* — three angels. It's finished,' Tammy said. 'That's why you invited us over. One last toast to what we tried before it's over.'

Malthus shook his head.

'How little you must think of me,' he said. 'I've been busy while you two have been resting. I'd like you to meet somebody.' He turned to face the door and raised his voice. 'You can come in now.'

The door opened again and in walked Eva Lynch, no longer dressed as a police officer. She looked at the two of them quickly before turning to Malthus.

'I knew they wouldn't want me,' she said. 'I can tell from their expressions.'

Sacha and Tammy both tried to talk at once.

'One at a time, please,' Malthus said.

'Is this a joke?' Tammy asked. 'Aren't there a few things you need to explain to Eva?'

'I thought the priority was to fill our vacancy before the deadline,' he answered. 'Eva was in the hospital, recovering from two miraculously healed bullet wounds, memory loss, delayed shook and a few other minor inconveniences. I bothered to check up on her, after you two left her so unceremoniously.'

'We thought it easier. Avoid explanations,' Sacha said. 'We knew she and her brother were alive, everyone else was… *out of the picture.*'

'So what do you know?' Tammy asked Eva. 'And what about the police?'

'Back to traffic? No, thank you. Besides, if it weren't for me and Peter, where would you to be? I know there's a darkness in this city, and I now know you two are fighting it. I want to help.'

'But did Malthus tell you…' Tammy started, then was interrupted by a voice from all around them. She and Sacha dipped their heads, while Eva looked around startled. Malthus did his best to seem inconspicuous.

'For now, you need to focus on the bigger picture,' the voice said. 'Explanations can follow, for now you need to move forward as three.'

'If I can ask,' Tammy said. 'Aren't there certain eligibility requirements built into the *Covenant*? Only certain… *entities* can take the role.'

'If I can help,' Malthus said. 'Miss Lynch, if you could give your full name. For the record.'

He moved to the side of the room while she answered.

'OK. It's Eva Clara Lynch. Eva is short for Evangeline. My mother's idea. It's an old family name — means something like good angel.'

Tammy and Sacha started to laugh, as Malthus brought across a tray on which stood four champagne flutes, each three-quarters full, bubbles sparkling and condensation forming on the sides. The four of them each took one, chinked glasses together then drank.

'Welcome to the angels,' the other voice came from all around.

'Why *the angels*?' Eva asked.

'You'll find out,' Sacha said, grabbing the bottle and topping up everyone's drink. 'You'll find out!' ♜

# THE MURDER COUPLE

*By Scott Pearson*

CARL RUSHED TOWARD THE DOOR as he heard footsteps approaching in the hallway outside their apartment. He stopped before stepping up onto the small landing and examined his hands, front and back, then rubbed his palms on his dirty sweatshirt.

As the door swung open, he held out his open hands and said, "Stop right there, Francis. I've gotta tell you something."

Francis stepped inside, coat folded over one arm, his unopened umbrella held in the other hand like a cane. Looking like a disappointed parent, he shook his head. "Don't bother, I know quite well what you've done." His voice was a soft counterpoint to Carl's growl.

Carl dropped his arms to his sides. "How could you?" He glanced over his shoulder toward the kitchen.

Francis stepped forward—eyes wide, eyebrows raised—brandishing his umbrella. “Just look at this!”

Carl turned back toward Francis. “What, your umbrella?”

“No, not the umbrella, this, this!” He poked the umbrella toward Carl, who backed away from the pointy tip—and the cigar stub impaled upon it. “You’ve done it again!” They stood staring at each other in silence for a moment.

Then Carl reached out, snatched the cigar from the umbrella, and jammed it into the corner of his mouth. “There, happy now?”

Francis stood frozen, his own mouth hanging open. “I most certainly am not. You may as well just go outside and lick the sidewalk as put that foul thing back in your mouth.”

Carl spit the cigar into his hand and threw it toward the ashtray on his nearby desk. He missed, and the cigar landed on the floor.

Francis stared at the stub on the carpet. “Are you going to pick that up?”

Carl clenched his fists. “No, Francis, will you just listen to me for a second? Something’s happened.”

“You mean there’s something else? What have you done?”

“It was an accident!” He shrugged. “Mostly.”

Francis opened the closet and set the umbrella inside. “Mostly? How can something be *mostly* an accident?” He took off his coat and hung it up.

“You just need to let me explain.”

"Can you explain while I'm in the kitchen? I've got hors d'oeuvres to make before your poker buddies arrive." Francis tried to step down from the landing, but Carl weaved back and forth, blocking his way.

Francis stopped and sighed, then feinted left before pivoting right and dodging down the steps. He shook a finger at Carl. "And you think I never pay attention to your sports games."

"Francis, please . . ."

But Francis breezed through the living room toward the kitchen. As he passed the poker table, he said, "Why don't you straighten those chips while I'm prepping."

Carl slumped onto the couch, leaned forward, head in his hands, and waited.

A moment later, Francis walked unevenly into the living room, blinking rapidly. He pointed back toward the kitchen. "There's a dead man in my kitchen."

"I know, Francis," Carl said without raising his head.

"With a knife in his back!"

"I know, Francis."

"One of my good knives, not the one you're allowed to use!"

"I know, Francis."

"It's my favorite knife for the crudité!"

"I—wait, no, I didn't know that. What's crudité again?"

"Raw sliced vegetables."

Carl sat up straight. "Oh, yeah, for that dip you make. You know, the guys love—"

Francis crossed his arms. "My whipped gorgonzola dip is not the subject at hand."

"Right, the dead guy." Carl leaned forward. "Didn't you see who it was?"

"He was face down, Carl. And in no condition to introduce himself. So who was it?"

"You're not going to like it, Francis."

"You think I'm liking this so far? I've got bacon to fry for my spinach puffs and I can't do that stepping over a corpse."

"Oh, the guys really do love those spinach puffs—"

"Just tell me who it is."

"Okay. But you have to let me explain. I was sticking up for you, Francis. Really, I was."

"Who is it, Carl?"

"And it was mostly an accident, like I said."

"Carl!"

"It's Mel."

Francis shrugged. "Mel who?"

Carl rolled his eyes. "Mel Tormé, obviously. Come on, how many Mels do you know?"

"Well, there's—" Francis stopped, putting a hand over his mouth before moving it to his cheek. "You didn't. You didn't murder my divorce lawyer."

"It was more of an accident than a murder."

"He was a good guy! Not like the others. They deserved—"

"We swore we'd never bring them up."

"We swore we'd never do it again after we got married!"

Carl clenched his teeth. "Have you forgotten we're both divorced now?"

"That's no reason."

"Then let's just say after what happened the last time, now we're even."

"We are not even close to even, mister! The cleaning costs alone—"

Carl jumped up from the couch. "Look, as much as I enjoy yelling at you, Francis, the guys are going to be here in an hour, and your crooked lawyer is dead in the kitchen."

Francis took a step forward. "He was not crooked."

Carl took a step closer. "He got you a lousy deal."

Francis put his hands on his hips. "He got me an amicable deal because I'm going to win Maria back."

Carl stuck a finger in Francis's face. "A lousy deal. Maria's never taking you back. And he wore a pinky ring like a mobster."

"That's—" Francis's response was cut off by a loud knock. As they both turned toward the door, it swung open revealing their friend Al in his police uniform.

"Sorry for busting in, guys, but I really need a bathroom. You could say it's a police emergency!"

Francis and Carl stared slack-jawed as Al hurried past them through the living room, their gaze following him in tandem as he disappeared down the hallway. When Al slammed the bathroom door shut, they turned toward each other, speechless for a moment before they scrambled for the kitchen.

"Jeez," Carl grumbled, "when you really want a cop, you can never find one, but—"

"Shush!" Francis snapped as they entered the kitchen. They stood over the body for a second, then Francis grabbed the feet. "Hurry up, we don't know how long he'll be in there."

"Why do I get the heavy end?"

"You know I've got a bad back, and besides, you reap what you sow."

"Fine." Carl shoved his hands under Mel's arms, heaved the torso off the floor with a grunt, and started dragging the body across the kitchen. After a few feet he stopped and stared at Francis.

"What?" Francis stood there, hunched over, knees bent, with Mel's ankles in his hands. Mel's knees were still on the floor.

"What?" Carl stamped his feet. "I've got this dead guy's head in my crotch, and you're carrying what he weighs from the knees down."

Grimacing, Francis choked up on Mel's legs until the lawyers knees were off the floor. "My back will have something to say to you later."

They wrestled the body out of the kitchen, and Carl, scuttling backward, angled toward the hallway as Francis turned the other way. The two stumbled to a stop, glaring at each other.

Francis tugged the legs in his direction. "Where are you going?"

"Your bedroom." Carl yanked back. "The last place anyone would look for a body."

"I will not have *your* victim in *my* bedroom." Francis leaned backward, tug-of-war style.

"So where are you going?"

"The closet." Francis tilted his head toward the landing. "Away from Al!"

"There's not enough room in there."

"Sure there is."

"Come on, he's getting heavier by the second." Carl started dragging the body toward the hallway, Francis's shoes sliding across the carpet.

"Absolutely not!" Francis hooked a foot on a leg of the poker table.

"Okay, okay, *my* bedroom, just hurry."

"We'll probably never find it again in there."

"Francis, if I had a hand free, I'd—"

At the sound of the toilet flushing, they both pulled frantically in opposite directions. They were still working against each other when Al appeared in the doorway. They froze, staring straight at him, dead body sagging between them, but Al was looking down at the front of his uniform, patting it with his hands.

“Oh good grief, I lost my badge again.” Al turned and disappeared back down the hallway without looking up.

Francis and Carl looked at one another. Francis said, “The closet’s closer.”

“Okay, go.” They hurried across the living room. “Steps! Steps!” Carl said just before Francis might have tripped onto the landing.

Francis stopped, exploring backward with one foot until he found the steps. After they maneuvered up onto the landing, Francis dropped Mel’s feet and opened the closet door. As Carl tried to push the body inside, Francis knelt down and guided the legs. Just as they dumped the body in and slammed the door, Al entered the living room. They hurried away from the closet.

Al waved his badge in the air. “Found it!” He put it back on his uniform jacket.

“That’s great, Al,” Francis said, smiling and nodding. “So I guess you’ll be getting right back to your beat?”

“Yeah, gotta keep those streets safe, right guys?”

“Those purse snatchers won’t chase themselves,” said Carl.

“No, no they won’t.” Al stepped up onto the landing, grabbed the doorknob, but turned back toward Carl and Francis. “Thanks for—”

“Good-bye now,” Carl said, waving. “Sorry you have to rush back to work.”

Francis was still smiling and nodding. "We'll see you later, next time we'll have pie and coffee, good-bye, have a nice shift!"

"Okay, okay, I get the hint." Al turned the knob but stopped before opening the door. He bent over and picked up something off the landing. "Hey, whose is this?" Al stood up and held out a gold pinkie ring.

Francis and Carl stood staring for a moment, then both pointed at the other.

"Oh, you guys," said Al, shaking his head. He looked closer at the ring. "It's got a *W* . . . no, it's an *M*!" He held it toward Francis. "An *M* for Maria, isn't that sweet."

That's when the closet door popped open and Mel flopped out onto the floor facedown at Al's feet, knife still sticking out of his back. Al's mouth dropped open like a broken ventriloquist doll.

"Stop him, Al, he's got my crudité knife!" Francis yelled.

Carl dragged his hands down his face to his chin. "I guess that was better than pointing at me and saying *He did it!*"

"Well, I'm sorry, Carl, I didn't have time to rehearse anything."

Al's gasping brought their attention back to the policeman standing over the body. He had one hand clasped to his chest. The ring tumbled out of his other hand, landing silently on the carpeting.

"Listen, Al, I can explain," Carl said. "It was an accident. Mostly . . ."

"Do you need a glass of water?" said Francis. "Let me get you a glass of water."

Al shook his head, mouth moving but no words coming out, then dropped like a bag of rocks, collapsing forward over the first body, motionless.

Carl gave Francis a little shove. "I told you we should have used your room."

"This is my fault now?"

"It's nobody's fault, Francis. It was an accident."

"Mostly."

"Yeah, exactly, mostly."

They stood looking at the bodies. After a moment without speaking, Francis clapped his hands together. "Well, time for the murder cleaning kit. Just like old times, eh?"

"Don't look so excited."

"Sorry, but you know how much I enjoy a good cleaning."

"Right. Why don't you get started, I'm gonna call the guys and cancel tonight."

While Francis scampered off for his supplies, Carl went to the phone. There was no answer at Charlie's, but he got ahold of Ray, and asked him to call Tony and try Charlie again. Just as he hung up, Francis returned to the living room wearing bright yellow rubber gloves that went nearly up to his elbows. He had a basket of cleaning supplies in one hand, a large rolled-up plastic tarp in the other, and a second tarp tucked under that arm.

"You just happen to have all that at hand, ready to go?"

"I like to be prepared for any cleaning emergency. Especially living with you."

"Har-dee-har-har," said Carl.

They unrolled and unfolded one of the tarps on the floor, right up to the bottom of the landing. Francis hummed a little tune as he straightened the tarp. He surveyed its placement, then rotated it ninety degrees clockwise and straightened it again. Standing back a step, he tilted his head left and right. "No, it was better the first—"

"Let's just get this over with." Carl bent over and grabbed handfuls of Al's uniform jacket. He looked up at Francis who was just standing there. "Well?"

"You didn't put on your rubber gloves."

"Oh, for crying out loud." Letting go of Al, Carl grabbed some gloves out of the basket and tugged them on. He got back in position and got ahold of Al again. Francis still stood upright. "Well, now what?"

"I'm worried about my back. Al's a lot bigger than Mel."

"You're always worried about something. Come on, gravity's on our side."

Francis leaned in to get a grip and nodded that he was ready.

"Okay, pull!" Carl said. They gave a good yank, and Al slid off Mel and down onto the tarp, but with his legs still up the stairs onto the landing.

"One more time!"

They pulled—and Francis froze with a yelp like a dog that just had its tail stepped on. "My back! I threw out my back!"

"I wish you could throw it out, it's a piece of junk."

"Very funny. Very helpful." He moved backward, his torso staying at a ninety-degree angle to his legs. He put both hands on his lower back, his elbows sticking up in the air.

"You look like a bird pecking at breadcrumbs."

"I'm glad you find my pain so amusing."

"Come on, Francis, I can't clean all this up by myself."

"You should have thought of that before you stabbed Mel."

"It was an accident."

"Mostly," they said in unison.

"I was sticking up for you!"

"Sure you were. Just give me my crudité knife." He held out one hand. "I think I can still reach the sink like this."

"Fine." Carl reached over Al's body, grabbed the knife in Mel's back, and yanked it out. Straightening up, he held it, handle first, toward Francis.

Francis, still doubled over, gingerly stretched one arm out, craning his neck back to see what he was doing, making the occasional whimpering noise. Just as he grabbed the handle, there was a loud knock. As they both turned toward the door, it swung open until it hit Mel's legs with a *thump*.

Carl's poker buddy Charlie marched in. "Sorry for busting in, guys, but I—" He stopped as he took in the scene before him, eyes going wide behind his black-framed glasses.

Francis pointed the knife at Carl and said, "He did it!"

"That's just great, Francis, thanks a lot."

"Well, why didn't you lock the door?"

"I didn't expect it to be Grand Central Station in here," said Carl. "Besides, why didn't *you* lock the door?"

"I've had my hands full!"

"And I haven't?" Carl shook his rubber-gloved fists in the air and turned toward Charlie. "And you! Doesn't anybody wait for a 'come in' anymore?"

Charlie leaned forward. "Is . . . is that Al?" He looked at Carl and shrugged. "So, are we playing poker or . . . ?"

"No, we're not playing poker." He flailed his arms around some more. "Now, in or out, close that door!"

Charlie and stepped in just far enough to be able to shut the door. He scratched the top of his head, messing his thick gray hair. "What the heck happened?"

Francis and Carl exchanged looks, then said together, "It was an accident. Mostly."

Charlie tugged his tie looser. "Well, I'm gonna need a drink."

"Help yourself," Carl said. "Beer's in the fridge."

"I need more than beer." Carefully stepping over the bodies, Charlie made his way to a tray—set up near the poker table—that held hard liquor, mixers, and an ice bucket. While he poured himself a glass full of vodka, he took the cover off the bucket and plunged a hand in to grab some ice.

Francis said, "Tongs for the ice!"

Charlie ignored this, pulled out a couple of ice cubes, and held them against his forehead as he knocked back some vodka.

Carl was folding the plastic tarp over Al. "Charlie, can you give me a hand over here? *Someone* conveniently threw his back out."

Francis shook his head, then squeaked in pain. "This is only convenient for my chiropractor. I'm singlehandedly putting his daughter through Vassar." He pointed his knife at Carl. "Wait, wait, let me get you some scissors."

Clenching his jaw, Carl held a roll of duct tape out toward Francis as he tore off a crooked strip and haphazardly stuck it on the tarp, barely holding it shut. Francis lowered the knife with a sigh. Carl unclenched his jaw. "So what do you say, Charlie?"

Charlie put his vodka on the poker table. "Yeah, sure, why not, long as I'm here."

Francis said, "Coaster!"

"Let it go, Francis," said Carl, but Charlie moved his glass onto a coaster and dropped the ice into the vodka.

Francis frowned. "You're not going to drink that now, are you?"

"Why?" Charlie said. "Do you want it?"

Carl laughed. Charlie took another drink. Francis opened his mouth, just sighed again, and hobbled toward the kitchen with his crudité knife, mumbling under his breath.

"So . . ." Charlie put his glass back down on the coaster and started rolling up his sleeves. "What gives? Didn't Al pay up from last time?"

Carl dropped the tape. "I forgot all about that."

"You can kiss that fifty bucks good-bye."

"I guess so." Carl taped up Al a little more, then they shoved him aside before spreading out the second tarp. "No, the big guy just had a heart attack when he saw . . ." He tilted his head at the other body.

"Yeah, I was wondering, who's the other stiff?" They rolled it off the landing onto the tarp.

"Mel."

"Mel Tormé?"

Carl chuckled. "That's what I said to Francis."

"You killed the Velvet Fog." Charlie suppressed a grin as they folded the tarp over the body. "That's a damn shame."

"Yeah, well, he provoked me." Carl ripped off some tape. "He shows up uninvited—"

"And starts singing 'The Christmas Song.' Middle of June!"

"Which I might have let go . . ." Carl affixed the tape across the tarp and sat back on the landing. "But he started scatting."

"You don't scat uninvited in another man's home. Everybody knows that."

They held straight faces as long as they could, then broke into snorting laughter.

Francis hobbled out of the kitchen, both hands on the small of his back, closer to standing straight. "What is going on in here? You're stacking bodies like cordwood but giggling like drunken schoolgirls."

Charlie took off his glasses and rubbed away tears. "Carl was just telling me why he killed Mel Tormé."

"It's all a big joke to you two. You know, you're both very comfortable around dead bodies, maybe you should have chosen different careers."

"Relax, Francis," said Carl. "We're just releasing some tension. You should try it sometime, you're like an overstretched rubber band."

"And I'm going to snap, is that it? Because I believe you're the one who snapped today."

"It was an accident!"

"Mostly," added Charlie. "Right? That's what I've heard."

Francis turned his wide-open eyes on Charlie. "What are you even doing here so early? Most poker nights everyone's late and I'm trying to keep hors d'oeuvres warm without drying them out."

"Oh, did you make those bacon things, I—"

"There are no spinach puffs! Only dead bodies and my misused crudité knife."

Charlie looked at Carl. "What's crudité?"

Carl said, "Sliced veggies."

"Right!" Charlie tilted his head to one side and pointed at Francis. "That dip of yours is—"

"There is no whipped gorgonzola dip!"

"Please, Francis," said Carl. "You're going to hyperventilate. Why don't we all just take a break and sit down?"

Carl and Charlie were both already in their seats at the poker table before Francis maneuvered his way to one of the chairs. They watched quietly as Francis tried to sit from the left side, then the right, then back to the left. After a couple more false starts, punctuated with various squeaks and moans, he finally eased himself down.

"Comfy?" Carl said.

Francis shrugged. "Maybe if you got me a pillow—"

"So, Charlie," said Carl, "why *are* you here so early?"

"Yeah, about that." Charlie took a drink of vodka. He cleared his throat. "Wait, you never answered my question."

Carl furrowed his brow. "What question?"

"Who's the other stiff?"

"I told you, it's Mel."

"My divorce lawyer," Francis added.

Charlie adjusted his glasses. "Huh, that's a coincidence." He rubbed his chin.

"How so?" said Francis.

"Well, Francis, the thing is . . ." Charlie pushed some poker chips around on the table. "I came here early to talk with you."

"Me?"

Charlie started restacking the chips. Carl reached out with one hand and pulled the chips away from Charlie. "For Pete's sake, just spit it out."

"All right, all right." Charlie glanced toward Mel's body before facing Francis. "I've been dating Maria."

"It's you?" blurted Carl.

"You what?" Francis said to Charlie, then he turned to Carl. "Wait, what did you say?"

Charlie said, "I just wanted to tell you before you heard it somewhere else."

Francis's kicked-puppy eyes stayed on his roommate. "And you knew about this, Carl?"

"No!"

"But you said—"

"Not specifically. But that's why Mel was here. He'd heard Maria was seeing someone, but he didn't know who. He was worried how you'd take it.

I told him he should be more worried about the lousy deal he got you. I told him that if this was serious, maybe he could renegotiate. I told you, I was sticking up for you."

"And then you killed him? He came by out of concern for a client, and you stabbed him in the back?"

"It was an accident!"

"Mostly?" said Charlie.

"Shut up," Francis and Carl said together.

"I admit I was angry at him," Carl said. "And I was waving the knife around, but I didn't pull it on him, I was using it. But when he turned his back on me, ignoring me, I took a step toward him, and . . . I slipped."

"You slipped the knife in his back."

"No, I slipped . . . on a pizza."

"On a pizza."

"Yeah, I was trying to cut a frozen pizza in half, and it fell on the floor. It was like stepping on ice. I slid forward with the knife in my hand—"

"Carl, Carl, Carl . . ." Francis put his face in his hands. "You were using my good knife on a frozen pizza?"

"I'm sorry, Francis."

"I didn't see any pizza in the kitchen."

"I cleaned it up."

"You cleaned it up. You left the body but picked up the pizza. I suppose

I should be grateful for small favors."

"I'm sorry, Francis." Carl turns on Charlie. "And you! How could you?"

"Me? I'm just a guy going on some dates, I'm not whacking people in the kitchen."

Francis moaned behind his hands. "I'm getting a sinus headache." He lowered one hand and raised the other to the bridge of his nose. "Heh. Heh. I'm all plugged up. Feh. Fmaa. Mngaaahhhh."

"Look what you've done," Carl said. "Now I've gotta listen to him honking all night."

"I came over here to let him know, man to—"

"Heh! Feh! Heh-hehhhh!"

"Man to goose. And I stayed to help with your mess. So don't put this on me. Besides, she's driving me nuts. It's always, *Francis* this and *Francis* that."

"Heh—feh?"

"*Francis* would've opened the door for me, *Francis* would've cooked for me, *Francis* would've washed the dishes. And I say to her, you should be happy I'm not Francis, you're the one who asked him to leave!" He started rolling up his sleeves. "But I don't think she misses you, Francis, I think she misses being waited on hand and foot. Don't get me wrong, she's a heck of a woman—you know what I mean!—but I say you got off easy." Charlie picked up the deck of cards. "So now I think the both of you need to shut up so we can play some Texas hold 'em. I'll ante up with Mel Tormé's pinkie ring." Charlie slammed the ring down on the table. "I found it; I can bet it."

Carl glared at Charlie. Francis, no longer honking, let his hand fall to the table. Carl looked at his roommate's long face and sad, downcast eyes. "Crudité?"

"What?" said Charlie.

"Francis . . ." Carl angled his head toward Charlie. "Crudité?

Francis blinked and raised his head. "Carl, I didn't have time to make . . . oh, I see. *Crudité*." Francis smiled and nodded.

"Guys," Charlie said, looking between them. "Why do you keep saying *crudité*?"

*Six months later . . .*

"Boy, oh, boy, Francis, this is quite the spread." Carl looked at a veritable smorgasbord laid across their table.

"Oh, it's nothing, really, mostly using up things from the freezer." Francis waved an arm dismissively, but he was smiling broadly. "I had to do something special . . . for our last meal as roommates."

"What? She said yes?"

"Yes! Maria said yes, and asked me to move right back in." He was practically bouncing on his feet. "I got her back, Carl!"

"Congratulations, buddy, really." They shook hands. "I'm sorry I ever doubted you."

"Water under the bridge. Now let's dig in before things get cold."

They both filled their plates with a variety of the table's offerings and ate ravenously without speaking.

"Well, we both have good appetites this evening," Francis said. "But I always get hungry when I'm cooking."

"I'm starving." Carl shoveled the last bite of food off his plate into his mouth and talked while chewing. "I burned a lot of calories this afternoon crossing off a name. I had to chase the guy down."

"Who?"

"That crazy client of yours, the one who kept demanding the new pictures."

"If you decide after the fact that you wanted to be cleanshaven in your wedding portrait, you don't get a free do-over, no matter how ugly your mustache was. Which I told him it was when he refused to comb it."

"Crudité," Carl said.

"Crudité indeed," Francis said.

"Now for seconds." Carl gestured around the table with his fork. "But what are all these dishes? They're delicious."

"A little bit of everything. I've been cooking all day. Here we've got a rich Bolognese, courtesy of Al. Then there are the slow-cooked ribs, that's Mel. And Charlie is the slightly sweet dish with the citrus glaze."

Carl sat quietly, eyes lingering over the table, and came to a decision. "I'll have some more of the Chuck à l'Orange." He waggled a finger at Francis's surprised expression. "And you think I never pay attention to your cooking shows." He sat back with his second helping and, talking with his mouth full again, said, "Now . . . who do you want for your wedding present?" ♜

# THE SHREVEPORT SLASHER

*By James A. Moore*

*September 7th, 1972, approximately 11:15 PM*

MR. DENNIS PHILIPS WAS HAVING a bad night. After drinking too many beers at the Hutch, his local watering hole, he had his car keys confiscated by the owner, one Todd Parsons. It was not the first time that Philips had been accused of drinking too much to be allowed to drive himself home. But according to several witnesses, this time around the difference of opinions led to a physical altercation.

It seems that Dennis was a man on a mission, and that mission included getting home without having to walk. No one was willing to pay for a cab to get him home, and the last of his money had been spent on a boilermaker roughly thirty minutes earlier. Despite threats, pleas, and promises to repay any loans, he never made it to his apartment.

It rained that night, and the banks of the Red River rose by over four inches.

His body was found the next day, or rather parts of it were. Sometime during the journey home, Dennis Philips was physically dismembered. What appeared to be bitemarks from "something large and ferocious" were found on several of his remaining parts. The remains were discovered by one Ellie Tidwell, a crossing guard at the Shreveport elementary school just after she had escorted several students across the street.

Police Detective Walter Harper of the Shreveport Police Department was the first investigator to arrive. According to eyewitnesses who wish to remain anonymous, the detective was physically ill after examining the body.

*September 9th, 1972, 3:30 AM*

Mark Tucker, age 37, was a big man. To call him a giant would barely be an exaggeration: at six feet, eleven inches and weighing in at three hundred and twenty-four pounds, the former Golden Gloves contender was an intimidating if familiar sight at the local branch of the First Union Bank of Shreveport. While Mark "Mack Truck" Tucker was a very large man, he was, by all accounts, an amiable sort when he wasn't working as the bouncer at Miss Kitty's Gentleman's Club, a slightly seedy strip bar with a pleasant name and a booming business catering to a clientele that believes beautiful women should be scantily clad. The ex-pugilist told many a person he could have been the heavyweight champion of the world, if only he could have found people willing to actually fight him.

Instead he was relegated to bouncer and cash delivery security guard for the local strip club, a job he handled easily enough. In the words of Franklin Pulver, the owner of Miss Kitty's, "No one in their right mind would ever think about trying to rob the Mack Truck." It's apparently true, as the man was never once approached despite the fact that he walked the four blocks to the bank in the predawn hours five nights a week on his way to make the late night deposit at the local bank, often carrying in excess of a thousand dollars in cold cash on his person.

When Mister Tucker failed to arrive at his apartment on September ninth his live-in girlfriend, Desiree Hammond, grew worried. Mark Tucker was nothing if not reliable in the extreme. After waiting until ten A.M, Ms. Hammond called the local police department to report her boyfriend missing. By that time, he had already been dead for several hours. No one could identify the remains until after Ms. Hammond's phone call.

Closed circuit cameras at the First Union Bank of Shreveport's recently installed Automatic Teller Machine verified that Tucker had, indeed, made the nightly deposit at the machine in question. The camera footage also shows several blurry partial images of what is believed to be his assailant that night, though darkness and heavy rains all but guaranteed poor visual quality. Of the visible evidence recorded on the security camera only seven pictures show evidence of an assault. The images, while grainy, clearly show Mister Tucker's last moments as a living member of the human race, as well as what can only be called a mysterious figure with unusual features.

The first of the images show Tucker turning to face whatever was behind him. It also shows a hand of extraordinary size reaching for him. That hand is clearly defined enough for viewers to see that each finger ends with a large talon, and that the hand appears to have an unusual amount of webbing between the fingers.

The second and third images show a humanoid shape that is unbelievably, even larger than Mark Tucker. According to several sources I checked with the best guess is that the figure is crouching, judging by the shadows that run behind that figure, and might stand as tall as seven and a half feet in height. In one of the two photos captured in this sequence the skin of the shape seems to show a pattern of heavy scales, thought there is some speculation that what is seen is actually a jacket.

The next image shows what is believed to be the head and face of the attacker, a triangular wedge that does not look at all human to this reporter, but could be said to resemble a reptile. Though the image is again grainy and not easily interpreted, there appears to be a ridge above the eye that does not appear human. This, again, leads to speculation as to whether or not the assailant might be wearing a mask of some sort.

It's the last two images that lead away from the possibility of dime store costumes, however. In the last frames showing the assault, Mark Tucker can barely be seen, but the shape of his attacker is much clearer, or rather the lowered back of the assailant is made clear and distinctly shows a thick extremity that simply does not belong on a humanoid form. In this case the appendage appears to be a prehensile tail.

For all of the speculation about costumes and hoaxes, it appears as if Mark Tucker was killed not by a man, but by a lizard man.

Convincing my editor, Jack DeZuniga of that fact could prove challenging, which is why I instead pushed the notion of the recession that is killing off the city of Shreveport after it lost both the General Motors plant and the business brought to the town by last decade's boom in the oil industry. It would not be the first time I convinced my editor that we needed a good human interest story. That's one of the excuses that works on him more often than not.

Of course, just because he agreed to do the piece wasn't a guarantee of arriving in style. I made it to Shreveport on September 11th by way of a Greyhound bus, settling my feet in the area at just after three in the morning, the witching hour.

Finding a hotel was easy enough, but finding a good hotel proved more challenging as there was a morticians' convention in town. I wound up staying at a motel across the street from the Shreveport police station, a point of interest only because police detective William Taylor made note of it when I caught his attention during my investigation into the Shreveport Slasher.

It was a fellow reporter from Shreveport who came up with the Slasher moniker. Edna Platt, much like me, tended to find stories of interest that most reporters seemed to overlook. She had already acquired a great deal of information on the deaths of Mark Tucker and Dennis Phillips when we met up for lunch. It was, she told me, my turn to buy. When it came to getting information for my case, I was glad to foot the bill.

We met over beers and burgers at the Sweet Spot, a bar that specialized in cheap drinks and surprisingly good food. Edna was good enough to bring copies of the photographs she had already managed to acquire from the coroner's office after I promised not to reveal her source.

The photographs offered more credence to the idea that the attacker was not human. At the sight of Mark Tucker's demise, a long trail of blood led from his remains toward the bank of the Red River, which runs alongside the road where the bank is located. Similarly, there are three very distinct footprints in the mud leading to where Dennis Philips was killed. The three prints moved as if they belonged to a man running. They are very deep tracks, pushed into soft mud brought about by the rain on the night of the Philips' murder.

The tracks were clear enough to see that they were not made by human footprints. Each had five toes, and deep marks at the front that once again seemed to indicate talons or claws. The marks were also indicative of something with a different structure altogether. The digits were widespread and the position at the front of the footprints seemed more like a paw than a human foot.

While Edna had done a lot of the research herself, we went together to meet up with Lance Hendricks, a doctor from the Louisiana State University, whose specialty was biology. The good doctor had made extensive studies in various fields of the animal kingdom, including reptiles. My initial plan was simply to see if the prints might be fakes, as so often was the case with claims of finding evidence for Big Foot, but to my surprise Doctor Hendricks looked at the photographic evidence and said that the prints seemed to be legitimate or among the best of the false claims he had run across in his career, he pointed to the placement of different pads on the print, and the structure and shape of the protruding bones within the marking.

He also pointed out that while the print might be a fake, it bore a powerful resemblance to the trail left behind by an American Alligator, though it was unlikely to have actually been left by one of the very large creatures, as the gait of the thing indicated a creature moving on two legs, not four.

It was just after nine PM when Edna dropped me off at my motel. I was tired, but restless. Rather than retire to my room, I decided to get a drink and a late-night snack at the closest watering hole, despite the heavy rainfall. The bar I chose was frequented by several police officers whose shift was ending. It was on their radios that I heard about the latest attack.

Dorothy Clemons was attacked outside her home, by what she claimed was a creature "the size of a bear, only scaly." The attack occurred as she was taking her trash out for the night, accompanied by her faithful canine companion, a one hundred-and fifty-three-pound Rottweiler named Alfie. Alfie was walking behind her, as he often did, and came to her rescue before matters could get out of hand.

Though Alfie was injured by whoever—or whatever – had tried to attack Ms. Clemons, he gave at least as good as he got.

Alfie was taken to the local emergency veterinarian's office, and is currently recovering at home, having received several stitches and a steak for his efforts. Ms. Clemons stated that she would surely have been killed if not for Alfie's intervention. As proof of her beliefs she pointed to the scratch marks along the side of Alfie's muzzle, and to the souvenir she was forced to give to the police before I could arrive at the scene. It seems that Alfie was able to take a bite out of his opponent during the fight, and that bite severed one long finger from the left hand of the attacker. According to Ms. Clemons, the finger was scaly, and had a long claw at the end of it.

I was able to look at the scene of the attack, and as had been seen at the previous sites, the attacker was not shy about leaving prints behind. The photos I took closely matched what had been seen in the other photographs, though in this case I could also see markings where the tail of the beast dragged through the muck. Said tail was thicker than my forearm, and though the impressions did not show it, I had little doubt of the reptilian nature of the appendage that made the marks on the ground.

As we were sharing information, I made a point of getting copies of my evidence to Edna. That worked out to my benefit, as Police Detective Walt Harper showed up at my motel room with three officers to confiscate the pictures I'd taken. It seems that my reporting of the news was looked at as interference into their investigation. Somedays it does not pay to be a journalist.

Despite the setback in my work, I persisted. I spent the first part of the day writing most of my article on the recession in Shreveport, and then after a late lunch, I was on my way back to the scene of the previous incidents. All three of the encounters with whatever was out in the wilds and trying to tear people apart had taken place near the Red River. What I needed now was a pattern to those crimes. It only took a few minutes to discern what that pattern was. Each incident took place after a hard rainfall. Louisiana was dealing with its wet season, when the rivers are likely to flood past the banks at the proverbial drop of a hat. I'd have bet my trusty fedora on that simple fact, and I'd have won.

The good news for me was that more rain was expected. That was also the bad news. I could see that the attacks had taken place along the side of the river, and that they were separated by distance and moving downstream at a steady pace, but I couldn't exactly predict with any accuracy where the next attack might take place. The best I could do was make a guess and pray I wasn't too far off the mark. The rough part of that scenario was that the police were likely doing the exact same thing. I just had to hope that my guesswork was better than theirs.

*September 14th, 11:43 PM*

Bruce Lazenby was intoxicated when he headed for home. On the bright side, he was a happy drunk, having just celebrated a promotion for the last three hours. On the darker side, he lived just off the river, and he made enough noise to garner the wrong sort of attention. In this case he caught the notice of Deena Garner, a woman who had to be up very early for her job as a waitress at the local diner. She came outside in her terrycloth bathrobe to let him know that his attempts at singing a sea shanty were not appreciated.

Before Mr. Lazenby could come up with a proper defense or even apologize, he was attacked by a creature that simply should not exist.

I heard the screams from Mister Lazenby and from his neighbor as at that precise moment I was less than a block away from the scene of the violence. Despite running as quickly as I could into the apartment complex where both people resided, I almost missed the action.

By the time I reached the spot, Bruce Lazenby was dead. I spotted the man's corpse a second before I saw the beast that had attacked him. Bruce Lazenby had been eviscerated. His ribcage was torn open, his internal organs spilled across the ground in front of his corpse, and directly behind him, towering over his remains, was a creature straight out of a nightmare.

The thing stood at least seven feet in height despite the fact that it was crouched down over its prey. The hands of the creature were drenched in blood. The left hand was missing a finger, but the stump looked uneven, and I do believe said digit was in process of growing back. The beast stared directly at me with eyes the color of molten gold. Those eyes were not human in the least, and neither was the face surrounding them. I cannot say what sort of lizard the features resembled, but they were definitely reptilian in nature. The snout of the thing was shorter than an alligator's, but the jaws were wide, powerful and predatory. The teeth I could see were long and sharp, and I had the impression that they could easily bite through a man's arm.

It looked to me like the thing was wearing the tattered remains of dress slacks. It was raining very hard by that point, and I can't guarantee that I actually saw clothing at all. I aimed my camera and took three pictures. My flash only went off twice, but both of the bright flares seemed to annoy and disorient the thing looking at me. I think it preferred the darkness.

That was all I had a chance to see before the creature charged toward me. I had exactly enough time to know I was a dead man before shots were fired. I could not tell you what sort of firearms were used as I was too busy staring my certain death in the face when the police unloaded a volley of bullets at the lizard-thing.

They hit their target. The creature charging in my direction was stopped by the force of the weapons striking it several times in the chest and at least once in the head. Though I can say with certainty that the hide of the thing was indeed scaly and looked heavy enough to stop any sort of weapon discharge, the bullets did, in fact, leave large holes in the body of the thing. It screeched and fell backward, and whether it was warm blooded or cold, it bled profusely.

In a perfect world I would be able to tell you that I saw the thing die, and that the police were quick to report what they had found and stopped, but it is sadly not a perfect world. Here are the facts that I can report, though without much substantiation.

Fact: I was saved from what I consider to be certain death by Police Detective Walt Harper and four uniformed members of the Shreveport Police Department. Those officers were as close as I was when the screaming started, though they came from a different direction and were far better prepared for the event than I was.

I was armed with a tape recorder and a Polaroid camera. They were armed with high caliber sidearms and two shotguns.

Fact: I was far happier to see them than they were to see me. My tape recorder and camera were confiscated, with the understanding that I could get them back at the end of a lengthy investigation.

Fact: I was given until exactly six AM to vacate my motel room. The detective in charge of the investigation made it a point to escort me to the Greyhound bus station and personally escorted me to my seat. He watched and waited as the bus in question left the station. I will also point out that a squad car followed said bus to the town limits and beyond. I took the hint and have not been back to Shreveport or the surrounding area since I was so politely but firmly asked to leave.

Fact: Edna Platt will not return my phone calls and has not responded to my attempts to contact her by mail. I have no doubt that a certain police detective is responsible for her silence.

One more fact for your consideration, though this one begs for conjecture: The hearse used by the Shreveport Coroner's office did not make it back from picking up the body of whatever it was that killed at least three people in that town and was gunning for me when it was shot by the local police. Though the police have offered no comment on the situation, rumors say that the hearse was found on its side near the Red River, with both the driver, Lawrence Edwards, and his assistant, Benjamin Rollins missing from their customary positions in the cab. Also missing was the bagged occupant placed in the back and heading for the coroner's offices for examination. The body bag which had been placed over said occupant was allegedly shredded and found at the scene.

Despite several attempts to reach either of the aforementioned men, I have so far been unsuccessful.

Rumor has it that the back of the hearse was opened with enough force to shatter the glass windows and bend the door out of shape to the point where it had to be replaced. I have found no one willing to confirm or deny these rumors. ♜

# THESE DAYS ARE OURS

*By Jason Henderson*

HAROLD SMELLED BACON WHEN HE awoke, and for a moment, in the haze between sleep and waking, he thought he was in the Philippines. He was late for duty and Lanford, the other cook in his outfit, had started without him. He cursed and shouted "Okay, okay, okay!" to himself, because he knew he was alone in the barracks because he had missed reveille somehow, and he was going to get it, and then his own voice brought him awake.

He felt heavy the way he always felt heavy when he awoke, but it was fine. He sat up in bed and looked across at the photographs on the wall and the floral-patterned curtains billowing gently in the wind. It was not 1931. It was 1955, and he winced when he remembered it was his birthday.

It was seven a.m., and he was forty-five today. He groaned. No, no. Don't feel sorry for yourself. Everyone turns forty-five. If they're *lucky.* He stood up and stretched and patted his not-at-all-twenty-one stomach. He was one of the lucky ones.

Harold found his robe on the back of the door and pulled it on, slipped into his slippers, and followed the smell of bacon downstairs. From one of the kids' rooms—he had three, a firecracker daughter, a smart son, and a driven son—a song was playing, some kind of bebop his didn't really know but that had wandered its way into his brain the way kids' music does. It hammered rhythmically like a piston, *One-o'clock-two-o'clock-three-o'clock-rock! Four-o'clock-five-o'clock-six-o'clock-rock!*

He thought of his oldest son, the *driven* one, and for some reason had one of those random snatches of memory. It was on Frances's second birthday, and Tom had decided to make her a gift of fresh apples and had picked all the apples off the tree out front. But of course he was too young to know the apples weren't ripe and that he'd destroyed a whole season of apples. He looked so happy and proud when he presented a basket of unripe apples. Harold had raged and Tom had cried all night. He didn't like to think of it, because gosh what a good kid, and gosh what a terrible father he could be. He blinked the guilt away. That had to be, what, 1945? The war was still on, right? Apples and Tom crying and Harold ashamed of his rages and the end of the war he wasn't a part of.

When he reached the bottom of the stairs, he felt a strange wave of vertigo pass over him. He lost all sound for a moment and had to grab the balustrade and was barely able to avoid stumbling over his older son's snow boots, which were thrown against the bottom of the stairs next to his daughter's ice-skates. He started to grumble, "Someone needs to get god-damned squared away!"

He closed his eyes, the vertigo passing, and when he opened his eyes, he looked across the living room at the open door to the kitchen.

His wife Minnie looked up at him as she came in through the screen door to the garden. "Oh, Harold!" she smiled. "You're not supposed to be up!"

"What?" He furrowed his brow. He gingerly stepped over Tom's boots and Frances's skates, spotting Reggie's basketball shoes neatly placed next to the front door. At least *the smart one* hadn't just piled his shoes at the bottom of the stairs.

Why would Tom even have his boots here? Harold tried to remember if Tom had visited and spent the night; the kid had his own place near the college. He didn't remember. "I feel strange," he said aloud.

"What's that, dear?" Minnie said as she flipped the bacon he suddenly smelled again. The song from upstairs had cut out and something else was playing, something else he didn't recognize at all. He shut the noise out. Families come with noise.

"I said I feel strange," he said, raising his voice slightly. "I wonder if I'm coming down…"

Where was the…

He still had his hand on the balustrade though he'd reached the bottom. Something was... was he dreaming?

"Where's the dining room?" he finally said. Wasn't there a...

"You're supposed to be in bed. I was going to get the kids up and bring you breakfast in bed," Minnie said as she emerged from the kitchen with a plate of bacon and eggs. "Oh, sit down, are you feeling well?"

"I *said* I wasn't..." he shook his head and followed her gesture to sit at the dining table in the dining area next to the living room.

"Dining area," he said. "Sure... sure."

Minnie sat down with a cup of coffee after setting one in front of him. "Happy birthday," she said. "We'll do something nice later."

She beamed. She really did. For a moment, with the sunlight streaming in from the window in the door, she was the same girl he had met on leave in 1932.

He laughed as he sopped a piece of bacon in egg, feeling himself again. "You were going to bring me breakfast in bed!" He loved the idea that they would still do something like that now that the kids were all practically grown. It was the kind of thing a five, seven and nine-year-old would love, but not a fifteen, seventeen –

"Oh, well, if I could drag Reggie and Frances out of bed themselves."

"I nearly tripped on Tom's clodhoppers," Harold said, thumbing back towards the stairs. For a moment he had a wave of vertigo again and thought of the dining room. What a strange dream he must have been having.

"Tom?" Minnie asked, sipping her coffee.

"Yeah, it's…" he shook his head. "I'm sorry. Did Tom stay here last night?"

"Tom…" Minnie seemed to search her memory. "Tom Lee, from the hardware supply?"

He laughed. "Minnie, where's your brain? Tom, our son."

She seemed to roll for a moment, her whole body, as though she were ill, and then it passed. Just like that it passed. But she looked at him with grave concern. When she finally spoke, the words were innocent and confused. "What are you talking about?"

Harold dropped the bacon, the hairs standing up on the back of his neck. "What do you… what do you mean?"

"Is Tom a name for Reggie?" she asked. "A nick-name that I haven't heard? You had a cousin Tom, right? He died changing a…"

Harold waved that away. "Yeah, changing a tractor tire in 1928." He didn't like to think about it. "We named Tom after him, after my cousin."

"I don't…" she stood up. Smoothed out her apron. "I don't know what you want me to say. But this isn't very funny."

He patted the air. He hated to see her worried and now she was clearly worried. What was wrong with her, that she didn't remember her first son? "Hang on," he said. "Okay."

He got up and headed for the stairs, remembering to step again over Tom's… over Frances's skates, because somehow the kid had snuck down and grabbed his boots. "You heard me, didn't you!" he shouted upstairs. *You heard me complaining that you left them.*

He tromped up until he reached the upstairs hallway, looking down at the bedrooms. The master bedroom on the right and on the left, the kids' rooms. Frances's door with its mum and a song was streaming out, *Saturday! What a day! Rockin' all week with you!*

And Reggie's room and he walked fast past Reggie's room and no this is wrong, there should be another room! He stopped at the window at the end of the hall pressed his chubby fingers against the glass.

How can there not be….

"No, no, this is wrong!" he shouted.

"Dad?" His daughter was standing in her door, rubbing her eyes. She was wearing frilly pink pajamas. "What's going on?"

He turned around, tightening his robe. "I'm looking for your brother."

"Reggie had a breakfast thing at the diner," she said. "Oh, gosh, we were gonna do breakfast in bed for you."

He clenched his fists. "No, I'm looking for Tom."

"Who's Tom?"

Harold wanted to throttle the girl. But no, this… "The room, the room is…" He waved her away. "It's okay, go back to sleep." He had to get out of here. He marched past her.

"Happy birthday!" he heard her shout.

He marched past Minnie and muttered, "I have to go somewhere," and grabbed the keys off the hook next to the door.

"But Harold, you're in your slippers!"

But he had to hurry, he didn't have time to change. Harold slammed the door behind him and made his way through scattered fall leaves. The apple tree was in full bloom. Tom had brought them a whole basket from that tree, and oh, how Harold had bellowed.

Harold got behind the wheel of the Desoto and headed out of the neighborhood, out onto Main. He passed his hardware store, which he was supposed to open in three hours. He laughed at himself, yes, Minnie was right, he would need to get home and change. But for now he needed to see Tom and figure out what was going on.

Milwaukee State University was ringed with apartment buildings that were charitably called lived-in. Most of them were firetraps, but Tom was lucky enough to have a nice ten-year-old garden apartment. He didn't see Tom's car in the lot when he pulled in, but Harold parked anyway, paddling in his slippers and stocking feet and robe up the metal stairs to Tom's apartment door. Number 5. That was it.

But the pair of girls who answered were not amused by the 45-year-old they found in front of them at 8 a.m., and he had to say, "No, I'm sorry, I'm looking for my… my son."

He didn't allow himself to think until he got back behind the wheel of the Desoto and sat there with his hands on the wheel. He looked at his own unshaven face in the mirror and tried to get his bearings.

The Ink Spots were wafting out of a window in the Apartment Complex.

We'll meet again, don't know where, don't know when…

What. The Hell. Was happening.

He started the car and drove past the hill overlooking Lake Michigan. He knew the kids came here to make out, they called it *watching the submarine races.* He turned on the radio as he drove. The ornate Order of the Leopard lodge emerged on his right, and he passed it. The cool air should have made him feel better, but it was no use.

I didn't imagine it. I didn't imagine it.

Then he thought: the *smart* one. Reggie had—what did Frances say? He had a breakfast thing at the diner.

He pulled away from the park, leaving the lake behind and throttling the Desoto, hurtling towards Benedict's Drive-in.

He pulled into the parking lot, and it was all wrong. He had met up with Reggie here before. They always parked in the back corner, and even at 8:30 there should be carhops in little Army caps skating all around the lot, so much so they were surely risking their life with every order. But no, it was just a parking lot. No drive-in at all.

He ran in and found his son and his friends at a booth, scrawling on some posterboard between bites of egg sandwich.

“Reggie!” Harold yelled as he flapped across the floor.

His second son looked up from a poster-board that said SCIENCE FAIR 1955. His eyes were wide below crazy red hair just like his brother’s and his mother’s. “Dad!”

“It’s… I need your help.”

Reggie climbed out of the booth as his buddies remained silent, staring at him. He knew how foolish he looked in his robe, but it didn’t matter. He pulled Reggie towards the jukebox. “I can’t explain it,” Harold said. “But this morning I’ve been looking for Tom and nobody’s helping.”

“Which Tom?”

That rage again. “Your *brother*. Tom.”

Reggie laughed. “Come on, what’s the gag?”

Harold backed away, struck again by a sense of vertigo, there were apples, there were apples, and they weren’t ripe.

“Happy birthday!” Reggie called as he ran back to the car.

He reached the Desoto and put his hands on the door and was overcome with shaking rage. “Tom. TOM!” he shouted.

A black car was parked next to the Desoto and the rear passenger window rolled down. He was about to apologize to whoever was about to go in and get an egg sandwich. He was rubbing his unshaven face and waiting for them to look at him in astonished embarrassment for him.

But it was no stranger. It was a man he had spent many evenings listening to. He had a neat gray suit and tie, no hat, and perfect white hair. "Harold," said Lyon Field. He was the Eminent One of Harold's Lodge, the Order of the Leopard. "What's going on?"

"Lyon," Harold said, throwing himself against Lyon's car door. "You've got to help me. You've got to. You… you helped with that thing with the crash, right?"

Lyon grimaced slightly. There had been an enormous pile-up on Hitch Highway last Winter, and Lyon had made the fault of some of the Order's brothers go away. But it wasn't something they discussed.

"I told you," came a man's voice from the front seat. "I told you."

"Why don't you get in," Lyon said. "You don't look like you feel like driving."

Harold nodded. His head was swimming. "Yeah… uh, okay."

The door opened, Lyon slid over, and Harold got into the car, settling into the dark bench seat.

"We got a call," Lyon said as the driver led the car onto the highway. "Your wife was worried about you, but you know, we hate to call a hospital when friends are better."

"Better?" Harold tried to make sense out of this. He looked in the front seat. The guy there had wiry gray hair and no jacket. He seemed very rumpled, though he had no room to talk in his bathrobe and slippers.

"Driver, take us to the lodge." Lyon folded his hands. "What seems to be the problem, Harold?"

"No one remembers my son," Harold said.

"Your son Reggie?" Lyon looked at the guy in front. "How many…?"

"It's one and one, a girl and a boy. That's it. We gotta have more scenes with the troublemaker."

"What did you say?" Harold said.

"Let's just get to the lodge," Lyon said. "No more talking. I mean it."

Twenty minutes later they were leading him in under the magnificent arches and columns of the temple-like Lodge of the Order of the Leopard. They didn't talk again, though Lyon helped Harold some, touching his elbow in that gentle, strong way of his. Finally they reached the inner sanctum, which was dark and lit only by the dusty streams of light from the stained glass.

"Why don't you sit," Lyon said, indicating a chair on the dais, the chair usually occupied by the Grand Viz, the second in command to Lyon. It was a comfortable chair.

Harold sat, clasping his hands together and feeling absurd and small in his robe. The gray-haired man in shirtsleeves paced nervously, looking at a clipboard he had in his hand. "I don't have time for this."

Lyon ran his hand carefully over his perfect head. "I received… the strangest visit this morning. From a man who said he had to fix things."

"Can we just move this along?" the gray-haired man said.

"I'm sorry, who are you?" Harold glared at the guy.

"Call me Sherwood," the guy said.

"I have only seen this once before," Lyon said. "But then I've only been Eminence for about fifteen years."

"Seen what?" Harold asked. "And what does this… Are you a doctor? Are you trying to commit me?"

"No," Sherwood chuckled. "God, no. We need you. Look. It's gonna be this way."

"Wait."

"No, you wait. Listen." Sherwood's wiry eyebrows turned down. "Now I am here to tell you that I'm sorry you noticed it, but it's not there. The dining room is *not there.* It *never was.* And Tom…"

"No!" Harold rose. "What the f—"

"You're not supposed to notice!"

"What are you?"

The guy puffed up. "I am your goddamn showrunner and the last thing I need is kibbitzing from *you.*"

"This is life now," Lyon said. "This is life."

"But I have a son. His name is Tom."

"Then do this," Sherwood said, handing over his clipboard. "You can bitch all about it, you can tell us all about it, but I want you to look at this clipboard. Take it, just walk out with it. And come back when you're done."

"Oh, I will," Harold said, taking the clipboard.

"Who was this son?"

"Tom," Harold said. The sheet on the clipboard said

**CHARACTERS**

**- FAMILY-**

**HAROLD (Father)**

**MINNIE (Mother)**

**REGGIE (Son)**

**FRANCES (Daughter)**

**- FRIENDS -**

**HANK (TROUBLEMAKER - LEAD THIS YEAR!)**

**KIRBY**

**FRANK**

**BENEDICT**

"This is… I'm out of here," Harold said. He needed to get home, change, and maybe start over. With the police this time. Who was in on this?

FAMILY?

He thought about the hallway that ended at the window. Because of course it did. But *no*.

"I'm not crazy. Tom, his shoes were… his shoes were on the stairs. He picked all the apples *he picked all the apples, and I was so… mad…*"

He glared at them and barreled through the door into the lobby and didn't notice until he reached the front door that he wasn't holding the clipboard anymore.

He stopped, looking down, and chuckled at his robe.

"Boy," said Lyon as he came out of the inner sanctum. "Gosh, Harold. Thanks for running over here to look at that busted pipe." He clapped a heavy hand on Harold's shoulder. "Always good to have a hardware man, eh? Sorry you didn't even have time to get out of your PJs!"

Harold nodded. "Sure. Just don't tell anyone." What a morning. He'd never heard Lyon so panicked. But heck, yes, Harold could fix a busted pipe. Yes sir.

It was a good birthday. Harold's family and friends gathered that evening and they all beamed at him. Minnie practically swooned when he thanked God for his children, Frances and Reggie, the firecracker daughter, and the smart son. ♜

# CONFESSIONS OF THE EX-FUTURE-MRS. X

*By Alethea Kontis*

HE WAS ONE IN A MILLION.

No, wait–that's not right. That's too many. Probably closer to the truth to say one in a billion, but it's still hard for me to believe that five other people on this planet could be that amazing. That unique. That happy. That loved. That insane.

How did we meet? I thought everybody knew that story. The short version: through a mutual friend, in a café halfway across the world. God, that feels like lifetimes ago, back before he was the man we'll call "Xavier Xanadu." Before the purple suits and the Albert Einstein hairdo. Before he was The Candy Man–if anyone can remember such a time–he was just a man, sitting at a table, sipping tea, and dreaming through rose-colored glasses.

But there was still magic. There was always magic.

To answer the question you're not asking: no. It wasn't love at first sight. I had a boatload of my own troubles in the World of Me, and had it been left to my devices there never would have been anything between us beyond that meeting. But he wore me down, infecting me with that contagious enthusiasm. He made me laugh like I hadn't laughed in ages. You know, that kind of addictive, honest belly-laugh that goes on forever and makes your stomach cramp and brings tears to your eyes. The first time I had cried in ages too. He made me laugh like I had when I was a child, when the world was innocent and wonderful.

But that was his gift.

How long were we together? More than three years. Less than five. I don't know exactly. I've never really wanted to add up everything I stole from him, and that time was definitely part of it. I know, I know…they say you can't steal something that's given freely, but they're wrong. You can. You can take it, knowing that you're taking it, and knowing that you won't, can't, give any of it back.

Those years of "us" were really all about me, and he made it that way. He gave me things I needed and things I wanted, and things it hadn't even occurred to me to need or want. He knew I had a sweet tooth and he encouraged that.

He opened the door, and I jumped through it.

He had a friend – back when he was called such by a mere handful and not the whole world – who got me a job as a reviewer. A food critic, a position that became more and more specific until I secured the cake assignment (excuse the pun) of reviewing only dessert shops and bakeries. I bathed in a chocolate-drizzled dream topped with whipped cream and raspberries.

Xavier saw my reaction to the sweet side of life, and he took it a step further. He made new berries. He created a haven where I really could bathe in chocolate if I wanted to, in my castle in the sky built on clouds of divinity. He presented me with the very first Xanadu Chocolate Decadence Bar as a birthday present.

He gave me the world, and I took it.

In a way, his exceptional generosity taught me how to take. And take, and take… until I was placing ridiculous demands on him just to see how high he would jump. Every time I took the bar up a notch, he cleared it.

Eventually, I was devoting my time to little else but trying to ruin what had become an essentially unbreakable relationship.

We are our own worst enemies: I became the worst of myself, and the dream girl that Xavier created betrayed him.

How were we together? I take it you're asking me what he was like. What do you think? Take the most grandiose, romantic version of what you've heard and multiply it times ten.

He was fantastic.

We were fantastic.

He understands children so well because he is one. He is a genius, but in so many ways he is still innocent. *Was* innocent.

He despises condescension, and he does not suffer fools. Life is too short. And magic was always drawn to him like a lodestone. His business cards should list Magic Magnet right beneath the Candy Man honorific.

There was so much magic permeating the air of that factory that nothing seemed out of the ordinary, no matter how strange. A tree that tasted like toothpaste. An edible flower that bloomed all the colors of the rainbow. I was approached by Minians who were: blue, gigantic, the size of insects, teleporting, invisible, flying. None of them gave me pause.

Much madness is divinest sense, after all.

Because of that, Xavier never ceased to be enraptured by the most mundane trivialities. Butterfly wings. Sunsets. The way rain slides down wet windows. Flickering candle flames. Wide, honest smiles and laughter.

Love.

Hope.

Honor.

Loyalty.

The Minians? Yes, he did always have the loyal Minians with their poetic souls, and he always will. You know that legend too, but again, my version differs slightly from the storybooks.

After the success of the Chocolate Decadence Bar, Xavier needed to expand his operations, and quickly. In his most humanitarian effort ever. and in some way as a show of generosity for my benefit, he hired half the population of that small, backward island in the South Pacific to help him run his factory. Then, of course, the volcano erupted, the rest of the population (including all the women and children) were lost, and Xavier rose from Philanthropist to Savior in the space of a few horrifying hours.

Caught up in the romance and…gratitude, I suppose…I asked him to marry me.

I'm still not sure why I did it. I deserved him then as little as I do now. Three days later I took a job halfway around the world and had an affair, just to prove how little.

You asked me not to pull any punches, didn't you? If you want to think I'm despicable and evil, you go right ahead. You wouldn't be wrong.

But everyone falls short when measured against the Xanadu standard. He is too generous, too kind, too loud, too colorful, too smart, too funny, too wise, too understanding, too passionate, too…everything. He's a goddamned angel.

The rest of us, well, our heels hit the ground when we walk.

Maybe what I said before was true, and maybe one of those seven other people on the planet is the perfect woman for him. And when they find each other, bells will ring across the globe and the world will sing about it and rejoice.

I won't leave the house that day. He deserves happiness. I just don't want to know about it.

Did I love him? Well, that's relative too, isn't it? I suppose, despite all the terrible things I did, that I loved Xavier as much as I was ever physically able to. I told him that I loved him; it wasn't entirely a lie. But it wasn't enough, of course. It was never enough.

I was never enough.

Perhaps that's why I fascinated him, me without any hope or honor or loyalty, and completely incapable of the depth and breadth of love he needed. Perhaps not.

How did it end?

I waited for him to do it, of course.

I wasn't completely stupid; I lived in a rainbow palace where every wish was granted and every desire was edible. And I could have kept that world.

Instead, I demanded more and more, taking and taking and holding the illusion of my love above his head until he finally, *finally* drew a line.

Condemn me if you will for how I ended it.

I think, perhaps, it would have been more heartless to stay.

Do I regret anything? Another hard question to answer. How can a person regret being herself?

There are things I miss, of course. (I do not miss the Minians. I always thought they were creepy, the way they followed me around with their baleful eyes and haunting chants.) I miss the factory and its nooks and crannies of adventure and instant gratification. I miss the way the world looked – as if all of us around him saw it through his eyes – full of light and color and soul. I miss the way the world smelled. The way it tasted. I miss the magic.

I miss…me. Or, rather, I miss the woman he thought I was. The woman he made me out to be. The woman I might even have been if the universe and my nature and everything else had been different. She was amazing, that woman. She was an incredible whirlwind of beauty and dynamite. She was talented and beautiful. She was full of hope and honor and loyalty and bottomless bounties of unconditional love. She believed in destiny, and life was her playground.

She was a dream, that woman.

I killed that dream.

I haven't seen him since that last visit halfway around the world – we kept up the pretense for a few weeks, but once the chocolate bunny crumbled, it was impossible to reassemble. He hasn't spoken to me since he found out about the affairs, and rightly so.

I still see him now and again – oh, not in person, of course. I see his face reflected on every angel in the architecture. I see his smile in every slice of lemon floating in a teacup like the teeth of the Cheshire Cat. I see his heart every time the sun paints the sky. I see the wonder in his eyes in every child who takes their first bite of a Xanadu Chocolate Decadence Bar. I hear his laugh when my daughter swings so high her tiny bare feet touch the sky.

I tell her that her mother was once a princess in a fairy tale. It's not entirely a lie. And when I hold her up so that she can catch the sun in her palm I tell her that she is one in a million.

I hope those odds never change. ♜

# CONTRIBUTORS

**Madeline Ashby** is a futurist and writer living in Toronto. She is the author of *Company Town*, a cyberpunk thriller set in Newfoundland, and the Machine Dynasty series, about a family of self-replicating humanoid robots who sometimes eat each other alive. With her husband, horror writer David Nickle, she is the co-editor of *Licence Expired: The Unauthorized James Bond*. This is her first horror story. You can find her on Twitter @MadelineAshby and at madelineashby.com, or on Instagram @MadAshby.

**Jeremiah Dylan Cook** is a horror writer whose work has been featured on the No Sleep Podcast. He's also had stories appear in anthologies from Ghost Orchid Press, Raw Dog Screaming Press, and Castle Bridge Media. In February 2021, he won Purple Wall Stories monthly writing competition, and in October 2018, he won First Prize in the Ligonier Valley Writers annual Halloween Flash Fiction Contest. Jeremiah completed his master's degree in the eldritch art of Writing Popular Fiction at Seton Hill University. While an undergraduate at St. John's University, he received the Mario Mezzacappa Memorial Award for Outstanding Achievement in Poetry and Prose. Jeremiah is a member of the Horror Writers Association and the managing editor of New Pulp Tales. He tweets @JeremiahCook1, and he posts reviews and writing updates on his website www.jeremiahdylancook.com. When not writing, Jeremiah is usually adventuring with his wife, playing board games, or doing the bidding of his black cat, Strider, heir to the throne of Cat-Gondor.

**Dennis K. Crosby** grew up in Oak Park, IL and completed his undergraduate work at the University of Illinois in Chicago. With a degree in Criminal Justice, he spent six years working as a Private Investigator. While working on a master's degree in Forensic Psychology, Dennis transitioned to social service where he worked with men and women experiencing challenges with mental health and addiction. He currently serves as Director of Apprenticeship Programs for a non-profit organization.

Dennis wrote dozens of short stories but did not pursue the finer points of the craft until later in life. After leaving Chicago and moving to San Diego, Dennis had the opportunity to get more involved in the writing community where he strengthened his skills. To further augment his writing skills, Dennis completed an MFA program at National University.

Dennis is currently working on the follow up to his bestselling urban fantasy novel, *Death's Legacy*.

Website: www.denniskcrosby.com

Twitter: www.twitter.com/denniskcrosby

Instagram: www.instagram.com/denniskcrosby/

Facebook: www.facebook.com/Denniskcrosby/

**Jason Henderson** is a Locus Best-selling author and Texas Lone Star List recipient. He is the host of the Castle of Horror and Castle Talk Podcasts, the editor of the Castle of Horror Anthology series, and the author of the Young Captain Nemo series from Macmillan Children's Books. His new 50s beach-party horror novel *Night of the Book Man* under the pseudonym Peyton Douglas, the first in the Surf Mystic series, debuted in 2020.

**Henry Herz** authored over 25 traditionally published short stories, including eight for the pro-pay markets Daily Science Fiction, Blackstone Publishing, Albert Whitman & Co., Air and Nothingness Press, Highlights for Children, and Ladybug Magazine. He edited three anthologies: BEYOND THE PALE (adult fantasy by Peter Beagle, Heather Brewer, Jim Butcher, Rachel Caine, Kami Garcia, Nancy Holder, and Jane Yolen), COMING OF AGE (Albert Whitman & Co., middle grade #ownvoices), and THE HITHERTO SECRET EXPERIMENTS OF MARIE CURIE (Blackstone Publishing, young adult horror by Mylo Carbia, Stacia Deutsch, Sarah Beth Durst, Alethea Kontis, Jonathan Maberry, Seanan McGuire, Scott Sigler, and Scott Westerfeld). Henry authored 11 traditionally published books for children.

Blog: www.henryherz.com

Twitter: www.twitter.com/HenryLHerz

Facebook: www.facebook.com/Henry.Herz

LinkedIn: www.linkedin.com/in/henrylherz/

Instagram: www.instagram.com/henry_herz/

**Tony Jones** has dined with royalty, supped Slings in Singapore and been taught by several Nobel Prize winners (though he could have paid more attention). He is a writer, reviewer and blogger based in the early 21st Century.

He's written *Doctor Who* audios for Big Finish and is currently focussed on writing short stories. Being part of *Castle of Horror* has inspired him to self-publish a few other supernatural stories for Kindle. Twitter: @helmstone

*New York Times* bestselling author **Alethea Kontis** is a princess, storm chaser, and Saturday Songwriter. Author of over 20 books and 40 short stories, Alethea is the recipient of the Jane Yolen MidList Author Grant, the Scribe Award, the Garden State Teen Book Award, and two-time winner of the Gelett Burgess Children's Book Award. She has been twice nominated for both the Andre Norton Nebula and the Dragon Award. She was an active contributor to *The Fireside Sessions*, a benefit EP created by Snow Patrol and her fellow Saturday Songwriters during lockdown 2020. Alethea also narrates stories for multiple award-winning online magazines and contributes regular YA book reviews to NPR. Born in Vermont, she currently resides on the Space Coast of Florida with her teddy bear, Charlie. Find out more about Princess Alethea and her wonderful world at aletheakontis.com.

**James A. "Jim" Moore** has been writing professionally for over twenty-five years. His works include over thirty novels, including the Stoker Nominated SERENITY FALLS trilogy, the SEVEN FORGES series, the TIDES OF WAR and BLOOD RED trilogies and many standalone horror titles as well as several licensed properties, such as BUFFY THE VAMPIRE SLAYER: CHAOS BLEEDS, and VAMPIRE: HOUSE OF SECRETS for White Wolf Games. He spent many years honing his skills with work in RPGs and in the comics field, but now works mostly on short stories and novels. His latest novel, THE GODLESS, comes out in September. You can find him at: @JamesAMoore on Twitter and www.facebook.com/james.a.moore1/ on Facebook.

**Rob Nisbet** lives near Brighton on the English south coast, just a dog walk away from the pink sea, green sky location used as the planet Thoros-Beta in Doctor Who. Perhaps it is living so close to this surreal environment that suggested his strange tale in this volume!

Rob has had over 60 stories in various publications, with romance and crime appearing under his wife's name. He has won several international story competitions and (back to the surreal) is currently working on a novel that he hopes will terrify ten-year-olds every time they look into a mirror. His Doctor Who connection extends to having written audio scripts which have been produced by Big Finish. The Thoros-Beta area is also an unofficial nudist beach – but he doesn't talk about that.

**Scott Pearson** is a full-time freelance writer and editor. He has published across a number of genres, such as lit fic, humor, mystery, urban fantasy, horror, and science fiction, including three *Star Trek* stories and two *Trek* novellas. Recent anthology publications include "The Ghosts of Glenmirror" in *Castle of Horror 4*, "In the Time of the Martians" in *Turning the Tied*, and "The Day It Came From Beyond Outer Space" in *Thrillling Adventure Yarns 2021*. He's the canon editor of the *Star Trek Adventures* role-playing game and the cowriter of the IMAX space documentaries *Space Next* and *Touch the Stars*. He is the co-developer, along with William Leisner, of *Tales of the Weird World War*, an alternate history/horror/sci-fi series which debuted in 2021. Scott lives in personable St. Paul, Minnesota, with his wife, Sandra, and their cat, Ripley. He and his daughter, Ella, cohost the podcast *Generations Geek*. Visit Scott online at scott-pearson.com and generationsgeek.com and follow him on Twitter @smichaelpearson.

**John Pritchard** has been fascinated by horror films and supernatural stories for as long as he can remember. At school his English teacher told him he had a morbid imagination and he's been putting it to good use ever since, writing the horror novels *Night Sisters*, *Angels of Mourning* and *The Witching Hour*, the fantasy epic *Dark Ages*, and several spooky Doctor Who audio dramas for Big Finish, two of which were nominated for Scribe Awards. As John Steiner he writes the *Furies* series of World War Two thrillers. He still enjoys his day job in hospital administration and likes reading about history, science and current affairs in his spare time. He tweets about movies, ideas and pleasing paragraphs at @MissFury1.

**Charles R. Rutledge** is the author of *Dracula's Revenge* and *Dracula's Ghost*, and the co-author of three books in the Griffin and Price series, written with James A. Moore. His short stories have appeared in over 30 anthologies. A child of the 1970s, Charles was raised on Dark Shadows, The Night Stalker, Friday Night Frights, Planet of the Apes, The Savage Sword of Conan, The Tomb of Dracula, and Enter the Dragon. He never wore tie-dyed shirts, but he did own a leisure suit. Find him on Twitter at @CRRutledge2.

**Heath Shelby** grew up on a steady diet of Universal monster movies and Hammer films before discovering modern day greats like Carpenter, Craven and Romero. This, along with comic books and science fiction staples such as Star Wars, Star Trek and Planet of the Apes, inspired Heath to read voraciously and write stories of his own. Over the years, the only thing that would rival Heath's love for horror and science fiction was music. Such was his love for music, Heath began working in radio at the age of 15. Today, Heath works as the Program Director, Music Director and on-air talent for a radio station in Searcy, Arkansas, where he lives with his wife of over 20 years, Jennifer; their son, Collin; their daughter, Caitlynn; their Maltese,

Claire; their rowdy Boston Terrier, Cocoa; and Uki, the Husky.

In his free time, you will find Heath cruising in his red Mustang; visiting his inspirations, his parents; Rokken with Dokken; hanging out at the nearest Margaritaville, scarfing down a Cheeseburger in Paradise or three; and praying that somehow, some way his beloved San Francisco 49ers will win at least one more Super Bowl during his lifetime.

Facebook: www.facebook.com/heathwshelby

Instagram: the_heath_shelby

Twitter: @heath_shelby

**In Churl Yo** has served as an editorial director and an award-winning creative consultant to several magazines during his career. He is currently Director of Omnichannel Operations at SagaCity Media in Seattle, Washington. Amazing Stories called his debut novel *Isonation* "a fast-paced post-pandemic story where nothing turns out to be quite what it seems." His follow-up novel *Austinites*, a literary nostalgia-infused trip through 1990's Austin, is available now. Born and raised in Texas, where he graduated from the University of Texas at Austin with a degree in Marketing, he made the move to cooler and greener climes out west with his wife and two children. Follow him on Twitter @inchurlyo.

**Bryan Young** works across many different media. He worked as a writer and producer of documentary films which were called "filmmaking gold" by *The New York Times*. He's also published comic books with Slave Labor Graphics and Image Comics. He's been a regular contributor for the ***Huffington Post***, ***StarWars.com***, ***Star Wars Insider magazine***, ***SYFY***, ***/Film***, and was the founder and editor in chief of the geek news and review site ***Big Shiny Robot!*** He co-authored ***Robotech: The Macross Saga RPG*** in 2019 and in 2020 he wrote a novel in the BattleTech Universe called ***Honor's Gauntlet***. Follow him on Twitter @swankmotron.

If you liked *The Castle of Horror Anthology Volume 5*, you might also enjoy reading the following titles available on Amazon from Castle Bridge Media:

***Austinites*** *By In Churl Yo*

***THE CASTLE OF HORROR ANTHOLOGY SERIES***
***Castle Of Horror Anthology Volume 1***
***Castle of Horror Anthology Volume 2: Holiday Horrors***
***Castle of Horror Anthology Volume 3: Scary Summer Stories***
***Castle of Horror Anthology Volume 4: Women Running From Houses***
*Edited By Jason Henderson*

***Castle of Horror Podcast Book of Great Horror: Our Favorites, Top Tens, and Bizarre Pleasures***
*Edited By Jason Henderson*

***FuturePast Sci-Fi Anthology***
*Edited by In Churl Yo*

***Isonation*** *By In Churl Yo*

***THE PATH***
***Book 1: The Blue-Spangled Blue*** *By David Bowles*
***Book 2: The Deepest Green*** *By David Bowles*

***Surf Mystic: Night of the Book Man*** *By Peyton Douglas*

***Nightwalkers: Gothic Horror Movies*** *By Bruce Lanier Wright*

Please remember to leave us your reviews on Amazon and Goodreads!

CASTLE BRIDGE MEDIA
DENVER, COLORADO, USA

**THANK YOU FOR SUPPORTING INDEPENDENT PUBLISHERS AND AUTHORS!**

castlebridgemedia.com